KV-676-292

# THE PENGUIN GUIDE TO AUSTRALIA 1989

ALAN TUCKER

*General Editor*

PENGUIN BOOKS

# PENGUIN BOOKS

Published by the Penguin Group
Viking Penguin Inc., 40 West 23rd Street,
New York, New York 10010, U.S.A.
Penguin Books Ltd, 27 Wright's Lane,
London W8 5TZ, England
Penguin Books Australia Ltd, Ringwood,
Victoria, Australia
Penguin Books Canada Ltd, 2801 John Street,
Markham, Ontario, Canada L3R 1B4
Penguin Books (N.Z.) Ltd, 182-190 Wairau Road,
Auckland 10, New Zealand

Penguin Books Ltd, Registered Offices:
Harmondsworth, Middlesex, England

First published in Penguin Books 1989
Published simultaneously in Canada

1   3   5   7   9   10   8   6   4   2

ISBN 0 14 019.905 5
ISSN 0897-6880

Printed in the United States of America by
R. R. Donnelley & Sons Company,
Harrisonburg, Virginia

Set in ITC Garamond Light
Designed by Beth Tondreau Design
Maps by General Cartography, Inc.
Illustrations by Bill Russell
Editorial services by Stephen Brewer Associates

# CONTRIBUTORS

DAVID SWINDELL, the author of several guidebooks on Australia and Sydney, has written extensively on Australia for *Travel and Leisure* magazine.

MIKE BINGHAM, a longtime resident of Tasmania, is the travel editor of *The Mercury,* Tasmania's largest newspaper, and its sister publication, *The Sunday Tasmanian.*

CHRIS BROCKIE, a stockman, rodeo contestant, and freelance journalist, has covered the Outback in depth since he moved there in 1972. He has been bureau chief for two major Australian newspaper groups.

SHIRLEY MAAS FOCKLER, a member of the Society of American Travel Writers, is a contributor to dozens of magazines and newspapers in North America and Oceania.

JANIS HADLEY, a resident of Perth, Western Australia, writes on travel for a variety of publications within Australia and overseas.

KERRY KENIHAN, an author and journalist for more than twenty years, lives in Adelaide, South Australia, and is a member of the Australian Society of Travel Writers.

IAN MARSHMAN, a lifelong resident of Melbourne, writes for many travel publications and is the deputy editor of Australia's *Traveltrade* magazine.

LEN RUTLEDGE, whose *Travelround* column was the longest-running travel column in Australia, is a contributor to newspapers and magazines in Australia, the Pacific, Asia, and Europe. He lives in Queensland.

# THE PENGUIN TRAVEL GUIDES

# THIS GUIDEBOOK

The Penguin Travel Guides are designed for people who are experienced travellers in search of exceptional information that will help them sharpen and deepen their enjoyment of the trips they take.

Where, for example, are the interesting, isolated, fun, charming, or romantic places to stay that are within your budget? The hotels described by our writers (each of whom is an experienced travel writer who either lives in or regularly tours the city or region of Australia he or she covers) are some of the special places, in all price ranges except for the lowest—not the run-of-the-mill, heavily marketed places on every travel agent's CRT display and in advertised airline and travel-agency packages. We indicate the approximate price level of each accommodation in our descriptions of it (no indication means it is moderate), and at the end of every chapter we supply contact information so that you can get precise, up-to-the-minute rates and make reservations.

*The Penguin Guide to Australia 1989* highlights the more rewarding parts of the country so that you can quickly and efficiently home in on a good itinerary.

Of course, the guides do far more than just help you choose a hotel and plan your trip. *The Penguin Guide to Australia 1989* is designed for use *in* Australia. Our Penguin Australia writers tell you what you really need to know, what you can't find out so easily on your own. They identify and describe the truly out-of-the-ordinary restaurants, shops, activities, and sights, and tell you the best way to "do" your destination.

Our writers are highly selective. They bring out the significance of the places they cover, capturing the personality and the underlying cultural and historical resonances of a city or region—making clear its special appeal. For exhaustive detailed coverage of cultural attractions, we suggest that you also use a supplementary reference-type guidebook—probably a locally produced publication—along with the Penguin Guide.

*The Penguin Guide to Australia 1989* is full of reliable and timely information, revised each year. We would like to know if you think we've left out some very special place.

ALAN TUCKER
*General Editor*
*Penguin Travel Guides*

40 West 23rd Street
New York, New York 10010
or
27 Wright's Lane
London W8 5TZ

# CONTENTS

## MAPS

# THE
# PENGUIN
# GUIDE TO
# AUSTRALIA
# 1989

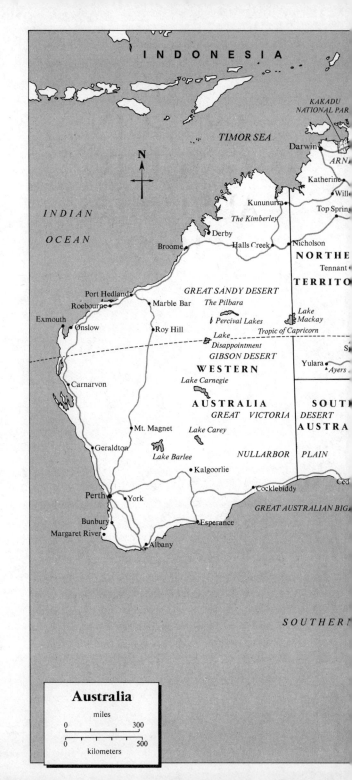

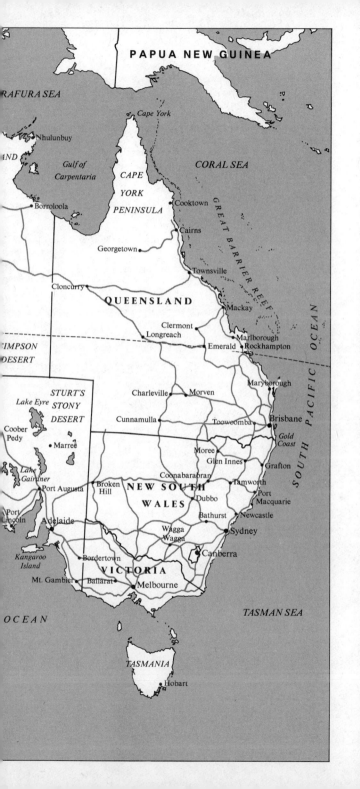

# OVERVIEW

*By David Swindell*

*David Swindell, an American journalist, has travelled extensively throughout Australia and written about the country for* Travel & Leisure, Frequent Flyer, America's Cup Challenge, *and other magazines. He is the author of several guidebooks on Australia.*

An ancient aboriginal myth—no one knows how many thousands of years old—attempts to explain how the first man and woman on earth managed to get together. The woman was travelling north, the man south, when they met on a plain.

The man asked, "Where are you from?"

The woman replied, "From the south. Where are you from?"

"From the north," he said. "Are you alone?"

"Yes."

"Then you will be my wife."

"Yes, I will be your woman."

It was all so simple then, but truth can be found in that myth even now in modern-day Australia. It illustrates the lack of formality and the straight-from-the-hip directness that is the charm of the Aussies. For those of us caught up in a more callous and strenuous world, the myth also helps explain why, of all the mysteries and peculiarities on this most unusual of continents, it is the Aussies themselves who are the most fun and the greatest attraction Down Under.

It is in this regard that Australia is so different from other places on earth. Traditional vacation spots almost demand that we visit them not for liaisons with the na-

5

tives but for their cultural or historical worth, or for their natural beauty. People packing for Paris, no doubt, have set their minds on seeing the Eiffel Tower and the Louvre. They are probably not anticipating long conversations in a pub with a neighborhood bloke.

But in Australia there are no ancient ruins, no Medieval cathedrals. No great battles were fought on its shores, and it is not a seat of world power. It is indeed, then, left to the Aussies to be Australia's greatest lure. Unpretentious, entertaining, and accommodating, Australians, far from having an inferiority complex about their distance and detachment, almost pity the poor folks who don't live in their lucky country.

And why not? It's a laid-back life Down Under—life in the tropics, where a winter's day might call for you to don a light jacket to walk on the beach; where a ceiling fan stirs an ocean breeze that cools better than any air conditioner; where sun, sand, and sea seem indistinguishable from one another; where the food is excellent and the beer is cold.

It's an unhurried place, too. No one seems to be dashing madly about, drivers don't honk their horns at each other and pedestrians, and when five o'clock comes work is over. Ambition may not be the Aussies' strong suit; living the good life, on the other hand, is on everyone's mind.

There are no better places in Australia to meet and "chat up" an Aussie than at a neighborhood pub or on the beach. A substantial portion of the population is bound to be at one or the other at any given time. Chat up means "talk to" in the Aussie parlance known as "strine," a peculiar form of English spoken only in Australia. As with any foreign language, it's a good idea to learn a few words and expressions to converse successfully with the natives.

Crocodile Dundee himself, the actor Paul Hogan, introduced many outsiders to their first words of "strine." In America and Canada, "G'day" became a familiar greeting. Hogan also told us a barbecue grill is simply called a "barby" where he comes from. But Croc left out a few other words and expressions in his 30-second spots for the Australian Tourist Commission that are equally handy to know Down Under. "Fair dinkum" is one—it means "the real thing." "He's a fair dinkum Aussie" tells us he's a homegrown boy. It's also a popular expression on tee-shirts sold around the country.

At the pub, several words and expressions will come in handy. First, know how to order a beer: A "schooner" is a large glass of beer, a "midi" a small one. If the bartender only has a "tinnie" it means beer is served by the can. Second, know how to order a round for your drinking buddies: "My shout, mate," is the proper response here. Important to know on the beach is that the swimsuit you're wearing is a "cozzie." Australia itself is often referred to fondly as "Oz."

Other key words that cry out for translation are "petrol"—gasoline; "boot" and "bonnet"—trunk and hood of a car; "brekkie"—breakfast; "tucker"—food; "pom"—an Englishman (from penal colony days, "Prisoner of Mother England"; thus, Queen Elizabeth, Princess Di, and all their countrymen are "poms"); "rock melon"—cantaloupe; "prawn"—shrimp; "crayfish"—lobster; "good on ya' "—good for you; "brolly"—umbrella; "lolly"—candy; "sheila"—girl; "bloke"—guy. The list goes on, but these few words will make you look much more informed.

And now to tackle "Waltzing Matilda." Who, outside Australia, has ever understood those lyrics? Understanding the song helps you better understand Australia. It is as essential to Australiana as "Home on the Range" is to Americana.

> Once a jolly swagman camped by a billabong
> Under the shade of a coolabah tree
> Down came a jumbuck to drink at the billabong
> Up jumped the swagman and grabbed him with glee
> And he sang as he shoved that jumbuck in his tucker bag
> You'll come a waltzing matilda with me

In the great Australian bush, or the Outback, as it is better known to non-Australians, a "swagman" is a hobo, a drifter who finds an honest day's work to his everlasting distaste. He is the type of guy who would much rather steal dinner than pay for it. A "billabong" is a pond, all the water left in an otherwise dried-up lake or river. In the vast Outback, a billabong is usually the only water to be found for hundreds of miles around.

A "coolabah" tree is a gum tree, which is also known as a eucalyptus tree, where all koalas live in Australia. In the bush, coolabahs provide what shade is to be had from the unrelenting sun.

A "jumbuck" is a sheep. In the song, the "swagman" apparently intended to have lamb chops for dinner, for he grabbed up the "jumbuck" and shoved him in his "tucker" (food) bag. And he sang, "You'll come a waltzing matilda with me."

There have never been many women in the Australian Outback, leaving the men to resort to their own devices when it comes to female companionship. The "swagman" was no doubt a lonely bloke. He'd sit around the campfire under an endless, starry Outback sky and drink whiskey until he was plastered. Then he'd grab "matilda" and waltz with her by the light of the moon, blissfully ignorant, for the night at least, that matilda was only the backpack that held all his worldly belongings.

## Australia's History

Australia's past has been checkered and its present is shaky, but Aussies are optimists. Few predict anything other than a bright future for a country that in 1988 celebrated 200 years of nationhood. The Australian Bicentennial actually marked the occasion when the first English colonists—the first whites—landed at present-day Sydney Harbour in January 1788. For the 70,000 or so years until then, Australia had been populated by aboriginals, as they became known to the outside world.

When the British lost the American colonies, it became imperative that a new location for prisoners be found. Naturally, one as far away as possible sufficed nicely for the Crown, and so Australia became England's newest and most dreaded penal colony. More than 700 prisoners were brought in that first boatload, and thousands more followed until the 1860s, when transportation of prisoners was halted forever.

Those prisoners and their jailers became the forefathers of white Australia. Many aboriginals were killed or died of imported European diseases—these people were totally wiped out in Tasmania—but enough remained to father later generations who are now just beginning to demand a place in Australian society.

Today, the government plays big brother to the aboriginals, many of whom live in ghetto conditions in the small towns and missions of the Outback. (Few are seen in city centers.) Only last year, the United Nations chided the Australian government for the squalid conditions in which many aboriginals live; a crowd of some 15,000 strong protested their plight at the Bicentennial Tall Ships Parade in Sydney on Australia Day, January 26, 1988.

In the 19th century Australia was closely tied to England's coattails. England was called "home" by just about every white person in the country, even though by mid-century most had been born in Australia. Few, in fact, ever set foot on English soil. Australia is still part of the Commonwealth, but many Aussies today resent the British presence and howl in derision if "God Save the Queen" is played as the national anthem.

Also in the last century, Australia had its own gold rush, which followed closely on the heels of the California Gold Rush of 1849. Indeed, many of the prospectors who panned California unsuccessfully made their way to the wilderness of Victoria hoping for better luck.

Today, the gold is mostly gone, and the Australian economy is a bit of a mess, with high inflation—about 8 percent annually—and unemployment at about 8 percent in a population of 16.5 million. The Aussie dollar, irreverently pegged the "Pacific peso," is a boon, however, for travellers exchanging U.S., Canadian, or New Zealand dollars or British pounds. At presstime, it was worth about 70 cents U.S., making it possible for some travellers to stay at better hotels or eat at top-notch restaurants and still remain within their budgets.

## The Visitor's Australia

There would still be plenty of reasons to travel to Australia were the place uninhabited—reasons like kangaroos, koalas, emus, wombats, Tasmanian devils, and platypuses. You may have seen all those in the zoo back home—and that's probably where you'll have to go to see them in Australia if you never venture out of the cities and into the bush. 'Roos, as they say in "strine," don't hop down Macquarie Street in Sydney or Collins Street in Melbourne.

Fortunately, there are some 500 splendid **national**

**parks** and **wildlife reserves** scattered around the nation, and at some the animals are tame enough to eat out of your hand. In the bush and out in the country, it's a common enough sight to see kangaroos bounding over fences in a paddock (pasture), koalas high in the gums, wombats scurrying here and there, and emus hightailing it across the plain. Platypuses are harder to find, and to see the disagreeable little Tasmanian devil in the wild you will indeed have to go to Tasmania.

Bushwalking, or hiking, is the best way to get close-up views of the rarefied flora and fauna that abound in Australia. There are 7,000 different wildflowers and 700 various kinds of eucalyptus trees alone. Apart from the cities and the desert, almost anywhere in the nation is a perfect place for a bushwalk. Most national parks have well-marked trails for treks of 20 minutes' to two days' duration.

Another perfect reason to visit Australia is the tropics, epitomized by the **Great Barrier Reef** that stretches 1,200 miles along the Queensland coast. "Going troppo" is how the Aussies explain a trip to the tropics. To go troppo means to leave the real world behind. What becomes important is not a commute to the office but a swim in the translucent waters of the South Pacific; not a meal on the run but a leisurely banquet of lobster or shrimp or oysters; not a sleepless night but a snooze under a mosquito net, with drowsiness brought on by the pounding of the surf or the rustling of the palms.

You can go troppo in the company of a crowd at the **Gold Coast**, Down Under's Waikiki, or alone or with someone special on an island in **The Whitsundays**, or in a beach cottage on the **Sunshine Coast**. And going troppo almost demands that you go snorkeling or diving on the Great Barrier Reef for a Technicolor trip beneath the waves, or sailing in the shimmering waters of the Coral Sea. Surrounded by tropical waters—the South Pacific and Indian oceans, the Arafura, Timor, and Coral seas, and the Gulf of Carpentaria—Australia has no end of places to go troppo.

Still another good reason to take the plunge Down Under is the country's surprisingly sophisticated city life. **Sydney**, on the east coast in the state of New South Wales, is the nation's most exciting city and Melbourne its grandest, but the other large metropolitan areas—Brisbane,

Perth, and Adelaide—are not without their own charms for visitors. Few sights in Australia are more exhilarating than the Sydney Opera House. Like the Statue of Liberty in New York, the Opera House is a symbol not only of the city but the nation, too. Its white sails, blinding against the harbor backdrop, represent the very hope of Australia that the future will be brighter than the past.

Grand old **Melbourne**, on the southeast coast in the state of Victoria, feels more European than other Australian cities. Forever locked in battle with Sydney as to which is the nation's premier city, Melbourne claims supremacy as the financial center of the nation—a claim Sydney bankers hotly dispute—and as the epicurean capital of the continent, a notion scoffed at by Sydney chefs. However, no one denies that Melbourne's Victorian Art Gallery is Australia's greatest repository of works by both the great masters and Australian artists, or that its theater, music, and cabaret scene is the most vibrant and trendsetting.

The spectacular **Great Ocean Road** winds westward from Melbourne along Victoria's southern coast past surf-battered cliffs, lonely beaches, and forests that stop only because the ocean begins. It easily rivals such scenic drives as California's Pacific Coast Highway and Italy's Amalfi Drive. **Phillip Island**, south of Melbourne, is one of Down Under's must-see spots, a wildlife refuge that claims koalas, fairy penguins, fur seals, wombats, and untold numbers of seabirds among its citizens.

And yet another very valid reason for visiting Australia must be mentioned: the forbidding **Outback**. A trip to the Northern Territory in the heart of the Outback—Queensland and other states have plenty of Outback, too—may not be for everyone, but it is the quintessential Australian experience. It's a tough place (except of course at the luxury resorts that have popped up in recent years), most of it a desert no-man's-land that promises a slow death to anyone who strays beyond what passes for civilization.

The aboriginals have survived here for eons, and indeed prospered until the white man stepped in to "civilize" them and convert them to Christianity. Aboriginal rock paintings around the Northern Territory depict their everyday life, which changed little for 20,000 years. One of the aboriginals' most holy places, **Ayers Rock** (known to the original Aussies as Uluru), is also one of Australia's top tourist attractions. The single rock, 5 miles in diameter at its base, soars 1,000 feet above the desert floor; nobody knows how deep it plummets underground. Its penchant for changing colors, from deep red to burnt orange, is legendary.

**Alice Springs**, immortalized by Neville Shute in *A Town Like Alice,* is the closest outcropping of civilization to Uluru. There's not a lot to do in this dusty hotbox of a town, but just having reached Alice is a monumental accomplishment for self-respecting world travellers. Alice would seem to some visitors the last place on earth, but it is a jumping-off point for even more exotic once-in-a-lifetime adventures that can only be experienced in the Red Centre of Australia. "Up the track" (up the road a few hundred miles) lies Darwin and the magnificent wildlife reserve known as **Kakadu**—Crocodile Dundee country. As rich in teeming wildlife as anywhere in Africa, the region is a new favorite among Aussies and their guests for bushwalking, camping, and going on safari in a four-wheel-drive vehicle.

**Tasmania**, too, "tiny Tassie," as Australia's smallest state is known, is a wealth of the unknown. Some areas of it are among the most treacherous places on earth and have never been fully explored, while others are as gentle as the English countryside they mimic. With beaches for swimming and mountains for skiing, Tasmania is another major reason to visit the land Down Under.

Though less visited by travellers from overseas, South Australia and far-flung Western Australia are filled with reasons to visit. **Adelaide** is a genteel city, brightly colored with flowers and sunshine. Just outside the city, in the Adelaide Hills, small wineries produce some of the boutique wines that are gaining world popularity, and in the **Barossa Valley**, 55 km (33 miles) northeast of the city, sprawling vineyards yield some of what are already the world's most respected wines.

**Perth** is best remembered as the setting for the last America's Cup Race (which actually was raced off nearby Fremantle, Western Australia's major port city). This Indian Ocean city is closer to Southeast Asia than it is to Sydney and is, indeed, about as far away as you can travel from anywhere on this planet and hope to find civilization. In the far north of the vast state of Western Australia, **The Kimberley**, a remote, sparsely populated, still largely unexplored region, is fast becoming one of Australia's most intriguing offbeat vacation destinations. The mountains and rivers in The Kimberley, geologists say, are among the oldest formations on earth.

On this smallest of continents, there is a world of things to do, see, experience, taste, smell, and remember for a lifetime. We tell you only about some of the best in this book. Undoubtedly you'll find others on your own. Australia is of course a big place, about the size of the continental United States, and no manageable book could completely catalog the many sights and attractions in this country.

You won't have to go far for advice. The natives are friendly, friendly enough to be concerned that you have a good time on their turf and friendly enough to insist that you see and do the things they think are Australia's best. Chat them up. They may be right.


## USEFUL FACTS

### *Entry Requirements*
A valid passport and Australian visa are required to enter Australia. Visas are available free from Australian government offices worldwide and can be applied for in person or through the mail. Citizens of New Zealand do not require a visa. No vaccinations are required before entering the country, unless the traveller is arriving from an infected nation as determined by the World Health Organization (the U.S., Canada, Great Britain, and New Zealand are not infected nations).

### *How to Get There*
There are several flights daily on a choice of airlines between the U.S. and Canada and Australia. Qantas (Australia's national airline), United, Continental, Hawaiian Air, Canadian International, Air New Zealand, and UTA French Airlines operate nonstop and direct flights between the continents. From Great Britain, Qantas and British Airways fly to Australia daily. From New Zealand, Qantas and Air New Zealand provide daily service.

### *Customs*
Visitors may bring into Australia their personal effects, and those over age 18 may bring in 250 cigarettes or 250

grams of tobacco and one liter of spirits. Dutiable goods
up to the value of A$400 are exempt from duty.

### Departure Tax
The departure tax is A$10, and must be paid in Australian
currency.

### Climate
Seasons are the reverse in the Southern Hemisphere of
what they are in the Northern Hemisphere; thus, summer
in Australia is December, January, and February, while
winter is June, July, and August. Many northerners find it
difficult to conceive of Christmas as the major summer
holiday. In a country about the same size as the continental United States, you will of course find variable weather.
Cold weather is rare, though; in winter the southern
cities—Sydney, Canberra, Melbourne, and Hobart—are
apt to be merely chilly, with lows in the 40s degrees F.
Highs run in the 50s and 60s degrees F. Rain in the
southern tier of Australia is also more common in winter
than summer, although torrential summer downpours do
occur. The high mountain ranges in New South Wales,
Victoria, and Tasmania generally have snow in winter, and
it is here that the nation's ski resorts are found. Summer
in Australia is hot everywhere. The best time to go trekking in the Outback is in the spring or fall, when temperatures are cooler and the flies of summer have ceased
their rampaging. The best time to visit the Great Barrier
Reef is any time—although winter is the wettest season.

### What to Wear
Aussies are hardly fashion mavens. They dress sensibly, as
dictated by the weather. For much of the year, this means
lightweight, cool clothes with shorts, tank top, and flip-
flops being favored by legions of the population. Few
occasions call for dressing up, but no one cares if someone wants to put on a jacket and tie or party dress for a
night at the opera or on the town. A lightweight jacket or
sweater is usually plenty for a winter night in the south.
An umbrella and raincoat might come in handy along the
coast but would be distinctly out of place in the nation's
midsection. A hat for protection against the sun will come
in handy everywhere, and those who plan to walk along

the Great Barrier Reef will need sturdy shoes to protect their feet against the cutting edge of the coral.

## Currency

The Australian dollar is the unit of currency in Australia and it is divided into 100 cents. All major credit cards are accepted in Australia at hotels, restaurants, and shops, and for air transportation and car rental. American Express, Diners Club, MasterCard, Visa, and Bankcard are the most widely recognized. Travellers' checks are also readily accepted; it is usually best to exchange them for Oz (Australian) dollars at banks, where rates are more favorable.

*Tipping.* Aussies are not big tippers, but the practice is catching on at finer restaurants around the country. When they tip, 10 percent is about the maximum. Cab drivers and bartenders don't expect tips, nor do airport porters. No service charges are added into Australian hotel and restaurant bills.

## Time Zones

There are three time zones in Australia: Eastern, Central, and Western. Eastern time is two hours ahead of Western and one-half hour ahead of Central. Clocks in Australia are advanced one hour during Daylight Saving Time, October–March. Brisbane, Cairns, Canberra, Hobart, Melbourne, and Sydney are in the Eastern time zone; Adelaide, Alice Springs, and Darwin are in the Central time zone; and Perth is in the Western time zone.

England, the United States, and Canada are all *behind* Australian time—London is behind Sydney by 9 hours, New York and Toronto by 14, California and B.C. by 17 hours, and Hawaii by 19 hours. To figure Australian time, *add* the difference. For example, when it's 5:00 P.M. in California it is 10:00 A.M. in Sydney—but the next calendar day. (In Australia and figuring time in the Western Hemisphere or Europe, *subtract* the difference.)

## Telephoning

The country code for Australia is 61.

## Electrical Current

The electrical current in Australia is 240/250 volts, AC 50 Hz. Power outlets are three-pronged. An adapter socket and voltage converter will be needed by Americans and

Canadians who want to run hair dryers, travel irons, shavers, and other small electrical appliances brought from home.

### Business Hours
Most banks are open 9:30 A.M.–4:00 P.M. Monday–Thursday and until 5:00 P.M. on Friday. Post office hours are 9:00 A.M.– 5:00 P.M. weekdays. Most stores and shops are open for business 9:00 A.M.–5:00 P.M. except Sunday. In bigger cities, some stores stay open late one night of the week.

### Public Holidays
In addition to the national holidays listed below, individual states celebrate local holidays that generally cause a shutdown. National holidays are: New Year's Day; Australia Day, January 26 or the following Monday; Good Friday; Easter; Easter Monday; Anzac Day, April 25; Queen's Birthday, a Monday in June; Christmas; Boxing Day, December 26.

### How to Get Around
Air, rail, and bus companies will get you just about anywhere you want to go Down Under. There are three domestic airlines with nationwide route networks: Ansett, Australian Airlines, and East-West Airlines. Numerous regional airlines in each state pick up where the majors leave off and fly to smaller cities and towns, sometimes in pretty small aircraft.

Railways of Australia is the national rail line that links most major cities. On long trips (such as the trip on the famed Indian-Pacific from Sydney to Perth, which takes 65 hours), trains are equipped with sleeping and dining cars.

Australia is crisscrossed with interstate and intrastate bus routes operated by three companies: Greyhound, Ansett Pioneer, and Deluxe. A bus trip from Sydney to Melbourne, for example, takes about 15 hours. Any travel agent can book domestic passage in Australia.

*Car Rental.* The major rental companies in Australia are Avis, Hertz, Budget, National, Thrifty, and Letz. Car-rental rates include unlimited mileage and some insurance, but drivers pay for gas and additional coverage. You might expect to pay about $A45 a day for a compact car and as much as $A65 a day for a full-size vehicle. Weekly and monthly rates reflect discounts. A valid driver's license and a major credit card are required to rent a car in Australia, and most agencies will not rent to people under age 21. It is the law that all passengers must wear seat belts, and penalties for driving while intoxicated are severe—with no allowances made for foreigners. Police in Australia can stop motorists at any time to administer an on-the-spot breath test. Those who fail or refuse the test are hauled off to jail. Take note: Aussies drive on the left-hand side of the road.

### Travel Bargains

Travel agents, airlines, the railway, and bus companies sell money-saving travel bargains that can reduce transportation costs in Australia. They are detailed in *The Aussie Holiday Book* (see below); Australian Tourist Commission offices also have information concerning discount travel. See Australia airfares, for example, slash as much as 30 percent off the price of a domestic economy-class air ticket for travel almost anywhere on the continent. Other air bargains represent additional savings. The Austrailpass allows unlimited first-class travel on trains in Australia for fixed periods of time. The 14-day pass costs A$440. Interstate bus lines sell similar discount tickets. Greyhound markets an Aussie Explorer ticket, which fixes the fares on certain routes at lower-than-normal rates. It's a good idea to ask a travel agent about these bargain tickets, because they are sold subject to conditions and restrictions, and some require purchase outside Australia.

### Information

U.S. residents can phone (800) 445-4400 for information about travel to Australia, and for a free copy of *The Aussie Holiday Book,* published annually by the Australian Tourist Commission, the national tourist office. The book contains information about tours, sights and attractions, accommodations, transportation, and other handy travel tips.

In Canada, contact the Australian Tourist Commission at 3080 Yonge Street, Toronto M4N 3N1, Ontario; (416) 487-2126. In the United Kingdom, contact the Australian Tourist Commission at 20 Saville Row, London W1X 1A3, England; (01) 434-4372. In New Zealand, contact the Australian Tourist Commission at Customs House, 29 Customs Street, West, Auckland, N.Z.; (09) 79-95-94.

In the United States, you may contact representatives of

Australian states at: New South Wales Tourist Commission, 2049 Century Park East, Los Angeles, CA 90067, Tel: (213) 552-9566; Victorian Tourism Commission, 2121 Avenue of the Stars, Los Angeles, CA 90067, Tel: (213) 553-6352; Northern Territory Tourist Commission, 2121 Avenue of the Stars, Los Angeles, CA 90067, Tel: (213) 277-7877; South Australian Department of Tourism, 2121 Avenue of the Stars, Los Angeles, CA 90067, Tel: (213) 552-2821; Tourism Tasmania, 2121 Avenue of the Stars, Los Angeles, CA 90067, Tel: (213) 552-3010; Western Australian Tourism Commission, 2121 Avenue of the Stars, Los Angeles, CA 90067, Tel: (213) 552-1987; Queensland Tourist and Travel Corporation, 611 North Larchmont Boulevard, Los Angeles, CA 90004, Tel: (213) 465-8418.

# BIBLIOGRAPHY

H. M. BARKER, *Camels and the Outback*. Camel drayman Barker provides a definitive account of the camel's role in exploration and frontier settlement.

D. L. BERNSTEIN, *First Tuesday in November* (1969). The total story of the Melbourne Cup, the horse race that annually brings the nation to a standstill.

GEOFFREY BLAINEY, *Triumph of the Nomads: A History of Ancient Australia* (1975). Carbon dating has identified aboriginal sites nearly 40,000 years old. Blainey describes the ancient settlement of the continent by people who created a lifestyle around a harsh, ever-changing environment. Their skills in finding water and as herbalists, trappers, and hunters are part of a description that also shows how rising seas led to the isolation of the first Australians.

JEFF CARTER, *People of the Inland* (1966). Rabbiters, 'roo shooters, drovers, bore sinkers, rodeo riders, and bush cooks are among the many unique Outback "identities" whose lives are described by Carter.

GAVIN CASEY AND TED MAYMAN, *The Mile That Midas Touched*. Water was once almost as precious as gold in Kalgoorlie, Australia's last great gold-rush town. This history traces the settlement from Patrick Hannan's 1893 find through development of both the deep mines of the Golden Mile and the water pipeline from mountains far to the west.

BRUCE CHATWIN, *The Songlines* (1987). A travelog/memoir/history focusing on the mythical "Dreamtime" of the aboriginals, when the ancestors walked across Australia singing the world into existence.

C. M. H. CLARK, *A History of Australia* (five volumes, 1981). This recent work is said to have "made Australians interested in reading about their history for the first time."

MARCUS CLARKE, *For the Term of His Natural Life* (1874). Published more than a century ago, this grim and powerful novel of life in an Australian penal colony is considered an Australian classic.

LEN EVANS, *Complete Book of Australian Wine* (1984). It takes 785 oversize pages to tell the history of Australia's wines, describe the wineries and regions, grape varieties, and white and red wines in the '80s. Beautiful illustrations.

A. B. FACEY, *A Fortunate Life* (1981). A Western Australian Everyman tells the story of his life: orphan boy on hardscrabble frontier farms, jackeroo on remote cattle stations, Anzac soldier in World War I, and family man in postwar Perth.

ERWIN H. J. AND GERDA E. E. FEEKEN, AND O.H.K. SPATE, *The Discovery and Exploration of Australia* (1970). The exploits of all of Australia's explorers, from the 17th-century Dutch to Frederick S. Drake-Brockman of 1901, are in this volume. It also contains a historical gazetteer of Australian place names.

MILES FRANKLIN, *My Brilliant Career* (1901) and *All That Swagger*. *Career* was the first novel by 21-year-old Franklin; the much later *Swagger* is considered her best. Both ring with her affection for Australian country life and feminist views.

MRS. AENEAS GUNN, *We of the Never-Never* (1908). The isolated life of a Northern Territory cattle station as described by Mrs. Gunn, who arrived at The Elsey in 1908 as a bride and departed a year later a widow.

ROBIN HILL, *Birds of Australia* (1967). A fine, illustrated introduction to the 700-plus species found Down Under. If the book or birds on the wing inspire you to birding, compact field guides are available on the spot.

DONALD HORNE, *The Lucky Country: Revisited* (1987). Hindsight of 1987 tempers the author's sometimes harsh look at the social and cultural climate of the 1960s. His topics range from the "first suburban nation" to "Australian ugliness."

ROBERT HUGHES, *The Fatal Shore: The Epic of Australia's Founding* (1987). The current best-selling analysis of The System, the scheme that transported 158,829 men and 24,568 women from England's prisons to penal settlements in Australia between 1788 and 1868. Grim reading.

BRIAN KENNEDY, *Silver, Sin, and Sixpenny Ale* (1978). This history of the silver mining town of Broken Hill—called "the Mecca of Unionism" and "industrial magnet of Australia"—starts with the claim-pegging days of 1883 and ends with the great labor strike of 1919–1920.

LEONIE KRAMER AND ADRIAN MITCHELL, EDS., *The Oxford Anthology of Australian Literature* (1984). A selection of both the best and the most representative in Australian letters.

FRANK LEECHMAN, *The Opal Book* (1961). A volume focused on the opal fields of White Cliffs, Lightning Ridge, and Coober Pedy: opal mining, myths and legends, and famous opals.

W. F. MANDLE, *Going It Alone* (1978). Varied unique incidents, from strikes to the death of the race horse Phar Lap, are used by Mandle to illustrate the development of national character in the isolated land Down Under.

MICHAEL MCKERNAN AND PETER STANLEY, EDS., *Anzac Day: Seventy Years On* (1986). Photography and words meld to plumb the meaning of Anzac Day, nearly three quarters of a century after Australians landed below the cliffs of Gallipoli.

ALAN MOOREHEAD, *Cooper's Creek* (1963). The story of the ill-fated Burke-Wills 1860 expedition to cross the continent from south to north and return.

EDWARD E. MORRIS, *A Dictionary of Austral English* (1898). Reprinted in the 1970s, this volume is considered unsurpassed as a historical record of entirely new words and altered English words in the Australian and New Zealand languages.

ANN MOYAL, *A Bright and Savage Land: Scientists in Colonial Australia* (1975). Australia, continent of "all things queer and opposite," was a paradise for the 18th- and 19th-century scientists whose work is described here. The account begins with naturalists and navigators and ends with experimenters and inventors. Sketches, paintings, and plates of the time provide illustration.

BILL NEIDJIE, STEPHEN DAVIS, AND ALLAN FOX, *Kakadu Man: Bill Neidjie* (1985). This little book contains the poetic, poignant response of Big Bill Neidjie, one of the last of the Bunitj people, to conflicting 1970s demands that tribal lands of Kakadu be made a national park or mined for uranium. (Park advocates won.)

PETER J. PHILLIPS, *Redgum and Paddlewheelers* (1980). Paddlewheelers on the Murray, Darling, and Murrumbidgee rivers aided in settlement and development of vast areas of interior Southeast Australia. This book tells the story of boats, captains, adventures, and disasters along the rivers.

PETER PIERCE, ED., *The Oxford Literary Guide to Australia*. A comprehensive and evocative account of the places lived in and celebrated by Australia's writers, listing more than 930 localities.

RHYS POLLARD, *The Cream Machine* (1972). A Vietnam War novel of Australian involvement, considered by many the best of its genre.

ERIC C. ROSS ROLLS, *They All Ran Wild* (1969). A tale of the ecological disasters wrought by foreign animals and plants Down Under. Rolls first looks at the ravages of the gray English rabbit, then follows with those of the hare, fox, trout, carp, sparrow, starling, feral pig, donkey, horse, camel, and goat. Not to mention the blackberry.

GEOFFREY SERLE, *The Creative Spirit in Australia* (1987). This volume provides newcomers to the Australian cultural scene with a Who's Who (and Why) in literary, visual, and performing arts.

MICHAEL SYMONS, *One Continuous Picnic: A History of Eating in Australia* (1982). Looks at food and eating habits as part of Australia's history and national character; traces the evolution of cookery from colonial damper bread to fluffy pavlova and beyond.

*Walkabout's Australia* (1964). A collection of the best stories published in *Walkabout,* a magazine that concentrated on the land and way of life. It begins with a 1934 article titled "Men, Sheep and Far Horizons" and ends with a 1964 feature on surfing and surfers.

PATRICK WHITE, *The Tree of Man* (1957). This novel by Australia's first Nobel Prize winner (1973) was also the first of White's work to draw universal acclaim overseas; Australian critics, however, raged at his concept of the national character.

JOHN YEOMANS, *The Other Taj Mahal* (1968). A look at the first ten years of squabbling, mistakes, and technical challenges in construction of the Sydney Opera House.

R. M. YOUNGER, *Australia! Australia!* (1987). Three detailed, pictorial volumes—*The Pioneer Years, March to Nationhood, Challenge and Achievement*—contain an overview of Australian history and cultural, social, and political development.

—*Shirley Maas Fockler*

# SYDNEY

*By David Swindell*

Sydney is a most distracting place. Imagine a city that combines the best of San Francisco and St. Tropez. Imagine a place where people take pride in their comfort and pleasure and hold them most dear. Imagine an urban sprawl of some 700 square miles trapped between sea and mountains, colored by eucalyptus trees, jacaranda, frangipani, hibiscus, and neon. Imagine all these things—and think Sydney.

It would be easy to call Sydney's more than three million people hedonistic. Tanned, slim, and topless, Sydneysiders by the thousands grease themselves up and broil in the sun that bakes this city most of the year. They congregate in pubs and never say no to another beer, especially if someone else is buying. They feast on the freshest seafood, dance at the trendiest clubs, and soak up opera, dance, and classical music as if they were Viennese.

But it is not a hedonistic city. There's nothing even vaguely sinister about the way Sydneysiders grapple with life. For most, it's fun, it's good to be alive, and it's great—the natives are happy to tell anyone who will listen—to live in a perfect place.

### MAJOR INTEREST

Sydney Harbour
The harbor ferries
Royal Botanic Gardens
Sydney Opera House
The Rocks, old penal-colony area
The old shopping arcades

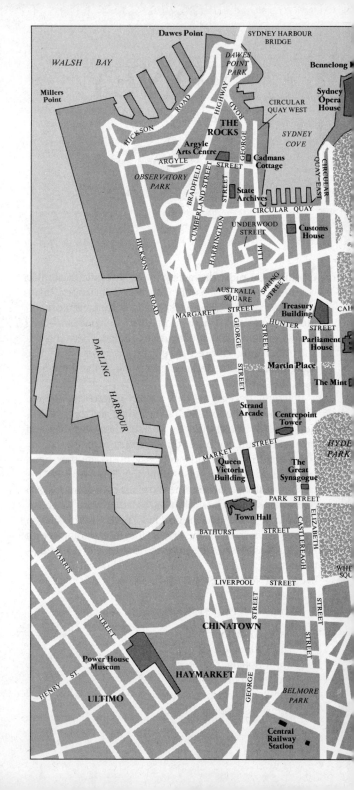

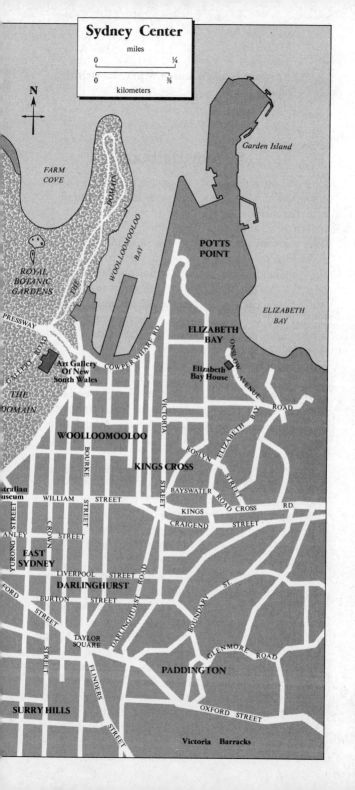

# Sydney Harbour

Of all the attractions that lure people to Sydney—and the city is the number-one tourist destination in Australia for overseas visitors—the greatest is Sydney Harbour. The harbor is a gift of nature, even more pleasing to the eye than the magnificent harbors in Rio and Cape Town. Sydneysiders use their harbor for much more than a shipping lane. They swim in it at any number of pleasant beaches—in the shadow of the downtown skyline—in water that is calm, mild, and clean. They live beside it in homes and condos as pricey as Manhattan or Mayfair apartments. They cross it in ferries. They attend the opera and dine at waterfront restaurants.

Indeed, the best place to get a first look at Sydney is from the harbor. That's easy enough to do on one of the ferries that operate every day of the year between **Circular Quay** and the harborside suburbs. The first ferry was launched in 1789, a year after Sydney—Australia's first white settlement—was founded. Ferries have plied harbor ever since.

The best of these trips is aboard the **ferry to Manly** (a Pacific Ocean suburb on the north head of the harbor entrance), which leaves from jetty 3. The half-hour voyage takes passengers past the Opera House and affords the best views of Sydney's skyline. On the way back, as an alternative, there's a hydrofoil that zooms atop the water and takes half the time of the ferry.

But for a more in-depth look at the city from the harbor, take a trip aboard one of the sightseeing boats operated by **Captain Cook Cruises**. Boats operate every day of the year from jetty 6 at Circular Quay, and you can usually board just by showing up a few minutes before sailing. A guide delivers a running commentary, pointing out places of interest. Highly recommended is the Coffee Cruise, which leaves the jetty daily at 10:00 A.M. and 2:15 P.M. and costs about A$18. In a two-and-a-half-hour trip, the cruise boat sails right around the harbor, a 21-square-mile area, past the city, and beyond to the beaches and outlying suburbs.

Many other cruises of various durations are available each day.

For those who might prefer a bit more privacy cruising around the harbor, the **Australian Sailing Club** charters yachts with or without a skipper for full- and half-day trips. In addition to full-size sailboats, the club rents dinghies, runabouts, catamarans, and even sailboards. (Call 960-3999 for information.)

Orienting yourself to Sydney from the water helps put the city in perspective. Keep in mind that this is a big city. To tackle such an overwhelming space, take it in stages. Good city maps are available free at the Travel Centre of New South Wales (corner of Pitt and Spring streets downtown). With a good map and a decent sense of direction—always use the water as a point of reference—it's hard to get lost in Sydney, despite its narrow downtown streets that reveal the founders' lack of concern for urban planning.

Most of the interesting sights in Sydney are in the city center, and with a strong constitution and sturdy shoes you can get to them on foot. The fainthearted can use the city's abundant taxis, buses, and trains to meander about, but it is advisable not to drive. As in all big cities, parking is scarce and lots are expensive.

## *EXPLORING SYDNEY*

A walk around Sydney Harbour from the **Art Gallery of New South Wales** to The Rocks covers many of the top sights and attractions in town. The art gallery, open daily, is on Art Gallery Road in a park called the Domain, just south of the Royal Botanic Gardens. It opened in the early part of the century and has been the repository of some of the finest works exhibited in Australia since. There is a fair representation of old masters, but it is the Australian works, some 20th century and contemporary, that attract the most attention here.

## The Royal Botanic Gardens

Toward the harbor a short distance north of the art gallery are the exquisite Royal Botanic Gardens. The gardens sit on the site of the first farm in Australia and have been functioning as a botanic garden since 1816. It would take days to explore the 74-acre gardens properly, but plenty can be absorbed just by strolling through. Planted everywhere in the gardens are both common and unusual flowers from Australia and around the world. Victorian fountains, statues, and monuments are sprinkled throughout the gardens.

It's hard to imagine a pulsating city just beyond the tranquility of these flowers and trees, but as the botanic gardens end, the Sydney Opera House comes into view at the northwest end of the gardens. The juxtaposition of Victorian gardens and 21st-century architecture provides a moment to be savored.

## Sydney Opera House

An international competition was held for the design of the Opera House in the late 1950s; a Danish architect, Jøern Utzon, won the contract. He designed the building in the shape of sails, in respect for the harbor on whose shore it was erected. Queen Elizabeth II opened the Opera House at an outlandish ceremony in 1973, and since then it has been the home of the Australian Opera and the Australian Ballet. Plays, concerts, and other shows are also staged here regularly.

Although the outside of the building is far more interesting than the inside, there are tours of the complex, including the backstage area, almost every day of the year. They're inexpensive and short enough not to be dull. Tickets to most of the shows can be purchased at the box office on the day of the performance. But if native Sydneysider Joan Sutherland—or any other big-name opera star—is singing, tickets are hard to come by.

Affordable lunches are served at the **Harbourside Restaurant** at the back of the Opera House; the cafeteria-style food is worth putting up with for the views across the water and of the graceful old **Sydney Harbour Bridge** (known to locals as "the coat-hanger" and rumored to have once had one Paul Hogan as one of its painters). Upscale meals are served at the **Bennelong Restaurant** here, but it's a dressy place most suitable for dinner before a performance.

# The Rocks

Circular Quay, where the ferries dock, is just beside the Opera House to the west, and beyond it a few blocks farther west lies Sydney's—and Australia's—most historic area, The Rocks. It was here 200 years ago that the first white settlement was established. Sydney itself was named after Thomas Townsend, Lord Sydney, the British Home and Colonial Secretary in the 1780s. It was through his office that plans to transport convicts to Australia were drawn up. There is no record, however, that he ever visited Australia.

The Rocks was neglected for many years, after it no longer served as the center of the settlement, and fell victim to such indignities as vandalism and the plague, but city fathers finally began redevelopment in 1970. Now The Rocks is a popular tourist area of historic homes, shops, and restaurants. The architecture demonstrates what happened when stuffy Victorian architects came face-to-face with the tropics, and for that alone The Rocks is worth a stroll.

The Rocks Visitor Centre at 104 George Street should be everyone's first stop. Maps of the district are available that point out places of interest and plot independent walking tours. A short orientation film is shown at the center, too. Visitors who prefer guided tours with commentary can join them at the center. Tours last a little over an hour and leave on the half hour from 10:30 A.M. to 2:30 P.M. daily.

Not every building at The Rocks is interesting. For some that have been restored, a peek at their exteriors will probably suffice. Others, however, are of interest even for people who have little knowledge of Australian history. **Cadman's Cottage** on George Street is Sydney's oldest building, erected in 1815–16 as a barracks for the governor's boat crew. It takes its name from John Cadman, government coxswain and later superintendent of government boats in Sydney, who lived in the cottage. Cadman's life sentence for horse-stealing had been commuted to transportation for life to Australia. He was pardoned in 1814 and eventually landed his government job. This petite dwelling is the only example of how people of modest means lived in Sydney in the early years of Australian nationhood.The house is now a museum that displays household items from the period (open every day but Monday). The site is still interesting to archaeologists, who dig there frequently in efforts to unearth more of Sydney's past.

Across George Street from Cadman's Cottage is Argyle Terrace, a small street whose workers' homes date back a century. The **Argyle Arts Centre**, the main attraction on the street now, houses small shops and boutiques and a few restaurants. It's a good spot to buy typically Aussie souvenirs, like stuffed koalas and platypuses, most of which seem to be made in Taiwan. Behind the arts center is a delightful little walk through Argyle Cut to the **Lord Nelson Hotel**, Sydney's oldest pub ("hotel" in Oz frequently means pub), which opened for business in 1842. Preservationists say it is a rare example of pure colonial Australian architecture. The entire neighborhood is full of colonial Australian homes, many of which, as on Argyle Cut, were built with convict labor.

Of interest back on Argyle Street is the 1840s **Orient Hotel**, another pub rich in Australian history. On this site in the latter part of the 18th century, so the story goes, Australia's first wedding was performed, a multiple wedding for seven brides and grooms—with their children in attendance.

Two shops, neither important historically, should be visited while strolling around The Rocks. The **Sydney Harbour Shop**, 123 George Street, is run by Ken Done, Australia's Andy Warhol. Original works by the whimsical painter are sold, none too cheap. The **Australian Fashion Design Centre**, 105 George Street, is a showcase for homegrown talent and sheep products. Woolen knitwear and other original clothing are sold by well-known Australian designers, none too cheap either. If an overseas visitor has an Australian family connection, he or she might consider one final stop in The Rocks. The State Archives on Harrington Street house all the convict transportation documents, and people are welcome to search their family tree for lost ancestors.

There is an alternative for people who find tackling Sydney on foot to be a bit too much walking. The **Sydney Explorer Bus** charges A$10 for a one-day ticket that allows passengers to get on and off as many times as they choose. It stops at 20 of the city's top attractions, including the Opera House, Royal Botanic Gardens, Art Gallery of New South Wales, Elizabeth Bay House, Australian Museum, Chinatown, Centrepoint Tower, and The Rocks. The bus is red, and stops are clearly marked around town. It runs daily between 9:30 A.M. and 5:00 P.M. and can be boarded at any stop.

## More Sights in Sydney

Other sights in Sydney are farther apart, although the main attractions are connected by the Explorer Bus. There is one perch in the city center for Empire State Building-like views of Sydney, **Centrepoint Tower**, known equally well as Sydney Tower. It sits on Pitt Street at the corner of Market and stands 1,000 feet above the pavement. On an average day the entire city as far away as the beaches and the Pacific Ocean can be seen from the 360-degree observation deck. On a supremely clear day, the Blue Mountains 60 miles to the west are quite visible. (There is a modest charge to ride the high-speed elevator to the top.)

The obligatory revolving restaurants in the tower serve up better views than eats, as usual in such places anywhere in the world, and numerous shops are located on the lower floors. Each year in June a marathon race up the 63 stories and almost 1,500 stairs to the top is the talk of the town. The record time is somewhere around seven minutes. Skip the tower's exhibit on UFOs. Enthralling—and free—views of the city are also seen from Dawes Point under the Sydney Harbour Bridge and from the roof of the **Australian Museum**.

The museum is a natural-history exhibit. It's far from the best such museum on earth, but its strong suit is its display of native flora and fauna. The section that traces aboriginal life from "Dreamtime," as the aboriginals call their very ancient history, is remarkable. For people with no idea of Australian history prior to the landing of the white man, a trip to the museum will provide some insight into this part of Australian lore. There is no admission charge to the museum, which is located on the corner of William and College streets near the downtown business district.

There are other museums in Sydney, but the city's devotion to life outdoors is reflected in most of these, and they are not of international caliber; they are, if anything,

a tad parochial. One, however, is worth visiting: the
**Power House Museum** on Harris Street in the nearby
suburb of Ultimo, just to the southwest of the city center.
This is a giant exhibition illustrating how many of the
machines we have come to rely on actually work. The
museum has recently upgraded its displays and is as
entertaining as it is informative. Planes, ships, trains, and
cars are dissected, explained, and exhibited. One popular
feature is an early steam engine built in the late 1700s.

Architecture buffs should stroll around some of the
Australian colonial and Victorian buildings and homes
that have been restored and preserved around the city.
**Elizabeth Bay House** is the city's most wonderful example of a home built in the colonial fashion. It dates from
1835 and was described at the time as the "finest house in
the colony." It still is.

The rooms have been carefully decorated with period
furnishings. Particularly beautiful for their simplicity are
the servants' rooms in the attic. A small display depicts the
life of a servant in colonial Australia, and throughout the
house are other exhibits about colonial life. The house
sits in a magnificent setting overlooking the harbor on
Onslow Avenue in the Elizabeth Bay section of the city
east of the Botanic Gardens. The house is closed on
Mondays.

Farther away from the downtown area is **Vaucluse
House**, every bit the rival of Elizabeth Bay House in terms
of beauty, artistry, and history. It was begun in 1803 but
rebuilt in the 1830s by the man known as the "Father of
the Australian Constitution," William Wentworth. The 15-
room house is built in a style that could only be called
Gothic Australian Colonial, and it is indeed one of a kind.
Twenty-seven acres of pleasant gardens surround the
house, which also overlooks the water. A cab ride to the
house is expensive, but the number 325 bus stops in front
of the house and continues to Circular Quay. There is a
modest entrance fee, and a tearoom that serves refresh-
ments and light meals.

Back in the city center, Victorian buildings that still
command more attention than modern-day steel office
towers are Town Hall (1889), the Queen Victoria Building
(1898; see the Shopping section to discover its new incarnation), the Great Synagogue (1878), and the Customs
House (1885). Predating the Victorian Age are Parliament

House (1827) and the Mint (1816), now a museum of decorative arts. These buildings, with the exception perhaps of the Great Synagogue and the Queen Victoria Building, are far more appealing from the outside and require no more than a cursory glance inside. The National Trust, which has saved more than a few of Sydney's grand old buildings and homes from the wrecker's ball, has information about these and other architecturally historic edifices available at its shop in the Queen Victoria Building. (See also the Inter-Continental Hotel under Accommodations, below.)

## Sydney Neighborhoods

Like the great cities of the world, Sydney is a coalition of neighborhoods, each with its own personality. Many are working-class neighborhoods with little to offer a visitor. Some, like **Chinatown** or **Newtown**—which is predominantly Greek—are ethnic. But others, particularly those close to downtown, provide the very heartbeat of the city. Most of these enticing neighborhoods are best toured on foot. There will be a pub every block or two where you might stop for a cool drink before heading onward.

One such neighborhood is **Kings Cross**, called The Cross, the sleazy Times-Square-like area east of the city center around Darlinghurst Road that comes alive at night and stays awake until dawn. Just to the south of The Cross is **Darlinghurst**, a bustling few blocks of cafés, restaurants, and boutiques. Follow Oxford Street away from the city center to what is Sydney's most vibrant neighborhood, **Paddington**, just southeast of Darlinghurst. A cross between New York's Greenwich Village and London's Earl's Court, "Paddo," as the locals call it, teems day and night. Oxford Street and the neighborhood's sidestreets are lined with shops, boutiques, bookstores, pubs, art galleries, and the city's most unusual and interesting stores.

There are other neighborhoods through which you might pass trekking around Sydney—Moore Park, location of the city's largest park, Centennial Park; Randwick, where the horse-racing track is located; Bondi, a neighborhood as well as a beach; Woollahra, with its quiet, tree-lined streets of terrace houses; and the peaceful harborside neighborhoods of Elizabeth Bay, Rushcutters Bay, and Darling Point, to name a few.

# THE SYDNEY BEACHES

To experience Sydney fully is to go to the beach. Even if you're not a beach person, go. Sydneysiders by the thousands would rather be on a beach close to home than perhaps anywhere else on the planet. If there is a national religion in Australia, it is sun worship. Not surprisingly, Aussies suffer a higher incidence of skin cancer than any other people on earth, which explains why it was they who invented zinc cream (it now comes in colors!).

Two types of beaches exist in the city: ocean beaches with surf and harbor beaches without surf. Sharks are not a problem. Beaches are netted and safe for swimming, but should the errant shark get in the swimming area, shark patrol lifeguards sound an alarm. There has been only one fatal shark attack in Sydney since the 1930s.

Trash is a problem, with the most popular beaches being the dirtiest. Bondi Beach, the most famous Australian beach, is a mess, despite the heroic efforts of cleaning crews who sift the sand regularly with goliath vacuum machines. Legions of people who use Bondi and other beaches seem not to mind the cans, cigarette butts, wrappers, and paper bags that litter otherwise beautiful seaside spaces. Naturally, there are no complaints from the sea gulls and pigeons. If trashy beaches are a concern, when you plan to go phone the beach pollution hotline—(02) 269-5450—to find out how bad conditions really are.

**Bondi Beach,** south along the Tasman Sea coast from the harbor entrance (South Head), is the granddaddy of Sydney beaches, easily reached from the city center by bus from Circular Quay and one of the few with a parking lot for the masses who drive to it on any given summer day. Beware the crowds on summer weekends, when the beachgoers are shoulder to shoulder, although many of those shoulders are fine to look at—on both sexes. Not since Annette and Frankie has a beach been the teen tease that Bondi is today. Add to that that it's topless, although families with tots frequent the beach, too. Bondi made history in the early 1950s when the young Queen Elizabeth watched her first surf carnival from its shores. The Aussies were so taken with the moment that a plaque was erected to mark the spot where Her Majesty stood. After

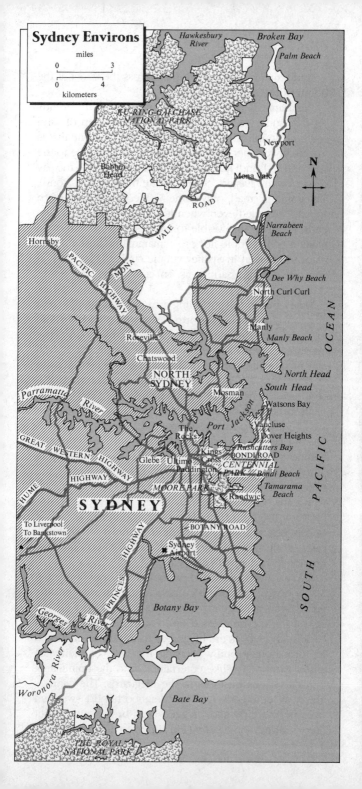

sunning, many retire to the pub across the street at the **Bondi Hotel** for a midi or two.

**Tamarama Beach**, called "Glamarama" by the trendy set that squeezes onto it, is a beautiful sweep of sand south of Bondi. It, too, is a topless beach, and one that is marginally cleaner than Bondi. City buses operate to the beach from Bondi Junction, which is connected to the city center by the Eastern Suburbs Line train. Unlike Bondi, Tamarama is small, only some 330 feet long, so it often appears crowded even when it's not. On summer weekends, it can be impossible to find a spot to spread out a blanket. Still, people flock to Tamarama because it is the place to be seen in Sydney yuppie circles. Leave early if you are driving; parking is on city streets and places disappear fast.

**Manly Beach** is a sprawling area north along the coast just above the harbor's North Head, with plenty of room for swimmers on one end and surfers on the other. The ocean surf here is often rough, but the beach is well patrolled by lifeguards who are quick to call in those who stray too far out. Take a ferry to Manly Beach from Circular Quay. The beach is a short walk from the pier.

All sorts of people show up at Manly, from families with kids, to teens, to lovers, to groups of friends. Nobody is out of place here. It's a clean beach, and the little park behind it supplies lots of shade under towering Norfolk pines when a break from the sun is needed. Across the street from the beach is the **Steyne Hotel**, which is a pub with a shady beer garden where lunch is served. Nearby, the **New Brighton Hotel** is another good place to stop at to cool down. There are several restaurants and sidewalk cafés along the pedestrian mall that connects the harborside ferry pier with the beach.

Surf carnivals are staged periodically at both Bondi and Manly beaches. These peculiarly Australian rites pit lifeguard against lifeguard in competition to see who can save a life the quickest. There is as much ceremony as contest, though, as the lifeguards march down the beach in formation, proudly carrying the flags of their surf clubs. It may look like entertainment to the uninitiated, but it's serious business to the lifeguards. The winners are near demigods in their neighborhoods, swooned over by the girls and bragged over by the moms, but there's always some young kid aiming to depose the king.

If opportunity knocks, don't miss this wonderful slice of Australiana. Phone the Surf Lifesaving Association, (02) 699-1126, to find out carnival dates.

If Manly Beach palls, just walk up the road north to the next beach—and the next, and the next.

Harbor beaches, again, have no surf and might be compared to lakeside beaches. The water is usually warmer than the ocean, and it is not uncommon to find people at a harbor beach on a sunny winter day in August. The easiest harbor beach to get to is **Camp Cove** near Watson's Bay, a suburb at the entrance of Sydney Harbour. Buses operate to Watson's Bay from various points in the city. Like all harbor beaches, it's small. All sorts of people use the beach, and it's topless.

Just beyond Camp Cove is **Lady Jane Beach**, where outright nudity is the norm. If you care to look, the views across the harbor are quite stunning. It's difficult to get to Lady Jane—you must walk along a path through the brush and descend a steep ladder to the beach—but such obstacles discourage few and the beach is both popular and crowded. Take food and water to Lady Jane, since it's a schlepp back to Camp Cove to get a Coke.

Sydney's most beautiful beach is **Palm Beach**, on the other side of the Hawkesbury River mouth at Broken Bay, north of town about an hour by car or nearly two hours by city bus (No. 190). It is a true tropical South Pacific beach, as gorgeous and lush as you might expect to find in Tahiti or Fiji. The surf seems always to be up, making Palm Beach a favorite with surfers. The southern end of the beach is where families with children congregate, while nudists have taken over the north end. Because it is out of town somewhat, the beach is rarely crowded. Incidentally, real estate in this part of Sydney commands some of the highest prices in Australia.

## *SPORTS*

Australia is a sports-mad nation. In Sydney, visitors can participate in such activities as parachuting and scuba diving, or the more tame sports of tennis and golf, to mention only a few. **Bushwalking**, that old Australian activity most everyone else calls hiking, is also a favorite Sydney pastime.

There are so many bushwalking clubs in Sydney that they've banded together into the Federation of Bushwalking Clubs, which has tons of information about hiking in the region and maps that point out the trails. Contact the organization at 176 Cumberland Street; Tel: (02) 27-4206. The staff there also has information about where to purchase the proper gear for a bushwalk.

It is impossible to say where the "best" trails for bushwalking are found in the region, but those in the **Royal National Park**, 30 km (18 miles) south of the city are certainly excellent. The park is the second oldest national park in the world, predated only by Yellowstone in the United States. Some of the trails lead to freshwater pools that are safe for swimming; try the walk to Woronora Dam and the river of the same name for a dip in some great swimming holes. But the first stop should be at the park's visitor center at the north entrance, where trail maps are available.

**Bicycling** is another easily accessible sport in Sydney, although in summer it is often too hot to bike during midday. The best place in the city for a bike trip is in **Centennial Park**, the huge expanse of green and lakes in Paddington that was opened in honor of Australia's first hundred years of colonial settlement. Bikes can be rented from an outfit called Centennial Park Hire, 50 Clovelly Road, Randwick, for less than A$20 a day. (Other bike rental shops can be found in the Yellow Pages.)

There are also bridle paths for **horseback riding** in Centennial Park. It will cost less than A$20 an hour to rent a horse for an escorted ride around the park, offered hourly from 9:00 A.M. to 5:00 P.M. every day. Two handy rental stables are Centennial Park Horse Hire at the Showgrounds on Long Road and Challis Riding School, 4 Challis Street, Randwick. Spectators should watch the papers to see when the horse races are on at Randwick, Rosehill, Warwick Farm, and Canterbury, Sydney's four tracks. Races are usually run at one of those tracks every Wednesday and Saturday. Trotting races are held on Friday nights at Harold Park in the nearby suburb of Glebe, just south of Ultimo.

Sydney's climate allows golfers and tennis players year-round access to greens and courts. There are dozens of places to play both sports. Those who belong to a golf club back home should check to see if there are reciprocating clubs in Sydney where they might play for free. If not, ask at the hotel front desk for the name of a club that welcomes non-members. Tennis enthusiasts should also ask at the hotel front desk for the location of the closest court.

Cricket is a major spectator sport in Sydney. If a match is on at the **Sydney Cricket Ground** at Moore Park, take it in; the whole carnival atmosphere is another experience that will enrich a trip to Sydney. Cricket season is October to March, and numerous games are played day and night.

## GETTING AROUND

The Urban Transit Authority (UTA) runs buses, trains, and ferries in a comprehensive route network that connects most points in the city with one another and with the outlying suburbs. Fares on buses and trains are based on distance. For information and timetables, phone Metro Trips at (02) 29-2622.

A Day Rover ticket, sold by the UTA, is valid for unlimited travel on buses, trains, and ferries for one day. Tickets are sold at rail and bus stations and at the Circular Quay ferry terminal. The UTA also operates harbor cruises seven days a week from Circular Quay. Tickets cost A$10 for the two-and-a-half-hour cruises, which provide a commentary on sights and attractions lining the harbor.

A bus to the airport is operated by the UTA from the Central Railway Station every 15 minutes, and from Circular Quay every half hour; tickets cost A$2.20. A free shopping bus, number 777, operates during normal business hours on weekdays and shuttles passengers around the city-center shopping district. It runs every 15 minutes or so; stops are clearly marked. Another free bus, number 666, operates from Hunter Street to the Art Gallery of New South Wales at approximately 30-minute intervals daily.

Taxis are readily available all over town and can be hailed from the street. They're usually waiting in front of hotels and are always lined up at the airport. Taxis are metered and drivers don't expect—but won't refuse—tips.

Hertz, Avis, Budget, National, and Letz are the major car-rental companies in Sydney. They have offices at the airport and along William Street in the city. Smaller companies, A.S.B. Car Rental, Bargain Rent-A-Car, Kings Cross

Rent-A-Car, Betta Rent-A-Car, Airport Rent-A-Car, and Rent A Bug, often have cheaper rates. All rates on rental cars include compulsory insurance, and most cover unlimited mileage.

Call the travel information hotline for details of what to see and do in Sydney. The line is open daily 8:00 A.M. to 6:00 P.M.; Tel: (02) 669-5111. Book theater tickets over the phone by calling Mitchell Bass at (02) 116-88.

Pick up the free publications *Where* and *This Week in Sydney* at your hotel or at the Travel Centre of New South Wales, at the corner of Pitt and Spring streets, for up-to-date listings of what to see and do.

## ACCOMMODATIONS

For visitors who like their accommodations top-of-the-line, Sydney has more deluxe and first-class hotels than any other city in Australia. But for those who aren't so particular, there are dozens of moderately priced hotels, motels, and apartments a visitor can call home for a while.

Deluxe hotels in Sydney are pricey by Australian standards but certainly not by American, Asian, or European. Many of the biggest ones are run by familiar companies— Hilton, Sheraton, Holiday Inn, Hyatt, Inter-Continental— that can usually be relied upon to supply decent service.

The telephone area code for Sydney is 02.

The top hotels in town are the Inter-Continental, the Regent, and the Sebel Town House. The **Inter-Continental** has the edge in being the newest and having the most character in terms of design, incorporating as it does the 19th-century Treasury Building, a gem of Victorian architecture. It's a fun hotel, too. Its glass-domed lobby, stuffed with leather sofas and outsize plants, has become a city-center meeting and conversation spot. Tea, coffee, and dainty finger sandwiches are served most of the day. Young execs from nearby office towers jam the **Tavern Bar** after work for a highball or two before heading home, and the **Top of the Treasury** has a cocktail lounge favored by the more sedate set as they sip drinks and savor harbor views—but it's dressy and a tad pricey that high up. At presstime, the Inter-Continental had the highest rates in town.

117 Macquarie Street, 2000. Tel: 251-2342; in U.S., (800)

327-0200; in Quebec and Ontario, (800) 268-3785; in the rest of Canada, (800) 368-3708.

Before the Inter-Continental came along four years ago, the most talked-about hotel in town was the **Regent**, still a smart place and one that costs almost as much as the Inter-Continental. It sits directly on the harbor near The Rocks and Circular Quay, and many rooms have exquisite views of the Opera House and the flotilla on the harbor.

199 George Street, 2000. Tel: 251-2851; in U.S., (800) 545-4000; in Canada, (800) 626-8222.

Show-biz types historically have favored the less-expensive **Sebel Town House**, a small inn-like hotel on Elizabeth Bay east along the harbor from the Botanic Gardens and in the shadow of the Kings Cross district. Service is impeccable, and rooms are spacious and airy. The two Bettes, Davis and Midler, are among the legion of famous guests in the not-so-distant past.

23 Elizabeth Bay Road, 2011. Tel: 357-1926; in U.S., (800) 223-6800; in Canada, (800) 341-8585.

In the city center are the two original deluxe hotels in Sydney, the **Hilton** and the **Sheraton-Wentworth**. Neither has anything architecturally to set it apart, but each can be counted on for efficient service and decent rooms—few, however, with views to match those at the Regent. For those who don't mind paying for a name, rates at the Hilton are as high as those at the Inter-Continental and Regent. The Sheraton is not as expensive.

Hilton. 259 Pitt Street, 2000. Tel: 266-0610; in U.S., (800) 445-8667.

Sheraton-Wentworth. 61-101 Phillip Street, 2000. Tel: 227-9133; in U.S. and Canada, (800) 325-3535.

There are less expensive rooms to be rented in Sydney for travellers who don't mind sacrificing lobby bars and rooms with views to save a few bucks. Most are clean, quiet, and safe, but some lean toward the scuzzy side.

Good, moderately priced hotels are the **Boulevard, Crest,** and **Sheraton Potts Point**, all located in or near Kings Cross and each accessible by train, bus, and taxi to the city center; **Rushcutter Travelodge**, a little bit out of the way beyond Kings Cross in the Rushcutters Bay neighborhood, but still served by public transportation; and the **Wynyard Travelodge** in the city center. The **Russell**

**Hotel** is on George Street in the city center, thus in the heart of downtown goings-on. It is not fancy, but it provides adequate accommodations for those not too fussy about decor and on-the-spot service.

Boulevard. 90 William Street, 2000. Tel: 357-2277; in U.S., (800) 421-0536; in Canada, (800) 251-2166.

Crest. 111 Darlinghurst Road, Kings Cross, 2011. Tel: 358-2755; in U.S., (800) 44-UTELL; in Canada, (800) 387-1338.

Sheraton Potts Point. 40 Macleay Street, Potts Point, 2011. Tel: 358-1955.

Rushcutter Travelodge. 110 Baywater Road, Rushcutters Bay, 2011. Tel: 331-2171; in U.S., (800) 421-0536; in Canada, (800) 251-2166.

Wynyard Travelodge. 7-9 York Street, 2000. Tel: 290-9888; in U.S., (800) 421-0536; in Canada, (800) 251-2166.

Russell. 143A George Street, Circular Quay, 2000. Tel: 241-3543.

Still cheaper hotels exist. Visitors who want to stay near the beach on the cheap should try the plain and simple **Breakers Motel** at Bondi Beach, which is about 9 km (5 miles) from downtown but just across the street from Sydney's most famous beach. The area is well served by public transportation.

164-176 Campbell, 2026. Tel: 309-3300.

Families or other groups travelling together can save money on accommodations by renting what the Aussies call self-catering apartments that have kitchens in which people can do their own cooking. The **York** on the perimeter of the city center is the most luxurious of these accommodations—with studios, one-, two-, and three-bedroom apartments to rent. Arrangements can be made for overnight or extended stays. The York has a restaurant, cocktail lounge, pool, spa, sauna, laundry room, and parking on the premises.

5 York Street, 2000. Tel: 264-7747; in U.S., (800) 44-UTELL; in Canada, (800) 387-1338.

Other well-appointed self-catering units are the **Carrington, Harbourside Holiday Apartments,** and **Park Apartments,** conveniently located on Oxford Street near shopping, restaurants, nightlife, and the city center. Less expensive apartments may be rented at the **Cosmopolitan Motor Inn** near Bondi Beach and **Grantham Lodge** at Potts Point near Kings Cross.

Carrington. 57-59 York Street, 2000. Tel: 290-1166.

Harbourside Holiday. 2a Henry Lawson Avenue, McMahons Point, 2060. Tel: 929-0399.

Park. 16–32 Oxford Street, 2000. Tel: 331-7728; in U.S., (800) 44-UTELL; in Canada, (800) 387-1338.

Cosmopolitan Motor Inn. 152–162 Campbell, Bondi Beach, 2062. Tel: 305–311.

Grantham Lodge. 1 Grantham Street, Potts Point, 2011. Tel: 357-2377.

One other hotel warrants a mention, although it is not in Sydney proper. It's the **Manly Pacific International** at the beachside resort of Manly, 7 km (4 miles) across the harbor from the city center. It sits right on the ocean beach, and guests need only cross the street for a swim in the South Pacific. It is a first-class hotel with nicely appointed rooms and private baths, three restaurants, four bars, a pool, spa, and gymnasium.

This is a popular hotel with those who want a vacation mix of city and beach life. No other top-of-the-line hotel in Sydney provides that advantage. Downtown is a 15-minute ride away by hydrofoil, 30 minutes by conventional ferry, and the ferry dock is a short walk from the hotel.

55 North Steyne, Manly, 2095. Tel: 977-7822; in U.S. and Canada, (800) 235-8222.

# DINING

It's easy to find a good meal in Sydney for just about any price imaginable at the hundreds and hundreds of restaurants in this Chicago-size city. The choice of cuisines served around town runs the gamut from Sri Lankan to Swedish, but Down Under down-home cooking is hard to beat for those who fancy meat-and-potato dishes, and worth a try for everybody.

Australian cuisine reflects the character of the nation and its people. It is hearty and unassuming—no fancy sauces or *nouvelle* portions here, just good basic food and plenty of it. The ingredients couldn't be fresher. Seafood fished from the seas surrounding the continent is rushed to Sydney tables daily. Beef and lamb from the great cattle and sheep stations of the Outback and fruits and vegetables from the farms of New South Wales also find their way to Sydney's restaurants in time for lunch or dinner. And Australian full-bodied, flavorful wines are gaining respect around the world.

Practically every section of the city has a good choice of places to dine, but some selectivity is required, and visitors should know a few ground rules about eating out in Sydney. There are two types of restaurants, those licensed to sell liquor and those that are not. The latter are called "BYO" (bring your own) and allow diners to bring in their own wine, beer, or spirits. All BYOs sell mixers, and some charge a modest corkage fee—a practice that infuriates the Aussies—to open and serve the wine. If the establishment is a BYO there will be a sign in the window or door advising that, and often recommending a liquor store not far away.

Tipping in Sydney restaurants seems quite subjective. At finer restaurants a 10 percent tip is adequate, but no waiter will chase a patron down the street after dinner demanding to be tipped. At smaller neighborhood places most diners do not tip. In any case, no service charge is added to restaurant bills, leaving it to the discretion of the customer whether or not to tip. Best advice: Tip 10 percent, although if you're dining with an Aussie you might be told, "Hell, mate, you'll only spoil 'em."

There is no dress code across Australia, and this applies to most Sydney restaurants. At the finer places, a coat and tie for men and cocktail dress for women is certainly not out of place, but an open shirt and nice slacks, or blouse and skirt, are just as acceptable. Shorts and jeans, while fine for a pub, beer garden, or McDonalds, are not appropriate for most upscale restaurants in the city, but many young people don jeans and other trendy getups to dine at places along Paddington's Oxford Street and at Kings Cross.

### Late-Night Dining

One last thing to know about dining out in Sydney is the early closing hours at many restaurants. Common practice is for kitchens to close at 10:00 P.M., although there are places that stay open later, maybe to around midnight. Such parochialism is out of place in Sydney and can be annoying, especially to New Yorkers, Montrealers, and Europeans used to dining late. It can certainly take the edge off an evening going from place to place only to be told the kitchen is closed, or, a favorite Sydney restaurateur's tactic, "Our kitchen closes in 15 minutes. Do you think you can be in and out in time?"

A few good restaurants that remain open later than 10:00 P.M. are suggested here. If you have a place in mind where you want to dine, however, call ahead to be sure how late the kitchen is open. **Cafe Opera** in the Inter-Continental Hotel is open seven days a week for breakfast, lunch, and dinner. It gets its name from its proximity to the Opera House, and many operagoers dine there before or after a performance. Its prix fixe buffet costs around A$20, an excellent value considering the lavish buffet and the right to return ceaselessly, and there is an extensive wine list as well as wine sold by the glass.

**Pasta Pasta** (107 Oxford Street) is also open seven days and remains open late on Friday and Saturday nights. **Rockefeller's** (227 Oxford Street) serves American-style hamburgers with names like "Washington Redskin" and "Atlanta Falcon," and barbecued chicken and ribs. Prices are moderate, and the place is open until 1:00 A.M. Friday and Saturday. Vegetarians also have a late-night venue available to them: **Laurie's** at Victoria Road and Burton Street, Darlinghurst, which is open until midnight seven days a week.

The **Bennelong** at the Opera House serves a late-night supper until 11:00 P.M., but Sydneysiders and local restaurant critics have grumbled about the food here since it opened 20 years ago. The establishment also serves lunch and dinner, which for two might cost A$60 or more, plus wine or drinks. **Bondi Bondi**, a new restaurant across the street from the beach, has caught on with Porsche-driving yuppies who favor the trendy, California-style cuisine. It's open until midnight daily. One major restaurant in the city is open 24 hours, **Bourbon and Beefsteak** on the main street, Darlinghurst Road, in Kings Cross. The menu is a rarefied mix of Tex-Mex and Aussie cooking, and the bartenders mix the spiciest Bloody Marys south of the Tropic of Capricorn.

### Dining on the Water

Dining on the water, or near it, is a tradition in Sydney, and an experience not to be missed by visitors. A company called Blue Line Cruises sails the *Southern Cross* from Circular Quay on luncheon and dinner cruises daily, and will cater breakfast cruises on request. The boat is licensed to sell liquor, and major credit cards are accepted. The *John Cadman* is another cruising restaurant that serves lunch and dinner afloat. The ship is a bit larger than the *Southern Cross,* allowing room for dancing onboard. The à la carte menu features international dishes, and there is a selection of Australian and imported wines. The ship leaves from jetty 6, Circular Quay.

Extremely popular with visitors is Captain Cook Cruises' Coffee Cruise, which sails daily throughout the year on a two-and-a-half-hour voyage across the harbor. A tour guide points out places of interest onshore. One generalization should be considered: Food served on these cruises is usually not of the quality found at restaurants on land.

Sydney's landmark restaurant on the water is, appropriately, a seafood establishment. It is **Doyle's on the Beach**, north across the harbor from the city center in the suburb of Watson's Bay. It is reachable by boat, city bus, or car. Views from Doyle's of the skyline across the harbor are exhilarating. The food served is hearty—and pricey, about A$60 for two people, plus drinks and wine. Australians seem to be just now discovering the succulence of Tasmanian trout, and it was Doyle's that first introduced it to Sydney. Service is poky, but that hasn't kept the masses away; always phone for reservations. Tel: 337-2007.

Another fine seafood restaurant, **Sails**, is located under the Sydney Harbour Bridge at McMahons Point on the north side of the harbor. It, too, sports fantastic city views, and there are tables outside for dining when the weather cooperates. John Dory, barramundi, Sydney rock oysters—all mouth-watering Aussie specialties—are on the menu. Reservations are a must here; Tel: 920-5793. The **Waterfront Restaurant** at The Rocks incorporates into its design a sailing ship, which actually isn't as corny as it sounds. Lunch is often served outside, and the seafood prepared by the chef comes directly from the fishing trawlers that tie up nearby every day.

### Ethnic Dining

Ethnic restaurants are legion in Sydney, with Italian leading the way and French not far behind. Chinese, Japanese, Thai, and Indian are also prolific. For Italian, **La Boheme**, 312 Crown Street, in Surry Hills, is hard to beat in the affordable category. A prix fixe of A$16 buys an entree (as Aussies call an appetizer), main course, salad or garlic bread, and coffee. The atmosphere is less than inspiring, but the food is interesting and the portions hefty. More expensive and equally good Italian food has been served at **Beppi's**, in East Sydney at the corner of Yurong and Stanley streets, for 30 years. Because it's an institution in Sydney, reservations are advised. Tel: 360-4558.

It's easy to see why Italian, Thai, and Chinese food is so popular in Sydney: There is a substantial population of each nationality living in the city. It's harder to explain the city's penchant for French cuisine. Perhaps it's a yearning for a touch of class or a craving for high-calorie sauces, but French restaurants proliferate, and most are priced the French way. Two of the best are also two of the most expensive places to eat in town.

**La Belle Helene**, 11 Hill Street in the North Sydney suburb of Roseville, is often touted as the top restaurant on the city's North Shore. There aren't many establishments of note over there, so that claim may well stand unchallenged. Even by Parisian standards, the chef's poached sausage rolled in crushed pistachio nuts is *très magnifique*. Dinner for two is expensive by Sydney standards, and the best way to get there is by car. Tel: 419-2970. Even more pricey is **Claude's**, 10 Oxford Street, routinely hailed as one of Australia's top restaurants. Seasonal dishes served at Claude's may bring tears to your eyes, either for the perfection of the food or the pain of the bill (prix fixe, A$100). Tel: 331-2325.

If you know where to look, French cuisine in Sydney does not have to be outrageously expensive. **Au Chabrol**, 248 Glenmore Road in Paddington, serves modern French cuisine at reasonable prices. Tel: 331-2551. **Pegrum's**, 36 Gurner Street in Paddington, is considered one of the inner city's best French restaurants. Tel: 360-4776.

Two Thai restaurants deserve a visit, and neither is expensive. **Siam**, 383 Oxford Street, serves exotic dishes that are elegantly spiced and expertly prepared; and **Thai Orchid**, 628 Crown Street in Surry Hills, is equally adept with its chile quail or chicken and coconut soup. There are Chinese restaurants galore in town. When you walk around Chinatown, in the city center, a peek or sniff in virtually every other door reveals a restaurant.

## Cafés

To join the ranks of Sydney café society, there are several places where you absolutely must be seen. This may all change when the new Hard Rock Café opens, but for now here are a few not-to-be-missed cafés and brasseries popular with the "in" crowd. The **Bayswater Brasserie** at Kings Cross is packed seven nights a week. People go there for full meals, or just coffee and cake or drinks. It's a good place for Sunday brunch, too.

Theatergoers frequent the **Wharf** at Pier 4 on Hickson Road, the main road that runs between Darling Harbour and Sydney Cove, roughly the boundary of The Rocks. It shares the renovated cargo shipping wharf that is now home to the Sydney Theatre Company. Pre-theater dinners and after-theater suppers are served. The younger set might prefer the **Music Café**, 199 William Street in Kings Cross, which serves drinks and light meals to go along with the music until 4:00 A.M. nightly. For late-night coffee or cappuccino, **Reggio Bar**, 135 Crown Street in East Sydney, is a crowd-pleaser.

### Australian Restaurants

When in Rome.... Might as well try some good Aussie cooking while you're in Sydney. Surprisingly, that won't be easy. Good Aussie restaurants are harder to find than Italian, French, or Chinese in the city proper. They become easier to find in far-flung suburbs where visitors are not likely to venture. A fairly new place is **Charlotte's**, 39 Elizabeth Bay Road, which tends to serve *nouvelle*-Aussie (daintily prepared tongue, for example), but for the basic Australian meat pie, **Convicts and Converts** in North Sydney has been satisfying customers for ten years. **Chez Oz**, 23 Craigend Street in Darlinghurst, and **Café Troppo**, 175 Glebe Point Road in Glebe, are restaurants near each other known for serving well-prepared Aussie cuisine. The latter is heavy on seafood—unusual dishes like barbecued bay octopus—but has vegetarian, beef, and lamb specialties nightly. (Both Oz and Troppo are near the city center and are accessible by public transportation.)

For a A\$5.95 investment, the book *Cheap Eats in Sydney* is a well-researched, well-written, and handy guide to some 750 of the city's best and not-so expensive restaurants. It is sold, along with other restaurant guides of course, in bookstores all over town.

As in cities everywhere, many restaurants in Sydney,

certainly the finer establishments, accept major credit cards.

# NIGHTLIFE

Come nightfall, Sydney remains Australia's most exciting city. It long ago shed the shy and retiring demeanor still possessed by other large cities in Australia that can't resist rolling up their sidewalks and putting everyone to bed at sunset. Sydney's hardcore night owls point to the Vietnam War era as the time when the city switched into high gear after dark. During the war years, legions of servicemen swarmed into Sydney for R & R, forever changing the face of the city at night.

## *Kings Cross*

Nowhere is this more apparent than in the Kings Cross area, where it all began for the fun-seeking soldiers. The Cross, as it is locally known, is Australia's Times Square. It is not as sinister, perhaps, as Times Square, a fact that is lost on self-respecting Aussies who wouldn't be caught dead there. In truth, The Cross is quite a lot of fun, tawdry perhaps, and dirty, but with a carnival atmosphere that is hard to resist.

In deference to those self-respecting Aussies, there are reasons to stay away from The Cross. Hookers lean on almost every lamppost, barkers block the sidewalk screaming invitations to come in and see trashy sex shows, and the dispossessed beg for dollars.

Kingpin of clubs at The Cross is **Les Girls**, which has been staging drag shows for the past 25 years. With its breathtaking costumes, male strippers, and zillionth incarnation of Judy Garland, the place is still a hoot and as fresh, old hands say, as it was on opening night. After the show, a disco remains open for the rest of the night. The club is just off Darlinghurst Road, the main street of The Cross, on Roslyn Street. One price covers two floor shows, dinner, and entrance to the disco. Prim American and Canadian visitors need not hide their faces when entering Les Girls. Drag is quite acceptable as entertainment in Australia.

Sydney's liveliest jazz club, **New Orleans**, is located at The Cross at 24 Darlinghurst Road. A combo plays here seven nights a week, and when its members are taking five, a guitarist/singer often stands in. Near The Cross in Potts Point is another of the city's favorite jazz clubs, **Jo Jo Ivory's** in the Sheraton Hotel. Its claims of serving excellent cajun food, however, will only amuse anyone who has ever dined in New Orleans.

The **Blue Moon Room**, 30 Darlinghurst Road, serves up live blues and Latin music, and there's a dance floor for those with happy feet. And for the dudes who can't live without a regular dose of loud music, the **Oz Rock Bar** has about the highest decibel level in town. It also sports a disco, a restaurant, and a lounge. A popular dance place at The Cross is the **Paradise Music Room**, 37 Darlinghurst Road, open until 3:00 A.M. for the disco crowd.

### Oxford Street/Taylor Square

The Oxford Street/Taylor Square area is another major entertainment center in Sydney. Here, too, the streets are buzzing well into the night with people going to clubs, restaurants that remain open late, and coffee and cappuccino houses.

The most popular place at Taylor Square is **Kinselas**, generally recognized as the city's top cabaret. It was once a funeral parlor; the room where the departed were laid out for a final viewing is now a restaurant serving pretty good French and Aussie *nouvelle cuisine.* The upstairs cabaret gets the best acts in town and is a favorite room for some of Australia's leading performers. A recent hit was a Motown review starring some of the best up-and-coming singers in the country. Patrons can eat during the show if they wish, but many choose just to drink. The upstairs bar is open even when the cabaret room is dark and is well worth a stop for a drink.

Nearby is the very seedy and very entertaining **Taxi Club**, 40 Flinders Street, which has a titillating air of danger about it. If ever a place couldn't decide which crowd to cater to, this is it. Don't be surprised if a Hell's Angels type enters the club with a society matron on his arm. This is one of the few clubs in Sydney where the public can come in and play the slots; most others are private. Those who don't gamble should visit the club for the crowd alone. But behave—the bouncers here have an unforgiving nature.

Down Oxford Street, below Taylor Square toward the city center, is Sydney's hottest disco, **The Midnight Shift**.

The music is the most up-to-date in Australia, and the laser light show is acclaimed as the nation's most technologically advanced. Non-dancers can prop themselves up at one of the club's three bars and watch the crowd, again quite an entertaining bunch. The Shift was once predominantly gay but now caters to a mixed crowd. For Sydney's younger players, it is one of the city's most in places, but those a bit older who might be offended at same-sex dancing partners might want to consider alternative entertainment.

### City Center
Head downtown if your pace is slower and more conservative than the clubs in either The Cross or the Taylor Square/Oxford Street area.

The Hilton on Pitt Street is a one-stop entertainment center for middle-of-the-roaders. There's a singer in the **America's Cup Bar** and often a live band in the **Henry the Ninth Bar**. Both rooms get a good-size crowd for cocktail hour and are open late for nightcaps.

The **Marble Bar** in the basement of the Hilton is a Sydney institution. There is usually live music there, too, but the real show is the architecture—a marriage of Renaissance, Roman, gaudy Australian, and risqué Victorian that in all probability comes together nowhere else on earth. Keep in mind that in a hotel, hotel prices are charged. The most expensive room in the Hilton, though, is **Juliana's**, a dressy, upscale nightclub where internationally known singers often perform. There's a dance floor as well, but the dance music is taped.

**Don Burrows Supper Club**, 199 George Street in the city center, is the place in Sydney for the 50-and-older cadre. A band plays until 2:00 or 3:00 A.M. most nights, and jazz bands are often on the bill. Dinner is served, too. It's expensive, from the A$12 cover charge to the A$6 ice cream, but the kind of people who frequent the place can obviously afford it. A less expensive place to hear jazz in the city center is at **Soup Plus**, 383 George Street, but the club, which also serves dinner, is not open late.

### Other Entertainment
There seems to be only one comedy club in Sydney, the **Comedy Store** on Margaret Street in the city center. It serves dinner with its show at 7:00 P.M., Wednesday

through Saturday nights. Unless you're Australian you probably won't know the comedians, whose humor is, quite naturally, Australian—which means some of the jokes will be lost on visitors from overseas. Nonetheless, there are plenty of universal laughs.

Sydney supports a number of legitimate theaters that stage plays and musicals by Australian writers as well as imports from Broadway and London's West End. At presstime, *Les Misérables,* at the Theatre Royal, is the big hit in town. Excellent shows are always playing at the Wharf Theatre, which is home to the renowned Sydney Theatre Company. The company specializes in performing new works and standards by Australian playwrights, and is generally acclaimed as the nation's leading theater group. Other theaters that stage lively shows and experimental productions are the Belvoir Street Theatre, Nimrod Theatre, Off-Broadway, and Q Theatre. Halftix on Martin Place, corner of Elizabeth Street, sells half-price tickets to most Sydney shows on the day of the performance.

Also highly acclaimed is the **Australian Opera**, which makes its home in the Sydney Opera House. It is one of the world's few major opera companies that performs a summer season, a plus for visitors from the Northern Hemisphere who can laze on the beach by day and listen to *La Traviata* by night. Because the opera is extraordinarily popular with the Aussies, always book in advance by stopping in at or calling the box office. Tel: 250-7111.

### At the Pubs

Describing the neighborhood pubs in Sydney stretches a writer's imagination. You could say they are as important to the city as the police and fire departments. There are pubs for every mood—rowdy ones for roughnecks, trendy ones for yuppies, loud ones for rock and rollers, dainty ones for grannies, sporty ones for sportsmen, gay ones for gays, and ones on the beach for that welcome beer after soaking up the relentless Aussie sun. Here are just some of Sydney's most interesting pubs:

The trendiest pubs in town at this writing are the **Lord Dudley** in Woollahra and **The Oaks** in Double Bay. It's wise to have a car to get to them, but parking is a problem.

Since most tourist areas of Sydney are best covered on foot, pubs are blessedly positioned a block or two apart, especially in the city center, Paddington, and The Rocks. At The Rocks, stop in at the **Orient Hotel** on Argyle Street for a breather and a beer, or at the **Lord Nelson** around the corner; in Paddington, try the 19th-century **London Tavern** on Underwood Street. There's a pub, too, in the **Bondi Hotel**, across the street from the city's most famous beach. On beach days, it is always crowded with refugees from the burning sands. The same is true of the **New Brighton Hotel** at Manly Beach.

Standing around a pub, beer in hand, is an art form in Australia and part of the fun of Sydney. Go into any pub in Sydney to meet the real Aussies. It won't be hard to strike up, or become part of, what seems for the moment a profound conversation. But don't forget your manners; generous Aussies will stand you a midi or two, so be sure to shout (buy) a round for your new mates.

Sydney's pubs have given birth to countless rock bands. Some, like Little River Band and Men At Work, became international sensations and helped familiarize the world with Australia, and any night of the week a band is playing somewhere at a pub in Sydney. The music costs no more than the price of a few midis (midsize glasses of beer). The Candy Harlots, Crash Politics, Loitering with Intent, The Lubricated Goats, and The Sexations are only a few of the scores of bands playing live in the pubs. Some of the music is dreadful, but most is quite good . . . and who knows which group will be Australia's next big rock band?

Some pub-clubs to watch are **The St. James**, 80 Castlereagh Street; **Hotel Manly**, opposite the wharf in Manly; **Lucy's Tavern**, 54 Castlereagh Street in the city center; **All Nations Club**, 50 Bayswater Road in Kings Cross; and **Hip Hop Club**, 11 Oxford Street, Paddington.

In every Friday's edition of the *Sydney Morning Herald* a schedule of the weekend and upcoming week's events at theaters, clubs, cabarets, galleries, and pubs is published. What's on at the Opera House and dates for concerts and other events are printed as well. The publication *Nightlife in Sydney,* published for the first time in 1988, bills itself as the "ultimate guide" to Sydney's clubs, cabarets, theater restaurants, and wining and dining nightspots. It is a handy booklet to purchase at bookstores in the city. Its reviews tend to be, as the Aussies say, spot-on, and its writers extend no mercy to mediocrity.

## SHOPS AND SHOPPING

Some vacation destinations are best known as shopping meccas, but Sydney does not number among them. True, there's plenty to buy and no dearth of places to shop, but bargains are rare, even on such Australian products as opals and woolen clothing. And since high shipping costs are passed on to consumers, imported goods are particularly expensive.

Nevertheless, it would be unfortunate not to do a little shopping in Sydney, even if you only buy a stuffed koala. There are shops in every area of town, but two areas are especially interesting: the city center, where the large department stores and shopping arcades are located, and Oxford Street in Paddington, the Soho-like part of the city where many of Australia's most trendy designers maintain boutiques.

The two large department stores in town are **Grace Brothers** on Pitt Street, the Marks and Spencer's of Sydney, and **David Jones**, rather more like Macy's—though it fancies itself more like Harrods—with locations at the corner of Elizabeth and Market streets and the corner of Castlereagh and Market streets. Like all other department stores, both sell a little bit of everything, and both seem to be having some sort of sale going on all the time. Neither particularly emphasizes Australian-made goods, although they carry books about the nation and the city and locally designed clothing. The stores are never crowded by New York or London standards, and salesclerks are generally helpful, attentive, and friendly.

### The Old Shopping Arcades

Two downtown shopping arcades are musts, as much tourist attractions as they are shopping centers: the **Strand Arcade** and the **Queen Victoria Building**. The QVB, as Sydneysiders call it, moved Pierre Cardin to comment, "It's the most beautiful shopping center in the world."

The Strand, which runs between Pitt and George streets in the city center, opened in 1891. Then as now it was a marvel to behold, with its cast-iron balustrades, stained-glass windows, glass-domed roof, and intricately crafted wood paneling that epitomizes the dedication to detail of Victorian carpenters. Only one original shop remains today, **Harris Coffee and Tea**, where customers have been resting weary feet and sipping tea and coffee for almost a century. Among the 80 or so other shops in the arcade that are special are **Jenny Kee's**, specializing in Australian-designed clothing, and **Moray's**, a hat shop where you are likely to find an Australian bushranger hat that simply cannot be purchased in any other country.

Even if you are not in the mood to shop, the QVB is a perfect place to stroll, have lunch or a drink, and people-watch. It is a massive building, occupying an entire block in the city center, on George Street between Market and Druitt streets. It was saved from destruction by concerned citizens who had the good sense to realize its architectural value. No edifice in London is more Victorian than the QVB. The building opened in the 1890s as a market and was lovingly restored throughout much of the 1980s. It has 190 shops and is one of the few places in Sydney open 24 hours a day seven days a week, although shopping hours pretty much follow normal opening hours for Sydney stores (9:00 A.M. to 5:30 P.M. Monday through Wednesday; 9:00 A.M. to somewhere between 7:30 P.M. and 9:00 P.M., depending on the store, Thursday and Friday; 9:00 A.M. to 4:00 P.M. Saturday).

Of particular interest in the QVB is the **Koala Bear Shop** on the second floor. It sells a wide range of Australian souvenirs, such as stuffed koalas, kangaroos, and platypuses as well as tee-shirts, boomerangs, and sheepskins. It also hawks duty-free opals and other goods. For aboriginal arts and crafts, visit the **Bindi Gallery** on the top level of the building; it sells traditional bark paintings by aboriginal artists, books about aboriginal life and mythology, prints, posters, cards, boomerangs, and **didgeridoos** (a didgeridoo is a traditional aboriginal wooden musical instrument). There's also a selection of jewelry and tee-shirts. **Australian Horizon**, on the second floor, stocks locally made gifts and souvenirs, and carries works made by Australian metal craftsmen. For opal shopping in the QVB, the **Skippy Opal Company** on the top floor has a wide range of the gems (90 percent of the world's opals come from Australia) at tax-free prices.

### Other Gem Shops

There are dozens of other duty-free jewelry shops in the city center where prices of opal and sapphire (another bountiful Australian gem) are somewhat reasonable. All claim to be competitively priced, but a peek into several of the shops will uncover no two prices alike. Try these: **Gemtec**, 250 Pitt Street; **E. Gregory Sherman**, 67 Castlereagh Street; **Opal Skymine** in Australia Square, a recreation of an Outback opal mine with a shop attached; and **Darrell James**, 73 Pitt Street, specialists in rare opals.

### The Rocks

The historical Rocks area of the city along Sydney Harbour has a few shops also worth a quick look. Its opal shop is **Flame Opals**, 119 George Street. **Argyle Centre** on Argyle Street houses some of the most noteworthy shops in The Rocks, including the Didgeridoo Shop, Aussie Ewe and Lamb Centre, Platypus Gallery, and the Lace Shop, all of which specialize in Australian-made products. Australian clothing—oilskin coats favored by men and women who work on sheep and cattle stations, lambskin coats, hacking jackets, moleskin jeans, bushranger hats, and kangaroo leather belts—is sold at **Morrison's**, 105 George Street.

### Oxford Street

Oxford Street is the place to go in Sydney to purchase something unusual or one-of-a-kind, and it is the city's most intriguing shopping district. Since most of the shops are on the same side of the road, it's an easy walk down the street, but it's more than a mile from the top of Oxford Street at Centennial Park to the Taylor Square area. Walkers should start at the Centennial Park end because the trek is largely downhill from that point. **Giovanni's Corner**, across the street from the park, is a good starting place to help summon up the necessary fortitude; they serve a Champagne breakfast, lunch, snacks, and coffee.

Clothing sold along the street tends to be tailored to the tastes of the young and hip. **Kake Gallery**, **Operator**, **J. Jackson Corp.**, **Dynamite**, and **The Academy** all fit this description. Many of the getups sold in Dynamite are designed by Stewart Membry, an Australian who also has a following in New York and London. His clothes are recognized by their bold patterns, such as polka dots and racing stripes.

William Street is a narrow side street running perpendicular to Oxford that is worth a short foray. **My Shop** sells whimsical, postmodern ceramics handmade by the owner, Irene Goverdovsky. Teapots in the shape of palm trees are top sellers. Across the street is the **Anti-Frantic**

**Center**, full of New-Age books and relaxation music. If by now you want to stop for a cold beer, just down the street on the corner of Underwood is the elegant old pub **London Tavern**, in business since 1875. Food is served in the garden bistro.

Back on Oxford Street, the **New Edition Bookshop**, which has an exhaustive supply of books about Sydney and Australia, is a good place to stop and browse and get a free copy of *The Paddington Book*. This little booklet, printed by the bookshop, contains a wealth of information about restaurants, hotels, galleries, attractions, and goings-on in the neighborhood.

On down Oxford Street is what may be one of Sydney's most interesting shops: **Coo-ee Australian Emporium**. The little store sells paintings by aboriginal artists expressly commissioned by the owner, Adrian Newstead. Sand paintings by the Pinturbi people of Central Australia are particularly wonderful. Such paintings were originally done on the desert sands for ceremonial purposes but in the last two decades have been laboriously transferred to canvas to be sold commercially. They cost in the A$800 range, but each painting is an original, even though the buyer is likely never to know the full story behind the work. Aboriginal artists tell what they want to and rarely divulge the tribal secrets that are painted into every scene.

Coo-ee also sells fabric designed by aboriginals and will copy a favorite shirt or dress in a few days for about A$65. Bark paintings are also for sale in the A$175 to A$230 range, depending on the work. Aboriginal wood carvings cost about A$50: boomerangs and non-returning throwing sticks made from mulga wood by people of the western deserts cost less.

# DAY TRIPS FROM SYDNEY

*By David Swindell*

The auto license plates in Australia proclaim New South Wales "The Premier State" in a reference to its place in Australian history as the nation's first European settlement. But the slogan goes a long way in expressing that, in terms of visitor attractions, the state is second to none Down Under.

There is, of course, no east of Sydney, but west beyond the Blue Mountains the beginnings of the Outback that stretches endlessly across the continent soon appear. Dry landscapes and the occasional tree, begging for water, are all that separate one rickety, dusty Outback town from another. **Dubbo**, some 335 km (200 miles) west of Sydney, is the classic Outback town, populated by sheep and cattle farmers who seem immune to the heat, dust, and flies. No one blinks in Dubbo when a kangaroo bounds across a paddock. **Broken Hill**, built on the riches of silver mining until that went bust, straddles the New South Wales-South Australia state line and is a stop on the Indian-Pacific rail line that links Sydney with Perth.

Head south from Sydney along the Pacific coast and you'll drive through semitropical rain forests that provide natural air-conditioning from the heat and look as they must have in prehistoric times. The cities and towns south of Sydney—**Wollongong, Kiama, Nowra**—couldn't be duller, but the beaches on the coast are perfect and much less crowded than those in Sydney.

On the northern coastal fringes of Sydney, **Palm Beach** is one of the city's posh neighborhoods, and its beach is a favorite of surfers. Nearby, about 45 km (26 miles) north of the city, is **Broken Bay**, which serves as the mouth of the **Hawkesbury River**. The river is one of Sydney's great recreational areas, to which boaters, swimmers, and picnickers flock on weekends.

Due north of Sydney are the gentle farmlands reminiscent of New England and the lush wine-growing regions of the Hunter Valley. The town of **Tamworth** is Australia's Nashville, the nation's country music capital. Fishermen zero in on the northern coastal town of **Coffs Harbour**, where marlin and other sport fish are abundant in the deep waters off the coast here.

Byron Bay, north of Coffs Harbour on the coast near the Queensland border, is an artsy, bohemian sort of enclave—and a surfer colony as well.

Full day cruises on the Hawkesbury River and extended tours to Coffs Harbour, Broken Hill, and Dubbo can be booked at the Travel Centre of New South Wales in Sydney.

The three day trips we suggest here, the Blue Mountains, Hunter Valley, and Canberra, are just that—suggestions. It's a big state to explore, and there's adventure in New South Wales any direction you travel.

**MAJOR INTEREST**

The Blue Mountains for scenery, nature, and
   hiking
Hunter Valley wineries, dining, and hot-air
   ballooning
Canberra, Australia's capital

## THE BLUE MOUNTAINS

When Sydney sizzles, many people head for the relative cool of the Blue Mountains, 100 km (60 miles) to the west of Sydney and visible on a clear day from such perches as Centrepoint Tower in the city. The mountains are an easy day trip by train or rental car. As many as a dozen trains a day leave Sydney's Central Railway Station bound for **Katoomba**, the largest town in the mountains, on the two-hour trip. Once in the mountains, however, you will need a car to get around. Several rental-car firms, including Budget, have outlets in Katoomba.

The Blue Mountains are the place to escape for solitude. Over the years, parts of the region have been "tarted up," as the Aussies say to explain the billboards and neon signs announcing another guesthouse, restaurant, or tourist attraction. But most of the region is pure, ecologically perfect, and little changed since it was formed 180 million years ago.

That leaves plenty of room to commune with nature, which is why bushwalking is the number-one sport in the Blue Mountains. The region is the closest wilderness area to Sydney, and for vacationers who do not intend to travel beyond the city, a trip here for a bushwalk is an excellent way to sample the famed Aussie bush, or Outback.

There are some 100 separate and well-marked trails in the Blue Mountains. A map available at the tourist information office at Echo Point in Katoomba is a must for would-be bushwalkers. Most bushwalks are designed for those in average shape; few are longer than four hours in duration. The easiest walk is the 10- to 20-minute stroll from the tourist information office in Katoomba along Echo Point to the Three Sisters, a rock formation on the edge of the town. This is also the starting point for the one-and-a-half-hour trek down the 860-step **Grand Staircase** into Jamieson Valley.

The steps descend into a quiet glen of ferns, trees, flowers, and moss-covered rocks. For those with abundant energy the trail winds around a cliff and comes out at Katoomba Falls, but hikers can give up before that and take a mountain-railway car back to the top. This **Scenic Railway** is a favorite trip of visitors to the Blue Mountains. More challenging walks are the three-and-half-hour trek along Federal Pass at Katoomba and the eight-hour hike along the Giant Staircase to the Ruined Castle, both rock formations. Again, these two bushwalks are designed for those in average shape.

Numerous scenic drives through the mountains have been mapped out as well. Signs along the roads point them out and all are equally spectacular; just turn down any marked road for magnificent mountain views.

On many of the roads there are well-marked scenic lookout points, and none is less compelling than another. For those who travel to Katoomba by train and don't have a car, **Queen Elizabeth Lookout** at Echo Point, adjacent to the tourist information office, provides an excellent peek at the **Three Sisters Formations**. An ancient aboriginal legend has it that the rocks were formed when three sisters were turned to stone by a witch doctor because they wanted to marry men of a different tribe. Unfortunately, the witch doctor died before he thought to turn them back into people, and to this day no one has figured out how to undo his curse.

Throughout the mountains are old country towns that date to the days in the last century when settlers made their way inland. Most picturesque is **Leura**, about 10 km (6 miles) from Katoomba. Most of the buildings on the town's one main street date to the 1920s or earlier and have been classified by the National Trust as landmarks. The few shops on this short street sell antiques, crafts, and gifts. The **Leura Resort** on Fitzroy Street serves lunch and dinner seven days a week and opens its garden bistro on warm days.

There are many other restaurants scattered about the Blue Mountains, but few are memorable. Most serve adequate food at moderate prices. In Katoomba, the **Clarendon**, 68 Lurline Street, serves good Aussie-style home cooking and turns itself into a dinner theater on Saturday nights. Nearby, **Steaks Down Under**, 122 Katoomba Street, lives up to its name. The most enticing restaurant, though not necessarily the best in terms of food, is at the **Hydro Majestic Grand Hotel** in the little town of Medlow Bath, a few miles west of Katoomba. The views from the restaurant's bay windows are splendid. The hotel itself, which opened in 1904, has seen grander days, but portions of the place are now being remodeled. It's a great place to visit to understand what a major resort the Blue Mountains were for Sydneysiders 50 years ago.

Most accommodations in the mountains are guesthouses or motels. Guesthouses are usually more appealing for an overnight stay. Some have fireplaces and cozy parlors and a restaurant. Rates are moderate. **The Carrington Hotel** in Katoomba is popular with city folks bent on a country weekend. The front-desk staff can arrange horseback riding, bushwalking, golf, tennis, and fishing.

Also in Katoomba, the **Katoomba Mountain Lodge** provides satisfactory lodging, as does **Balmoral House** at 196 Bathurst Road.

**Crystal Lodge**, 19 Abbotsford Road, is the only health resort in the Blue Mountains. The staff at this redone mansion indulge guests in beauty therapy, t'ai chi, and hypnosis, and allow them to soak in herbal baths and bob in a flotation tank. They'll also plan bushwalks. Only vegetarian food is served in the restaurant.

More information about a day trip or longer jaunt to the Blue Mountains can be obtained in Sydney by stopping in at the Travel Centre of New South Wales, corner of Pitt and Spring streets.

## *HUNTER VALLEY*

The Hunter Valley, three hours' drive north of Sydney, is one of Australia's two major wine-producing areas, the other being South Australia's Barossa Valley. In truth, only a small portion of the Hunter is given over to wine producing, but for visitors the vineyards and wineries, some which have been in business for a century or more, are all that matters.

The trip to the Hunter Valley is rather like a trip out of San Francisco to the wine-growing areas of Napa and Sonoma. Like those regions, the Hunter is rich in wineries that open their doors for tours, tastings, and purchasing, and hidden country inns and appealing restaurants round out the valley's allure for those who care to venture beyond Sydney for a weekend.

The valley's location between the Pacific Ocean and the Great Dividing Range provides the perfect Mediterranean climate for grape growing. Australians, like the Americans and unlike the French, name their wines by grape type (varietal), and in the Hunter several types can be relied on to produce excellent wines. For white wines, Hunter growers are famous for semillon and chardonnay. The semillons produce a fine dry wine, while the chardonnays yield a respectable white "Burgundy." For red wines, the best buys from the Hunter are pinot noir and cabernet sauvignon. The red "Bordeaux" produced from the cabernet sauvignon grapes grown in the Hunter are especially good, and some are being exported overseas.

There are other good wine types produced in the Hunter Valley, but it's hard to go wrong with these four. Growers at each winery, however, are more than glad to comment on the quality of their wines.

**Cessnock** is the main town in the vineyard region of the valley; most of the wineries open to the public are within a few miles of town. The Hunter Valley Wine Society, 4 Wollembi Road, has information and maps to the wineries. The information office is open seven days a week.

The most famous producer in the Hunter Valley is **Tyrells**, which is one of the few Australian wineries still operated by the original family. It has been in business for some 130 years at the same location on Broke Road. The family has to some degree resisted advances of the high-tech world of mass production, and still uses hand presses, and wooden casks to mature their wine. Tyrells is open 9:00 A.M. to 5:00 P.M. every day but Sunday.

**McWilliams Mount Pleasant**, another producer that has been in business for a century, is just outside Cessnock on Marrowbone Road. The McWilliams name is well respected for its quality pinot noir. Guided tours of the winery are conducted every day but Sunday. **Lake's Folly** is a newcomer to the Hunter, opening for business in 1963, but it has already established itself as a top producer of both chardonnay and cabernet sauvignon wines. The winery, on Branxton Road, is open weekdays.

Acclaimed as the top place to stay and dine in the vineyard area is **Pepper's Guesthouse** on Ekert's Road. It is quite luxurious without being too pricey (about A$100 per night); its French restaurant is open daily for lunch and dinner. For novices in Australian wines, the wine list here presents the best of the Hunter. For reservations, Tel: (049) 98-7596.

Two other restaurants in the vineyard region can also be recommended. **Blaxland's** on Broke Road also serves French cuisine at moderate prices, about A$50 for two. **Pokolbin Cellars** is located in the Hungerford Hill Wine Village, another winery open to the public for tours, tastings, and purchasing, on Broke Road. The restaurant is French, and meals cost about the same as at Blaxland's. Drive back into Cessnock to find restaurants that serve non-French, less-expensive meals.

Like its Sonoma counterpart, and like wine-producing

regions in France, the Hunter Valley is a popular haunt for **hot-air ballooning**. Balloon Aloft operates its hot-air machines from the Hungerford Hill Wine Village, and Balloon Flights Australia is based at the Pokolbin Trading Post on Broke Road. Both send their balloons up in the early morning for scenic flights over the valley.

More information about the Hunter Valley is available at the Travel Centre of New South Wales in Sydney. The staff will be happy to map out the best route to Cessnock.

# CANBERRA

Essentially, Canberra is mentioned here for the record only. It is the Australian capital and, as such, is perhaps most interesting for Australians. It's strictly a company town, the company being the Australian government.

Americans might be interested to note that the planned town was designed by their countryman Walter Burley Griffin in the early part of this century. It sits on a diplomatically chosen site halfway between Sydney and Melbourne, which shared the glory as co-capitals until then. Parliament first convened in Canberra, believed to be an old aboriginal word meaning "meeting place," in 1927.

This city of 250,000 people is the kind of sleepy place where people work hard by day and return home to their families and the television set at night. It's a quiet, safe, and—some even have said—boring town.

But for travellers who have a penchant for visiting well-planned capital cities that sit in the middle of nowhere, Canberra is an easy day trip by car, bus, plane, or train from Sydney. A car is the best idea, because Canberra sprawls and it is often too cold, too hot, or too wet to walk around without handy transportation. There are city buses and cabs.

The new Parliament House was designed by a New York architectural firm that won an international competition, the same way Burley Griffin got the job to design the old Parliament House. The sessions are open to the public almost every day of the year.

The Australian War Memorial opened during World War II and chronicles the nation's participation in all its wars up to Vietnam. Of particular interest are the Gallip-

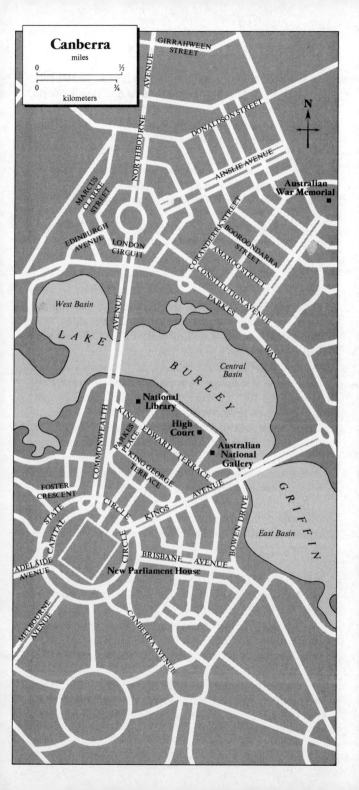

## Canberra

miles

0 ——— ½

0 ——— ¾

kilometers

GIRRAHWEEN STREET

NORTHBOURNE AVENUE

DONALDSON STREET

AINSLIE AVENUE

**Australian War Memorial** ■

MARCUS CLARKE STREET

EDINBURGH AVENUE

LONDON CIRCUIT

CORANDERRK STREET

BOOROONDARRA STREET

AMAROO STREET

CONSTITUTION AVENUE

PARKES WAY

*West Basin*

LAKE

*Central Basin*

BURLEY

**National Library** ■

KING EDWARD TERRACE

**High Court** ■

PARKES PLACE

KING GEORGE TERRACE

**Australian National Gallery** ■

PARKES AVENUE

COMMONWEALTH AVENUE

FOSTER CRESCENT

STATE CIRCLE

CAPITAL CIRCLE

KINGS AVENUE

GRIFFIN

*East Basin*

BOWEN DRIVE

ADELAIDE AVENUE

BRISBANE AVENUE

**New Parliament House**

MELBOURNE AVENUE

CANBERRA AVENUE

N

oli exhibition, which retells the story, already a Mel Gibson movie, of Australia's most famous and deadly World War I conflict, and a Japanese submarine, captured in Sydney Harbour during World War II.

The **Australian National Gallery**, next door to the High Court, perhaps the most appealing exhibit for non-Australians, displays a superb collection of paintings by Australian artists; some A$50 million was spent gathering those and other works by artists from around the world. The gallery is particularly strong in post-World War II artists. Nearby, the **National Library**, with its rare books and early Australian manuscripts collections, also has wide appeal.

Most accommodations in the city fall into the motel range, but there are some full-service hotels: the **Canberra Parkroyal, Noah's Lakeside International**—which has the town's only casino—and **Canberra City Travelodge**.

Several restaurants are noteworthy. The **Charcoal Restaurant** serves thick steaks, has a good Australian wine list, and accepts major credit cards. Canberra's yuppies hang out at the **Fringe Benefits Brasserie**, so named because it is a fairly typical expense-account establishment. It, too, serves grilled steaks and chops, and is happy to accept most credit cards. For upmarket Chinese food downtown, **Imperial Court** is about the only choice.

Visitors to the capital should stop at the Canberra Tourist Bureau in Jolimont Centre, Northbourne Avenue, for a map and other information about the city.

But unless you're a capital freak or bent on seeing everything in Australia, your vacation time—after uncounted hours in the air to get here—is better spent in Sydney.

## ACCOMMODATIONS REFERENCE

▶ **Balmoral House**. 196 Bathurst Road, **Katoomba**, N.S.W. 2780. Tel: (047) 82-22-64.

▶ **Canberra City Travelodge**. 74 Northbourne Avenue, **Canberra**, A.C.T. 2600. Tel: (062) 49-6911; in U.S., (800) 421-0536; in California, (800) 252-2155; in Canada, (800) 251-2166.

▶ **Canberra Parkroyal**. 102 Northbourne Ave., **Canberra**, A.C.T. 2601. Tel: (062) 49-1411; Telex: 61516.

▶ **Carrington Hotel**. Katoomba Street, **Katoomba**, N.S.W. 2780, Tel: (047) 82-1111.

► **Crystal Lodge**. 19 Abbotsford Road, **Katoomba**, N.S.W. 2780. Tel: (047) 82-5122.

► **Katoomba Mountain Lodge**. 21 Lurlane Street, **Katoomba**, N.S.W. 2780. Tel: (047) 82-3933.

► **Noah's Lakeside International**. London Circuit, **Canberra**, A.C.T. 2601. Tel: (062) 47-6244.

► **Pepper's Guesthouse**. Ekerts Road, **Pokolbin**, N.S.W. 2321. Tel: (049) 98-7596.

# QUEENSLAND
## THE GREAT BARRIER REEF AND OUTBACK

*By Len Rutledge*

*Len Rutledge, a resident of Queensland for the last 19 years, has run his own newspaper in Cairns and produced the longest-running syndicated travel column in Australia. He publishes a tourism magazine in Townsville and writes for publications throughout the Pacific area and Europe.*

Queensland, the "Sunshine State," attracts more travellers than anywhere else in Australia, leaving aside Sydney, the major gateway to the country. First and foremost in Queensland, of course, is the Great Barrier Reef and the resorts for which it is the setting. Also contributing to its appeal are the incredibly good weather, the great and uncrowded beaches, and interesting wildlife and flora. The Outback areas of Northern Queensland, the Crocodile Dundee-type places like Cooktown, add even more to the attraction of Queensland.

We cover Queensland—an immense geographical area—in several steps, starting at the south with the city of Brisbane, the Gold Coast to its south, and the Sunshine Coast just to its north. To the north of this area is the southern end of the Great Barrier Reef, and at that point we discuss the Reef in general. Next, to the north, is what we call the Central Great Barrier Reef, in the Townsville area (including its Outback area), followed by the North-

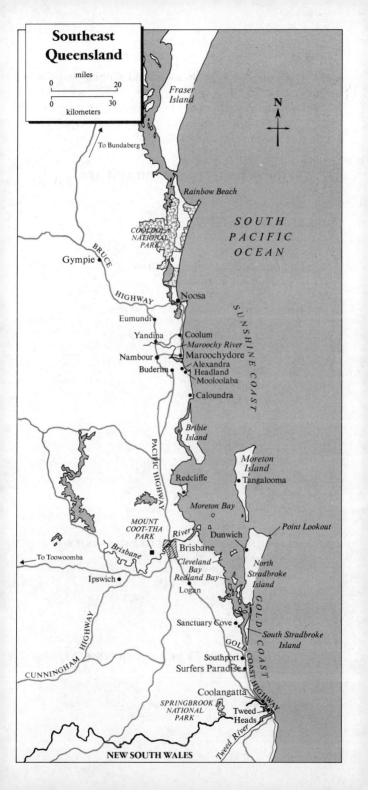

## Southeast Queensland

miles
0       20

kilometers
0       30

N

To Bundaberg

*Fraser Island*

*Rainbow Beach*

*COOLOOLA NATIONAL PARK*

SOUTH
PACIFIC
OCEAN

BRUCE

Gympie

HIGHWAY

Noosa

Eumundi

Yandina   Coolum
*Maroochy River*
Maroochydore

Nambour   Alexandra
Buderim   Headland
Mooloolaba

Caloundra

*S U N S H I N E   C O A S T*

*Bribie Island*

PACIFIC HIGHWAY

Redcliffe

*Moreton Island*
Tangalooma

*Moreton Bay*

*MOUNT COOT-THA PARK*

River

Dunwich

*Point Lookout*

*Brisbane*

Brisbane

To Toowoomba

*Cleveland Bay*
Redland Bay

*North Stradbroke Island*

Ipswich

Logan

*GOLD COAST*

Sanctuary Cove

*South Stradbroke Island*

CUNNINGHAM HIGHWAY

Southport
Surfers Paradise

GOLD

COAST HIGHWAY

Coolangatta

*SPRINGBROOK NATIONAL PARK*

Tweed Heads

*Tweed River*

**NEW SOUTH WALES**

ern Great Barrier Reef area—around Cairns—and the Outback there.

Finally, at the northern tip of Queensland, we cover the Cape York Peninsula, closer to Papua New Guinea than any other point in Australia.

### MAJOR INTEREST IN THE BRISBANE AREA

**Brisbane**
Queen Street Mall
Queensland Cultural Centre
Mount Coot-tha
Botanic Gardens and Planetarium
Lone Pine Koala Sanctuary

**Gold Coast**
The surf beaches
Downtown Surfers Paradise
Sea World
Sanctuary Cove
Dreamworld
Currumbin Sanctuary

**Sunshine Coast**
The surf beaches
Noosa Heads
Buderim
Sunshine Plantation
Fraser Island

### MAJOR INTEREST ON THE GREAT BARRIER REEF
Coral viewing
Marine life
Diving
Staying on the reef
Underwater photography

### MAJOR INTEREST IN THE SOUTHERN REEF REGION

Heron Island
Rockhampton Victorian cityscapes
Capricorn Coast

MAJOR INTEREST IN THE CENTRAL REEF
REGION

**Townsville**
Great Barrier Reef Wonderland
Sunshine
Flinders Mall and Flinders Street East

Mission Beach (for peace and tranquillity)
Charters Towers and the Outback
Other island resorts
Aboriginal culture

**On the Water**
Magnetic Island
Four Seasons Barrier Reef Resort
Whitsunday island resorts
Sailing the Whitsundays
Deep-sea fishing

MAJOR INTEREST IN THE NORTHERN REEF
REGION

**Cairns**
Shopping
Restaurants

**Around Cairns**
Trips to the Great Barrier Reef
Kuranda Railway and Village
Green and Fitzroy islands
The Marlin Coast
Port Douglas
Marlin fishing
Cooktown
Cape York

# BRISBANE, THE GOLD COAST, AND THE SUNSHINE COAST

Queenslanders are different from other Australians. You notice it as soon as you cross the border, but the farther north or west you go, the more obvious it becomes. Maybe it's the tropical heat that slows people down; perhaps the magnificent beaches make people less interested in the office; or it could be that they are all slightly mad to want to live in a state that others say is five years behind the rest of Australia.

Some call Queensland the "deep north," others think of it as paradise—but there's no denying that Queensland has become Australia's vacation playground. Brisbane is Queensland's capital and the state's largest city. The nearby Gold Coast is the major holiday center, with about three million visitors each year. The Sunshine Coast just up the shore, however, is emerging as a major competitor.

Together, these three areas of southeast Queensland constitute the third-largest population center in Australia and the most visited tourist destination in the whole country outside Sydney.

## *BRISBANE*

Brisbane is the hardest Australian city to characterize. This, the third-largest city in the country, is still labeled by many as a large country town (but some people say the same about Melbourne). Others see it as nothing more than a gateway to Queensland's other attractions. They are wrong; Brisbane today is a modern subtropical city that's well worth a visit.

Perhaps what finally convinced the people of Brisbane that their city is special was the staging of World Expo 88, a world's fair of international status. Expo was the cause of extensive building, including a new airport and many new facilities for visitors.

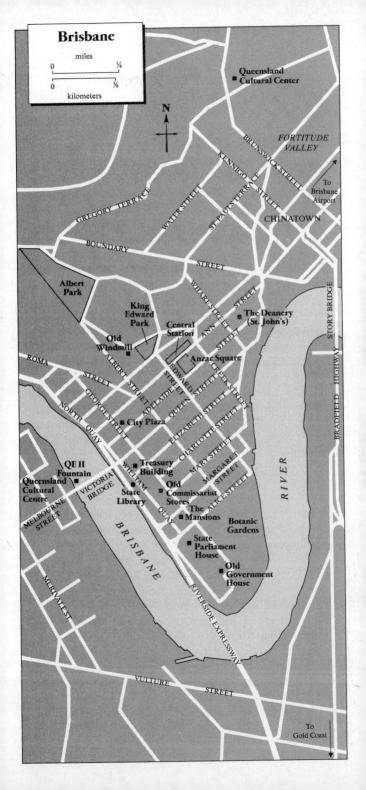

# The City Center

The center of Brisbane is generally made up of undistinguished high-rise buildings, although some attempt is now being made to take advantage of the attractive banks of the Brisbane River. The city lies 30 km (18 miles) upriver from Moreton Bay, set in undulating countryside. Town planning was not high on the priority list until fairly recently, so much of the suburban area is a hodgepodge of development, lacking in broad thoroughfares and other distinctive urban features. Even in the city center on the river's north side the main streets are too narrow, and the Brisbane City Council seems to be undecided as to whether to carry on with further downtown freeway development or to encourage a traffic-free area. In the past it's done both, so a long stretch of river is dominated by an elevated freeway that leads commuters to midtown traffic chaos.

But this doesn't mean that central Brisbane is entirely unattractive. The **Queen Street Mall**, which was hurriedly constructed in 1982 prior to the Commonwealth Games, has been nicely developed and recently extended. Downtown remains a major shopping area. Central Brisbane is best explored by walking. Start at the **Hilton International Hotel** and the Wintergarden shopping center on the Mall. Two blocks west on Ann Street, next to St. John's Cathedral, is the Deanery, the site of the proclamation in 1859 declaring Queensland a separate colony from New South Wales. Close by is Anzac Square, with its eternal flame of remembrance, and opposite is the Central Railway Station and Brisbane's best hotel, the **Sheraton Brisbane Hotel and Towers**.

Walk through King Edward Park to **The Old Windmill** and Wickham Park. The Old Windmill, originally used to grind grain, dates from 1829, making it one of the city's oldest buildings. Past the park is King George Square, the Neoclassical City Hall, and the reputable **Mayfair Crest International Hotel**. Now walk via City Plaza shopping center to the Italian Renaissance-style Treasury Building at Queen and George streets. If you crave a meal in an opulent 19th-century setting, stop off at **Agatha Christies** restaurant above City Plaza.

George and William streets contain numerous government offices, including the state's Parliament House

(1868) and the Old Government House (1862). Just opposite here, the **Botanic Gardens** provide 45 pleasant acres for strolling and relaxing.

A National Trust "Historic Walks" brochure will throw more light on the items of historical interest in the city. It's available from Old Government House, some hotels, and other visitor information centers. General city information is available from a kiosk in the Queen Street Mall.

You can take a bus tour with Boomerang Tours, which offers morning, afternoon, or all-day tours; their phone number is (07) 221-9922. Also, the City Council offers the "City Lookabout Tour," a three-hour bus trip taking in nearly 100 interesting sites. Superior Tours has limousine service for that extra-special tour; phone them at (07) 368-3857.

One of the few commercial tourist attractions in the city center is the **Wilderness Walk** in Koala House, corner of Adelaide and Creek streets. This is an indoor display of woodland rain forest and coastal wetland, complete with some live koalas.

The city provides plenty of shopping opportunities. The new Myer Centre, for example, is Australia's largest city-center shopping development. **Queensland Aboriginal Creations** on George Street is a good place for original handicrafts and artifacts; **Baa Baa Black Sheep** in the Queen Street Mall specializes in Australian woolen products; and **Koala Homeland** in the Wintergarden complex has a particularly wide range of Australian-made gifts.

For those with more expensive tastes, **The Town Gallery** on Elizabeth Street has a good collection of art by distinguished Australian artists; **Eilishas Antiques** in The Mansions has some quality pieces; and **Endors** on Edward Street offers excellent Australian opals, other gems, and fine jewelry.

Brisbane doesn't boast such renowned restaurants as do Melbourne, Sydney, and even Adelaide, but the city does have several good places to eat, some of which we mention as we go along. Of the hotel restaurants, **Denisons** at the Sheraton, **Olivers** at the Mayfair Crest, and The **Drawing Room** at the Brisbane City Travelodge on Roma Street are all excellent.

**Allegro** in Central Station Plaza has good food and a classical music tradition. **Harrower's** on Coronation Drive at the edge of downtown provides sophisticated dining overlooking the Brisbane River. **Michael's on the Mall** has good wine and atmosphere. Any of these would be unlikely to disappoint you. For something a little more relaxed, try the courtyard of **Faces**, Given Terrace, Paddington (2 km/1¼ miles west of the city), or **Jimmys on the Mall** in the Queen Street Mall for good seafood in a casual atmosphere.

Seafood is excellent everywhere in Queensland, but many of the names on the menu will appear strange. Shrimps are known as banana prawns, while Moreton Bay bugs are a type of bay lobster. Among the fish species are barramundi, a delicious perch; coral trout and coral cod from the Great Barrier Reef; and mud crab or mangrove crab.

For action into the early morning hours **Spillanes** at the Mayfair Crest, **The Red Parrot** at the Hilton, and **Reflections** at the Sheraton are all satisfactory. For more contact with the locals try **Bonaparte's Hotel** in Fortitude Valley north of the city center, **Rosie's Tavern** on Edward Street, or **Fridays** at the Riverside Centre.

The **Warana Festival**, Brisbane's annual fun and culture fest, takes place for two weeks every September.

# Southside

The south bank of the Brisbane River is an area transformed. The huge **Queensland Cultural Centre** is a superb permanent facility, while much of the remaining riverbank has been occupied by the World Expo 88 site. Access from the city center is via Victoria Bridge from the Queen Street Mall or by train to South Brisbane Station.

The Cultural Centre has several components. The **Queensland Art Gallery**, with its wide-ranging Australian and European collection, is open daily; guided tours are available at 2:00 P.M. each day. The **Performing Arts Complex** comprises a series of auditoriums and other facilities for classical and popular performing arts and exhibitions. The **Queensland Museum** has displays emphasizing the natural, human, and technological history of Queensland. Two cafés at the Centre, the bistro-style **Lyrebird Restaurant** and the delightful **Fountain Room**, provide a wide dining choice. The complex will soon be completed with the opening of the State Library.

On the Southside, vegetarian cuisine in a charming

setting is available at **Squirrels Restaurant** on Melbourne Street. The **Cordelia Street Antique and Art Centre** features some of the best antiques in Brisbane. It's also worth considering the Southside for accommodation. Several new hotels and serviced apartments were built for Expo 88; demand has now slackened so prices are good. **Hillcrest Central Apartments** on Vulture Street and **Riverview Gardens Apartments** on River Terrace are two well-equipped properties particularly suited to families.

## Fortitude Valley/Newstead

Fortitude Valley is immediately north of the central city. This area once rivaled downtown as a shopping district and for some time was the major nightlife area. Today there are a few department stores here, a recently renovated Chinatown with some good restaurants, and the city's exhibition grounds, which spring to life for a week in August. There is still nightlife, although some of it borders on the seedy.

**Newstead Park** is a pleasant and historic riverside area just a little farther north (its Newstead House, built in 1846, is the oldest home in Brisbane). In Chester Street is the beautiful and equally historic **Roseville Restaurant**, serving lunch and tea Tuesday to Friday and dinner Tuesday to Saturday. Newstead's relaxed **Breakfast Creek Wharf** probably has Brisbane's best seafood. The nearby **Breakfast Creek Hotel** is a real Brisbane institution, a public bar where beer is served off the wood, with great steaks and a relaxed garden for eating and drinking. ("Hotel" in Australia most frequently denotes a bar, often with attached accommodation.)

For shopping in Fortitude Valley there is **The Potters' Gallery** for unusual quality pieces and **Pierrot**, an art and craft center where you can meet and watch artists at work.

## Around Brisbane

**Mount Coot-tha**, a little under 8 km (5 miles) west of the city center, is the highest point in the suburban area, and there are many lookouts, tracks, and facilities here. The **Summit Restaurant** has good food and a dazzling view at night. Around the foothills are the **Mount Coot-tha Bo-**

tanic Gardens and the Sir Thomas Brisbane Planetarium, which together have developed into one of Brisbane's most popular attractions. Buses connect them with the city.

At the Lone Pine Koala Sanctuary, 11 km (6½ miles) southwest of the city center, you can cuddle koalas, hand-feed kangaroos, and see wombats, emus, and platypuses. The best way to get there is on the M.V. *Captain Cook,* which sails from the Riverside Centre, Eagle Street, Brisbane, at 12:50 P.M. every day.

Among the Moreton Bay Islands east of Brisbane, North Stradbroke Island has good beaches, interesting headlands, and fascinating freshwater lakes. Car ferries operate the 13 km (7¾ miles) from either Cleveland or Redland Bay (20 km/12 miles southeast of Brisbane) to Dunwich on the island approximately every hour. Various accommodation exists on the island, with the Anchorage Village Beach Resort probably the best choice.

St. Helena Island is a tiny island where you can see the ruins of St. Helena prison, one of Queensland's most severe penal settlements, which operated on the island from 1867 until 1932. Day trips operate from Breakfast Creek on Saturdays and Sundays. Moreton Island has, on the western side, the Tangalooma Resort, once an old whaling station. Accommodation at the resort is good, but many visitors prefer merely to take the day trip from Brisbane. The resort catamaran leaves Hamilton Game Fishing Wharf in Brisbane daily at 9:30 A.M..

Bribie Island, one hour by bus north of Brisbane, is reached by a bridge to the southern end of the island. Upwards of 8,000 people call this island, with its good surfing and calm channel toward the mainland, home.

The M.V. *Brisbane Explorer,* a fully air-conditioned modern cruise ship with accommodation for 170 passengers in self-contained double cabins, is a comfortable way to cruise Moreton Bay. The ship does a four-day Gold Coast cruise and a two-day Moreton Bay cruise each week. It leaves from Admiralty Wharf near Story Bridge in Brisbane; Tel: (07) 844-3533.

# THE GOLD COAST

The Gold Coast's surf beach and its nine months of almost guaranteed sunshine would be enough to drag many tourists to the area. Of course, that's how it all began, but the attractions have increased to such an extent that for many visitors the beach hardly rates. In its place are shopping, dining, nightclubbing, golfing, touring, boating, and gambling. Most of these man-made attractions reflect the incredible growth that has transformed sand dunes and swamps into arcades, hotels, and more.

Gold Coast bus tours are available through Ansett Pioneer and Intertour, as well as other bus services. Check with the Queensland Government Travel Centre at 196 Adelaide Street, Brisbane, for full details.

The Gold Coast is both a region and a city. In general terms it stretches the 50-odd km (about 30 miles) from the Coomera River in the north to the Tweed River in the south. Its undisputed center is Surfers Paradise.

## Surfers Paradise

"Big, brassy, bright, but barely beautiful" sums up the town of Surfers Paradise. It's where the bodies are brownest, the bikinis are smallest, the shops are the swankiest, and the action is coolest. Along the strip, skyscraping apartment blocks, hotels, and vacation rentals jostle for space as in Waikiki and Miami Beach.

At street level there is color and movement in a kaleidoscope of neon signs, take-out food places, designer boutiques, tourist joints, and tacky souvenir shops. But just as you might be about to dismiss Surfers as a second-rate international beach resort, try walking down Orchid Avenue late afternoon or early evening, and suddenly a more sophisticated, elegant, cosmopolitan Surfers Paradise will emerge.

The main part of Surfers Paradise is a three- or four-block stretch between the surf beach and the Nerang River. The central spine of this is the Gold Coast Highway linking Brisbane with New South Wales. In downtown Surfers, the traffic on the highway is nonstop, the side-

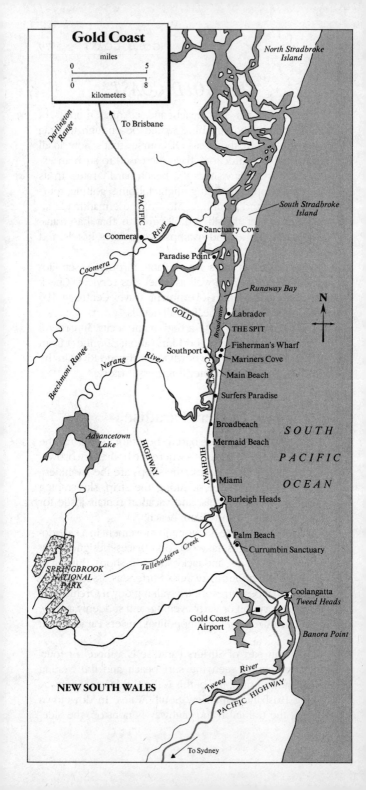

walks can be crowded, and the holiday spirit mixes un-
easily with the commercial hustle.

Some relief comes in the arcades that lead from the
highway toward the beach. Here you will find the best
shops, take-out food, souvenirs, and duty-free shopping.
The newest arcade and one of the best is **Holiday City
Galleria** surrounding the high-rise A.N.A. Hotel. Nearby
are the **Forum** and **Dolphin Arcade**. Each contains clothing stores, restaurants, fast-food outlets, souvenir shops,
and so forth. There are all the usual designer-label boutiques, high-class jewelry, quality souvenirs, and Australian fashions. These are places for browsing and personal
discovery, not for guidebook recommendations. The
other major complex is **Paradise Centre**, which has 120
specialty shops, a supermarket, more than 30 places to
eat, five bars, and the **Ramada Hotel**.

Down one side of the Paradise Centre, Cavill Avenue
turns into Cavill Mall, with outdoor restaurants and a few
garden areas, and this in turn leads directly to the beach.
Midway, **Orchid Avenue** leads off to the left. Here the
pace is slower, the streetscape more appealing, the outdoor cafés more inviting. Have a drink by the Forum
fountain and watch a good cross-section of the world
shuffle by.

This whole area is packed with restaurants. **Bogarts** has
an intimate atmosphere, a delightful piano bar, and a
good, varied menu; the **River Inn Seafood Restaurant** has
good service; **Danny's** has outstanding Italian food and
live Latin music; **The Loft** features elegant, affordable
dining and the chance to bring your own favorite wine.
There are another hundred or so restaurants in Surfers
Paradise, and it's hard to make a serious mistake.

It's the same with accommodation. The **Ramada**, the
**A.N.A.**, and the **Gold Coast International** are all fine
hotels with good rooms, excellent restaurants and bars,
and satisfactory service. Alongside these are scores of
high-rise vacation apartments that have full cooking facilities and are ideal for those staying a few days. Down-
market are a huge range of motels and guesthouses.
Despite this, accommodation can be very tight at Christ-
mastime and during midyear school holiday times (June
and September). Prices also rise frighteningly at these
times.

# North from Surfers

Main Beach, The Spit, and Southport are immediately north of Surfers Paradise. **Southport** was the original town on the Gold Coast, and it's still more of a real town than most other areas. It lacks the glamour and life of Surfers Paradise and pretty much goes about its own business.

Southport is sheltered from the ocean by a long sand promontory called **The Spit**, and between The Spit and the mainland is a bay called the Broadwater. This area has recently received major development. Leading the way is **Sea World**, a huge aquatic amusement center that is the largest man-made attraction on the Gold Coast. There are dolphin and water-ski shows, a monorail train, roller coasters, thrill rides, and eating outlets. For theme park addicts it's one of the best around.

Nearby, the **Gold Coast Sheraton Mirage Hotel** sets the standard by which all other Gold Coast hotels are judged. This delightful property has a prime beachfront location and its own shopping and marina complex. While it's somewhat away from the Surfers Paradise action, a ten-minute limousine ride can fix that. Mariners Cove and Fishermans Wharf add further attraction to this area with their shops, outdoor eateries, and boardwalks. Farther north along the wide tidal Broadwater you come to **Runaway Bay** and **Paradise Point**, where there are several large marinas. This is real water-sport territory. The warm, calm water is perfect for water-skiing, jet-skiing, catamaran-sailing, sailboarding, parasailing, fishing, paraflying, and cruising.

Power boats and other sports equipment can be rented from several outlets along this section of waterfront. Trips operate from here to **Tipplers Resort** on **South Stradbroke Island** for lunch and swimming and farther north to Dunwich on North Stradbroke Island. These waters are excellent for fishing; flathead and whiting are best from December to March, while bream, snapper, and tailor are caught from May to August.

Naturally, this area is big on seafood restaurants. **Grumpy's Wharf** and **Yacht Harbour Seafood Restaurant**, both on The Spit opposite the Sheraton Hotel, are excellent, while **Holy Mackeral** and **David's Fishermans Basket**, both at Southport, are also highly recommended. Two other places that usually get rave reviews are **Scampi's on the Beach** at Labrador and **Le Noumea,** a French-style B.Y.O. restaurant at Southport. All are relaxed and casual—in fact, it's hard to find a formal restaurant in these parts.

Farther north again is **Sanctuary Cove Resort,** aiming to become Australia's top address. The development consists of a **Hyatt Regency Hotel,** exclusive residences for 1,400 families, a top marina, and extensive sporting facilities. The development was opened with the help of Frank Sinatra and Whitney Houston in early 1988. This undoubtedly ranks among Australia's top resorts.

A few kilometers (a couple of miles) from here, **Dreamworld,** a Disneyland-style theme park, has become Australia's best attended man-made attraction. For kids of all ages, nothing here beats it.

## South from Surfers

The surf-pounded sand strip runs south from Surfers Paradise for 25 km (15 miles) through Broadbeach, Mermaid Beach, Miami, Burleigh Heads, and Palm Beach to Coolangatta. No single center comes near to rivaling Surfers Paradise, but together they offer a variety of attractions and accommodations that is quite impressive.

**Broadbeach** is the first major center. It marks the end of the beachfront high-rise clutter. There is a great beach, two surf lifesaving clubs, the **Pacific Fair Shopping Centre**—the largest shopping complex on the coast—and the **Conrad International Hotel and Jupiters Casino.** The Conrad is built on its own island in the Nerang River and is a complete holiday center in itself. There are four licensed restaurants, a 24-hour casino with more than 100 gaming tables, a 1,000-seat show room featuring girls and feathers, a nightclub, pool, spas, tennis courts, and full gymnasium and health club. It is an unusual mixture of sophistication and beach vacation resort; elegant style rubs shoulders with beachwear here.

The Conrad Hotel is huge by Australian standards, and the casino is one of the most open and relaxed in Australia. Patrons can arrive by road or by boat via some of the area's hundreds of canals. Inland from here are some of Australia's most expensive houses, built on artificial keys that ultimately connect with the Nerang River and the

Broadwater. Half-day cruises operate throughout the region from the Nerang River jetty at the end of Cavill Avenue.

Development south from here is more spread out, and some areas become faintly scruffy. **Burleigh Heads** provides the next cluster of high rises, overlooking a lovely surf beach and rocky promontory. There is a small national park here with walks and picnic tables. The highway continues south past the Gold Coast Airport to **Coolangatta** on the New South Wales border. This is a pleasant town with a good beach and lots of surfing. There is little artificial sophistication, and so some people prefer it to the hype of Surfers.

Along the way south, among numerous commercial tourist attractions you will have passed the **Currumbin Sanctuary**, owned by the National Trust of Queensland and well worth a visit. The well-known lorikeets (a type of parrot) feed in the early morning and late afternoon, but there are so many varieties of birds and animals that a visit any time is a delight.

The hinterland area to the west has long been overshadowed by the beach, but now it is being seen as a major attraction. Within 40 km (25 miles) of the coast you can be at 3,960 feet in lovely mountain country with huge beech trees, lovely waterfalls, and charming old-world resorts. Coach tours to these areas operate from all Gold Coast accommodations.

## *THE SUNSHINE COAST*

The Sunshine Coast north of Brisbane claims to be the fastest-growing region in Australia. The attractions are the beach, the weather, and the relatively unspoiled nature of the area. Unfortunately there are already signs that this will become all-too-equal competition for the neon-lit Gold Coast. If that happens, the Sunshine area will have lost much of its original charm.

The Sunshine Coast is about 45 miles long, with several seaside centers separated by fairly sparse development. But already the gaps are closing. Before too long it will be a continuous ribbon of development joining Caloundra, Maroochydore, Coolum, and Noosa. Each of these towns

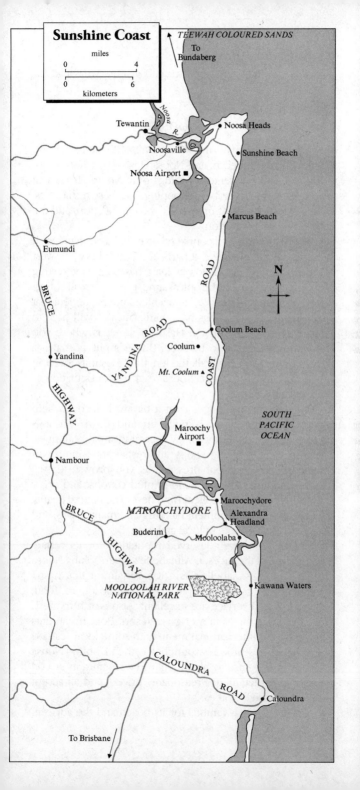

has its devotees, but sophisticated visitors will head for Noosa.

# Noosa

Noosa vaguely covers the small towns of Tewantin, Noosaville, Sunshine Beach, and Noosa Heads. For those wishing to be in the center of things only **Noosa Heads** will suffice. Here is the best shopping, the best restaurants, the widest choice of up-market accommodation, and the only real sophistication.

Sophistication is of course relative. No Australian beach resort has the elegance of parts of the Riviera or the West Indies, but Noosa Heads at least has some interesting architecture, a real subtropical atmosphere, a small collection of "beautiful people," and a nice understatement that implies there are things happening but you will have to search for them yourself. Hastings Street is where you must be, the place to be seen. But let's put Noosa into perspective: You can walk the length of Hastings Street in five minutes. The entire Noosa *area* has a population of fewer than 25,000.

Anyone staying longer than a day will need no help with shopping hints. Wander up and down Hastings Street and you will find many charming small boutiques, hairdressers, souvenir shops, and restaurants. Shops will welcome you without pressure as you browse. Casual wear abounds; sandals, hand-printed cottons, and original jewelry are all excellent buys here. The natural beauty of the Noosa environment has attracted many artists, and their work is for sale in local galleries.

Noosa has a well-deserved reputation for its restaurants. One of the nicest is **Annabelle's**, overlooking Noosa Main Beach. Annabelle's is a top restaurant that hasn't been ruined by a big reputation; its atmosphere, food, wine list, and service are excellent. Also worth trying is **Michelle's** at the Netanya Noosa Resort. Both restaurants have a good international menu with some local seafood specialties. If seafood is your choice, then **Dooleys Noosa Heads** is also sure to please. All three restaurants are on Hastings Street, all are reasonably priced, and all accept diners in casual clothes.

Noosa Heads is famous for its beach and the adjacent

**Noosa National Park** and **Sunshine Beach**, the latter for the best and most consistent waves on the Sunshine Coast, but the Noosa River and lake system inland are the biggest attraction here for many. Enthusiasts can hire a boat, canoe, or houseboat for fishing or sightseeing, but most visitors will be content to take a tour. Tours come in several shapes and sizes. The *Noosa Queen* offers a four-and-a-half-hour cruise with barbecue lunch on the Noosa River and Lake Cooroibah. The *Cooloola Queen,* the *Everglades Express,* and the *Kookaburra Jet* do something similar. All tour operators pick up guests at their hotels.

The other major tour is to the **Colored Sands of Teewah** and **Rainbow Beach**, a 36-mile expanse of glorious beach immediately north of Noosa, across the Noosa River. Tours operate each day in four-wheel-drive vehicles that travel the beach to Double Island Point. The beach is lined with 200-foot-high cliffs. Day trips usually include lunch, a swim, and a visit to one of the freshwater lakes.

For those not put off by a long day, the 12-hour trip to **Fraser Island** about 65 km (40 miles) north of the coast is good value. Fraser Island is the world's largest sand island, now protected from sand-miners after a bitter struggle. There are superb beaches, towering sand dunes, and clear freshwater lakes and streams. The island is closed to individuals, and the only way to visit it is with one of the tour groups operating out of Noosa. Tourism is strictly controlled, and each tour operator is restricted to a certain area. All, however, will show you the beaches, the pristine rain forest, and the lakes. Fishing is great, but swimming can be dangerous. Visitors often see dingoes (native dogs) and brumbies (wild horses). The cost of the full day runs to about A$70.

Noosa accommodation is good and reasonably priced, except for a few weeks at Christmas and during the September school holidays. The best accommodation is at the **Netanya Noosa Resort**, which has a beachfront position on Hastings Street. There are one- and two-bedroom suites and penthouses with private balconies, saunas, and full kitchen facilities. The **Noosa International** is larger but still very attractive. Most units have two bedrooms and two bathrooms and a fully equipped kitchen and laundry. Its disadvantage is that it's a ten-minute walk to the beach, but the two pools, three spa pools, and two saunas are some compensation, and there is a courtesy bus service.

Two other Hastings Street hotels, cheaper but still excellent, are the **Seahaven Beachfront Resort** and the **Terrace Gardens Quality Inn**. Both have self-contained units with availability of restaurants, bars, barbecue facilities, pools, and—of course—the beach.

# Elsewhere on the Sunshine Coast

Noosa is not the largest center nor the only holiday spot in this part of Australia. The coast region stretches south for about 40 miles and inland to the ranges. Visitors can enjoy time in many other places, such as:

**Caloundra**, at the southern end of the beach strip. There are several good beaches here in what is very much a family vacation town. Gamblers will enjoy the new Corbould Park horse racecourse.

**Maroochydore**, covering the three centers of Maroochydore, Alexandra Headland, and Mooloolaba north of Caloundra. These towns have grown dramatically in recent years and now have good shopping, entertainment, and accommodation options. The beach is still the prime attraction here, though, and there is a choice between surfing and swimming. Two restaurants with good reputations are **Fronds** on the beach in Mooloolaba and **La Promenade** in Maroochydore. There are cruises on the Maroochy River, and a newly opened golf center is fun. The nightclubs **My Place** and **Galaxy** are popular after-dark venues for the young at heart.

**Buderim**, a delightful little hillside town inland from Maroochydore. There are some dramatic views from Buderim toward the coast. Try **Portofino's** for dinner.

**Sunshine Plantation**, the biggest tourist attraction in this region. This strange combination of pineapple farm, rain-forest area, tourist infrastructure, and educational facility draws over a million visitors a year. Next door is the CSR Macadamia Nut Factory. Try the fresh tropical fruit parfaits, sundaes, and drinks.

**Nambour**, settled in 1860, a working town with sugarcane trains crossing the main street and a sweet smell of prosperity. This is the real world, one content to do without the hype of the coast. A wide range of tropical produce is grown in the surrounding area.

**Coolum**, back on the coast, a small population center about to be thrust into the limelight with the opening of a huge **Hyatt Regency Coolum**. This will become the largest and most prestigious resort on the coast and is bound to draw other development.

**Yandina** and **Eumundi**, two small towns just southwest of Noosa Heads, with rich history, art, and culture. The Saturday morning Eumundi craft market is justly famous, while at Yandina, the **Fairhill Native Plants** (a botanic garden), the Ginger Factory, and **T Trees Restaurant** are all worthy additions to the delightful landscape.

# SOUTHERN GREAT BARRIER REEF

The Great Barrier Reef is one of Australia's best-known attractions, yet few visitors have an accurate picture of what the reef is like and even fewer appreciate the problems associated with seeing it. The Great Barrier Reef is a 1,200-mile-long chain of coral reefs paralleling the Queensland coast, the majority above water only at the lowest of tides. The reef is a sensational underwater attraction that man is only now starting to penetrate. Fortunately, man's development of reef-viewing facilities has been rapid, so that under normal weather conditions everyone who wants to can now experience this unique environment, whether they swim and scuba dive or not.

## The Reef

The Great Barrier Reef is coral, a huge system built by tiny animals just a few millimeters in size that live and die in this marine environment. The living coral polyps excrete a limy skeleton; when they die, this remains. New polyps grow on their dead predecessors, and in this way a reef is slowly built up.

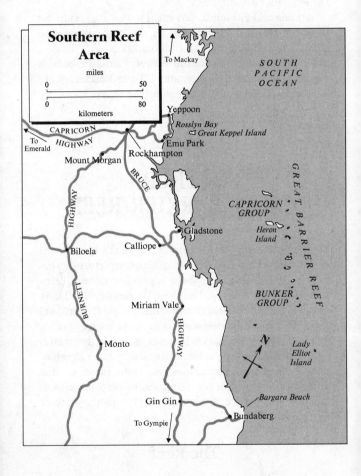

## Southern Reef Area

miles
0                   50

kilometers
0                   80

To Mackay

SOUTH
PACIFIC
OCEAN

Yeppoon
Rosslyn Bay
Great Keppel Island

CAPRICORN
HIGHWAY
To Emerald
Emu Park
Rockhampton

Mount Morgan

BRUCE

GREAT BARRIER REEF

CAPRICORN
GROUP

Gladstone
Heron Island

Calliope

Biloela

BURNETT

BUNKER
GROUP

Miriam Vale

Monto

Lady Elliot Island

HIGHWAY

N

Gin Gin

Bargara Beach
Bundaberg

To Gympie

Coral requires warm, clean, salty water for proper growth. The outer edge of the Australian continental shelf provides near-perfect conditions. This is where the reef is best and viewing most spectacular. The reef has few islands. Coral cannot live above water, but sometimes dead coral rubble and coral sand will accumulate inside a reef and rise above water level. Over time this can become colonized, first with grass, which attracts sea birds, then later with shrubs and trees, which grow from seeds carried by the birds.

Unfortunately the tourism industry isn't always precise with its terms, so "reef-island" cannot necessarily be translated into "coral cay." In fact, most of the popular resort islands are continental-type islands, that is, the tips of offshore mountain ranges. Some of these have fringing reef that can be quite spectacular, but that doesn't constitute the Great Barrier Reef.

The first thing you see on the reef is coral. It comes in a bewildering variety of shapes, sizes, and colors. Many visitors are initially disappointed that there is so much "dead" coral everywhere. This is due in part to the staghorn corals that make up the largest proportion of coral on the reef. The staghorns provide shelter to fish and other animals, but unfortunately they are easily broken by storms and man.

So the reef flats and some lagoon areas are a wasteland, and it's not until you approach the outer edges of the reefs that you see the more spectacular pieces: delicately colored ferns, huge lumps of brain coral, and some of the soft corals that don't actually take part in the building process but add their beauty to the underwater garden.

The Great Barrier Reef would be nothing much more than a giant breakwater for the Pacific Ocean if it were not for the prolific marine life that inhabits all reefs. The fish come in an extraordinary variety of colors and shapes, and some have rather strange behavior patterns as well. For visitors they represent the second major reef attraction, and the development of semi-submersible vessels and underwater observatories means that the fish can be seen much more readily than in the past.

Colors are of immense value to reef fish as warning or camouflage. Many have vivid bands, spots, or patches that break up their outline and confuse predators. Some reef fish can even change color to match their surroundings.

Other fish have intimate relationships with larger creatures. Some small wrasse fish are cleaners taking parasites from larger fish. Even eels and huge manta rays visit these "cleaning stations" for service. Other fish live within the poisonous tentacles of the giant anemone in complete safety. Reef visitors can often see all this fascinating activity. In some parts visitors can see giant groupers. These amazing fish can become semi-tame and will swim with divers and wait to be fed. They can grow up to ten feet in length and weigh more than 880 pounds.

Then there are the numerous colorful shells. One of the most common is the ringed money cowrie, while the most interesting is undoubtedly the giant clam. There are at least 50 species of cowries in Australian reef waters and various varieties of sand-dwelling volutes.

## Gateways to the Reef

The Great Barrier Reef starts just south of the Tropic of Capricorn and goes north almost to Papua New Guinea. The main reefs are 250 km (150 miles) off the coast from Rockhampton at the southern end, but as you travel north the distance becomes smaller. While it is possible to reach the reef from many coastal centers, visitors would do well to head for one of the following:

**Townsville** is the research capital of the reef, and it is becoming the tourist capital as well. The city is home to the Great Barrier Reef Marine Park Authority, the Australian Institute of Marine Science, James Cook University, the Great Barrier Reef Wonderland, the offshore Four Seasons Barrier Reef Resort, and Fantasy Island. From Townsville you have the choice of a day trip to floating Fantasy Island, to Orpheus Island, Palm Island, or an overnight or longer stay on the Four Seasons Barrier Reef Resort on John Brewer Reef.

**Cairns** was the first center to take advantage of the Great Barrier Reef, and more day visitors go to the reef from here than from any other mainland city. Visitors have a choice of going to Fitzroy Island, a mainland island with good fringing reef, to Green Island, a true coral cay with visitor facilities, or to one of two outer reefs that have pontoons and semi-submersible submarines.

**Brisbane** is hundreds of miles south of the Great Barrier Reef, yet it is an important gateway because of its access to Bundaberg and Gladstone, which in turn are gateways to Lady Elliot Island and Heron Island, the two southernmost reef islands.

## Staying on the Reef

There are only four alternatives if you wish to stay *on* the Great Barrier Reef: Lady Elliot Island, Heron Island, Green Island, or the Four Seasons Barrier Reef Resort. The first three are coral cays that have limited mid-market accommodation; the fourth is a large floating luxury hotel—the first such hotel in the world.

**Heron Island** is generally considered the nicest coral cay. It is quite a way off the coast, so there are no day-trippers. Access is via helicopter from Gladstone Airport (A$140 one way) or boat from Gladstone Marina (A$65 one way). Transfers are not included in resort fees. The island is a haven for snorkelers and scuba divers.

**Lady Elliot Island** is 92 km (55 miles) from Bundaberg and transfers are by air (A$120 round trip). The island is still developing, so this is not the place for those seeking luxury. Some cabins have private facilities, while roomy safari tents offer an economical alternative.

**Green Island**, 25 km (15 miles) off Cairns and con-nected by catamaran (cost included in resort tariff), has been popular for thirty years. The facilities have recently been upgraded, and in the evening this is one of the nicest islands around.

The **Four Seasons Barrier Reef Resort**, 70 km (42 miles) off Townsville at **John Brewer Reef**, opened in early 1988. The 200-room floating hotel is 13 feet above the reef, yet it offers facilities equal to many mainland resorts. There are a marina, a floating tennis court, a large pool, underwater video cameras, a semi-submersible sub-marine, shops, restaurants, bars and disco, game-fishing boats, and dive boats. Connections are by helicopter from Townsville airport (A$200 round trip) or by catamaran from Ross Creek, Townsville (A$70 round trip).

## Visiting the Reef

For those who are short on time or for those with special interests, other facilities exist for visiting the reef.

Day trips on fast catamarans are available to various

reefs. Daily trips operate from the Whitsunday Islands, Townsville, Mission Beach, Cairns, and Port Douglas, while boats operate from Mackay several days a week, and from Great Keppel Island, Orpheus Island, and Lizard Island for guests at those resorts.

Extended cruises are also available. The *Elizabeth E II* cruises from Mackay, visiting some of the Whitsunday islands and the Great Barrier Reef on a four-day itinerary; Tel: 079-574-281. Roylen Cruises has a somewhat similar cruise with a five-day itinerary. Both leave Mackay Harbour on Monday morning (Tel: 079-553-066).

The *Coral Cat* operates from Hamilton Island and cruises the Whitsunday Passage; weather permitting, a full day is spent on the reef. The *Coral Princess* cruises from Townsville to Cairns and back (four days, three nights each way); this catamaran stops at several inshore islands and resorts, but also visits reefs and cays on the Great Barrier Reef. Departure from Townsville is on Friday, and departure from Cairns is on Tuesday.

# Diving the Reef

The Great Barrier Reef provides some of the best diving in the world, and there are plenty of opportunities to use the facilities of local professional experts. Local knowledge is an essential ingredient. The warm, clear water may look perfect, but there are currents, the coral is sharp, and there are other dangers similar to those at home.

Fortunately most island resorts now have trained dive masters, charter-boat operators are familiar with the reef and know the dangers, and most dive tours are excellently run. Australia has a good safety record, and most operators will require a diving-oriented medical certificate together with an acceptable diving qualification before you will be permitted to rent gear or enter the water.

Many resorts operate basic-training courses that allow you to shallow-dive with a group to see a little of the reef. Some resorts and a number of mainland centers provide facilities for full accreditation. This will take five to seven days. Diving tours operate from several centers along the coast. Those from Townsville north are considered to be the best, while Heron Island in the south and Lizard

Island in the north are also two very popular island dive locations.

Virtually all of the Great Barrier Reef is a marine national park controlled by the Great Barrier Reef Marine Park Authority. There are a number of rules as to where you can go and what you can do, so check with local divers. If you intend to camp on a privately owned island, seek the approval of the owner, or, if it is government-owned, obtain a permit from the National Parks and Wildlife Service. (This can take several weeks.)

Spearfishing in scuba gear is generally prohibited, and minimum sizes apply to about 50 species of crabs and fish. Some species, like turtles, clams, dugong (sea cow), and triton shell, are totally protected.

Tanks and weight belts are universally available on a rental basis from resorts and gateway city dive operators.

# Weather

The weather plays a vital part in the enjoyment of the Great Barrier Reef. Few visitors will want to battle with rain, high wind, or huge seas to reach a suitable vantage point. Divers hope for clear skies and light winds so that visibility will be at its best. Sailors want small seas and consistent breezes.

During the Great Barrier Reef's winter (June-September) the southeast Trade Winds blow parallel to the Queensland coast. They are dry, mild (10-20 knots), and constant. Cruising yachts sail northward, spinnakers flying.

In summer (December-March) the northeast monsoons, saturated with moisture after their long Pacific voyage, deluge the reef and coast with sudden, heavy showers. Thunderstorms are common, with the occasional cyclone. Rain can last for three or four days, then there can be a week of fine weather. At this time the humidity is high and southern Australians stay away. Many visitors from the Northern Hemisphere are less disturbed by this weather, especially if they come from the northeast United States or Canada.

The transition periods of April-May and October-November are often warm, sunny, and languid.

There are considerable weather differences within the reef region. Records indicate that over the past 80 years the Cairns region has had more cyclones than other areas of the coast, yet the number in recent years has been small. Likewise, Cairns has more rainy days than most other areas.

All of Australia's tropical coastline has a problem with marine stingers. These jellyfish (Portuguese men-of-war) are found close inshore between November and April each year. Some inflict a painful sting, while one variety can be fatal. Understandably, locals avoid ocean swimming while stingers are around, and you should too. Swimming is safe in filtered rock pools and also within netted areas on many beaches.

# THE SOUTHERN GREAT BARRIER REEF REGION

The Great Barrier Reef reaches its southern extremity at Lady Elliot Island, offshore from Bundaberg. There is a group of reefs and islands running north to just above the Tropic of Capricorn, then there is a big gap until the central reef region around Townsville. Relatively speaking, the southern reef region is small, stretching a mere 120 miles along the coast. It is important, however, because this section of reef has great pressure put on it by the big population centers farther south. On the coast, the cities of Bundaberg, Gladstone, and Rockhampton are gateways to individual islands, while at the same time they go about their business of being regional and industrial centers.

## The Islands

**Lady Elliot Island** is the southernmost coral cay on the Great Barrier Reef. In the past the island has been underdeveloped, so it has often been overlooked, but recent improvements have brought it into prominence. The island is 320 km (192 miles) north of Brisbane and 92 km (55 miles) northeast of Bundaberg. Flights are available from Brisbane and the Gold Coast to Bundaberg, with a transfer to Lady Elliot Island by Sunstate Airlines.

Accommodation on **Lady Elliot Island** is provided in comfortable cabins and safari tents, and meals are served in the dining room or on a terrace overlooking the reef.

There is a store and a dive shop. Snorkelling and diving equipment is available for hire, and you can dive straight off the beach.

**Heron Island** is known worldwide by divers for its clear waters and variety of dives, but you don't have to partake in the sport to enjoy this lovely coral cay. The island is 70 km (42 miles) offshore, with launch and helicopter connections from Gladstone.

As is the case with most Queensland islands, the accommodation on Heron Island has recently been expanded and improved, but none of these southern islands is up to full international luxury standard. Then again, neither are the prices; you can get accommodation and meals for around A$120 a day.

Heron Island is alive with bird life and shaded by pandanus (or screw pines) and coconut palms. It is also home to green turtles and loggerhead turtles, which lay their eggs here from November to March. The resort has the usual facilities: dive shop, reef walks, beach, semi-submersible submarine, fishing trips, pool, bar, and entertainment.

**Great Keppel Island**, a mainland type island far from the Great Barrier Reef, is reached by air from Rockhampton or by launch from Rosslyn Bay (A$12 one way). The main resort of **Great Keppel Island**, owned by Australian Airways, has been heavily promoted as a young people's enclave, but in reality it is also visited by families and people of all ages. The accent, however, is on organized activities, and for participants there is never a dull moment: swimming, snorkeling, fishing, sailing, paraflying, sailboarding, golf, tennis, squash, archery, spas, and bars. At night the island has a show in the Sand Bar, dancing at the Wreck Bar disco, and "gentle" music at the Sunset Lounge. At Keppel Island you can "get wrecked" right around the clock.

# The Mainland

**Bundaberg**, the access point to Lady Elliot Island, is a major sugar-producing center. The city of about 40,000 is famous for its rum distillery. You can tour the rum distillery as well as several sugar mills; for something different, visit **Tropical Wines** on Gin Gin Road, which produces dessert-style wines from fresh Queensland fruit.

**Bargara Beach**, 13 km (7¾ miles) north of the city, provides some of the last surf on the route north. The **Don Pancho Beach Resort** offers good facilities and access to the beach and a golf course. Nearby **Mon Repos Environmental Park** has a famous turtle rookery, where between mid-January and late March thousands of young turtles hatch and head for the sea.

**Gladstone** is not everyone's idea of a tourist city. It is one of the busiest ports in Australia, exporting coal and aluminum and importing bauxite. Gladstone is important for visitors only because it is the departure point for Heron Island. There is a range of moderately priced motel-style accommodation in town, with the **Country Comfort Motel** being one of the best.

**Rockhampton**, situated astride the Tropic of Capricorn, is a solid city of 55,000 with many memories of its past: Rockhampton had an early gold rush, though today cattle is the big industry. Quay Street has one of Australia's best Victorian commercial streetscapes; more than 20 buildings here have National Trust classification. A National Trust walking-tour brochure is available from hotels and visitor-information outlets.

Right in the center of the shopping and business area, **Duthies Leichhardt Hotel** is a well-known and popular property, moderately priced. Three streets away, the **Riverside International Motel** is now throwing down the challenge for the position of best accommodation in town. Those wanting history should try the beautiful old **Criterion Hotel**, reasonably priced.

Rockhampton has always been a "civilized" town, so it's no surprise to find that the **Pilbeam Theatre/Art Gallery** complex on Victoria Parade is one of the best around. Also worth seeing are the **Botanic Gardens**, south near the airport.

There are several places to visit just outside Rockhampton; bus tours operate from the city. Some 38 km (23 miles) southeast is **Mount Morgan**, an old mining town with a huge gold and copper open-cut mine 990 feet deep. The mine has operated off and on for more than a hundred years. Mine inspections take place 9:30 A.M. and 1:30 P.M. daily. About 30 km (18 miles) north of Rockhampton, the **Berserker Range** has several limestone caves and a museum; guided tours are available. Some 260 km (156 miles) inland is the attractive town of **Emer-**

ald, and some 50 km (30 miles) farther on are the sapphire, topaz, and amethyst gem fields of Central Queensland. For those inclined, at the **Mt. Hay Gemstone Tourist Park** you can select your pick, shovel, and bucket and try your luck at a dig. Alternatively, visit the **Miners Heritage Walk-In Mine** at Rubyvale, the gem fields' largest underground hand mine. For those who have no luck, rough and cut sapphires are available for sale. Between Rockhampton and Emerald you see evidence of the huge open-cut coal mines that dot this area, providing Australia with large amounts of export dollars.

**Yeppoon** is the major center for the 24-mile stretch of beach to the east of Rockhampton known as the **Capricorn Coast**. This area has long been popular with local vacationers looking for wide, sandy beaches and a quiet, relaxed time.

There are sporting facilities and some interesting scenic drives in this area. From **Rosslyn Bay** you can visit Great Keppel Island and the **Middle Island Underwater Observatory**.

Accommodation and restaurants in this area are adequate rather than spectacular; at most times of the year you should select accommodation by cruising along the coast road and choosing something that appeals to you.

Yeppoon has been thrust into prominence by the construction of the **Capricorn Iwasaki Resort** just north of the town. The reasonably priced, Japanese-owned resort is built within 20,000 acres of parkland and wildlife sanctuaries and has restaurants, nightclubs, swimming pool, spa, sauna, 18-hole golf course, and 9 miles of beach. The resort initially met considerable local opposition, but since the first stage opened (in 1987) there have been fewer problems. At present, guests are Australian and Japanese, with a handful of other international visitors.

# THE CENTRAL GREAT BARRIER REEF REGION

This region has become one of the most popular and fastest-growing tourist areas in Australia. It combines some of the best sections of the Great Barrier Reef with lovely islands, good beaches, lush tropical rain forest, fascinating Outback country, and Australia's sunniest city. This is the beginning of North Queensland—where people are slower, time has less meaning, and there exists a friendliness now missing from much of the world.

Australian aboriginals have lived here for thousands of years, but Western knowledge of the area started with Captain Cook, who sailed the coast here in 1770, naming many islands, capes, and bays. You will see more black faces here than in most areas of the country. These are aboriginal people now living within the general community: Torres Strait islanders, who have left their small isolated islands and settled on the mainland, and South Seas islanders, who are mainly descendants of forced laborers brought in to work the sugar fields in the late 1800s. There is also a large Italian population who first arrived after World War I to work on the sugar farms and who now own the majority of the area's sugar industry.

## *TOWNSVILLE*

Townsville (population 115,000) is very much the "big city" of North Queensland; you have to travel 1,400 km (840 miles) to Brisbane to find anything larger. Some North Queenslanders have never done this. Townsville is undergoing significant growth these days, with a lot of developments not yet completed, and the town seems to be in the process of defining its personality.

Visitors come to Townsville for the weather and the reef. The city has a perfect warm-to-hot winter climate (April–October) with clear days and balmy nights. Sunshine is guaranteed; in fact, the city receives more sunshine hours than any other large center in Australia.

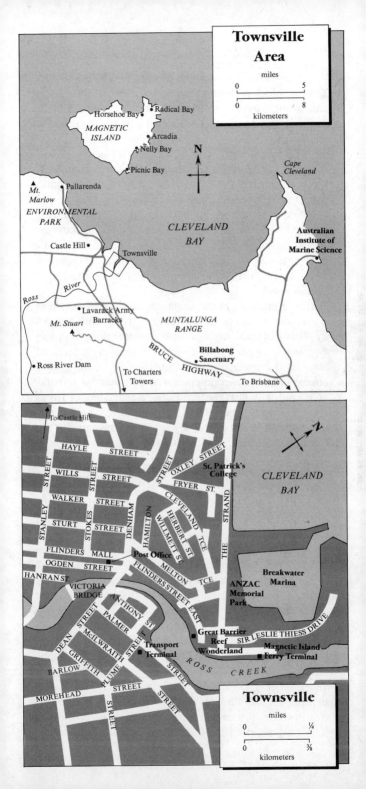

**Flinders Mall** is the perfect introduction to Townsville. The two-block pedestrian precinct is crowded with palms and tropical trees, fountains, street-size chess and backgammon games, seats, children's playground equipment, and an amphitheater. Here too are the main stores, fashion boutiques, and shopping arcades. It's here you will find the **Townsville International Hotel**, the boardwalk food fair, and the **Perc Tucker Art Gallery**, with its good collection of North Queensland art.

Flinders Mall leads to Flinders Street East, a nicely preserved tourist precinct with restaurants, art, souvenir shops, and nightclubs. Old-style lampposts, many beautifully restored old buildings, and tropical landscaping add to the appeal. At the far end is the **Great Barrier Reef Wonderland**.

The "aquarium" at the Great Barrier Reef Wonderland is operated by the Great Barrier Reef Marine Park Authority. This major facility is a huge seawater tank complete with waves and tides, which holds a living coral reef and associated marine environment. Because of the fragile nature of this environment the achievement is remarkable, and it is also the most spectacular view of living coral that most people will see anywhere. This experience should be on everyone's list. Then you can visit the Great Barrier Reef itself, with sufficient knowledge to fully appreciate what you see.

Flinders Mall, Flinders Street East, and the Great Barrier Reef Wonderland are the best areas for visitors to shop. Many shops here open longer than the five-and-a-half-day Australian norm. Aboriginal artifacts, coral, artworks, and tropical beachwear are popular buys here. The aboriginal-owned **Australian Collection** is known throughout Australia for its good, genuine pieces.

The **Sheraton Breakwater Casino/Hotel**, on the waterfront, is the city's best hotel. The 200-room property overlooks the Pacific Ocean, Magnetic Island (see Other Islands, below), and a huge new marina. Nearby are a new ferry terminal for the Magnetic Island catamaran, an overwater restaurant, a helicopter base for scenic flights, and shopping and commercial centers. Some of Townsville's other good hotels are along a nearby section of beach. Best are the high-rise **Townsville Travelodge** and the low-rise **Townsville Reef International**. Both have lush gardens, pools, and excellent bars and restaurants.

The Travelodge has a good open-air jazz session every Saturday afternoon.

The best restaurant in town is probably **Melton's** at the Sheraton. Jackets and ties are not mandatory, but most male patrons wear either or both. Other fine hotel restaurants are **Cassis** on the roof of the Townsville Travelodge, **Flutes** in the Reef International, and **Margeaux** at the Townsville International. Dress at these restaurants is definitely relaxed.

North Queensland is famous for tropical fruits and seafood. Most menus have examples of these dishes while some restaurants specialize in them. Most restaurants have good fresh prawns, Moreton Bay "bugs," mud crabs, and two local fish, barramundi and coral trout. **Mariners** and **Admiral's** are two very popular eat-as-much-as-you-like seafood smorgasbords where there is some music and atmosphere—but the emphasis is on quantity. **Higgins** on Flinders Street East is noisy and fun, with a blackboard menu, while the nearby **Metro** serves good vegetarian food.

Several places feature contemporary Australian rock music. Best are the Dalrymple Hotel, the Seaview Hotel, and the Speakeasy, while the top discos are The Bank and The Terrace—both on Flinders Street East—Heaven at the Criterion Hotel, and Elizas at the Crown Hotel in South Townsville. East Street and the Sheraton Lobby Lounge are popular quieter spots for talking, drinking, and dancing.

Townsville has several other must-see attractions. **Castle Hill**, which dominates the central city, has a lookout providing spectacular city and island views. The nearby **Townsville Environmental Park** is recognized as one of the world's most important waterbird sanctuaries, while **Billabong Sanctuary** is an attractive home for tropical wildlife, including the much-feared crocodile and the cuddly koala.

## THE CENTRAL REEF

The Central Great Barrier Reef stretches more or less parallel to the coast roughly from Mackay to Mission Beach. Major access to the reef is from Townsville, the Whitsundays, Mackay, and Mission Beach.

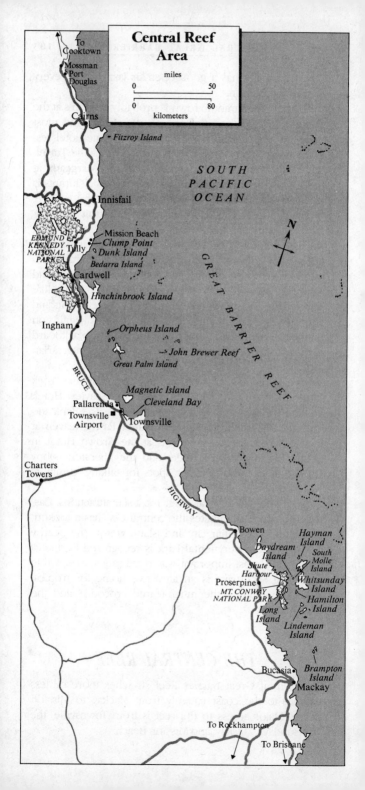

## Central Reef Area

miles
0                  50

kilometers
0                  80

To Cooktown

Mossman
Port
Douglas

Cairns

*Fitzroy Island*

SOUTH
PACIFIC
OCEAN

Innisfail

Mission Beach
*Clump Point*
*Dunk Island*
*Bedarra Island*

*EDMUND
KENNEDY
NATIONAL
PARK*

Tully

Cardwell

*Hinchinbrook Island*

GREAT BARRIER REEF

N

Ingham

*Orpheus Island*

*John Brewer Reef*

*Great Palm Island*

BRUCE

*Magnetic Island*
*Cleveland Bay*

Pallarenda
Townsville
Airport

Townsville

Charters
Towers

HIGHWAY

Bowen

*Hayman
Island*

*Daydream
Island*

*Shute
Harbour*

South
Molle
Island

Proserpine

*MT. CONWAY
NATIONAL PARK*

*Whitsunday
Island*

*Hamilton
Island*

*Long
Island*

*Lindeman
Island*

Bucasia

*Brampton
Island*

Mackay

To Rockhampton

To Brisbane

# Seeing the Central Reef

**John Brewer Reef** off Townsville is the most developed of all the reefs along the coast. This is home to Fantasy Island, a floating "donut" with drinking, eating, swimming, diving, lounging facilities, and underwater observatories. John Brewer is also home to the Four Seasons Barrier Reef Resort floating hotel, which gives you the only opportunity anywhere to stay above the reef itself. (See Staying on the Reef, above.)

The floating hotel and Fantasy Island are linked to Townsville by the 450-seat, high-speed *Reef Link* catamaran (90 minutes) or helicopter (20 minutes). Coral viewing can be done in a semi-submersible submarine. Similar day trips are offered by the M.V. *Quickcat* from Clump Point near Mission Beach and by various boats on different days in the Whitsundays and Mackay. The cost is about A$75.

Air Whitsunday pioneered air trips to the reef some years ago, and the company now operates float planes from Airlie Beach to Hardy Lagoon and, as Reef-World Airways, from Townsville to Davies Reef. At each location there is a mini-semi-submersible vessel for coral viewing. Other trips don't actually visit the Great Barrier Reef, but you still see good coral. From Townsville, Pure Pleasure Cruises operates daily to Orpheus Island for coral viewing and island exploring, while Westmark Marine operates to Palm Island (see Other Islands, below). The cost runs A$50–$75.

In the Whitsunday area, there is an underwater observatory on Hook Island.

# Diving the Central Reef

The Central Reef has three types of dive: coastal reefs, wrecks, and outer reef drop-offs. It's important to understand what type of dive is being offered by the numerous operators.

It's possible to dive the coastal reefs and some wrecks on day trips, but the outer reefs require extended tours. Experts rave about the diving on the outer reef wall, where drop-offs plunge 165 feet or more, and where water clarity is almost unbelievably outstanding.

From Townsville, day trips are available to Fantasy

Island, to Orpheus Island, and to the *Yongala* wreck. The *Yongala* is considered by many to be the best wreck dive on the reef because of the amount of sea life there. Unfortunately, though, the wreck is in fairly exposed waters, so winds and strong tides can affect comfort and water clarity. On a good day this may be the ultimate dive experience.

A number of extended trips also operate. The Dive Bell has the 66-foot M.V. *Hero* on two-, three-, and four-day trips. Mike Ball Watersports operates M.V. *Watersport* and M.V. *Supersport,* while the *Coral Princess* does a five-day trip and is available for charter. All boats provide cylinders and weight belts, with other gear available for hire. Dive trips are usually heavily booked, so plan ahead. (Coral Princess Cruises, 78 Primrose St., Belgian Gardens 4810; Tel: 077-724-675. Dive Bell, 141 Ingham Road, Townsville 4810; Tel: 077-211-155. Mike Ball Watersports, 252 Walker St. 4810; Tel: 077-723-022. Pro Dive, Great Barrier Reef Wonderland, 4810; Tel: 077-211-760.

Learning-to-dive facilities are excellent. Short, hold-hands courses are available at some of the resorts and at Fantasy Island. Full-certificate courses are also readily available; these give you a qualification that is recognized all over the world.

# Fishing

The reef is a fisherman's paradise. The variety of fish and the near certainty of a good catch will appeal to most sportsmen. Reef fishing trips depart daily from Townsville, less frequently from other centers. They can last for 8, 12, or 15 hours. Some are little more than drinking binges, but others are for serious fishermen. Local travel agents will be happy to provide details and make recommendations. Try Tropic Sands (Tel: 077-751-767) or Reef Adventure Charters (Tel: 077-752-759).

There is also a rapidly growing **game-fishing** industry based in Townsville. The exciting Cape Bowling Green fishing grounds offer marlin, sailfish, and other large game fish. Most boats are light tackle, and several world records have been posted. Good catches have been made as early as March, but the best season appears to be from June to November. There are several fishing competitions in the August-to-October period. Visitors can hire a game-fishing boat complete with crew, tackle, bait, meals, and drinks from about A$1,000 a day for up to eight passengers. Sometimes a single seat may be organized on a charter or regular trip. Try Australian Pacific Charters (Tel: 077-818-809) or Aussie Game Fishing Agencies (Tel: 077-731-912).

# THE WHITSUNDAY ISLANDS

The 70-odd islands of the Whitsunday group and Whitsunday Passage, which separates them, are probably the best and most beautiful places in Australia to spend a holiday on water.

Most of the islands have been declared wholly or largely parkland, and many have fringing reef. All are within 50 km (30 miles) of Shute Harbour near Proserpine, which is about halfway between Townsville and Mackay to the south. Shute is the jumping-off point for island cruises and yacht hire. The islands are not on the Great Barrier Reef, but they provide facilities for getting to the reef.

The principal mainland center for this region is **Airlie Beach**, next to Shute Harbour, a small attractive waterfront town with a rapidly growing tourism infrastructure. Airlie Beach is three hours south of Townsville by bus (services are operated by all major coach companies). There is a small airport with some commuter flights.

Air access to the islands is via Ansett Airlines to **Hamilton Island**. Direct flights operate from Brisbane, Sydney, and several other northern and western centers.

## Whitsunday Island Resorts

The Whitsunday Island resorts each has a specific niche in the marketplace.

**Hayman Island** is very up-market, sophisticated, and expensive. No costs have been spared to make this a luxury resort. There is an air of elegance, of good living for its own sake, of indulgence. Food, service, and facilities are excellent. If you have reached the top, Hayman is for you. The 230-room resort has elegant furnishings, tropical gardens, a huge man-made swimming lagoon, and a choice of four sophisticated restaurants. Rooms are on the expensive side.

Major access is from near the Hamilton Island airstrip by luxury launch (40 minutes), but you can also travel via Shute Harbour or by seaplane from Townsville.

**Hamilton Island** is more difficult to define. It started out up-market, changed direction, and now caters to mid-range to luxury. This is by far the largest resort off the Queensland coast, with high-rise and low-rise buildings, a marina, a deer park, a good airport, a nice beach, a huge pool, a shopping village, and throbbing nightlife. Building continues. Hamilton guests come in a variety of ages, backgrounds, and interests. The island is diverse enough to satisfy all—except those looking for peace and quiet. The resort has seven restaurants of varying standards, as well as fast-food outlets and a supermarket. All accommodations are less than five years old.

You can fly direct to Hamilton Island from Townsville, or use the high-speed catamaran from Shute Harbour (30 minutes).

**South Molle Island**, now operated by Ansett Airlines, is one of the older resorts, but extensive rebuilding has kept it in good condition. The island has long stretches of sandy coral beach, good water-sport facilities, walking tracks, and a golf course. Food leans toward quantity rather than quality, but prices are reasonable and guests enjoy the relaxed, friendly atmosphere.

Prices here are much lower than on Hayman and much of Hamilton, so the island attracts family groups, young people, and mid-market Australians looking for sun, sea, and excitement. There is nightly entertainment and a resident band. Travel is via the Hamilton Island airstrip or Shute Harbour (20 minutes).

**Daydream Island** is a smaller resort than South Molle—in keeping with the size of the island. Recent accommodation additions have kept it competitive; the new units have more privacy. Daydream attracts a mid-market clientele similar to that of South Molle. Most activities center around the large pool and organized evening entertainment, although there are several nice beaches and opportunities for water sports. Regular boats operate from Shute Harbour (20 minutes).

**Long Island** is the only island with more than one

resort. The **Palm Bay Resort** provides basic accommodation for those seeking an island without frills or entertainment. Some 2 km (about a mile) away, **Contiki's Whitsunday Resort** provides an action-packed vacation for 18–35-year-olds.

**Lindeman Island** is the oldest of the resorts and the most southerly in the Whitsunday group. The resort has had several different owners who have completely rebuilt facilities; it currently aims at the upper-middle-class market. There are plenty of activities and good dining in two restaurants and at the poolside barbecue area. During the day there is golf, tennis, and water sports, while at night a disco operates on the beach. The island is reached by air from Mackay or Proserpine or boat from Shute Harbour, Hamilton Island, or Mackay.

# Whitsunday Mainland

Airlie Beach is the mainland accommodation center in this area, and, together with adjoining **Cannonvale**, there are many good places to choose from. The area is extremely attractive, with timbered mountains, extensive water views, and pretty settlements. **Conway Range National Park** is nearby, with lush rain forest and some nice walking trails.

Major resorts here are **Whitsunday Terraces**, **Coral Sea**, **Club Crocodile**, and **Whitsunday Wanderers**. All these places have a feeling of space, the tropics, and vacation getaway. All can be contacted simply by writing Airlie Beach, Queensland, on the envelope (Airlie is *that* small).

Day access to the islands from the mainland here is excellent. Buses connect with Shute Harbour for boat day-trip departures. It's a very professional operation; you can visit just one or a variety of islands in a day. Other water-based attractions here are yacht and motor cruises that go nowhere in particular. They call at a deserted beach, give you time for some snorkelling, and generally just offer a relaxed day in the sun. At least half a dozen of these trips leave the Shute Harbour jetty every day, so telephone around when you get there to see which suits you best. Try the *Apollo* (Tel: 079-466-922), the *Gretel* (Tel: 079-466-224), or the *Nari* (Tel: 079-466-991).

# Sailing

Shute Harbour is the center of Australia's bareboat yacht-charter business. That's simply because the Whitsunday area provides ideal weather, temperature, and the attractions to keep "boaties" happy.

Bareboat chartering in the Whitsundays is only ten years old, yet facilities are outstanding. It's not yet possible, however, to equate the Whitsundays with the Bahamas, the Riviera, or the Aegean; the Whitsundays' attraction is their solitude and the large number of uninhabited islands, with a sprinkling of resorts.

Three types of chartering are available. Absolute novices can charter a boat complete with skipper, who will do most of the work and take you to the best fishing, snorkelling, and sightseeing locations. If you're keen, he'll also teach you how to handle the boat yourself and let you have some practice.

For those able to sail but who need a little help, some companies have flotilla cruises during the peak season where you travel in a group with an experienced skipper close by. It's good moral support, and it can be fun being with people who enjoy a similar lifestyle.

Then there are the true bareboat charters, where you cruise at your own pace wherever you wish to go. All you need is food and a chart to get back to your starting point at the end of the rental period. Some skill and experience help, but generally the weather and sea conditions are kind.

Major companies in the charter business here are Australian Bareboat Charters, Shute Harbour (Tel: 079-469-381); Cumberland Charter Yachts, Airlie Beach (Tel: 079-466-230); Hamilton Island Charters, Hamilton Island (Tel: 079-469-144); Whitsunday Rent-a-Yacht, Shute Harbour (Tel: 079-469-232).

Then there are sailing opportunities for anyone on large crewed vessels. Many of these are day trips, but others are for longer periods. Two of the best known vessels are *Gretel,* an America's Cup challenger of some years back, and the maxi-yacht *Apollo.* Both depart Shute Harbour daily. The ketch *Cygnus* and the brigantine *Golden Plover* operate weekly sailing holidays, the sloop *Lodestone* does three-day beachcomber cruises, while the 74-foot ketch *Pegasus* and 70-foot motor cruiser *Nocturne* do eight-day trips between May and November.

## OTHER ISLANDS IN THE CENTRAL REEF AREA

Apart from the Whitsundays there are other islands in the Central Reef region popular with visitors. All provide sunshine, sand beaches, clear water, relaxation, and good facilities.

**Brampton Island** is mountainous with lush forests and fringing reef. The island is a national park, and its **Brampton Island Resort** is mid-market. There are many secluded sand beaches and sports facilities on the island.

The island is reached by air (15 minutes) or launch from **Mackay**, a nice city (surrounded by sugar cane) some 400 km (240 miles) south of Townsville. Mackay has Australia's largest bulk-sugar loading terminal, while just south of the city there is a major coal-loading port. There are regular boat trips to the reef and southern Whitsunday Islands from Mackay, and some nice beaches north of the city. Good accommodation in Mackay is found at the **White Lace Motel**. For a beach-resort atmosphere try **Kohuna Village Resort** at Bucasia (15 minutes north of the city). A series of *bures* (individual hut/villas) are perched right on the beachfront. Each *bure* is tastefully decorated and has its own bathroom and kitchen facilities. There is generally a festive family atmosphere at Kohuna.

**Magnetic Island** is one of Australia's best-kept secrets. The island is larger than many along the coast and has a permanent population of about 2,500. Many of the residents commute to Townsville daily by fast catamaran (20 minutes). The island was named in 1770 by Captain Cook, who thought his ship's compass was affected by the rocky promontories. No one since has agreed.

There are fine beaches, good bushwalking trails, and several little resort towns on the eastern side. The island has two well-priced hotels, three or four nice family resorts, a multitude of self-contained holiday units, and a variety of other accommodations. **Arcadia Resort Hotel**, on the beach at Geoffrey Bay, and **Latitude 19**, about a km (half a mile) inland from Nelly Bay, are two well-kept properties with good rooms, swimming pools, bars, restaurants, and other vacation facilities.

One of the joys of Magnetic Island is being able to move from bay to bay as the heart dictates. There is a good bus service with helpful drivers who will stop almost anywhere, or you can hire small MiniMoke vehicles (which carry four people), mini-motorcycles, and bicycles. Sporting facilities include golf, bowling, tennis, horseback riding, and, of course, all types of water sports. There are lifesaving clubs at Picnic Bay and Alma Bay.

Hayles and Westmark Marine both operate catamaran services to the island from downtown Townsville about every 90 minutes. Hayles also has a car ferry to the island.

**Orpheus Island** is north of Townsville and is connected to it by a float-plane service (20 minutes). **Orpheus Island Resort** is small and exclusive and has won several industry awards for excellence. Expensive and classy, it is a place for enjoying good food and wine, relaxing on the beach, around the pool, or in the spa, and meeting people who, like you, wish to escape reality for a short while.

**Hinchinbrook Island** is North Queensland's biggest island and one of the most spectacular. There are high mountains, thick forests, and narrow channels winding through mangroves. Most of the island remains untouched by development. The small **Hinchinbrook Island Resort** is on the northern end, connected to Cardwell on the mainland by speedboat (30 minutes) and Townsville by seaplane (30 minutes). Accommodation is in individual cabins scattered on the hillside, with a central pool and bar/restaurant area. A maximum of 30 guests can enjoy the beauty and solitude of this island. There are no telephones, radios, or television sets—and there is a great beach.

**Dunk Island** provides the prettiest venue for any of the resorts. Lush rain forest, good beaches, and a hillside national park combine to provide an idyllic setting. It was on Dunk that E. J. Banfield lived and wrote *The Confessions of a Beachcomber* early this century. The island environment is remarkably little changed today.

The **Dunk Island Resort** has been extensively redeveloped in recent years, and refurbishing continues. Dunk can accommodate 400 people—and often does. It is extremely popular with the southern Australian package vacationer looking for an up-market holiday. There are a growing number of international visitors, however. The tariff is all-inclusive, except for a few exotic sports such as game fishing and target shooting.

Two lovely beaches, two pools, two restaurants, several bars, and activity centers mean that the resort never feels crowded. The older style single-story beachfront units are the most desirable accommodations for many.

Access is by air from Townsville or Cairns (40 minutes), boat from Clump Point near Mission Beach (30 minutes), or water taxi from Mission Beach (10 minutes).

**Bedarra Island** is exclusive. It has two small luxury resorts: **Bedarra Bay** and **Bedarra Hideaway**, where no children or day-trippers are allowed. Each takes a maximum of 32 guests; both are operated by Australian Airlines. The resorts provide first-class facilities and cuisine as well as peace and privacy. They are expensive, but the service merits the prices. Access is by launch from Dunk Island.

**Palm Island.** No resort exists on Great Palm Island, and in fact you cannot at present stay overnight on the island. The main interest on the island is the 3,500 aboriginal people. The island is run by an elected Island Council, and considerable debate rages about the desirability of developing tourism. Access is by air from Townsville (20 minutes), with several flights daily. A cruise also operates from Townsville two days a week. There is a bus that takes you to the town on the island; you are welcome to visit the store and wander around. A few souvenirs are available, but it's the opportunity to observe an aboriginal community that will have the most appeal.

# THE NORTH QUEENSLAND OUTBACK

There is probably more mystery, intrigue, and romance written about life in the Australian Outback than any other area of the country.

As far as visitors are concerned, the Outback is anywhere inland where there are few people. You can be on the edge of the Outback only 70 km (42 miles) inland from Townsville. All the ingredients are there: isolation, great wildlife, old mining towns, huge cattle properties, and Outback characters.

This is *Thorn Birds* country, with some Crocodile Dundee thrown in. Some people call it the real Australia. Certainly the people, the country, and the lifestyle are real—but as foreign to the average Australian as to the overseas visitor. It's fascinating, it's intriguing, but it's a life few would want to live. In other words, it's something for a short visit.

You can rent a car or camper van in Townsville and drive into the Outback, but for most people the environment is too strange and daunting to do that. You will probably want to take a tour with locals who know the country and can make you feel comfortable.

## Charters Towers

This town of about 7,000 people is the largest and most interesting remnant of a past era. From 1872 to 1916 this was a fabulously rich gold-mining city, with a peak population of about 35,000 and a local name of "The World." Today beautiful old buildings, several museums, and a restored stock exchange are a lasting reminder of those days. You still occasionally see "ringers" (local cowboys) on horseback hitching horses to posts in the main street, just as they did 100 years ago. The 1980s have seen gold fever return to Charters Towers, but this time it is big companies developing recently discovered deposits. Plans are in the works to re-create an area of old gold-mining activity, but at present visitors cannot actually see mining at close hand.

Charters Towers is accessible from Townsville on day trips. Brolga Tours has a coach departure two days a week, and Rundle Air combines a visit to Charters Towers with lunch on a cattle station fronting the Burdekin River.

## Touring the Outback

For those with the time, Australian Explorer Tours operates a three-day/two-night Outback and Rain Forest Tour, which visits Charters Towers, then heads north into the wonderful country of the Great Basalt Wall and the upper reaches of the Burdekin River. You can see loads of wildlife, visit working cattle stations, stay in bush camps, see Australia's highest single-drop waterfall, and travel through a lush rain-forest national park. Departures are from Townsville on Sundays; bookings are essential. (Australian Explorer Tours, c/o The Travel Co., Northtown 4810; Tel: 077-715-024. Brolga Tours, 293 Ingham Road 4810; Tel: 077-797-799. Rundle Air, Townsville Airport 4810; Tel: 077-796-933.)

## NORTHWARD UP THE COAST

The road northward from Townsville to Cairns is one of the most interesting sections of the Bruce Highway in Queensland. It's good self-drive country. The trip can be made in about four hours, but there are numerous points of interest along the way that can extend the time to several days. Australian Explorer Tours has a Townsville–Cairns connection that takes two days; express buses make the trip in half a day. While the road parallels the coast, for most of its length it is miles inland, so the beach suburbs north of Townsville are bypassed. At Rollingstone, 50 km (30 miles) from Townsville, there is good river swimming; a side road leads to Balgal Beach, where there is excellent fishing; the beach is 6 km (3½ miles) off the highway.

Farther north a road to the left climbs the rain-forest-covered ranges to the **Crystal Creek/Mount Spec National Park**, with its bushwalks, swimming holes, lookouts, and village of Paluma (20 km/12 miles off the highway). Some 20 km (12 miles) farther a sign indicates **Jourama Falls National Park**, a very popular river swimming spot (6 km/3½ miles off the highway).

Ingham, 120 km (72 miles) northwest of Townsville, is a sugar-producing town with large Italian influence. Inland is Wallaman Falls and beautiful rain forest, while on the coast **Forrest Beach** and **Taylors Beach** have good swimming.

The Bruce Highway now climbs high above the coast, providing a spectacular view of rugged Hinchinbrook Island and the mangrove-flanked passages of Hinchinbrook Channel, then takes you back to the coast at the vacation center of **Cardwell**.

Stop and look at the National Parks Information Centre

near the jetty at Cardwell and consider a boat trip either to the Hinchinbrook Island Resort or through the Hinchinbrook Channel to the mangrove boardwalks. Just north of Cardwell, the **Edmund Kennedy National Park** has interesting mangroves, huge paperbark trees, swamps, and again, boardwalks, but it also has mosquitoes. **Murray Falls** are another pleasant detour 15 km (9 miles) off the highway.

**Tully**, the wettest place in Australia, will drench you with 14 feet of rain a year, while nearby **Mission Beach** gives you solitude and tranquillity. The almost 5-mile-long beach is fringed with coconut palms and rain forest, and at times you may be entirely alone. That's rather surprising when you learn that there are three excellent resorts and a range of other accommodations along this beautiful stretch of coastline. (Dunk Island is just offshore, for example.)

# CAIRNS AND THE NORTHERN GREAT BARRIER REEF REGION

If Australia is the tourist flavor of the year, Cairns is the top pick of the month. This most northerly Queensland city has been recently engulfed by world tourism, and it's not quite sure it likes all the consequences.

It has gained high-rise hotels, a greatly expanded tourism infrastructure, and a wide range of expensive but generally tacky visitor-oriented clothing, jewelry, and souvenir shops; it has lost much of its slow pace, its isolation, and its small-town gregariousness. Cairns is nonetheless widely perceived (except in Townsville) to be more relaxed and casual than Townsville, and to have more of a festive atmosphere about it. Cairns—and Far North Queensland in general—has its own lifestyle, quite different even from Southern Queensland.

Those Queensland natives who knew Cairns, Port Douglas, and Cooktown ten years ago are sad to see the passing of an era. Those who visit today for the first time find an area attuned to tourism and generally able to fulfill the expectations of most visitors. And yet—these towns, especially Cookstown, are a long way from St-Tropez.

Nothing, however, has yet changed the region's lovely wet, green rain forests, its clear water and extensive reefs, and its wide, sandy beaches, where you can still find peace and solitude.

# CAIRNS

Cairns (pronounced "Cans") is one of the fastest-growing cities in Australia, and the growth is almost entirely due to tourism. Five years ago the Australian government built a modern international airport in the city, and shortly afterward the state of Queensland decided to increase the marketing of the airport as the northern gateway to Australia from North America and Asia. The airport has been hugely successful, and international tourism into the region has boomed. Accommodations, day tours, restaurants, shopping, car rentals, and reef facilities have all strained to meet demand.

A pattern that has repeated itself around the world quickly emerged. Locals respond to the initial demand by building mediocre development in a hurry, local governments adopt a liberal attitude to town planning and building regulations, and then international developers move in, pushing real-estate prices sky-high. That's Cairns today. There is no end in sight to the growth, but there are indications that future development may be of a higher standard. The Hilton International, which opened in late 1987, and the Parkroyal (mid-1988) should help raise both building and service standards and set Cairns on the road toward becoming a real international destination.

The Cairns region has far more interest than the city of Cairns, but many visitors base themselves in the city and sightsee on day trips. The only real alternatives are to stay at one of the northern beach resorts or at Port Douglas.

The annual **Fun in the Sun Festival** is held in October. May to October has the best weather, but this is also the peak season, when accommodation is often tight.

Central Cairns is built on flat land between the railway station and the shoreline. There are wide streets with huge shade trees, and sidewalks along which casually

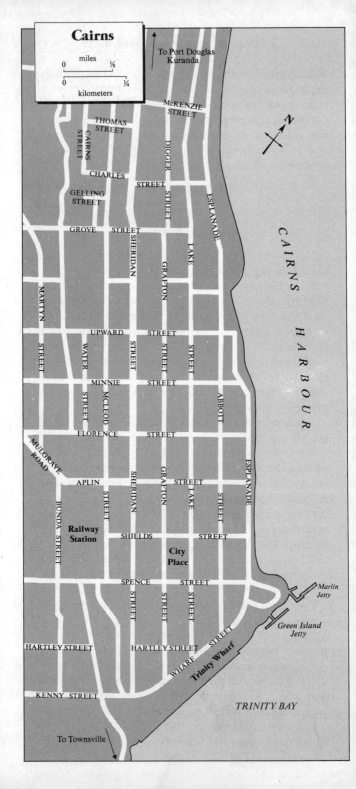

dressed people stroll. The center of Cairns is **City Place**, a small pedestrian precinct formed by closing a street intersection and converting the legs into cul-de-sacs. The main retail shopping area is the two blocks on each side toward Trinity Bay and two blocks south toward Trinity Inlet.

Visitors are inevitably drawn to the waterfront, so walk down Shields Street to the Esplanade. Most visitors are disappointed to find that the water here is very shallow and there is no beach. At low tide there is mangrove mud stretching for hundreds of yards, but the numerous water birds are some compensation. The Esplanade has been largely taken over by backpackers who flock to the city for the warm weather. It's a real cosmopolitan scene; everyone is relaxed and happy. The backpackers have encouraged a series of cheap eateries.

There is a walkway along the seashore, so head south on it toward the inlet. The area to your left is under development as a marina, while the **Pacific International Hotel** on the right was the best property in Cairns until 12 months ago.

Ahead was where Cairns started in 1876 as a small port for the gold and tin mines developing in the interior. Later this colorful area was known as the Barbary Coast, and no genteel visitor ventured there after dark. Most of the sleaziness has now gone—along with many of the fine old buildings with wide wrought-iron balconies, unfortunately.

Turn left into Marlin Parade and walk to Marlin Jetty. The major glamour activity in Cairns is big-game fishing. The reef waters northeast of the city produce huge fish, some weighing over 1000 pounds. The season lasts from September to November and, despite the high cost, most boats are booked well in advance. At other times of the year you can see their sleek lines bobbing against the jetty; one look shows it is a multimillion-dollar industry. (For details see the Northern Reef and Marlin Fishing section below.)

Overlooking this area is the **Hilton International** opened in late 1987 and doing very nicely in its lovely waterfront position. Just across the road is the even newer **Parkroyal**—not waterfront but having the advantage of a major shopping complex right next door. This whole area is changing almost daily. The old

Wharf Number 1 site next door opened in late 1987 as a cruise liner terminal and retail/office complex called Trinity Wharf. On the ground floor is a bus terminal now used by all express operators, and nearby is the mini-railway station for the Kuranda train. This is also the departure area for daily boat cruises to Green Island, Michaelmas Cay, Hastings Reef, and Fitzroy Island, and for charter boats for fishing, snorkeling, and diving trips to the Outer Reef. It's also a great place for seafood restaurants, with **Tawny's** on Marlin Parade, the ever-popular and moderately priced **Barnacle Bill's** on the Esplanade, and **Benji's** on Spence Street—three of the best.

A walk along Lake Street will lead you back to City Place. On the way you pass several arcades and shopping centers full of giftware and fashion shops, and small eating places.

Cairns must have some of the best dining-out facilities of any provincial city in Australia, but many close early and there is a disappointing lack of good open-air dining. To some extent this is because for six months of the year Cairns has a very hot and wet climate (December to May), but for the other six months open-air dining would be ideal.

Seafood and tropical fruit are the two local specialties, and these are extensively used, even at so-called international-style restaurants such as **Verandahs** on Shields Street and **It's Williams** on Sheridan Street.

Nightlife has not grown in line with the recent tourism development, so Cairns is not the place for a wild nighttime vacation. The cocktail bar at the Hilton is busy early in the evening and **Milliways** on Grafton Street and **Yanki** on Lake Street provide early-morning sustenance and some entertainment. Young-at-heart visitors will enjoy the discos at **Scandals**, **The Nest**, and **House On The Hill**.

There are some other attractions in the city: Windows on the Reef, an audiovisual show that simulates a 100-foot night dive (near the ferry terminal); the House of 10,000 Shells on Abbott Street; and the Cairns Museum, housed at City Place, which contains aboriginal artifacts.

It's as a visitor shopping center that central Cairns excels. There are souvenirs of substance at **Bong on the Reef** and **Cairns Resort Store**, both at Trinity Wharf; **Gumnut Creations** on Shields Street has some exclusive hand-painted resort wear; **Koala Craft** on Aplin Street has arts and crafts.

The laid-back lifestyle of the Cairns region is good for artists; examples of their work can be seen in many galleries. **Grafton House Galleries**, the **Upstairs Gallery**, and the **Pottery Place** are good examples. Art of a different kind is also featured: The **Big Boomerang** in Rusty's Bazaar has Australian aboriginal and Papua New Guinean artifacts; the **Niugini Gallery** specializes in artifacts and village handicrafts from Papua New Guinea; **Asian Connections** combines the art of Papua New Guinea with that of Indonesia, Thailand, India, and China.

For locally produced arts and crafts, a visit to the market at **Rusty's Bazaar** on Saturday morning could be rewarding—Cairns may well be the tee-shirt capital of Australia.

## AROUND CAIRNS

Cairns is in the wet tropics, so it's not surprising that there is lush tropical growth in some parts. The best place to see this is in the **Centenary Lakes/Flecker Botanical Gardens/Whitfield Range Environmental Park** region about 3 km (2 miles) from the city center. These facilities are more or less contiguous, and they combine lakes, formal gardens, parkland, and mountain walks. Don't visit in the rain or during the mosquito-breeding season, but otherwise it's a delight.

In the opposite direction, the Blue Water Coral Factory in Aumuller Street less than 3 km (2 miles) from the city center is interesting for those wanting coral souvenirs or shell jewelry. The paddlesteamer S.S. *Louisa* departs morning and afternoon from the Marlin Jetty for a desultory and uneventful trip along the mangrove-lined estuary.

## The Beaches North of Cairns

For some people, Cairns City has the huge disadvantage of having no beach. It's not until you travel north to the **Marlin Coast** that white-sand beaches and swimmable water appear. Each of these northern beaches between 20 and 35 km (12 and 27 miles) north along the coast from

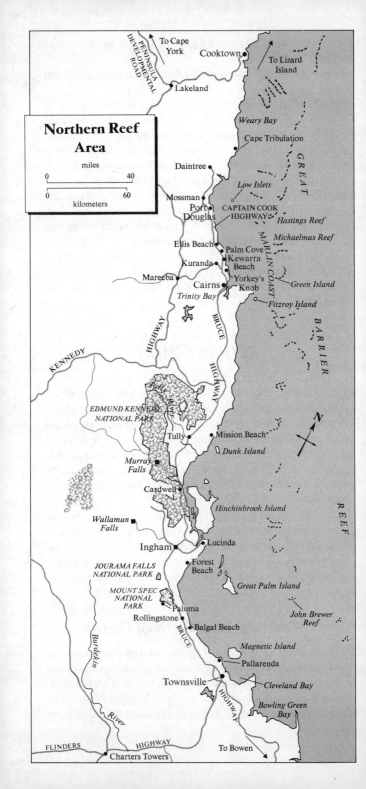

## Northern Reef Area

miles
0 — 40

kilometers
0 — 60

Cairns has developed its own character. Visitors can choose between Yorkeys Knob, Trinity Beach, Kewarra Beach, Clifton Beach, Palm Cove, and Ellis Beach. All these centers have local communities, shops, and resorts or other accommodations. There are regular bus services connecting each to Cairns.

Some of the best accommodation is at **Palm Cove**, with the large **Ramada Reef Resort** and the small, exclusive **Reef House** offering expensive up-market accommodation in a delightful setting. The Paradise Village Shopping Centre will meet ordinary needs, and it's all set amid huge paperbark trees, palms, and the delightful beach.

The **Kewarra Beach Resort** is another excellent low-rise, bungalow development with a touch of the exotic—and a gorgeous crescent beach. The huge lobby and delightful open restaurant add to the great beachfront site.

**Cairns Colonial Club**, situated closer to Cairns, has an ambience similar to Kewarra Beach Resort's, but caters to a younger and more energetic clientele; free transfers to and from the city and the airport.

As with all of northern Australia, these inviting beaches are plagued by dangerous box jellyfish from November through April. To combat the menace, five stinger-resistant floating net enclosures have recently been built along the coast, and these have proved to be effective. It is unwise to swim without protection, so use the enclosures or the hotel pool.

# Green Island and Fitzroy Island

While Cairns receives much publicity, it is actually the Cairns *region* that visitors rave about. The combination of reef, islands, rain forest, and lush rolling farm country is unique.

About 27 km (16 miles) offshore from Cairns is **Green Island**, a true coral cay. There is a small resort on the island (the **Green Island Reef Resort**), but most environmental pressure comes from the hundreds of day-trippers who flock there on numerous tours. The beaches are lovely, the water is clear, but unfortunately the coral that surrounds the island has been extensively damaged and is now generally poor. This has been overcome by operators now going to Michaelmas Cay or one of the nearby reefs as part of a Green Island/Reef day trip.

**Fitzroy Island** is the other resort island near Cairns. This is a larger, continental island with some good budget accommodation (**Fitzroy Island Resort**) and reasonably good coral just offshore. It can be combined with Green Island in a day. Boats leave the Cairns foreshore at various times with various companies. The largest operator by far is Great Adventures. Your hotel will tell you what is happening during the time you visit.

# Kuranda Railway and Village

One of the best excursions available from Cairns is the Kuranda rail trip. The one and a half hours it takes to reach Kuranda is full of fun, top sights, 15 tunnels, 40 gorges, and great anticipation. Trains leave at least once a day from Cairns and from the Freshwater Connection (10 km/6 miles) out. It is worth paying the extra to be in the commentary car. On the trip up the best views are had from the right-hand-side seats. Kuranda railway station, with its tropical flowers and ferns, is pretty, but the adjacent little village is an even greater delight. On some days you can catch an afternoon train back to Cairns, and there are also regular buses.

There is a particularly colorful Sunday morning market at Kuranda and a smaller version on Wednesdays. See **Heritage Homestead** with the old DC-3 crashed beside the entrance. Inside there is a small museum and café. Next door is the **Australian Butterfly Sanctuary**, with its huge walk-through enclosure (guided tours on the hour). Nearby, the **Kuranda Wildlife Noctarium** displays nocturnal animals of the rain forest in their active, natural state. The various species coexist and interrelate just as they do in the wild. There is also a river cruise and a fish and reef museum. Finally, don't miss the **Tjapukai Aboriginal Dance Theatre**; this is one of the few opportunities in Australia to see aboriginal dance talent blended with modern theater technique. The one-hour performance is excellent.

Kuranda has some delightful casual restaurants, the usual tourist shops, and some outstanding art at the **Kuranda Gallery**. Make a point of seeing some of the works of Jo Anne Hook.

Inland from here the Atherton Tableland offers an escape from the coastal heat, with some of Australia's most delightful waterfalls and several interesting lakes and other facilities. There are numerous Tableland trips from Cairns with different operators, so check around for price and availability.

For action seekers, the one-day **whitewater rafting** trip on the Tully River is excellent. Two companies operate basically similar trips from Cairns and Townsville: Raging Thunder (Tel: 070-514-911) and Raft and Rain Forest (Tel: 070-517-105).

# PORT DOUGLAS AND CAPE TRIBULATION

The road north of Cairns, from just south of Ellis Beach, runs right along the coast, passing lovely beaches and dramatic scenery. Between Cairns and Port Douglas there are two animal attractions: **Wild World**, which has birds, reptiles, kangaroos, and crocodiles, and **Hartley's Creek Zoo**, which has Charlie the Crocodile.

**Port Douglas** was once a sleepy backwater in a delightful location. Now it has been "discovered," and visitors have flooded in, forcing many of the locals to leave. It's still a very pretty town, with nice country pubs and one of the best beaches around. But Port Douglas has changed. It's impossible to build a A$200-million resort in a town of 600 people and expect it to remain the same.

The **Sheraton Mirage Resort**, while it has swept away the old Port Douglas, is in fact a masterpiece of resort design and could well be the best hotel on the Queensland coast. It is one of the few Australian resorts that is almost self-sufficient: There are swimming, golf, tennis, a gymnasium, and water activities of various types. Yet it's possible to find a quiet corner at the resort and make believe you are in your own tropical paradise.

For many years Port Douglas has had at least two well-publicized expensive restaurants: the **Nautilus Restaurant** and **The Island Point Restaurant**. Both still exist and each has a bigger reputation than before, but they may be having difficulty maintaining standards as the town changes.

Port Douglas has developed into a departure point for cruises, due largely to great work by the Quicksilver Connections Company, which has a daily trip to **Low Isles**, a small coral cay surrounded by 50 acres of reef; a daily trip to **Agincourt Reef**, where there is a floating pontoon, an underwater observatory, and a semi-submersible submarine; and a regular day cruise to **Cooktown**, allowing about four hours to see this isolated town (see below). All these trips are excellent. Also worth doing is the Bally Hooley Express rail tour from Port Douglas through sugar farms to Mossman.

After Port Douglas the road continues up along the coast to Mossman, a pretty sugar town, then farther north to Daintree. Just outside Mossman there is a national park with the beautiful river and waterfalls of **Mossman Gorge**. This is one of those rare places of great natural grandeur. You can stay here in the modern **Silky Oaks Colonial Lodge**. Just before Daintree a dirt road leads to the Daintree Ferry, where there are tours on the river to see rain forest and what most people hope to see: crocodiles.

After passing the ferry landing the road continues at a reasonable standard to **Cape Tribulation**—a virgin promontory named by Captain Cook as he ran his ship on to the Endeavour Reef. This area is not for everyone. There are few facilities, just grand untouched beach, rain forest, and fresh mountain streams. There are tours to Tribulation from Cairns and Port Douglas, and if you are confident enough you could drive *this* far in a conventional vehicle. For an organized tour, contact Australian Pacific Tours (Tel: 070-519-299); Ansett Trailways (Tel: 070-518-966); or Tropic Wings Tours (Tel: 070-518-433).

**Crocodylus Village**, while not luxurious, provides a suitable environment for the night. This is basically a backpacker's hostel, but the timber huts covered by modern tenting seem to suit the area.

North of here the road deteriorates rapidly. Despite massive opposition from conservationists and the general public, the state government and local council in 1976 bulldozed a goat track through primeval forest, causing severe destruction to the region and probably damage to the nearby reef. The road, which was only ever negotiable by four-wheel-drive vehicles, is now totally impassable for many months of the year.

# COOKTOWN AND LIZARD ISLAND

Cooktown was Australia's first British settlement. After Cook unexpectedly had a close encounter with the Great Barrier Reef in 1770, he beached the boat for repairs where Cooktown now stands. The repairs took six weeks, so Cook and his naturalist, Joseph Banks, had plenty of time to study the flora and fauna of the strange new land. It was here that Cook named the kangaroo, and the majority of specimens that Cook took back to England came from the Cooktown area.

Little happened from then until 1873, when James Mulligan discovered gold in the nearby Palmer River. It turned out to be one of the richest gold rushes in history. By 1885 Cooktown's population exceeded 35,000, including about 18,000 Chinese. Now the gold is gone. A few years ago the population was down to 800, but now it's growing again. Cooktown is slowly discovering tourism.

Cooktown is 340 rough-road km (204 miles) north of Cairns. It's accessible by air from Cairns, but the best way to travel is by fast catamaran north from Port Douglas, a two-and-a-half-hour trip on the Quicksilver Cooktown Connection.

Cooktown is a place to visit for atmosphere. There are some things to see, but just walking along the main street and sitting in a local pub ("hotel") is the best way to appreciate that this is a frontier town different from just about anywhere else in the world. Everything is done at half pace in Cooktown. That's the pace the visitor should work at, too.

Among the sights is the **James Cook Historical Museum** in the Sir Joseph Banks Gardens. The exhibit is nothing very special, but the building (which was once a Catholic convent school) is interesting. Another old-time building worth seeing is what is now the Westpac Bank on the main street. On the edge of town, the old cemetery contains many memories, and the Chinese Shrine is another striking reminder of a past era. So too is the Botanic Gardens, originally established in the 1870s and now being restored. You can ride or walk to the top of Grassy Hill and stand where Cook did as he searched for a way through the reefs to open water.

One of the most surprising finds in Cooktown is the **Sovereign Hotel**. The original building, now gone, was built in 1874, but in 1987 the Sovereign was transformed into a small resort, with tropical gardens, pool, cocktail bar, restaurant, and large resort units. It just might tempt you into staying the night—or a month. But Cooktown is not East Hampton, Muskoka, or Saint-Tropez; you wouldn't be surprised to see either Crocodile Dundee or the crocodile stride into a "hotel" here.

**Lizard Island**, some 100 km (60 miles) north of Cooktown, is the most northerly of the coastal island resorts. The **Lizard Island Lodge** is expensive and not overly luxurious, but the beaches and clear water are wonderful. During the marlin-fishing season (from August through October) you need to book months ahead to get a room. At present there is no regular connection from Cooktown to the island, although there are almost daily flights from Cairns. At times there is an aerial Cairns/Lizard Island/Cooktown/Cairns day tour, allowing you to see glimpses of this wide area, but you are not doing justice to a region that requires time for you to adjust to the pace, the history, and the isolation.

# THE NORTHERN REEF AND MARLIN FISHING

James Cook was a superb navigator and consummate seaman. He sailed from England to Tahiti, circumnavigated and charted New Zealand, and sailed 1,800 miles along the eastern coast of Australia before running aground on the northern section of the Great Barrier Reef.

Since that day the Great Barrier Reef has become the graveyard for more than 500 ships. Today, however, thousands of visitors safely visit the reef each day. Fast boats travel daily from Cairns and Port Douglas to platforms above the reef. Here underwater observatories or semi-submersible submarines provide excellent viewing. Current costs are about A$80 for the day.

Scuba-diving trips are also frequent. Coral Sea Diving Services operates various packages from Port Douglas on the dive boat *Aquanaut*. In Cairns, Down Under Aquatics operates daily to the reef in a fast catamaran. Reef Ex-

plorer Cruises operates two vessels up the coast from
Cairns to Cooktown, Lizard Island, and even as far as
**Thursday Island** off the tip of Cape York. Most divers take
a portion of each tour, returning to Cairns by air. For
something a little different, the 53-foot yacht *Schehera-
zade* operates an eight-day itinerary to the Outer Reef
and Lizard Island for a maximum of six guests. All these
boats carry diving equipment, compressor, and radio and
provide all meals. (Coral Sea Diving Services; Tel: 070-
985-254. Down Under Aquatics; Tel: 070-516-566. Reef
Explorer Cruises; Tel: 070-516-566.)

Cairns is gateway to the great black-marlin fishing
grounds of the Coral Sea. These days about 95 percent of
the big fish are released. The catch is photographed
alongside, then tagged with a plastic capsule that helps
the fishery authorities plot populations and migrations.
Marlin fishing is expensive. Boats nudge A$1,500 a day,
and that's usually for only four to six passengers. Bottom
fishing is much cheaper, and boats are available to take
up to 30 passengers. Lines, bait, and other necessities are
provided. For information, contact the Cairns Game Fishing Club (Tel: 070-515-979).

For the really keen fisherman a visit to **Bloomfield
Lodge** south of Cooktown will be a great experience. The
lodge is open from May to January and provides opportunities to fish for both bottom and open-sea species.

# CAPE YORK

From Cairns a huge triangle of land—harsh and lonely—
points north toward Papua New Guinea. This is Cape York
Peninsula, one of the wildest, least developed areas of
Australia outside of the deserts.

This area is anything but desert. The eastern highlands
(Great Dividing Range) extend along the eastern side of
Cape York Peninsula to within 120 miles of the tip. Monsoonal rains between December and April, and other
rains during the year, keep most rivers here flowing
constantly. Rain forests occur on the eastern slopes and

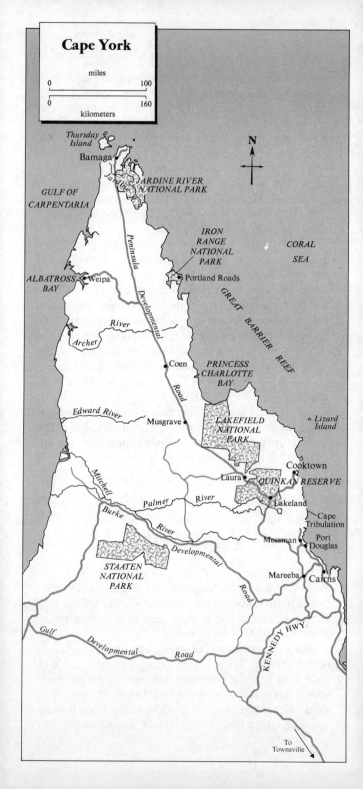

## Cape York

miles
0 — 100

kilometers
0 — 160

N

*Thursday Island*

Bamaga

**JARDINE RIVER NATIONAL PARK**

*Jardine R.*

*GULF OF CARPENTARIA*

*IRON RANGE NATIONAL PARK*

*CORAL SEA*

*Peninsula*

*Developmental*

Portland Roads

*ALBATROSS BAY*

Weipa

*River*

*Archer*

*GREAT BARRIER REEF*

Coen

*PRINCESS CHARLOTTE BAY*

*Edward River*

Musgrave

**LAKEFIELD NATIONAL PARK**

*Lizard Island*

*Mitchell*

Laura

Cooktown

*QUINKAN RESERVE*

*Palmer*

*River*

Lakeland

*Burke*

*River*

Cape Tribulation

*Developmental*

Mossman

Port Douglas

**STAATEN NATIONAL PARK**

Mareeba

Cairns

*Road*

*Gulf*

*Developmental*

*Road*

*KENNEDY HWY.*

To Townsville

lowlands, while the swamps and low country to the west are flooded for several months each year.

Visitors are attracted to this region for a variety of reasons. One is simply because it remains a challenge. Roads are poor and facilities are sparse, but the sense of achievement in penetrating the area—then returning to civilization—is great. Cape York excursions aren't for would-be adventurers, but for the truly bold.

## The Road to the Cape

The journey from Cairns to Cape York along the Peninsula Development Road is still one of Australia's great road (or track) adventures. The distance of about 1,000 km (600 miles) will take three or four days in good weather but can take months during the December-to-May wet season. Access is not possible in a conventional vehicle except in exceptional circumstances, and even those inexperienced with four-wheel-drive vehicles would be foolish to try in the best of machines.

Fortunately there are numerous tour companies that offer trips to Cape York. Some are in normal four-wheel-drive landcruiser-type vehicles, others use special vehicles such as Unimogs. Some trips are one-way with the other leg done by air, while others are 12- to 14-day road round trips from Cairns. (Some of the better Cape York tour operators in Cairns are AAT Kings, 070-311-155; Independent Safaris, 070-545-279; New Look Adventures, 070-517-934.)

The road north from Cairns leads inland to Mareeba, then north toward **Lakeland**. Lakeland Downs was the vision of a millionaire who dreamed of producing corn, sorghum, and other crops on 75,000 acres of cleared country. But the country refused to be tamed, and a fortune was lost. The township survived the bad times, and today it's the gateway to Cape York Peninsula, with a hotel/motel, trailer park, store, and service station.

North of here, the craggy **Palmer Range** is an impressive sight. This is Quinkan country, from which aboriginal people were driven by white men some 120 years ago. The black people, in huge cave paintings, have left a wonderful story that has amazed anthropologists. The area is a reserve, but visitors are welcome to use the walking tracks that lead to some art sites.

The next town is **Laura**, founded in the 1870s to serve the gold-rush track from Cooktown to the Palmer River, but now a small settlement with a resident population of about 100. To the north stretches the **Lakefield National Park**, a vast area of rain forest, paperbark woodland, swamp, mangrove, open grassy plains, and mud flats. In the wet season the rivers overflow and join to form massive lakes. In the dry season there is still enough water to support a wealth of wildlife: Water birds, crocodiles, parrots, kangaroos, wallabies, and dingoes are all common. Swimming here can be distinctly and dramatically unhealthy.

After driving through Lakefield you rejoin the main track at **Musgrave Homestead**, now a roadhouse but originally a telegraph station opened in 1887 on the amazing Overland Telegraph Line, which extended right up the spine of Cape York Peninsula and eventually, by submarine cable, to Thursday Island off the peninsula tip. The small town of **Coen** farther north is a relative oasis of civilization; it has a school, a few shops, a hotel, a police station, and so on.

From here north it is a slow grind. The track deteriorates even more, and each creek crossing seems harder than the last. For visitors, though, the sense of achievement continues to increase with the true wilderness experience of Cape York.

The country now changes from bloodwood to ironbark scrub to healthland, and to the east there is the wonderful rain forest of **Iron Range National Park**. Amazing 10-foot-high magnetic ant hills dot the countryside. In parts you can find palm-like pandanus plants providing food for the flocks of cockatoos. There are also pitcher plants that trap unsuspecting insects, and over 50 varieties of orchids.

After three days' hard driving you will be amazed to find the town of **Bamaga** and finally to see the waters of Torres Strait. Bamaga dates from 1946, when a group of black islanders moved to the mainland from their overcrowded island off the coast of Papua New Guinea. It is now a progressive town with schools and even a small college. Tourism has reached this area via an old World War II airfield, originally built by the United States Army Air Corps but now partially reopened as Bamaga's airport.

Remote, undeveloped **Thursday Island** is less than two hours away by speedboat.

The nicely run **Cape York Wilderness Lodge** is linked by bus to Bamaga, about 30 km (16 miles) away. **Punsand Bay Private Reserve** is close by. The tip of Cape York is a short drive from Bamaga. This is the most northerly part of mainland Australia, and one steeped in history. Malays, Chinese, Dutch, Spanish, Portuguese, and Japanese all visited this area, but it was left to Captain Cook to raise the British flag on Possession Island in 1770 and claim the whole of eastern Australia for Britain.

## GETTING AROUND

*Brisbane* has Australia's most modern airport, and it is accessible from anywhere in Australia. There are good international connections from New Zealand, North America, Asia, and Europe. A bus service operates to city hotels; taxis are also available.

There are express trains to Brisbane from Sydney, and intrastate services from many parts of Queensland. All major coach companies have express services to Brisbane. There is a Transit Centre at Roma Street for all major services. Brisbane has an electric rail network and an extensive bus system.

Rental cars are readily available at the airport and the Transit Centre; driving is easy from here to the Gold or Sunshine coasts. There are good coach connections to the Gold Coast and Sunshine Coast, and day tours are also available. A hovercraft operates from Brisbane Airport to Southport Spit. The Gold Coast airport at Coolangatta is served by direct flights from Sydney, Melbourne, and some other southern ports. The Sunshine Coast airport has limited services. Transport within the Gold Coast area is excellent, with various tourist bus services linking most attractions; in the Sunshine Coast it is more limited. Hotels/motels are the best sources of current information. Taxis are available everywhere.

*Bundaberg, Gladstone,* and *Rockhampton* all have air service from Brisbane. Each city is on the east-coast rail and road network, so there are good rail and bus services from both north and south, but watch out for times, because some services arrive very early in the morning.

Rental cars are available and cost about A$9 to the city center.

Though each center offers some day and extended tours, there are no organized tours that cover this region completely. Lack of facilities usually means lack of demand, so it's clear that touring the region is not high on local priorities. More common is a flight to one of the gateway centers, then a stay on one of the islands or in the Yeppoon area.

You can fly to *Townsville* from almost anywhere, with direct services from Brisbane, Sydney, Cairns, Mt. Isa, Alice Springs, and Adelaide, among others. There is a good cheap airport-to-city bus connection that passes many hotels and motels. Rental cars are available from four companies at the airport and from city depots. Mackay and Hamilton Island both have air services from Brisbane and Townsville. Townsville, Mackay, Bowen, and Cardwell are served by "The Sunlander" and "Queenslander," air-conditioned trains from Brisbane. Townsville is also the terminus for "The Inlander" from **Mount Isa** west in the Outback. All the major express-bus companies have several daily services through the region.

*Cairns* has become an important northern gateway into Australia, with direct flights from North America, New Zealand, Papua New Guinea, Japan, and Asia. It is also a major hub for the domestic air network, with flights to southern capitals, Alice Springs, Ayers Rock, and Darwin. There is an airport shuttle bus that travels past many of the major hotels/motels.

The city is the northern terminal for the east-coast railway and all east-coast bus systems. Because it is the most northerly sizeable city on the east coast, it is also the starting or finishing point for several one-way tours that travel to and from Brisbane, Sydney, or Melbourne.

This is a good place to have a rental car because traffic is light and it's easy to find your way around. Cars are available at the airport and downtown. All the majors are there plus several "cheapie" operators. It's also possible to hire a four-wheel-drive vehicle or campervan.

*Port Douglas* has a hovercraft service from Cairns airport, and there is also a bus. A bus service runs to Kuranda and on to several towns on the Atherton Tableland.

There are a large number of tours available from

Cairns. Your hotel will be pleased to advise on destinations and companies. One not previously mentioned, for example, is Ocean Free, a luxury cruising yacht that does day trips to Michaelmas Cay and the Great Barrier Reef from the Marlin Jetty.

## ACCOMMODATIONS REFERENCE

▶ **A.N.A. Hotel.** 22 View Avenue, **Surfers Paradise**, Qld. 4217. Tel: (075) 386-485; in U.S. and Canada, (800) HOLIDAY; Telex: AA 44655.

▶ **Anchorage Village Beach Resort. North Stradbroke Island**, Qld. Tel: (075) 498-266; Telex: AA 40472.

▶ **Arcadia Resort Hotel.** 7 Marine Parade, Arcadia Bay, **Magnetic Island**, Qld. 2700. Tel: (077) 785-177; in U.S., (213) 465-8418.

▶ **Bedarra Bay** and **Bedarra Hideaway. Bedarra Island**, via Townsville, Qld. 4810. Tel: in U.S., (800) 551-2012 or (800) 445-0190; in Canada, (800) 235-8222.

▶ **Bloomfield Lodge.** Via **Cooktown**, Qld. 4871. Tel: (070) 519-687.

▶ **Brampton Island Resort Hotel.** Via **Mackay**, Qld. 4740. Tel: (079) 572-959.

▶ **Brisbane City Travelodge.** Roma Street, **Brisbane**, Qld. 4000. Tel: (07) 238-2222; in U.S., (800) 44-UTELL; in Canada, (800) 387-1338; Telex: AA 141778.

▶ **Cairns Colonial Club.** 18–26 Cannon Street, **Manunda**, Cairns, Qld. 4870. Tel: (070) 535-111; in U.S., (800) 551-2012; Telex: CC Club 48221.

▶ **Cairns Parkroyal.** Abbott Street, **Cairns**, Qld. 4870. Tel: (070) 311-300.

▶ **Cape York Wilderness Lodge.** c/o Air Queensland, 62 Abbott Street, **Cairns**, Qld. 4870. Tel: (070) 504-205.

▶ **Capricorn Iwasaki Resort.** Farnborough Road, **Yeppoon**, Qld. 4703. Tel: (079) 390-211.

▶ **Club Crocodile Resort.** Shute Harbour Road, **Airlie Beach**, Qld. 4802. Tel: (079) 467-155.

▶ **Conrad International Hotel.** Gold Coast Highway, Broadbeach Island, **Broadbeach**, Qld. 4218. Tel: (075) 921-133; in U.S., (212) 697-9370 or (800) 223-1146; Telex: AA 145127.

▶ **Contiki's Whitsunday Resort. Long Island**, Qld. 4741. Tel: (079) 469-400.

▶ **Coral Sea Resort.** 25 Ocean View Avenue, **Airlie Beach,** Qld. 4802. Tel: (079) 466-458.

▶ **Country Comfort Motel.** 100 Goondoon Street, **Gladstone,** Qld. 4680. Tel: (079) 724-499.

▶ **Criterion Hotel.** Quay Street, **Rockhampton,** Qld. 4700. Tel: (079) 221-225.

▶ **Crocodylus Village.** Cow Bay, **Cape Tribulation,** Qld. Tel: (070) 311-366.

▶ **Daydream Island Resort. Airlie Beach,** Qld. 4802. Tel: (079) 469-200; Telex: AA 48519.

▶ **Don Pancho Beach Resort.** 62 Miller Street, Kelly's Beach, **Bargara,** Qld. 4670. Tel: (071) 792-146; Telex: 46510.

▶ **Dunk Island Resort.** Via **Townsville,** Qld. 4810. Tel: (070) 688-199.

▶ **Duthies Leichhardt Hotel.** Corner Denham Street and Bolsover Street, **Rockhampton,** Qld. 4700. Tel: (079) 276-733.

▶ **Fitzroy Island Resort.** Via **Cairns,** Qld. 4870. Tel: (070) 519-588; in U.S., (800) 6-ANSETT or (800) 4-ANSETT; in Canada, (800) 268-6370.

▶ **Four Seasons Barrier Reef Resort.** 55 Lavender Street, **Milsons Point,** N.S.W. 2061. Tel: (077) 709-111; in U.S., (800) 654-9153 or (800) 922-3559; in Canada, (800) 654-9058.

▶ **Gold Coast International.** Gold Coast Highway, **Surfers Paradise,** Qld. 4217. Tel: (075) 921-200; in U.S., (800) 44-UTELL; in Canada, (800) 387-1338; Telex: AA 42142.

▶ **Gold Coast Sheraton Mirage Hotel.** The Spit, Sea World Drive, **Southport,** Qld. 4215. Tel: (008) 222-229; in U.S. and Canada, (800) 325-3535.

▶ **Great Keppel Island Resort.** Via **Rockhampton,** Qld. 4700. Tel: (079) 391-744; in U.S., (800) 551-2012 or (800) 445-0190.

▶ **Green Island Reef Resort.** Via **Cairns,** Qld. 4870. Tel: (070) 514-644; in U.S., (714) 675-7306, collect.

▶ **Hamilton Island Resort.** Via **Airlie Beach,** Qld. 4801. Tel: (079) 469-144; in U.S. and Canada, (800) 268-1469.

▶ **Hayman Island Resort.** Via **Airlie Beach,** Qld. 4801. Tel: (079) 469-100; in U.S., (800) 4-ANSETT or (800) 6-ANSETT; in Canada, (800) 268-6370.

▶ **Heron Island Resort.** Via **Gladstone,** Qld. 4680. Tel: (079) 781-488; in Brisbane, (07) 268-8224; in U.S., (800) 551-2012.

▶ **Hillcrest Central Apartments.** 311 Vulture Street, South Brisbane, Qld. 4000. Tel: (07) 846-3000.

▶ **Hilton International Brisbane.** 190 Elizabeth Street, Brisbane, Qld. 4000. Tel: (07) 231-3131; in U.S., (800) 445-8667; in Canada, (800) 268-9275; Telex: AA 140981.

▶ **Hilton International Cairns.** Wharf Street, Cairns, Qld. 4870. Tel: (070) 521-599; in U.S., (800) 445-8667; Telex: AA 48292.

▶ **Hinchinbrook Island Resort.** Via Townsville, Qld. 4816. Tel: (070) 668-585; Telex: AA 148971.

▶ **Hyatt Regency-Coolum.** P.O. Box 78, Coolum Beach, Qld. 4573. Tel: (071) 462-777; in U.S. and Canada, (800) 228-9000; Telex: 70963.

▶ **Hyatt Regency at Sanctuary Cove.** Casey Road, Hope Island, Qld. 4212. Tel: (075) 30-1234; in U.S. and Canada, (800) 228-9000.

▶ **Kewarra Beach Resort.** Kewarra Road, Kewarra Beach, Cairns, Qld. 4871. Tel: (070) 576-666.

▶ **Kohuna Resort.** Bucasia, via Mackay, Qld. 4740. Tel: (079) 548-555.

▶ **Lady Elliot Island Resort.** Via Bundaberg, Qld. 4670. Tel: (071) 722-322; in Brisbane, (07) 229-7661; in U.S., (213) 465-8418.

▶ **Latitude 19 Resort.** Mandalay Avenue, Magnetic Island, Qld. 4810. Tel: (077) 785-200; in U.S., (213) 465-8418.

▶ **Lindeman Island Resort.** Via Mackay, Qld. 4741. Tel: (079) 469-333; in U.S., (800) 551-2012.

▶ **Lizard Island Lodge.** c/o Air Queensland, 62 Abbott Street, Cairns, Qld. 4870. Tel: (070) 504-205; in U.S., (800) 551-2012 or (800) 445-0190.

▶ **Mayfair Crest International.** King George Square, Brisbane, Qld. 4000. Tel: (07) 229-9111; in U.S., (800) 44-UTELL; in Canada, (800) 387-1338; Telex: AA 41320.

▶ **Netanya Noosa Resort.** 75 Hastings Street, Noosa Heads, Qld. 4567. Tel: (071) 474-722; Telex: 43507.

▶ **Noosa International.** Edgar Bennett Avenue, Noosa Heads, Qld. 4567. Tel: (071) 474-822.

▶ **Orpheus Island Resort.** Via Townsville, Qld. 4810. Tel: (077) 777-377; in U.S. and Canada, (800) 235-8222.

▶ **Pacific International Hotel.** 43 The Esplanade, Cairns, Qld. 4870. Tel: (070) 517-888; in U.S., (800) 44-UTELL; Telex: AA 48274.

▶ **Palm Bay Resort.** Long Island, Qld. 4741. Tel: (079) 469-233.

▶ **Punsand Bay Private Reserve.** Via Bamaga, **Punsand Bay**, Qld. Tel: (070) 691-722.

▶ **Ramada Hotel.** Paradise Centre, Gold Coast Highway, **Surfers Paradise**, Qld. 4217. Tel: (075) 593-499; in U.S., (800) 228-2828; in Canada, (416) 485-2692 (call collect); Telex: AA 42936.

▶ **Ramada Reef Resort.** Corner Veivers Road and The Esplanade, **Palm Cove**, Qld. 4871. Tel: (070) 553-999; in U.S., (800) 228-2828; in Canada, (416) 485-2692 (call collect); Telex: AA 48342.

▶ **Reef House Resort.** Williams Esplanade, **Palm Cove**, Qld. 4871. Tel: (070) 553-612; Telex: AA 48478.

▶ **Riverside International.** 86 Victoria Parade, **Rockhampton**, Qld. 4700. Tel: (079) 279-933.

▶ **Riverview Gardens Apartments.** 26 River Terrace, **South Brisbane**, Qld. 4000. Tel: (07) 846-3100.

▶ **Seahaven Beachfront Resort.** Hastings Street, **Noosa Heads**, Qld. 4567. Tel: (071) 473-422.

▶ **Sheraton Breakwater Casino/Hotel.** Sir Leslie Theiss Drive, **Townsville**, Qld. 4810. Tel: (077) 724-066; in U.S. and Canada, (800) 325-3535; Telex: AA 47999.

▶ **Sheraton Brisbane Hotel and Towers**, 249 Turbot Street, **Brisbane**, Qld. 4000. Tel: (07) 835-3535; in U.S. and Canada, (800) 325-3535; Telex: AA 44944.

▶ **Sheraton Mirage Resort.** Port Douglas Road, **Port Douglas**, Qld. 4871. Tel: (070) 985-888; in U.S. and Canada, (800) 325-3535; Telex: AA 48888.

▶ **Silky Oaks Colonial Lodge.** Finlay Vale Road, **Mossman**, Qld. 4873. Tel: (070) 981-666; Telex: AA 46110.

▶ **South Molle Island Resort.** Shute Harbour, via **Airlie Beach**, Qld. 4810. Tel: (079) 469-433; in U.S., (800) 4-ANSETT or (800) 6-ANSETT; in Canada, (800) 268-6370.

▶ **Southbank Motor Inn.** 23–29 Palmer Street, **South Townsville**, Qld. 4810. Tel: (077) 211-474.

▶ **Sovereign Hotel.** Charlotte Street, **Cooktown**, Qld. 4871. Tel: (070) 695-400.

▶ **Tangalooma Resort.** Moreton Island, Qld. 4004. Tel: (075) 482-666; Telex: 43375.

▶ **Terrace Gardens Quality Inn.** 1–6 Hastings Street, **Noosa Heads**, Qld. 4567. Tel: (071) 473-077.

▶ **Tipplers Island Resort.** Tipplers Parade, **South Stradbroke Island**, Qld. 4216. Tel: (075) 573-311.

▶ **Townsville International Hotel.** Flinders Mall, **Townsville**, Qld. 4810. Tel: (077) 722-477; Telex: AA 47076.

▶ **Townsville Reef International.** 63/64 The Strand, Townsville, Qld. 4810. Tel: (077) 211-777.

▶ **Townsville Travelodge.** 75 The Strand, Townsville, Qld. 4810. Tel: (077) 724-255; in U.S., (212) 247-7950 or (800) 344-1212; Telex: AA 47166.

▶ **White Lace Motel.** Nebo Road, Mackay, Qld. 4740. Tel: (079) 514-466.

▶ **Whitsunday Terraces Resort.** Golden Orchid Drive, Airlie Beach, Qld. 4802. Tel: (079) 466-788; in U.S. and Canada, (800) 528-1234; Telex: AA 48529.

▶ **Whitsunday Wanderers Resort.** Shute Harbour Road, Airlie Beach, Qld. 4802. Tel: (079) 466-446.

# NORTHERN TERRITORY

## THE RED CENTRE AND THE TOP END

*By Chris Brockie*

*Chris Brockie worked on Australian cattle stations until an automobile accident forced him to find less rugged work in journalism, first with the Australian Broadcasting Corporation and then as bureau chief for two major newspaper groups. Originally a New Zealander, he has lived and worked mostly in the Australian Outback, particularly the Northern Territory, since 1972; he now lives in Canberra and works as a free-lance journalist.*

For many years only the hardiest and most intrepid traveller visited the Northern Territory. This was partly due to its inaccessibility—the tyranny of distance is Australia's greatest natural enemy—and partly because Territorians did not see tourism as a viable industry. After all, if Australians didn't want to visit, then surely nobody from overseas would either.

All this has changed. Territorians now realize that the benefits they took for granted do interest others. The same spirit of adventure that attracted the early explorers and travellers is what attracts today's visitor to this timeless territory.

MAJOR INTEREST

**The Red Centre**
The beauty of Ayers Rock
The Olgas and Uluru National Park
The natural grandeur of Palm Valley
The raw Outback towns
Aboriginal culture

**The Top End**
Darwin's relaxed lifestyle
Crocodiles
Bathurst and Melville islands; the Tiwi people
The natural beauty and wildlife of Kakadu National
    Park
Yachting and marlin fishing at Nhulunbuy
The Katherine Gorge

Born of "bloody hard yakka" (bloody is the Great Australian Adjective, yakka a colloquialism for work), the Northern Territory has evolved from a pioneering cattle-raising region to a mining-oriented land where tourism is the second-largest industry.

In fact, Territorians have a philosophy that goes something like this: "If you can't dig it up and sell it to them, get them to come and look at it."

The Territory's roots are essentially British, yet many see in it what Hollywood once portrayed as the American West. It is now often referred to as the "The Last Frontier."

And it is big. Covering about 487,627 square miles, it is about twice the size of Texas and just over five times the size of the United Kingdom.

About two-thirds of the Territory lies north of the Tropic of Capricorn, just north of Alice Springs, but it is not until you near Katherine in the north that you become aware that there are really two areas as distinct as fire and water: the Red Centre and the Top End.

In between are the Barkly Tablelands (running east into Queensland) and the small mining town of Tennant Creek, guarded by the Devil's Marbles and by the sometimes huge termite (white ant) mounds.

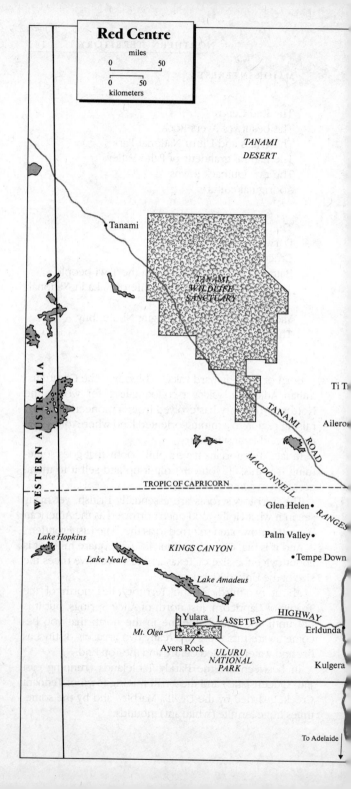

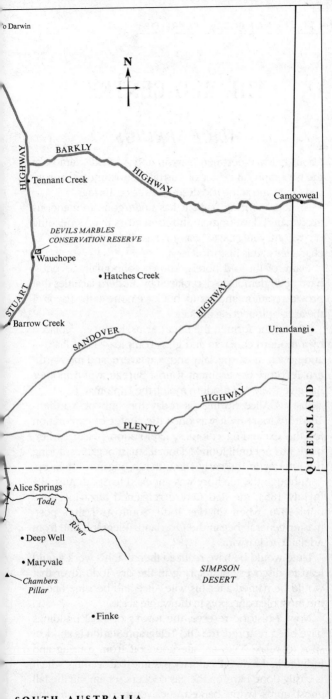

# THE RED CENTRE

## *ALICE SPRINGS*

About halfway between Darwin and Adelaide, almost at the geographical center of Australia, surrounded by iron-red sands and semi-arid desert, lies Alice Springs.

An ideal touring base, it has undergone tremendous growth and development in recent years that, depending on whom you talk to, has or has not led to a loss of character in this historical town.

Many of the old hotels, known colloquially as pubs, have been demolished, replaced by modern facilities that provide comfort and luxury but have none of the flavor of the area's pioneering heritage.

One of the former, the Stuart Arms, has been replaced by a modern concrete and glass complex—Ford Plaza—and now houses specialty shops, a tavern, and the Northern Territory Government Tourist Bureau, while another has given way to a modern motel, the **Diplomat**.

Just as Alice Springs is today the hub of Northern Territory tourism, it was once the center of exploration for the expanding colonies. Exploration began earlier, but it was not until John McDouall Stuart began exploring the interior in the early 1860s that it began to open up.

Although the territory was annexed to South Australia in July 1863, the Red Centre remained terra incognita until 1870, when Charles Todd, South Australia's postmaster general, began the Overland Telegraph line from Adelaide to Darwin.

Little would he have realized then that his work would lead to discovery of a spring in the dry Todd River that would be named after his wife Alice and become one of the most pleasant spots in the whole area.

Now a historic reserve, the town's original buildings have been restored; the **Old Telegraph Station** is an ideal spot to relax. Take an afternoon off from touring and indulge in the Aussie culinary pastime, barbecuing, which is easily done here on the gas cookers set among the tall ghost gums (white-barked eucalyptus trees) lining the Todd River. Ingredients for your B.B.Q. can be ordered from your hotel kitchen in a hamper stuffed with lean Centralian beef steaks, sausages, wine, breads, and other tasty morsels.

The station became operational in 1872, yet it wasn't until 1889, when the South Australian government sent people northward looking for suitable railheads, that the site where Alice Springs now stands was established as a settlement (originally called Stuart, and 3 km/2 miles south of the telegraph station). The first train arrived only in 1929; until then camels were the major mode of transport.

There are constant reminders of the camel connection. The train from Adelaide, **the Ghan**, is named in memory of the early cameleers, many of whom were Afghans who used to ply the route before the railway was built. In 1980 the original narrow-gauge line was replaced by a standard-gauge railway. There are now two Ghan trains, the old and the new.

At **MacDonnel Siding**, about 10 km (6 miles) south of Alice Springs, the Ghan Preservation Society has established a living museum where diesel and steam locomotives and passenger and dining cars from the old Ghan have been restored. About 19 miles of the old track remains, and the Society now runs excursion trips to Ewaninga Siding.

There is also the annual **Camel Cup** race meeting, usually in April. Now an international event, since 1987 it has created especially keen competition between teams from Alice Springs and Virginia City, Nevada.

For an enlightening look at the Alice, as it's called, and to help imagine some of its lost character, spend a couple of hours on the **Heritage Walk**. Starting in Todd Mall (formerly Todd Street) at what was Alice Springs's first mission hospital, Adelaide House (opened in 1926)— and which then became an accommodation and convalescent house for bush women and children from 1939 until 1961—wind your way in and out of history. Move into Hartley Street, where you will find, among other things, the Old Court House, the Residency, and the old Stuart Gaol—the oldest building still remaining in the town area. The **Residency** was built in 1926–27 for John Charles Cawood, Alice Springs's first government resident. It is now owned and operated by the Museums and Art Galleries Board of the Northern Territory.

The **Royal Flying Doctor Service** (RFDS) was set up in 1928 by the Reverend John Flynn to provide a "mantle of safety" to isolated areas throughout Australia. When Flynn died in 1951, the service covered about five million square miles. The Alice Springs base opened in 1939. Visitors can view a short film that details the RFDS history and activities and see a collection of historic photographs and other memorabilia.

The only way for many Outback children, isolated by distance, to receive an education is through regular radio contact with a teacher at the Alice Springs base of the **School of the Air**. The crackle of radio conversations helps you to realize that more than six hundred miles may separate teacher and student.

Other places worth visiting in Alice Springs are **Panorama Guth**, which houses a 360-degree painted panoramic landscape depicting the Central Australian landscape as well as artifacts from the early pioneering days; **Diarama Village**, depicting the legends and myths of the aboriginal people; **Pitchi Richi Sanctuary**, a large outdoor museum featuring birds, flowers, and sculptures; and **Olive Pink Flora Reserve**, which has as its subject Central Australia's plant life.

Although Alice Springs has no public transport, all of these places can be comfortably seen in a day because they are all within easy walking distance of the town center. However, it is still better to take a tour of the town's major attractions with one of the locally based tour operators; an especially enjoyable way is by the Cobb & Co. horse-drawn coach.

Shopping is relaxed here and confined mainly to Todd Street/Mall. **Aboriginal Arts Australia** on Todd Street (not the Mall), set up by the Australian government to help market traditional aboriginal arts and crafts, has a large range of traditional and contemporary works, ranging from bark and sand paintings to carvings, weavings, and **didgeridoos**—traditional aboriginal musical instruments up to six feet long and about two inches in diameter. Usually they are made from hollow tree branches and played by blowing and sucking air through them.

Most other gift and souvenir shops around town offer traditional aboriginal works, too, along with some fine examples of locally produced pottery, textiles, and other handicrafts.

Traveller's checks can be cashed at the Westpac, ANZ, and State banks, where no charge is made on either Australian or overseas transactions; the Commonwealth or National banks, which charge A$2 and A$5, respectively, on each overseas transaction; or at Lasseters Casino.

Many of the better restaurants are in-house at the hotels, but otherwise the **Stuart Auto Museum Restaurant**, an upscale establishment with dishes like grilled buffalo in witchetty-grub (a kind of caterpillar, rich in protein and a traditional aboriginal food source), and **Angelina's Grill Room** (at the same museum venue; see Around Alice Springs, below) are both recommended. Both are closed Sundays.

For more traditional-style cuisine, step back into the culinary wonders of the early pioneers with a menu of beef, buffalo, and barramundi (an Australian lungfish) at the **Overlander Steakhouse** on Hartley Street.

Much of Alice Springs's nightlife revolves around pubs and clubs. Most, at some time during the week, have some form of live entertainment. Perhaps, however, the most notable and enjoyable would be **The Old Alice Inn**, formerly the Todd Tavern, in Todd Mall. The Inn is actually five bars, including the up-market Maxim's Bar and Restaurant, Melba's Piano Bar, and Dimensions Nitespot. **Dimensions** would undoubtedly be the favorite among Alice Springs's younger visitors. Monday evenings it sees a jam session, on Thursdays, Fridays, and Saturdays it becomes a disco, and on Sundays it becomes the place to hear folk music.

At the other end of town is the **Alice Junction Tavern** at the Heavitree Gap Tourist Resort. Here jazz lovers are entertained Saturday to Wednesday, and on Friday nights and late Saturday nights the disco lovers have their turn. There is country-and-western music Saturday nights and Sunday afternoons.

## Staying in Alice Springs

The Northern Territory's very diverse nature has been re-created, probably unwittingly, in the range of available accommodation. But because the Alice is used more as a base than a straight destination it makes little difference which you choose.

However, after a day touring the dusty Outback you

may feel you need a little extra style and comfort, away from the commercial center, and this can be found at the **Sheraton** (which is a touch sterile) or at **Lasseters Hotel Casino** along Barrett Drive (Lasseters is a licensed gambling casino with opulent decor and strict dress standards). They are expensive by comparison with the average, at more than A$100 a night, but recommended. And they have great meals, from formal dining to café snacks.

With few exceptions, hotels and motels are serviced by tour operators with transfer or pickup and setdown services.

We list several more ordinary hotels/motels in the Accommodations Reference section at the end of the chapter. Hotel rates average about A$70 to A$80 a night (room only) for a single. Most provide in-house videos, have their own restaurants, and are fully air-conditioned—a prerequisite for comfortable living in the Territory. Most have swimming pools and saunas.

# Around Alice Springs

**Chateau Hornsby**, 15 km (9 miles) out of Alice off the south Stuart Highway, is the Territory's first and only commercial winery. On Sundays, Tuesdays, and Fridays you can take a camel to dinner here, care of Frontier Tours. For about an hour you trek down the Todd River on the back of a camel, swaying with each step but enjoying the different perspective this mode of transport gives of the surrounding country. At the winery you are then given a tour of the cellar and a wine tasting before sitting down to dinner.

Chateau Hornsby is an experience not to be forgotten, especially when the entertainment comes from the world's leading master of a uniquely Northern Territory instrument, the Fosterphone. Five nights a week Ted Egan plays his Fosterphone (a carton of Foster's lager tuned by drinking the carton's contents), sings, and tells yarns in a fashion never thought possible throughout the rest of the civilized world. Join in for a chorus of his popular "Oh They've Got Some Bloody Good Drinkers in the Northern Territory."

The **Stuart Auto Museum**, just a few minutes out of town off the Ross Highway, houses a fine collection of fully restored automobiles dating from 1911. It also has a large collection of motor bikes, as well as motoring memorabilia.

There are many gorges and parks within a short drive of the Alice that require a half to full day to explore. However, it is not until you get about 100 km (60 miles) or more out that you find the more spectacular sights: Kings Canyon, Chambers Pillar, Glen Helen Gorge, Arltunga, and Palm Valley.

**Chambers Pillar**, discovered in 1869 by explorer John McDouall Stuart, lies abut 150 km (90 miles) south; you need a four-wheel drive to get there along the Maryvale Station road. Sitting atop a domed hill, the cream-colored pillar is about 495 feet in circumference and stands as a lonely sentinel some 165 feet tall. Since its discovery it has served as a signpost to explorers and adventurers. The aboriginals have various names for it, one of which is "Idracowra"; they all mean "place of the adulterous male."

From a lonely wedge-tailed eagle gliding the thermals above you to the fragile plant and prehistoric life of Palm Valley and Kings Canyon, you are aware of how minuscule your place in the world is.

**Palm Valley**, 155 km (96 miles) west from Alice Springs and accessible only by four-wheel drive, is part of the 89,000-acre Finke Gorge National Park. *Livistonia mariae* palms, thousands of years old and found nowhere else in the world, help take you back in time as you walk among the rock pools.

Some 30 of the 300 plant species here are considered among the world's rarest. Except for barbecue and toilet facilities, there are no other amenities. Allow at least a full day for the return trip. Camping is allowed. Some 320 km (200 miles) southwest of the Alice is an almost biblical setting: **Kings Canyon**, a living natural-history museum where a multitude of plants—including one considered to be a living fossil—grows among the rugged landforms and trapped pools of water. There are no facilities in the canyon proper, and until recently the only accommodation nearby was at Wallara Ranch, about 80 km (50 miles) away. Now, however, visitors may stay at the three-star **Kings Canyon Wilderness Lodge** which is just 5 km (3 miles) away and opened in late 1987.

Even at **Arltunga**, amid the rugged MacDonnell Ranges

110 km (66 miles) west of the Alice, where the atmosphere is more modern, you feel like a bit player on the mammoth stage of history. Just over 100 years ago gold was discovered here but, as at many goldfields, the yield soon petered out. Sitting among the excavated rubble you can almost hear the long-dead miners chipping away at the rock in search of an elusive dream. Or without too much effort you may hear the battery crushing the gold-bearing ore brought in from the diggings. And if this doesn't work take a walk among the recently restored stone buildings.

If you can't hear the history in the wind, Gary and Elaine Bohning will relate and embellish it as you sit at the bar of what has been described as the "loneliest pub in the world," where it is not uncommon for stockmen from surrounding cattle stations to be found drinking and telling tales of their exploits.

After you look over the relics of this once-profitable mining camp, the Bohnings may show you the Christmas Nugget, a four-ounce nugget they found on Christmas Day in 1980. Tiring of city life, the Bohnings moved to Arltunga in 1980 to prospect for gold among the old diggings. For years the road from Alice Springs had been rough, but not enough to deter visitors from making their way to the ruins. Eventually the Bohnings began to receive numerous visitors, and this led to the establishment of their pub and a campsite.

While it's possible to drive yourself to these places, it's best to take one of the specially organized tours. These are usually for small groups, with the guide often being the owner/operator—someone who has spent years living and working in the area. These tours from Alice Springs are relatively inexpensive; there are many day excursions available from about A$45.

One of the better, comprehensive, and more flexible tours is the Saltbush Package offered by Spinifex Tours; it includes a one-day tour of Palm Valley, a day tour of the gorges in and around the MacDonnell Ranges, a day tour of town attractions (including Chateau Hornsby), and a three-day tour of Ayers Rock, the Olgas (see below), and Kings Canyon.

# ULURU NATIONAL PARK

Uluru National Park, which includes Ayers Rock and the Olgas, has been one of the most controversial areas in Australia's recent history since it was handed back to the traditional aboriginal owners in October 1985.

The 520-square-mile national park bearing the aboriginal name for Ayers Rock has been leased back from its aboriginal owners and is managed by the Australian National Parks and Wildlife Service.

## Yulara

The Territory's only true resort town—Yulara, just outside the park boundary—is a self-sufficient township (the Territory's fourth-largest community) and a self-contained destination capable of accommodating up to 5,000 visitors a day. Fears have been expressed by some Alice Springs operators that aggressive promotion of Yulara is having a detrimental effect on the tourism trade in Alice Springs. The fears are justified: Yulara is now serviced regularly and directly by most major and secondary airlines and coach (bus) companies. And for people driving up the newly paved Stuart Highway from South Australia in search of a relaxing holiday mingled with the Outback experience, Uluru/Yulara is closer than Alice Springs.

About 500 km (300 miles) southeast of the Alice, Yulara is a comfortable four to five hours by car, or 45 minutes by air, from Alice Springs. The drive down passes through the heart of Australian cattle country, studded with grazing Brahman, Herefords, Shorthorns, and horses, and dotted with groves of shady desert oak.

Yulara, a conglomeration of vacation facilities constructed improbably in the middle of the Outback near Ayers Rock and the Olga Mountains, has every amenity you expect of a resort, from shops to its own pub, the **Ernest Giles Tavern**, which is frequented by visitors and is the local watering hole for the resort's workers.

Accommodation ranges from the international-class **Sheraton** to the more moderate **Four Seasons** to the **Ayers Rock Lodge**—and down to the camping ground.

Yulara is not short on the elegance befitting its resort status, with V.I.P. Hire Cars offering privately escorted tours with fully trained, uniformed chauffeurs in late-model air-conditioned limousines 24 hours a day.

# The Olgas

Apart from the ironical luxury of being driven around the Outback in a limousine, consider having a formal dinner (likewise arranged at Yulara) at the mysterious mountains, **The Olgas**. Wining and dining and being waited on at a portable table, set with crisp white linen and polished silverware and illuminated by gas lamps as the sun drops behind the jumbled Olgas—which the aboriginals call Kata Tjuta, "place of many heads"—is not just ironical or elegant, it is fun.

In legend Mount Olga is home of the giant serpent, Wanambi, who lives in a cave below. When angry the monster blows gusts of wind through the gorges; when happy Wanambi changes into a rainbow, spreading himself across the more than 30 magnificent domes.

Like Ayers Rock, the Olgas are steeped in aboriginal myth, with everything having its origins in the Dreamtime, the aboriginal creation myth. They are more spectacular, more eerie, more interesting than Ayers Rock—although not as challenging.

# Ayers Rock

Ayers Rock is nonetheless what attracts people to Yulara. Before this multimillion-dollar resort was built, long before Uluru was handed back to the aboriginals, people came to Ayers Rock. It was—and still is—a challenge. It has to be climbed, like Mount Everest, because it is there. Some Europeans, like the aboriginals, say a spiritual aura emanates from within this the world's largest monolith.

The dangers that confront visitors to the Territory cannot be stressed too often. In recent years at the Olgas and Kings Canyon there have been several deaths of people ill-prepared for the elements. All could have been avoided. Some victims died of thirst, others from being unable to withstand the often grueling climbs.

At least a liter of water per person should be taken on short walks, and four liters a day should be drunk in hot weather.

Climbing Ayers Rock is dangerous: Sufferers of heart

complaints—including high blood pressure and angina—asthmatics, and those who fear heights or are prone to dizziness should not make the climb. If you are generally unfit, or have doubts, do not attempt it.

There is ample evidence of those who have lost their lives on Ayers Rock; memorial plaques are fixed permanently to the rock at the place where the climb starts.

# The Aboriginal Culture

Europeans and North Americans, no matter how hard they try, have difficulty understanding the relationship aboriginals have with the land. Theirs is an ancient culture, and one that should be respected.

With World Heritage status, Uluru is Australia's first Aboriginal National Park, and since the handover there have been some dramatic changes made to protect the local inhabitants and the fragile natural milieu here.

In 1986 the small Mititjulu community near the rock was closed to the public. As one publication aptly put it, "... with rapidly increasing numbers of tourists they were being mistaken for one of the park's attractions. Dozens of buses would arrive every day to see them and their homes and to photograph them as if they were a rare species of wildlife...."

A compact understanding of the aboriginal culture can be gained instead in a visit to the **Maruku Arts and Craft Centre** just behind the park's entry station, where you can view *Uluru,* a film made by the local Mititjulu, which tells the history of their land and the importance of Tjukurpa—existence itself.

Because of the complex issues that surround the park and its traditional owners, there are some rules that must be adhered to, although many non-aboriginals, particularly Australians, resent them.

Most aboriginals do not like their photographs to be taken because, it is said, they lose their inner spirit. In Uluru there is a policy of *Don't ask.* Also, if you have plans to sell or publish any photographs taken within the park, formal permission *must* be obtained, in advance, from the Australian National Parks and Wildlife Service. Commercial photography is defined as any photography for anything other than private use. (The same conditions apply to Kakadu National Park.) Assistance with applications from commercial photographers can be obtained through the Northern Territory Tourist Commission.

One of the greatest crimes against the traditional owners is entering a sacred site. These are clearly marked within the park and are protected under Northern Territory and Commonwealth legislation.

A large portion of the area surrounding the park, excluding Yulara, is aboriginal land to which entry is prohibited without a permit.

# THE TOP END

Whatever you do, don't leave the insect repellent, sunscreen, sturdy walking shoes, and sun hat you've been carting around the Red Centre (which takes its name from the predominantly red, iron-rich sands) behind when you head into the Top End. The flies and sun are just as fierce there as they are in the Centre, despite the difference in climate.

The Top End summer—October through April—is called the "Wet." The air is hot and humid and the average rainfall is between 40 and 52 inches. And because of its high humidity and temperatures—in the mid-to-high 30s C (90s F)—it is referred to by locals as the "suicide season."

Not surprisingly, winter here is the "Dry," when little if any rain falls. Humidity is low and temperatures average 31 degrees C (86 degrees F). It is during the Dry when most prefer to visit, but the Wet provides more interesting and enduring memories, especially at Kakadu and at Katherine Gorge.

Unlike the Centre, where the prolific wildlife is often hidden from the searing heat, the Top End is a large walkthrough botanical and zoological garden.

## *DARWIN*

When the aircraft cabin begins to feel steamy, as the plane's air conditioner struggles to adjust to the high humidity outside, you know you're heading into Darwin.

It was not until the fifth attempt at settlement here that success came, with the setting up of Palmerston. The harbor was called Port Darwin after Charles Darwin, who was aboard the *Beagle* when it explored the harbor; the town officially became Darwin in 1911.

Considered Australia's Asian gateway, Darwin was almost forgotten until 1872, when the Overland Telegraph from South Australia opened. Darwin's importance increased then because the telegraph was the main communications link between Australia and Britain in those days, and Darwin became the access point for mainland Asia.

Today Darwin is a multicultural city with more than 40 nationalities making up the population, although it does have a distinctive Asian quality about it. A walk through the **Smith Street Mall** in the city center on a Saturday morning is ideal for buying bargain-priced sarongs and other Asian-type crafts from the street vendors.

Darwin is not like any other Australian city. Its history has been turbulent. In 1942 the Japanese bombed the city 60 times. Cyclones, a fact of life for Top End residents, have ravaged the city many times, the worst being on Christmas Eve 1974, when Cyclone Tracy's 174-mph winds roared in from the Timor Sea and flattened over 90 percent of the city, injuring more than 150 people and killing 65.

Such is the nature of Darwinites that after evacuation most returned to pick up their lives and rebuild the city. Unlike Alice Springs, which physically draws its character from the harsh Outback, Darwin's character is in the makeup of its people and their lifestyle: casual, relaxed, friendly, and fond of drink. So wide is the range of beer available that ordering becomes an exercise in remembering the primary colors. Blue is for Foster's lager; green is Victoria bitter; white is Carlton draught; and cold gold is Castlemaine XXXX ("Four X," supposedly so-named because Australians can't spell "beer"), and so on. Sinking a tinnie (a can of beer) is a real pastime in Darwin, the climate being a common partial excuse.

Darwin's worship of beer has led to the Beer Can Regatta each June, where rules two and three state: "Thou Shalt Build Thy Craft of Cans" and "Thy Craft Shall Float by Cans Alone." Drowning is prohibited and it is decreed that everyone "shall have a bloody good time."

Being a coastal settlement, Darwin centers many of its activities and attractions around water. For an unusual

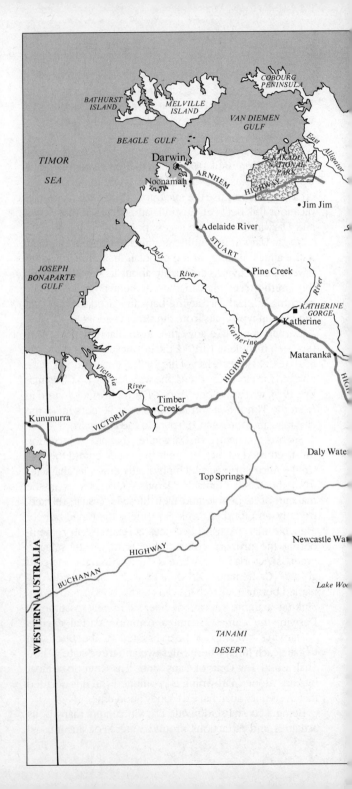

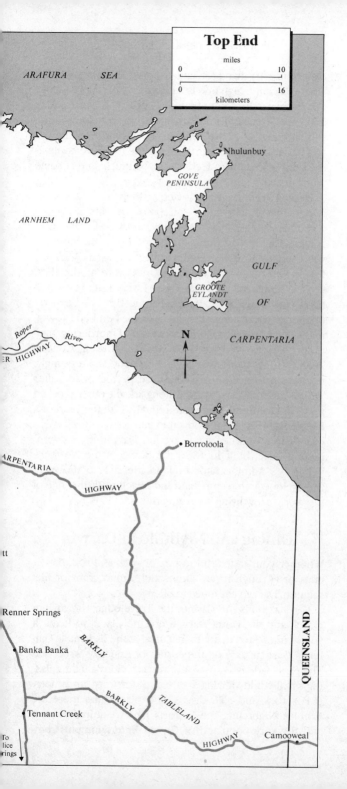

experience try hand-feeding fish: On the foreshore off **Doctor's Gully**, high tide is feeding time for thousands of fish as they swarm in to be fed on bread, octopus, squid, and other treats. Visitors are welcome to help feed the fish, although they are sometimes reticent in taking tidbits from strangers (over the years the fish have come to trust the woman who feeds them, so much so that some will roll over to be scratched).

Darwin's remoteness attracted not only adventurers and speculators—today called entrepreneurs—but also unsavory characters such as thieves and vagabonds. The once-remote **Fannie Bay Gaol**, surrounded now by suburbia, was used for almost a century until 1979, when Berrimah Prison was finished. Its gallows (they were modeled on those at England's Newgate Prison) were built in 1952 to hang two convicted murders. Fannie Bay has been re-opened as a museum. After the Japanese bombed Darwin, many of its prisoners, some convicted of murdering Japanese pearlers, were set free. Again, following Cyclone Tracy in 1974, many inmates were pardoned. Interestingly, not one prisoner attempted to escape the prison after Tracy's ravages. Many worked alongside the other shocked survivors to rebuild the shattered city. Like the Territory, Fannie Bay Gaol was unconventional.

A couple of other sights around Darwin are **Government House**, built in 1869, the home of the Northern Territory's Administrator built in the style of Darwin's pre-cyclone architecture, and **Indo Pacific Marine**, one of the world's few living coral aquariums.

## Dining and Nightlife in Darwin

Whether your tastes run to jazz or rock and roll, barbecues or an English pub atmosphere, mud crabs or filet mignon, Darwin has much to offer.

For jazz buffs the **Casino**, the **Travelodge**, the **Atrium Hotel**, and the **Hotel Darwin** are the places to head. If you're interested in art, then a meal at the Esplanade Gallery's **Garden Café** on the corner of Knuckey Street and The Esplanade is a must. Here you can enjoy a light, relaxing meal while viewing a variety of territory landscapes.

For rock and roll, discos, and piano bars there are **Fannies Nightclub**, the **Victoria Hotel**, **Squires Tavern**, and the very popular **Hot Gossip Entertainment Com-**

**plex** in Cavenagh Street, where you can dance the night away at **Scandals** or enjoy the more sophisticated atmosphere of **Whispers Cocktail and Piano Bar**.

The Sheraton has provided an English-pub environment at what, appropriately, is called **The Pub**.

Darwin has its share of ethnic restaurants that serve excellent food, but you may want to eat Australian. **Gabby's Bar and Bistro** in Cavenagh Street gives you the "true flavor of the Territory" with its crocodile and buffalo dishes.

For mud crabs and barramundi take a sunset cruise on the *Billy J* to Mandorah, where you will be entertained with an aboriginal corroboree and your meal is cooked in traditional style, in glowing, red-hot coals.

## Swimming in the Darwin Area

The Top End has many beautiful and secluded beaches, some quite close to Darwin. Many have grassed areas shaded by tall trees. At **Casuarina Free Beach** it is quite legal to bathe in the buff. A casino overlooks the popular **Mindil Beach**, which stretches for several miles; you can rent boats here for an hour or longer. Other popular Darwin beaches are Vesteys, Casuarina (different from the free beach), Nightcliff, and Fannie Bay.

Top End beaches can be dangerous for the unwary. In addition to crocodiles, sharks also inhabit the coastal waters. However, perhaps the most dangerous inhabitants are the sea wasps, jellyfish that infest much of Australia's tropical coast during the Wet. Although not absolutely necessary (it may draw a bit of a giggle from some people) during the Dry, you might want to wear a pair of nylon panty-hose when swimming in Australia's warmer waters. Divers often wear them to protect their legs from being stung by jellyfish.

## Crocodiles

Crocodiles are endemic to the Top End. There are two species, the freshwater crocodile, which is largely harmless unless provoked, and the more feared, dangerous saltwater crocodile.

The crocodiles are a fascinating part of the Top End. They can move quickly and without warning. A two-and-a-half-hour cruise aboard the *Adelaide River Queen* along the Adelaide River in Kakadu National Park gives you a first-hand look at the crocodiles in their natural environment. With food to entice them, the crocodiles slip menacingly from the mud banks into the water, then, often without warning and with jaws snapping, leap high out of the water to snatch their meal and quickly disappear.

Crocodiles also have the ability to jump right into your boat. Do not swim in waters marked with croc signs, and be watchful when moving around riverbanks. Ignoring these warnings can be fatal. Unlike many other dangerous species found throughout the Territory, such as snakes and spiders, saltwater crocodiles are not likely to retreat from danger.

Visitors can now take out insurance against crocodile attack. The Northern Territory Insurance Office has, for a small fee, introduced "croc cover," although to collect the attack has to be fatal.

However, if crocodiles really interest you and a closer look is needed, then Darwin's **Northern Territory Museum of Arts and Sciences** and the **Crocodile Farm** are both worth a visit. The museum houses an extensive range of historical items relating to the Northern Territory, and also has extensive displays from around Southeast Asia. The museum's art gallery has a large selection of original works by Australian artists, and hosts regular exhibitions.

The Crocodile Farm is about a 30-minute drive south from Darwin along the Stuart Highway. Australia's first commercial croc farm, it has more than 7,000 crocodiles, from hatchlings a few inches long to 13-foot giants.

The most infamous, yet the most beloved of Territory crocs, Sweetheart, a 16½-foot-long, 1,716-pound monster, is preserved at the Darwin Museum. Sweetheart, renowned for attacking boats, died in 1979 (he accidentally drowned after being captured for relocation to a quieter part of the Finniss River).

So popular is the Sweetheart legend the **Diamond Beach Casino** has named a bar after him and has a six-foot neon replica lazing in a giant cocktail glass overlooking the gaming floor. The Diamond Beach Casino, at Mindil Beach, is quite up-market, with superb views of the Botanic Gardens and a relaxing 2-mile-long beach, and of course has licensed gaming floors. (For other accommodations at Darwin, see the Accommodations Reference section at the end of the chapter.)

# BATHURST AND MELVILLE ISLANDS

A short 80-km (48-mile) plane ride north of Darwin aboard Air North's "Gooney Bird" (a DC-3) will take you to Bathurst and Melville islands, home of the Tiwi people.

Unlike the Centralian aboriginal communities, which are essentially off-limits, those of the Top End show an intense desire to have their culture shared with others. Perhaps the finest example is to be found among the Tiwi, although, as at other aboriginal communities, individual visitors must have entry permits.

However, Darwin-based Tiwi Tours and Australian Kakadu Tours both provide an opportunity to visit the islands for half a day or as long as three days. You will have a chance to mingle with the people and obtain some of the finest examples of north Australian aboriginal art and craft available.

Tiwi Tours offer half and day tours of both islands, while Australian Kakadu Tours offer one- , two- , and three-day tours that supply an aboriginal guide to help you hunt and gather traditional foods. If you wish to visit both islands it means crossing the narrow Apsley Strait from Bathurst Island. Be prepared to get wet; the trip is often made in an open boat.

The Tiwi were the first to feel the wrath of the Japanese, when the Japanese bombers strafed the islands on their way to bomb Darwin. Australia's first Japanese P.O.W. was captured on Melville Island by a Tiwi, Matthias Ulungura, after crash-landing there.

The Tiwi are renowned for their colorful screen-printed fabrics, which have graced the covers of many international fashion magazines. Clothes and fabrics manufactured by the Tiwi are sold throughout Australia under the labels Tiwi Designs, Jilmarra, and Bima Wear.

Translated, Tiwi means "people; we the people" or "we, the chosen people." Their culture differs from that of the mainland aboriginals, and until the late 1800s the Tiwi had little contact with the mainland. On both islands visitors find themselves becoming, albeit for a short time, part of the community. The openness of the Tiwi is such that you are welcome to join in whatever they are doing; you need only ask.

You will also find yourself absorbed in the island's history and hear lighthearted but nonetheless serious tales, like the one about the bishop who had 150 wives.

On Melville Island, where a large Caribbean pine plantation has been established, you can swim at **Taracumbie Falls**—no crocodiles here—before heading off in a minibus along the often dusty track to Milikapiti, where you visit an aboriginal burial site, with its colorful, carved *pukamani* poles. The islands so capture the imagination that you feel a little like Ernest Hemingway. And you certainly won't want to leave.

## *KAKADU NATIONAL PARK*

An Australian politician once remarked that much of the 3,268,250-acre Kakadu, 300 km (180 miles) east of Darwin, was nothing but "clapped-out buffalo country."

Certainly there has been constant degradation of this World Heritage area by feral buffalo and other introduced animal and plant species, but the beauty of Kakadu lies in its intrinsic value to everyone. It is as rich in aboriginal history as it is in mineral wealth and natural beauty—and many interests are eyeing that mineral wealth.

Kakadu is home to about a third of all the bird species in Australia, more than 20 species of frog, some 45 species of fish—28 of which can be found in the Magela and Nourlangie creeks alone—saltwater and freshwater crocodiles, and countless other species of animals, plants, and insects. To appreciate Kakadu takes time, to understand it would take a millennium. Kakadu is waterfalls cascading from the ancient rock formations of the Arnhem Land Escarpment; it is a storybook of aboriginal history and mythology; it is tidal flats and estuaries surrounded by mangrove swamps; it is fishing for barramundi in the billabongs (water holes) and rivers; it is grassy plains and rain forests filled with birds, insects, reptiles, and other animal life; it is indeed a World Heritage Environment.

Such is the nature of Kakadu that several specialist tours are available catering separately to the photographer, the bird watcher, or the fisherman. There are also several companies offering half- and full-day aerial tours. One of the best ways in which to experience Kakadu's Wetlands is on a Wild Goose Tour to **Bamurru Djadjam** in the heart of the park. These six-hour tours start and end at the Four Seasons Cooinda and are led by one of the area's traditional aboriginal owners. They lead you on a discovery of aboriginal culture, explaining the importance placed on birds and animals in aboriginal life. You will learn about the days of the buffalo shooters and how the delicate balance of nature was upset by the feral water buffalo.

If you drive to Kakadu we suggest a four-wheel-drive vehicle. Check road conditions by contacting the park headquarters or, in Darwin, the Northern Territory Emergency Service. During the Wet (November to April), and at other times after sudden storms, most roads are impassable for long periods.

Access from Darwin is via the paved Arnhem Highway, which turns east off the Stuart Highway 35 km (21 miles) south of Darwin.

The Wet leaves a lasting impression on visitors, but unfortunately much of the park becomes inaccessible as the large floodplains become inland seas. The two largest of these are Magela and Yellow Waters, with Magela often extending for 80 square miles. Yet, despite this, during the Wet much of Kakadu becomes (especially toward the end of the season) an almost sheer carpet of green and gold and pink, as lilies and grasses flower, and huge flocks of water birds begin moving about in search of food. It is interesting to see traditional enemies, such as snakes and mice, sharing the same branch as they take shelter from the floods.

Road conditions within the park vary, and despite the apparent closeness of a site it may take hours to reach. During the Dry it takes 45 minutes to drive the 40 km (24 miles) to the East Alligator area from the park's headquarters, yet it takes three to four hours to get to Jim Jim Falls, 70 km (42 miles) from the Kakadu Highway.

There are several camping spots within the park, with standard accommodation at either the **Four Seasons Cooinda**, via Jabiru, or the **Kakadu Holiday Village** (part of the South Alligator Motor Inn) on the Arnhem Highway.

Geologically Kakadu is more than 100 million years young, or more than 200 million years old—depending on what rocks you happen to sit on. For the aboriginals it is as old as life itself, the Dreamtime.

The aboriginals have no written history as we know it:

There are no books written by the tribal elders to teach the younger generation their history; for them history is recorded in the mind and handed down in song and dance, or by drawings.

At **Ubirr** (Obiri Rock), featured in the film *Crocodile Dundee,* journey back to . . . when, nobody knows—but it is thought that the oldest paintings here may be more than 20,000 years old, making them possibly the oldest artworks known. The best time to see these ancient masterpieces is in the early morning or late afternoon, when it is cool.

Actually, that is the best time to do almost everything in the Northern Territory.

From the ancient to the nuclear: That is another face of Kakadu. The A\$350-million Ranger uranium mine here is Australia's largest, and the world's second largest producer of the ore.

Kakadu Air Services has set up an information center at Jabiru Airport—**Jabiru Township** was established to service the Ranger, Nabarlek, Jabiluka, and Koongarra mines—and offers free tours of the Ranger mine. The tour provides an interesting view of the mine's operations and is an opportunity to seek answers about the mine, uranium, land-ownership, conservation, and other issues from the mine operators' perspective.

# *NHULUNBUY*

Some 650 km (390 miles) east of Darwin, at the far northeastern point of Arnhem Land, is Gove Peninsula, of which Nhulunbuy is the region's focal point.

Once bauxite mining began here in the early 1970s, on land leased from the Arnhem Land Reserve, a support town was needed.

Today Nhulunbuy is a thriving community of about 6,000 people. It is about two hours by jet from Darwin; it is not recommended to drive there, as the only road in is from Katherine, and it requires considerable experience with Outback conditions to negotiate it. There are, however, a few tour operators that will take you there by boat from Darwin.

Its weather is monsoonal and, as at Darwin, venomous

jellyfish infest the water during the Wet, making swimming impossible.

It is an attractive place; like many areas of the northern coast it was once visited by fishermen from Macassar, Indonesia, searching for trepang (bêche-de-mer or sea slugs). Until European settlement, those Malaysian fishermen were often the only contact Top End aboriginals had with the outside world.

Just off its coast the Arafura Sea meets the Gulf of Carpentaria, and the township acts like a magnet to yachts sailing around Australia or, for that matter, around the world. Drinking at the yacht club in Melville Bay can be as rewarding as sailing with these people, to whom Gove is a supply depot. And as you sit on the veranda drinking the inevitable tinnie, gaze seaward and dream of big marlin. The club is just a short drive from the town center. As is the case with most licensed clubs in Australia, you must be signed in by a member or pass as a bonafide traveller. If you want to spend some time here, the locals will see to it that you get in.

In recent years, usually in November, Gove has hosted the Northern Territory's Gove Game Classic, a fishing competition that attracts game fishermen from around Australia. One of the purposes behind the classic has been to promote and prove the developing marlin grounds off Truant Bank, about 60 km (36 miles) from Nhulunbuy. The first marlin taken there in competition was only in 1984, but reports of marlin in the area are frequent, including the story of a 2,860-pound body—headless and gutted—being found in the hold of a Taiwanese fishing boat. The fishing season for black marlin and sailfish is short, November through December, and charter boats operating from Gove are hard to come by. However, with sufficient lead time, at least three months, you will probably be able to secure one. The only way to do so is to telephone (089) 872-445.

Nhulunbuy is small and isolated. Some say it is the ideal place to live. An oasis of palms and tropical plants, the township is girthed by white, sandy beaches, mangrove swamps, and tropical forest. Much of the immediate countryside is flat. As in Darwin, there are two seasons, the Wet and the Dry. During the coolest months, June and July, the temperature averages about 26 degrees

C (77 degrees F), and in November and December rises to about 32 degrees (90 degrees F).

Because, like much of the territory, the area can be inhospitable, it is recommended that you see it on an organized tour. One of the best is conducted by aboriginal artist Terry Yumbulu and other aboriginal guides. Limited to no more than six people, Terry's three- and four-day tours become an intimate exploration of the area, including a trip to some of the islands off Gove—some of which few whites have ever set foot on.

Apart from visiting ancient burial sites and viewing "galleries" of ancient cave paintings in the Gove area, you will see natural breeding lakes for turtles, crocodiles, and other sea creatures. You may even see some of the giant stingray that inhabit the waters.

(See the Accommodations section at the end of the chapter for places to stay here.)

# *KATHERINE*

Author Neville Shute brought recognition to Central Australia, particularly Alice Springs, with his book *A Town Like Alice.* Like other parts of the Northern Territory, Katherine, 300 km (180 miles) "down the Track" (the Stuart Highway) from Darwin, has also been immortalized in fiction—in Mrs. Aeneas (Jeannie) Gunn's novel *We of the Never-Never,* published in 1908 and made into a film in 1981. A remarkable woman, Jeannie Gunn was the wife of the manager of Elsey Station and the first white woman to set foot in the area.

Like Alice Springs, Katherine began life as a repeater station for the Overland Telegraph. Katherine and Alice Springs are similar in many other ways. They are both centers of the large pastoral industries in their regions, and both have a large aboriginal population. Katherine is a significant grain-growing region, but, unlike the Alice, has not yet had its frontier spirit altered by tourism. As one of Australia's fastest-growing areas, however, with the establishment of the nearby Tindall Royal Australian Air Force Base being a large contributor, it may soon change.

Set on the banks of the Katherine River—named by John McDouall Stuart in 1862 after Katherine Chambers, the daughter of one of his expedition's backers—it was one of the territory's earliest settlements.

The single most popular attraction here is **Katherine Gorge**, actually 13 gorges, 32 km (19 miles) from the town. However, most visitors usually see only the first two.

As you cruise through the first of the gorges in specially designed flat-bottomed boats, past sloping, tree-lined banks, you may feel a little disappointed, wondering what all the fuss is about. But beyond the rock barrier that separates the first from the second gorge (you have to change boats) the mood changes. Here the sides are vertical, rising a sheer 300 feet, and the gorge takes a series of 90-degree turns. Normally the near-three-mile cruise of both gorges ends at the next rocky bar; however, it is possible to go farther into the gorge system.

Because of the land barriers between the gorges, boats usually have to be carried across them during the Dry and left for use—until the Wet, when they are retrieved before the Katherine River turns into a torrent of angry water.

To get to Katherine it is perhaps best to pick up a rental car, preferably a four-wheel drive for off-road exploration, in Darwin. Have it booked to meet you at your hotel or at the airport. Access to Katherine from Kakadu is via the partly paved Kakadu Highway that comes out at Pine Creek, just a few miles north of Katherine.

After a day exploring Katherine Gorge we suggest you drive 100 km (60 miles) farther south to Mataranka to stay at the **Mataranka Homestead**, 7 km (4½ miles) off the Stuart Highway on the Roper Highway.

Established in 1916 by the Northern Territory's Administrator of the day, Dr. Gilruth, as an experimental cattle station, it is here that a replica of the Elsey Station homestead has been built. Nearby are the **Mataranka Thermal Pools**, where the water is a constant 34 degrees C (93 degrees F). A swim in the pools is relaxing and refreshing despite the territory's hot weather. Mataranka is surrounded by a forest of towering paperbark trees and cabbage palms.

## GETTING AROUND
Despite its isolation, getting to the Territory poses few problems. Most visitors, even those headed first to Darwin, come in from the south—that is, from Sydney, Mel-

bourne, or Adelaide—and through Alice Springs, either by air, road, or rail.

Darwin has the territory's only international air facilities (despite the fact that U.S. military aircraft servicing the joint American/Australian base of Pine Gap land at Alice Springs) which mainly services Southeast Asia. The crowded, humid, and inadequate facilities are shared with domestic passengers.

Australia's two major domestic airlines, Ansett and Australian, have regular daily flights to Alice Springs and Darwin from major southern capitals and major secondary ports. Darwin is also serviced daily, with regular flights from Alice Springs and major Southeast Asian cities.

You can expect a flight of between two and three hours from the major southern capitals to Alice Springs and another two hours to Darwin. Ansett, Australian, and East-West Airlines have regular flights to Ayers Rock. Katherine is serviced by flights from Darwin and Alice Springs.

Facilities at all Northern Territory airports are, to say the least, casual and, with few exceptions, crowded.

If you have time it is worth considering rail or road transport into the Territory. Alice Springs is serviced by two direct trains: "The Ghan" from Adelaide and "The Alice" from Sydney. In Queensland you can catch "The Sunlander" from Brisbane to Townsville, connecting there with "The Inlander" west to **Mount Isa**, from where you finish your trip to Darwin by bus.

*The Ghan.* Most rail travellers opt for the new **Ghan**, which, unlike its infamous narrow-gaged predecessor that took up to a week to reach Alice Springs from Adelaide, takes just 24 hours and has all facilities such as dining car, sleepers, etc. A trip on the Ghan is a self-contained adventure where the confinement, along with the common interest of travelling to the Northern Territory, leads to a sharing of personal experience with people from diverse cultures and backgrounds. Many lifelong friendships have been forged after a cross-country journey aboard the Ghan.

Despite fervent efforts by the Northern Territory government in recent years, Alice Springs and Darwin are still not connected by rail.

*Driving.* There are three main roads into the territory: the Stuart Highway from Adelaide, the Barkly from Brisbane via Mount Isa in Queensland, and the Victoria from

Western Australia via Kununurra (for which see the Western Australia chapter). Driving gives you the freedom to visit areas of interest as well as the advantage of staying at each place as long as you wish.

However, the long distances involved—for example, over 1,000 km (600 miles) from Adelaide in South Australia to Alice Springs—can be dangerous if you are unaccustomed to long-distance driving. Also, breakdown problems are compounded by the distances, sometimes over 200 km (120 miles) between garages (roadhouses).

Unfamiliar road conditions, wandering livestock, kangaroos, and roadtrains (massive road transporters hauling up to three trailers laden with livestock or other freight) all pose dangers for driving in the territory.

About two-thirds of the Territory's roads are unpaved, and we suggest that you drive at half the normal highway speed.

Before leaving on a trip contact the local police station for information on road conditions. Some tracks may be closed or restricted to four-wheel-drive vehicles. Also inform someone of your destination and likely time of arrival. Once there, telephone to let them know you have arrived.

The major bus companies—Greyhound, Stateliner, Ansett Pioneer, and Deluxe Coachlines—have regular services linking the territory with all important towns.

## ACCOMMODATIONS REFERENCE

▶ **Ayers Rock Lodge**. Yulara, N.T. 5751. Tel: (089) 56-2170; Telex: 81089.

▶ **Beaufort Hotel**. The Esplanade, **Darwin**, N.T. 5790. Tel: (089) 82-9911; in U.S., (800) 44-UTELL; in Canada, (800) 387-1338; Telex: 85818. An up-market hotel that has its own gym and specialty shops, and houses a business center.

▶ **Darwin Travelodge**. 122 The Esplanade, **Darwin**, N.T. 5790. Tel: (089) 81-5388; in U.S., (800) 44-UTELL; in Canada, (800) 387-1338; Telex: 85273.

▶ **Diamond Beach Hotel Casino**. Girluth Avenue, **Mindil Beach**, N.T. 5790. Tel: (089) 81-7755; Telex: 85214.

▶ **Diplomat Motor Inn**. Corner Hartley Street and Gregory Terrace, **Alice Springs**, N.T. 5750. Tel: (089) 52-8977; Telex: 81044.

▶ **Four Seasons**. Stephens Road, **Alice Springs**, N.T.

5750. Tel: (089) 52-6100; in U.S., (800) 44-UTELL; in Canada, (800) 387-1338; Telex: 81051. A member of the upscale chain.

▶ **Four Seasons Cooinda. Jim Jim Jabiru**, N.T. 5796. Tel: (089) 79-0145; in U.S., (800) 44-UTELL; in Canada, (800) 387-1338; Telex: 85463.

▶ **Four Seasons Darwin.** Dashwood Crescent, **Darwin**, N.T. 5790. Tel: (089) 81-5333; in U.S., (800) 44-UTELL; in Canada, (800) 387-1338; Telex: AA 85309.

▶ **Four Seasons Yulara Resort.** Yulara Drive, **Yulara**, N.T. 5751. Tel: (089) 56-2100; in U.S., (800) 44-UTELL; in Canada, (800) 387-1338; Telex: AA 81367.

▶ **Hideaway Safari Lodge and Motel.** Prospect Road, **Gove**, N.T. 5797. Tel: (089) 87-1833; Telex: 85594DN116. As the name suggests, hidden away from the town center. However, it is close to the airport and provides excellent value for the money.

▶ **Kakadu Holiday Village.** Arnhem Highway, **Kakadu National Park**, N.T. 5796. Tel: (089) 79-0166; Telex: 85732.

▶ **Lasseters Hotel Casino.** Barrett Drive, **Alice Springs**, N.T. 5750. Tel: (089) 52-5066; Telex: 81126.

▶ **Marrakai Apartments.** 93 Smith Street, **Darwin**, N.T. 5790. Tel: (089) 82-3711; Telex: 85502. Fully serviced apartments with rates for long- or short-term stays.

▶ **Mataranka Homestead Tourist Resort. Mataranka**, N.T. 5780. Tel: (089) 75-4544; Telex: 85425.

▶ **Oasis Motel.** 10 Gap Road, **Alice Springs**, N.T. 5750. Tel: (089) 52-1444; Telex: AA 81245. Recently refurbished with upgraded rooms; excellent value for the money.

▶ **Sheraton Alice Springs.** Barrett Drive, **Alice Springs**, N.T. 5750. Tel: (089) 52-8000; in U.S. and Canada, (800) 325-3535; Telex: 81091.

▶ **Sheraton Ayers Rock.** Yulara Drive, **Yulara**, N.T. 5751. Tel: (089) 562-200; in U.S. and Canada, (800) 325-3535; Telex: AA 81108.

▶ **Sheraton Darwin.** 32 Mitchell Street, **Darwin**, N.T. 5790. Tel: (089) 82-0000; in U.S. and Canada, (800) 325-3535; Telex: 85991. Up-market, right in the heart of Darwin.

▶ **Walkabout Hotel.** Westal Street, **Nhulunbuy**, N.T. 5797. Tel: (089) 87-1777; Telex: 85133. Right in the town center. Not the Walkabout Hotel depicted in *Crocodile Dundee*.

# TASMANIA

*By Mike Bingham*

*Mike Bingham, a longtime resident of Tasmania and a member of the Society of Australian Travel Writers, is travel editor of* The Mercury, *Tasmania's largest newspaper, and of its sister publication,* The Sunday Tasmanian.

While the rest of Australia basks in the image of golden beaches, *Crocodile Dundee,* the Outback, and the vitality of Sydney, the island of Tasmania, the smallest and most remote of the states, maintains a laid-back lifestyle, one that belies its brutal and repressive beginnings as a British penal settlement.

Tasmania was discovered by the Dutch explorer Abel Tasman in 1642, but it was ignored by his countrymen, and Tasman's voyage was rated a failure. It was another 130 years before the next European arrived, and not until 1803 that the British established a settlement on the site of the present Hobart in the south of the island; even then they did so only to block any attempt by French explorers to claim it for France, and to gain another dumping ground for convicts.

There were 24 convicts in the first party; over 60,000 more followed before transportation ended here in 1851. Discipline was harsh, with the chain gang, the lash, and the noose always present. Some convicts died trying to escape, others became bushrangers, and still others stowed away on American whalers. One Irish prisoner escaped to become governor of Montana. But most eventually gained their freedom and helped establish the new colony.

Hobart's dock area, Sullivans Cove, rough-and-tumble home to the international whaling fleets of the 19th cen-

tury, retains much of its old charm, though the bustle and
bawdy excitement have long disappeared—except, perhaps, in late December and early January when the city
welcomes the fleet at the end of the Sydney–Hobart yacht
race, one of the world's great ocean classics.

Overlooking one side of the cove is Battery Point, so-
named because of the gun emplacements that protected
the infant colony from French and Russian explorers in
the 19th century. It too was a hive of maritime activity,
filled with shipbuilding yards, chandlers, pubs, and seedy
residential areas. Much of it still stands—now a trendy
area of restored dwellings, craft shops, restaurants, and
historic pubs.

Tasmania, some 200 miles south of the Australian mainland, lacked the industrial base and transport advantages
of Australia's other eastern states, and thus developed
much more slowly. These seeming disadvantages have
produced a lasting benefit, particularly for the visitor,
because, unlike the other states, Tasmania retains superb
and substantial echoes of its colonial past: the penal
settlement at Port Arthur, quaint villages and towns rich
in Georgian architecture, elegant colonial mansions, and
the Hobart port area, Sullivans Cove. Three 19th-century
docks—Victoria Dock, Constitution Dock, and Water-
men's Dock—sit just a few yards from the city's commercial heart, and these days are home to the fishing fleet and
cruising yachts.

Tasmania's total population is small, only 480,000, and
so are its major cities (Hobart has 175,000 inhabitants and
Launceston 70,000). Life here lacks many of the urban
pressures experienced on the mainland. Hobart's city
traffic peak, for example, lasts only for about ten minutes
twice a day, and some city workers still go home during
their one-hour lunch break.

Tasmania's other major attraction, and one even more
enduring than the relics of its colonial beginnings, is the
extraordinary wilderness contained in its 26,000 square
miles. Boasting Australia's oldest conservation authority,
it now has 14 national parks, the largest and most rugged
of which is the **South West National Park**, a World Heritage area. The state has been at the center of fierce
conservation debates in recent years over attempts to
dam its wild rivers and log some of the world's finest
examples of temperate rain forests. Experiencing the wil-

derness, either through a one-day flight from Hobart, a 12-day rafting trip, or a seven-day walk, is one of the best reasons for visiting the state.

Unlike that in the rest of Australia, the scenery is a rapidly changing blend and is frequently spectacular. Less than an hour often separates sandy beaches from craggy mountains, or a city from impenetrable wilderness.

MAJOR INTEREST

Surviving remnants of the colonial past
Wilderness areas and adventure tours

**Hobart**
Sullivans Cove dock area's shops and restaurants
Battery Point area's winding streets
Views from Mount Wellington

**Tasmania outside Hobart**
Old Port Arthur prison settlement
Richmond historic village
Driving tours from Hobart to Launceston
Cradle Mountain–Lake St. Clair National Park
Farm and colonial cottage accommodations
Penny Royal World Heritage Park in Launceston
South West National Park

# The Food and Wine of Tasmania

Tasmania offers chefs an abundance of excellent raw materials. Its seafood—especially crustaceans and mollusks, such as crayfish (which in Australia are lobsters), abalone, oysters, mussels, and scallops—is exported around the world and is of a very high standard. Inland waters contain fine trout, both brown and rainbow. One of the state's newest and most promising industries is the farming of Atlantic salmon and the fabled sea-run trout. Other tasty deep-sea fish well worth trying include trevalla, trevally, stripey trumpeter, and orange roughy.

The cool Tasmanian climate is ideal for growing a wide range of fruits and vegetables; visitors should especially look for berry fruits, such as strawberries, raspberries, and blueberries. The state also is renowned for its dairy foods, the best coming from King Island in the far northwest. Particularly good are the cream, cheddar, and a famous brie, but these can be difficult to obtain because of strong mainland and overseas demand.

Tasmania's lamb, too, is of a high standard, and there is an increasing demand for local game meats such as venison, hare, quail, duck, and spatchcock.

The Tasmanian wine industry is new but very promising. Tasmania has a cooler climate than most grape-growing districts on the mainland, and the resultant wines are elegant and delicately flavored. The best wines are generally produced by the state's big three: Pipers Brook, Heemskerk, and Moorilla Estate. Even so, the term "big" is a relative one, and total production here is still on quite a small scale. Most vineyards don't have much in terms of cellar-door tastings, and the best places to purchase local wines are in the better restaurants and bottleshops. The exception is St. Matthias Vineyard, located in the pretty Tamar Valley to the north of Launceston. Visitors are welcome, and many different Tasmanian wines are available for tasting and purchasing. The best bottleshops are at Aberfeldy Cellars in Hobart, the Royal Oak Hotel in Launceston, and the Gateway Inn in Devonport.

# HOBART
## Sullivans Cove

The water dominates Hobart, as it does any great maritime city, and a tour of Hobart should begin at the docks around Sullivans Cove, which in the 19th century time of whalers and tall-masted trading vessels earned a reputation as one of the busiest and wildest ports in the Pacific. Things are quieter there now, but the port is still alive with fishing vessels, yachts, ships that service Australia's Antarctic bases, and the occasional cruise ship that graces the docks.

The warehouses that line both Salamanca Place and Victoria Dock have found new uses as restaurants, art galleries, and shops for the many skilled craftspeople who have gravitated to Tasmania. There's a street market in Salamanca Place on Saturday mornings, but the best woodwork, jewelry, pottery, and weaving are in the little shops, where visitors can often watch the local artists at work. To gain an idea of the range and quality of their work, visit the Crafts Council of Tasmania Gallery, and

## Hobart

miles

0     ¼

kilometers

0     ⅜

RIVER DERWENT

N

Macquarie Wharf

SULLIVANS COVE

EVANS STREET

HUNTER STREET

Victoria Dock

Constitution Dock

Wharf

Elizabeth Street Pier

Franklin

Watermans Dock

Princes Wharf

CASTRAY ESPLANADE

SALAMANCA PLACE

BATTERY POINT

Van Diemens Land Memorial

■ Folk Museum

Tasmanian ■ Maritime Museum

■ Theatre Royal

CAMPBELL STREET

MARKET PLACE

DUNN STREET

Tasmanian Museum & Art Gallery ■

Town Hall ■

Customs House ■

St. Davids Cathedral ■

St. Davids Park

SANDY BAY ROAD

ELIZABETH STREET

ARGYLE STREET

MURRAY STREET

HARRINGTON STREET

STREET

STREET

STREET

MACQUARIE STREET

DAVEY STREET

COLLINS STREET

LIVERPOOL STREET

■ Anglesea Barracks

the workshops of jewelers **Phill Mason** and **Jon de Jonge**. A particularly interesting art gallery is in the University of Tasmania's Arts School in the renovated IXL jam factory across the road from Victoria Dock.

# The City Center

Hobart's two main thoroughfares, **Davey Street** and **Macquarie Street**, each have more than 30 buildings classified by the National Trust. Particularly worth visiting are the Anglesea Barracks, the oldest military establishment in Australia. It is still used by the Army, and there are tours every Tuesday morning at 11:00. Other fine examples of colonial architecture are the Customs House, St. Davids Cathedral, and the Town Hall.

The **Tasmanian Museum and Art Gallery** houses some outstanding examples of colonial art and furniture, and has interesting displays on Antarctic exploration, Tasmanian aboriginals, and the state's maritime history.

The Theatre Royal (1837), in Campbell Street, described by Sir Laurence Olivier as the "greatest little theatre in the world," is Australia's oldest theater. It was gutted by fire in 1984 but has been totally restored.

# Battery Point

This hodgepodge of winding streets, tiny cottages, grand mansions, restaurants, quaint shops, and old pubs that rises above Salamanca Place is far more easily explored on foot than by car. The area features some fine bed-and-breakfast accommodations in colonial buildings. **Barton Cottage**, built in 1850, is among the most delightful, with its attic bedrooms.

Take a guided walking tour, or pick up a free brochure and find your own way about. As with most of Hobart, the streets are safe, even in the evening. Allow two or three hours for a leisurely stroll, and browse the antique shops en route for colonial bric-a-brac. Battery Point has its own village green—the tiny Arthurs Circus—and the magnificent St. Georges Church, as well as a number of excellent museums.

The **Van Diemens Land Folk Museum**, in a fine colonial mansion built in 1834, is located in Hampden Road. Many of the rooms have been furnished and decorated to reflect the lifestyle of the first settlers, and the outbuildings contain period vehicles and tools. Secheron House, with its wide verandas and classic design, is regarded by many as the best example of Georgian architecture in Hobart. These days it houses the **Maritime Museum**, a vast collection of maritime memorabilia and models covering everything nautical from the whaling days right up to the present.

## Dining in Hobart

Tasmania for many years was considered a backwater when it came to good restaurants, but fortunately that situation has been rectified. Even so, opening hours and standards of service can leave something to be desired.

When it comes to seafood the most famous name in Tasmania is **Mures**. George and Jill Mure established their reputation with Mures Fish House in Battery Point; they now also have a fish center at Victoria Dock, right in the heart of Sullivans Cove. As well as the top-class Mures Upper Deck restaurant, this contains a sushi bar, a bistro, specialty shops, and a fish-processing facility.

**Prossers on the Beach**, located in Sandy Bay (see below), is doing great things with seafood, and has quickly built up a reputation for its innovative menu. The atmosphere here is relaxed elegance, and the view over the water makes it one of Hobart's most appealing daytime restaurants. The ritziest place in town, however, is **Sullivans**, located in the new Sheraton Hobart Hotel (see below). The service is impeccable, and the menu contains a wide range of local dishes as well as recipes that use American grain-fed beef. Also at the more formal end of the scale are **Dear Friends** and the **Revolving Restaurant** at the Wrest Point Hotel-Casino (see below). The latter is worth a visit for the views alone; its weekday businessmen's lunches offer particularly good value.

## Staying in Hobart

The new **Sheraton Hobart**, in Hobart on Davey Street, is the best thing that has happened to the city in the way of accommodations for many years. About 4 km (2½ miles) down the Derwent River from Hobart in the trendy riverside suburb of **Sandy Bay** is the **Wrest Point Hotel Casino**, built 15 years ago and the first casino in Australia. It is indicative of Tasmania's north–south rivalry that Australia's second casino opened a few years later in Launceston in the north: the **Federal Country Club**. Both casinos offer four-star accommodation and are the centers of nightlife in the two cities—if *anything* can really be called nightlife in Tasmania.

Also noteworthy is the recently renovated **Hadleys Hotel** in Hobart. If was from there in 1911 that Norwegian explorer Roald Amundsen telegraphed the world to proclaim his successful expedition to the South Pole.

## Mount Wellington and Mount Nelson

Mount Wellington (about 4,000 feet), Hobart's most famous landmark, is regarded with great fondness by the locals. Its moods vary from brooding and menacing to kindly and protective, and the panoramic view of Hobart is well worth the 30-minute drive to the top.

Less ambitious, but still worthwhile, is the 15-minute drive to the top of Mount Nelson. Apart from the view, there are tearooms and relics of the old signal station used in the communications chain linking Hobart and Port Arthur.

## *DAY TRIPS FROM HOBART*
### Port Arthur

Tasmania, or Van Diemen's Land, as it was known until 1856, was initially settled as a penal colony, and the best-known of the old prison settlements is Port Arthur, established in 1830.

If visitors to Tasmania see no other attraction, they should at least experience the eerie serenity and stark beauty of Port Arthur, which is 110 km (70 miles) southeast of Hobart. Cross the Tasman Bridge from the city center and follow the Arthur Highway. Allow 90 minutes for the drive along the winding road. A few minutes in the solitary-confinement cell of the Model Prison is sufficient to know what it must have been like to spend half a lifetime or more at His Majesty's pleasure in one of the world's most dehumanizing outposts. It's quite easy to spend a day wandering around the ruins and restored buildings—the asylum, church, penitentiary, commandant's house, hospital, and so forth—and there are also boat trips to the Isle of the Dead, where nearly 2,000 convicts and free settlers were buried on a remarkably small piece of land.

Also worth seeing in the area is the **Remarkable Cave**. This cave, part of a stunningly rugged coastline on the Tasman Peninsula, faces the Tasman Sea and is reached by a steep flight of steps from the headland above. Even when the sea seems relatively calm elsewhere, it still "boils" into the cave. Nearby **Eaglehawk Neck** is a narrow stretch of land connecting the Tasman Peninsula to the Tasmanian mainland. Convicts attempting to escape from the penal settlement at Port Arthur had the option of swimming through cold, rough seas over considerable distances or attempting to elude the dogs and guards here at the Neck; none is known to have escaped. On Sundays it is worth stopping off at the **Lufra Hotel** on Eaglehawk Neck for the "craybake"—a lunch of freshly cooked lobster. (For accommodations in the Port Arthur area, see Colonial Cottages, below.)

# Richmond

Richmond; 27 km (16 miles) northeast of Hobart, was founded in 1824 as a stopping point on the old road from Hobart to Port Arthur, and it quickly became one of the colony's most important rural centers. In a state that has many charming historic villages, Richmond is perhaps the most charming, and certainly the best preserved.

The convict-built **Richmond Bridge** is the oldest in Australia. Local legend has it that the bridge is haunted by the ghost of a particularly harsh overseer who was murdered there by convicts and thrown into the river.

Sandstone cottages, Georgian mansions, and Gothic churches abound. Of particular interest is the Richmond jail, which predates anything at Port Arthur by about five years. Many of the other old buildings have been restored as private homes, shops, and art galleries. Richmond is second only to Hobart's Salamanca Place for those interested in arts and crafts. **Saddlers Court Gallery** is worth visiting for its excellent selection of paintings by Tas-

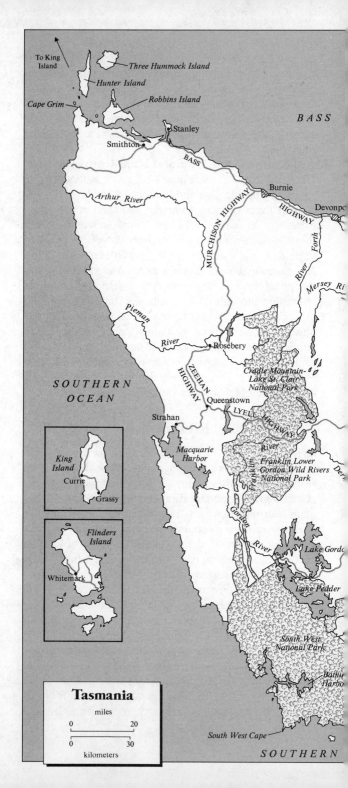

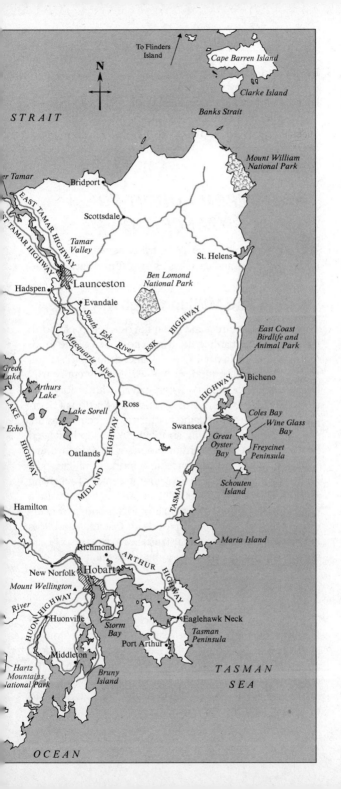

manian artists, and for the opportunity it provides to examine and buy work by two of the state's best potters, Les Blakebrough and Derek Smith.

**Prospect House** makes wonderful use of local game, and also offers accommodations in a colonial-style building.

# FROM HOBART TO LAUNCESTON

There are a number of ways to travel between the state's two major cities, and each has its own attractions:

## The Midland Highway

This is the most direct and by far the quickest route north to Launceston, enabling the trip to be done in little more than two hours. It would be a shame, though, to stay on the fast lane of the modern highway for the entire trip, because some of the byways are paved with history. The town of **Oatlands** has Australia's largest collection of Georgian architecture, and gained notoriety last century as the starting point of the futile aboriginal roundup instigated by Governor George Arthur (founder of Port Arthur).

Farther north is **Ross**, once an important military post and coaching stop. These days it is the center of a thriving wool industry but nonetheless a sleepy town with a convict-built bridge to rival that of Richmond, and many other relics of its colonial past. Both Oatlands and Ross are classified by the National Trust. Leave five or six hours for this trip if you want to do some sightseeing.

## The East Coast

Travelling from Hobart to Launceston via the Tasman Highway on the east coast extends the driving time to about five or six hours, and there's not as much history along this route. The compensation is the beauty of the coastline, particularly in the vicinity of the Freycinet Peninsula and St. Helens. If you've got the time, a detour to Coles Bay and the **Freycinet Peninsula National Park** is well worthwhile. The wallabies will eat out of your hand, and there are many hiking trails of varying duration and difficulty. Especially appealing is the walk to **Wine Glass Bay**—about an hour each way.

If you want to do any serious walking or sightseeing on the east coast, the trip to Launceston will take more than a day. Accommodation is available in a number of the coastal towns near the park. There are reasonable two- and three-star motels and, especially around **Swansea**, some excellent colonial-cottage accommodations, such as **Rose Cottage**.

Nearby **Bicheno**, which began its existence in 1803 as a port for sealers and whalers, is another attractive seaside town, with fine beaches and comfortable motels; the **Beachfront Motel** (Tel: 003-751-111) organizes "cray-bakes" for guests. Just outside Bicheno is the **East Coast Birdlife and Animal Park**, set in natural coastal bushland. There are wallabies and kangaroos to hand-feed, emus, native birds, and, of course, Tasmanian devils—but not to handfeed.

# The West Coast

It is possible also to travel between Hobart and Launceston via **Queenstown** on Tasmania's wild west coast and Burnie on the northwest coast. This trip is certainly much longer than a day trip, though; also, the weather can be far from hospitable and the driving conditions hazardous. If you do go this way, stay overnight at **Queenstown** or nearby Strahan and take the river cruise along the Gordon River and Macquarie Harbour. It's one of the best ways of experiencing at first hand just what the wilderness the conservationists fought for is all about.

Near Queenstown is the **Cradle Mountain–Lake St. Clair National Park. Cradle Mountain Lodge**, at the northern end of the vast park, offers comfortable log-cabin-style accommodations on the edge of the wilderness. It's lights-out at 11:00 when the generator cuts off, but the compensations are enormous: hearty, fireside meals in the dining room and abundant wildlife. Each night a smorgasbord of fresh fruit and vegetables lures opossums, wallabies, and even the occasional Tasmanian devil to feast under a spotlight outside the lodge.

## Staying out on the Island

The best of the conventional accommodations in Tasmania are offered by the **Four Seasons Group** and the **Innkeepers Group**, both of which list moderate to first-class properties throughout Tasmania.

Another option is to spend a night or two at a host farm. Many are listed with Homehost Tasmania Propriety, Ltd. (P.O. Box 550, Rosny Park, Tasmania 7018. Tel: 002-445-442); for about A$45 per couple they provide lodging and a cooked breakfast. Most of the farms are small—50 to 200 acres—and operate a mix of crops, dairying, and livestock for meat production. Some, like **Holly Tree Farm** at Middleton, 40 minutes south of Hobart, also produce fruit and flowers on a small scale. A herd of tame donkeys, two pet sheep, chickens, ducks, and rabbits in the bottom paddock are a bonus for visitors. Holly Tree Farm has two guest rooms, both with en-suite facilities, and, as at many of the farms in the group, your hosts will prepare a hearty country dinner if you ask.

## *LAUNCESTON AND THE NORTH*

Launceston, founded in 1805, is Tasmania's second largest and second oldest city. It rapidly developed into a river port of considerable importance, and into the commercial center of a rich agricultural district.

The town has magnificent public and private gardens, including the 30-acre City Park, with its enormous oaks and elms dating back to the 1820s. There are also many buildings to delight those interested in history and grand architecture. The **Queen Victoria Museum and Art Gallery**, opened in 1891, was built to celebrate the queen's Jubilee. It houses outstanding exhibitions of Tasmanian flora and fauna, aboriginal and convict relics, and both early and contemporary art. There is also a Chinese joss house that was built during the mining boom last century and was donated to the museum by the Chinese families of northeastern Tasmania.

The city's Customs House is considered by many to be its most attractive building, and though it isn't open to the public its magnificence is a reminder of the days when

Launceston was a prosperous port. The **Old Umbrella Shop**, the last genuine period shop in Tasmania, was built entirely from Tasmanian blackwood in the 1860s. As well as housing a fine collection of umbrellas not for sale, the shop sells umbrellas and other knickknacks and serves as an information center for the National Trust.

Launceston's **Penny Royal World** complex is one of Tasmania's most imaginative tourism creations. A working corn mill that was originally located near Cressy, south of Launceston, was moved stone by stone and reconstructed at Launceston. The complex also has a 19th-century gunpowder mill, a cannon foundry, a restored tramway, a replica paddle steamer, a museum, and a lake complete with old ships. There are accommodations on the grounds. (There are also four-star accommodations here at the **Federal Country Club**, Launceston's casino.)

The reputation of Launceston's restaurants has slipped a bit in recent years, particularly in comparison with those in Hobart, but there is still some very good food to be had here. The best seafood is at **Shrimps**; **Rowells** offers French cuisine in a reasonably formal atmosphere. (Both are in George Street in the city center and are moderately expensive by Tasmanian standards, moderate by mainland standards.) **The Gorge**, in a delightful setting in the Cataract Gorge not far from the center of Launceston, offers everything from a quick snack to a formal meal.

## Colonial Cottages

In keeping with its reputation as Australia's most history-conscious state, Tasmania has developed a fine network of self-contained accommodations based in colonial cottages. Typical is **Ivy Cottage**, in the center of Launceston. It has two bedrooms, a living room, a fully equipped kitchen, and a bathroom. The shelves are lined with 19th-century books and bric-a-brac, and guests are encouraged to make use of the lovely vegetable garden in the back.

Other cottages of merit include **Molecombe Cottage** in Launceston, **Wagner Cottage** and **Rose Cottage** near Swansea on the East Coast, and **Emma's Cottage** at Hamilton, and there are many more around the state. They may not have all the facilities of international-standard hotels, and the floors may sometimes creak, but if you want to stay somewhere with a bit of atmosphere and a lived-in feeling they are hard to beat.

## Around Launceston

Launceston is worth using as a base for a few days to visit the many historic villages in the north. **Evandale**, 18 km (11 miles) south of Launceston, and **Hadspen**, 11 km (7 miles) west of Launceston, are both small settlements that still retain much of their 19th-century charm. Browse for antiques, and enjoy the leisurely pace of life.

**Clarendon**, near Evandale, is one of Australia's most magnificent Georgian mansions. Built in 1838 as a residence for the wealthy merchant James Cox, it is now owned by the National Trust, which is progressively restoring the house and surroundings to their full 19th-century grandeur. It is open to the public daily except during July.

**Entally House**, at Hadspen, just a few miles west of Launceston, is a delightful whitewashed country house set among beautiful gardens and interesting outbuildings, including a bluestone church and a two-story coach house. Entally was built in 1820 by Thomas Reibey, whose mother arrived in Sydney as a 13-year-old convict and became a highly successful businesswoman. His son, also named Thomas, was Premier of Tasmania, a fact that clearly demonstrates how quickly descendants of convicts could gain high standing in colonies, which lacked the rigid social structure of their English homeland.

## *THE NORTHWEST COAST*

Tasmania's northwest coast is a rich agricultural area that produces fine fruit and vegetables and top-class dairy foods. Of particular interest is **Stanley**, the oldest settlement in the northwest, founded in 1826 as the headquarters for the Van Diemens Land Company, a mighty London-based outfit set up to breed fine-wool sheep in the colony. The town is dominated by the Nut, a huge volcanic outcrop that these days can be reached by cable car. In town are many fine examples of colonial architecture, as well as some excellent craft shops.

**Cape Grim**, on the northwestern extremity of Tasmania, is reputed to have the cleanest air in the world, and is used by scientists as a monitoring station to provide baseline data for experiments on atmospheric pollution worldwide.

## THE WILDERNESS

You don't have to be an experienced backpacker or mountain-climber to experience and enjoy Tasmania's wilderness areas. Access can be as quick and comfortable as a one-day aerial outing, including transfers to and from your hotel, a cruise on a remote harbor, and a barbecue.

The **South West National Park**, listed as a World Heritage area, is a 40-minute flight from Hobart by light plane. Par-Avion Wilderness Tours operates a day trip that begins with a flight along the rugged southern coast before landing near the shores of Bathurst Harbour. A professional guide will be on hand to explain the wilderness and to arrange a boat tour through the crisp clean air and awesome silence of this harbor, surrounded by mountain ranges. All waterproof and safety gear are provided, as is a barbecue lunch. The return flight goes over the spectacular Federation Peak and makes its way back to Hobart over the farms of the Huon Valley. The tour, which has guests back in their Hobart hotels by 5:00 P.M., costs A$220. Contact Par-Avion Wilderness Tours, Cambridge Aerodrome, Hobart; Tel: (002) 48-5390.

Also from Hobart, Tasair operates a two-hour flight over the southwest, with a landing on a remote ocean beach. Ideal for those with limited time, the round trip takes less than three hours and costs A$98. Contact Tasair, Cambridge Aerodrome, Hobart; Tel: (002) 48-5088.

The ultimate wilderness experiences—rafting down the wild Franklin River, or trekking into the national park—are only for those with a week or ten days to spare. Open Spaces, a Hobart company, has a four-day trip that begins with a floatplane flight from Strahan to the Lower Gordon River, followed by a walk through a rain forest to the Franklin River, and a chance to test your **river rafting** skills. Tours leave weekly from November to April and the all-inclusive cost is A$580. Contact Open Spaces, 28 Criterion Street, Hobart; Tel: (002) 31-0983.

Open Spaces also conducts a series of one-day wilderness tours from Hobart. The minimum number of passengers is two. One such tour is through the **Hartz Mountains National Park**, south of Hobart. It includes a walk to the summit of Mt. Hartz for a sweeping view of the southwest wilderness. Transport to and from Hobart, and lunch, is included in the A$49 cost. The tours leave at 8:30 A.M. and return by 6:00 P.M. They operate from November to April.

Tasmania's rivers and lakes, many within two hours' drive of Hobart and Launceston, provide good **trout fishing**. The majority of the highland lakes have shallow edges and fish can be seen feeding in water only a few inches deep. **London Lakes** in the center of the state are Australia's largest privately owned trout-fishing waters, and the well-stocked lakes are a delight for fly fishing. The accommodation, limited to ten people, is first-class, at an all-inclusive A$264 a day. Limo and helicopter transfers are available from Devonport, Launceston, and Hobart airports. (**London Lakes Fly Fishers Lodge**, Post Office, Bronte Park; Tel: 002-89-1159.)

## GETTING AROUND

Tasmania is one hour by air from Melbourne; direct flights from Sydney take about 90 minutes. Qantas operates a once-weekly service from Auckland to Hobart via Melbourne (Mondays); and Air New Zealand operates between Christchurch and Hobart on Saturdays.

The island has two major jet airports—at Hobart and Launceston—as well as smaller airports at Burnie and Devonport on the northwest coast. There are daily flights connecting all of these with Melbourne, while Hobart and Launceston are also linked to Sydney.

Other access to the state is provided by the *Abel Tasman,* an overnight vehicular ferry service that plies between Melbourne and Devonport. All accommodation is in cabins, and there are a number of restaurants and entertainment areas on board.

Late summer and autumn are the best times to visit Tasmania, as well as early February when schools reopen and accommodation problems disappear. The temperature varies around the island: The east coast is generally the warmest and driest, and the west coast and central highlands are often the coldest and certainly the wettest. Many North Americans who have visited Tasmania compare the climate in Hobart and Launceston with that of Seattle in the United States and Vancouver in British Columbia, Canada.

Summer temperatures can climb to the mid to high 20s C (high 70s to the low 80s F), and the usually dry autumns peak at about 18 or 19 degrees C (65 degrees F). Temperatures in winter can drop to below freezing at night, especially in the highlands, but during the day they range from about 12 to 14 degrees C (53 to 60 degrees F). Nights are cool year-round, however, and it is advisable to have a light jacket or sweater handy. In the wilderness areas, be prepared for sudden changes in the weather.

The roads in Tasmania are good but, taxis apart, the public transport system is poor, so plan on renting a car. In an island just 200 miles from north to south, and just a little bit wider, driving is fun.

Gasoline prices in Tasmania are among Australia's highest at about A$.65 a liter, but the compactness of the island lessens the impact on the wallet. Launceston in the north is only a two-hour drive from Hobart in the south. Hobart to Strahan on the rugged west coast is about four and a half hours, Hobart to Port Arthur on the Tasman Peninsula is about 90 minutes, and Hobart to the historic village of Richmond is a mere 25 minutes.

## ACCOMMODATIONS REFERENCE

▶ **Barton Cottage**. 72 Hampden Road, **Battery Point**, Tasmania 7004. Tel: (002) 236-808.

▶ **Cradle Mountain Lodge. Cradle Mountain**, Tasmania 7306. Tel: (004) 921-303.

▶ **Emma's Cottage**. "Uralla," Main Road, **Hamilton**. Tasmania 7460. Tel: (002) 863-270.

▶ **Federal Country Club Hotel**. Country Club Avenue, Prospectvale, **Launceston**, Tasmania 7250. Tel: (003) 448-855.

▶ **Four Seasons Great Northern Motor Inn**. 3 Earl Street, **Launceston**, Tasmania 7250. Tel: (003) 319-999; in U.S., (800) 654-9153; in Canada, (800) 644-9058; Telex: AA 58877.

▶ **Hadley's Hotel**. 34 Murray Street, **Hobart**, Tasmania 7000. Tel: (002) 234-355; Telex: AA 58355.

▶ **Holly Tree Farm. Middleton**, Tasmania 7163. Tel: (002) 921-680.

▶ **Innkeepers Colonial Motor Inn**. 31 Elizabeth Street,

Launceston, Tasmania 7250. Tel: (003) 316-588; in U.S., (800) 44-UTELL; in Canada, (800) 387-1338; Telex: AA 58667.

▶ **Innkeepers Penny Royal Watermill.** 47 Patterson Street, **Launceston,** Tasmania 7250. Tel: (003) 316-699; in U.S., (800) 44-UTELL; in Canada, (800) 387-1338; Telex: AA 58605.

▶ **Ivy Cottage.** 17 York Street, **Launceston,** Tasmania 7250. Tel: (003) 318-431.

▶ **Molecombe Cottage.** 23 Kenyon Street, **Newstead** (Launceston), Tasmania 7250. Tel: (003) 311-355 or 317-481.

▶ **Prospect House. Richmond,** Tasmania 7025. Tel: (002) 622-207.

▶ **Rose Cottage. Lisdillon,** Tasmania 7190. Tel: (002) 578-331.

▶ **Sheraton Hobart Hotel.** 1 Davey Street, **Hobart,** Tasmania 7000. Tel: (002) 234-499; in U.S., (800) 325-3535; Telex: AA 58037.

▶ **Wagner Cottage. Swansea,** Tasmania 7190. Tel: (002) 577-576.

▶ **Wrest Point Hotel Casino.** 410 Sandy Bay Road, **Sandy Bay** (Hobart), Tasmania 7000. Tel: (002) 250 112; in U.S., (800) 44-UTELL; in Canada, (800) 387-1338; Telex: AA 58115.

# MELBOURNE AND VICTORIA

*By Ian Marshman*

*Ian Marshman, a lifetime resident of Melbourne, is deputy editor of* Traveltrade, *the country's leading travel-industry publication, and has hosted his own travel-oriented radio talk show. He is the author of a major study of tourism in Australia.*

**M**arvellous Melbourne, Australia's industrial, financial, and commercial heart, is also one of the world's most intact Victorian cities. Dubbed by newspapers in Europe and North America as "marvellous" in the 1880s, Melbourne at that time had the most rapid growth of any city in the Western World.

From a few ragged tents and small sheep runs in the 1840s, the city expanded to stage the Great Exhibition of 1888, which celebrated the first century of Australia's European settlement. The catalyst for the growth was the discovery of gold in 1854 at Ballarat and Bendigo in Victoria, the biggest gold rush the world had then experienced. As the mines and creeks of California became increasingly less lucrative, the richest alluvial and surface gold-mining regions ever discovered lured miners to Victoria from North America, Europe, and China.

Melbourne's boom lasted until the great crash of the 1890s, an event that far exceeded the financial crises of

1929 and 1987. The boom over, Melbourne never rivaled New York or London as a world capital, but evolved instead into a 20th-century metropolis that still retains much of the charm of the previous century; i.e., an architecture and overall visual style that reflect gold-generated wealth and the boom. Gothic cathedrals reminiscent of Paris or Vienna, steel and glass skyscrapers, and rivers like European canals create a stylish and beautiful city.

Melbourne is also the gateway to Phillip Island, with its highly entertaining "Penguin Parade," and the spectacular Great Ocean Road. The "most European" of Australia's cities, Melbourne is home to nearly 3 million people who have moved here from throughout the world to enjoy its temperate climate and, in contrast to its slightly larger rival, Sydney, a quiet, undemanding lifestyle.

Melbourne's proximity to the great Australian wilderness allows easy access to snow-covered mountains in winter and rolling surf in summer.

### MAJOR INTEREST

**Melbourne**
Victorian-era terrace houses with iron-lacework verandas
Quiet, small-town ambience
Cosmopolitan ethnic makeup, restaurants

**Victoria outside Melbourne**
Phillip Island: the Penguin Parade, wildlife, beaches
The Great Ocean Road's scenery and nature

## *MELBOURNE*

Nearly every writer who has attempted to capture on paper the spirit of Melbourne has devoted pages to space: space to move and breathe clean fresh air and enjoy a personal freedom not common in most of the modern world. Despite its size and key role as a business and industrial center, the city has retained the feel of an outsized country town. It's easy to feel at home in Melbourne. The people are friendly, the pace is slow, the restaurants are good, the weather is temperate. Life seems easy.

Melbourne is Australia's Detroit, with five vehicle manufacturers; it's the center of the oil and gas industry, with refineries and shipping; it's the country's biggest shipping terminal; and it's the retail heart of the country. It was the first Australian landfall for the millions who came from Europe via South Africa's Cape of Good Hope, and the destination for nearly one million postwar immigrants fleeing a war-devastated Europe; more recently thousands have made a new home in its suburbs as an alternative to the rice fields and sprawling cities of Southeast Asia. There are nearly a hundred languages in daily use here, but every person you meet will say "G'day," and all will extoll the virtues of their hometown.

Melbourne was Australia's capital from 1901 to 1927, and over the years has been host to hundreds of thousands of American troops—and to General Douglas MacArthur, who initially based his headquarters here for the fight to regain the Philippines and Singapore during World War II.

Today Melbourne is a hub of the Australian film industry (albeit with rivals in Sydney and Adelaide), the center of Australian fashion and art, and the only city in the world to grant its citizens a public holiday to attend a horse race. The **Melbourne Cup**, staged since 1867, carries more than A$1,000,000 prize money, and is the major attraction of a racing carnival the first week of each November, with the big race at Flemington on Tuesday. It's "anything goes" on racing day, as people dress to the nines in everything from top hats to beachwear and don't mind guzzling Champagne at lavish parking-lot parties. Not even the U.S. presidential elections, held on the same day, divert attention from the big race.

The first Melburnian was John Batman (the Australian-born son of a transported English convict), who purchased much of the region from local aboriginal tribes for a handful of beads and trinkets. It was never a destination for convicts, but settled by people who chose it as a home in the wake of the gold rush and 19th-century land booms. The boom mentality is still in evidence, with most residents choosing to sell and buy their own homes at auctions, a system of land transfer uncommon outside Australia. Sociologists say the auction system reflects Melburnians' propensity to take a gamble, to let it ride—even with their homes. It often seems that little has changed

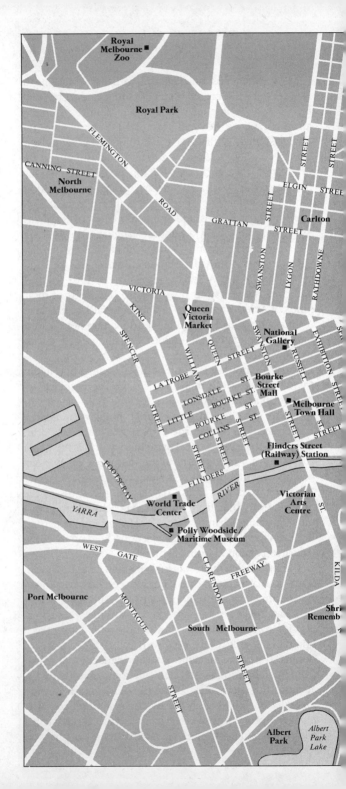

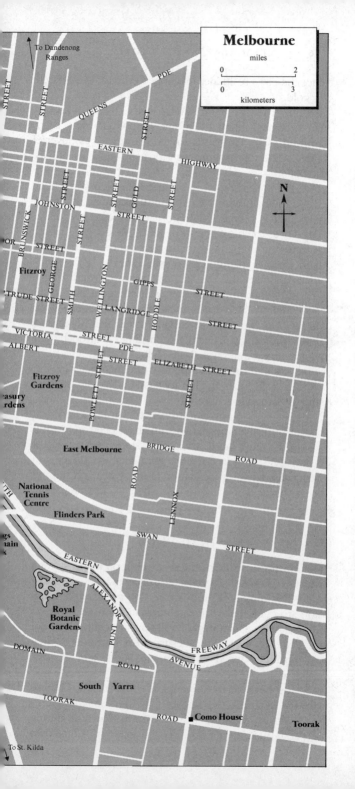

since the city's residents abandoned everything to search for gold.

Melbourne is sometimes described as the most Australian of cities, being the home of both Foster's lager (brewed at the Carlton & United Brewery, on Bouverie Street at the top end of Swanston) and Australian Rules football.

"Aussie Rules footy" is a rugged modern version of Gaelic football, which arrived in Australia via the gold-fields and is played from February to September each year. Try to catch a game at the MCG (Melbourne Cricket Ground), an immense stadium near the central business district that can handle 120,000-plus crowds.

Like all cities, this one has its famous sons and daughters. In Melbourne's case they include opera star Dame Nellie Melba (1861–1931); rock stars Olivia Newton-John, Men at Work, and Little River Band; actors Mel Gibson and Sigrid Thornton; business tycoon Rupert Murdoch; and Wimbledon winner Pat Cash. Melbourne has also been home to some famous temporary residents, including the young naval officer Lyndon Johnson and Prince Charles, who went to school here.

Melbourne's trams, reminiscent of San Francisco's cable cars, travel a huge network and have been an integral part of the city's public transport system for most of this century. It's easy to catch a tram: Signal the driver at a designated stop, but be careful of cars when you step off the curbside, and even more so when you leave the tram.

# In the City

Melbourne is a fully planned city built on a grid system, with the commercial section measuring exactly one square mile. The central city too is based on a grid, with Swanston Street on the north/south axis and Bourke Street on the east/west axis. Bourke is the major retail street, but the better shops and arcades front Collins Street. **Chinatown**, with its dozens of restaurants, is only a block away on Little Bourke Street.

In the heart of this precinct the **Museum of Chinese History** captures the impact that Chinese immigrants have had on Australia, from the earliest arrivals during the gold rush to the traders who make up Chinatown today. The city's major boulevard, St. Kilda Road, begins just south of Swanston Street.

From the center of the city, a number 8 tram will take you to **South Yarra**'s rows of terrace houses, with their verandas covered in cast-iron lace, and Toorak, the neighborhood that is home to some of Australia's wealthiest residents.

**St. Kilda Beach** is 6 km (3¾ miles) south of Flinders Street Station, the sandstone edifice that dominates the southern gateway to the commercial district. The trip to the beach takes about 20 minutes on a number 15 or 16 tram. (You can ride a tram all day in Melbourne for A$2–$3.) From its position as the city's premier suburb a century ago, **St. Kilda** regressed into Melbourne's red-light area in the 1970s, with a high incidence of drug-related street crime. However, in more recent times St. Kilda has been gentrified, and now offers a cosmopolitan mix of the bohemian and the trendy with its ethnic restaurants, 19th-century mansions converted into chic apartments, and palm-studded beach-front parks that give it an Art Deco atmosphere. St. Kilda's Acland Street is great for a Sunday stroll; it has dozens of Jewish cake shops and intellectual bookshops. Craftsmen sell their work each Sunday on the beach-front Esplanade, and it's common to find artists capturing St. Kilda on canvas.

A highlight of a visit to the city is the famous **Royal Melbourne Zoo**, which displays animals in their natural habitat. The zoo, housing about 4,000 species, is the third oldest in the world (dating to 1857) and is in Royal Park, only a few minutes north of the city center in the suburb of Parkville. The most popular animal resident is Mzuri, the world's first gorilla born as a result of artificial insemination. There is a bear enclosure and the world's biggest butterfly house, where visitors stroll through a lush tropical jungle as the butterflies fly free around them. The zoo is a great place to see native Australian species: kangaroos, emus, wombats, platypuses, and koalas—animals that won't be found anywhere else in Melbourne.

## Parks

Melbourne's parks constitute one of the biggest urban networks anywhere and range from the open sports fields of Royal Park to the 102.5-acre **Royal Botanic Gar-**

dens. The Botanic, on the southern banks of the Yarra River, is home to 12,000 plant species and plenty of ducks and other wildlife. The adjoining Fitzroy and Treasury gardens at the eastern end of Flinders and Collins streets provide a place of solitude in the heart of the city. Albert Park Lake in South Melbourne is a former swamp turned into a home for ducks, black swans, and small yachts.

One of the newest attractions in town is the **National Tennis Centre** in Flinders Park, just southeast of the city center, home of the Australian Open. The center is also used to stage rock concerts and other big events and is considered one of the best tennis facilities in existence.

Historic attractions in Melbourne worth a stop include the sailing ship *Polly Woodside* and the **Melbourne Maritime Museum,** on the south bank of the river opposite the World Trade Centre. The deep-water, square-rigged ship is one of the last of its type still afloat.

A good way to see the Port of Melbourne is from the decks of the 1933 steam tug *Wattle,* which cruises from 11 North Wharf on Flinders Street.

Melbourne was once a wealthy city, and many historic mansions remain from the time when gold-rich miners and wool-wealthy graziers built city houses to rival any in Europe and North America. **Como,** in South Yarra, was the home of a single family for more than a century. It is a fine example of the elegant, iron-lace-fronted homes that housed the privileged during the last century. Its acres of Victorian gardens and authentic period furnishings, including many of the family's possessions, accurately capture the colonial period. **Ripponlea** in Elsternwick (south out of the city via St. Kilda Road) is an even grander house, built in the Romanesque style with a huge fernery set in nearly ten acres of gardens.

The Shrine of Remembrance in King's Domain park dominates St. Kilda Road and provides the backdrop to the city's commercial district as you look south. It was built as a memorial to World War I soldiers, but the Acropolis-type structure has become a permanent reminder of the horrors of war. Some of the best views of the city can be seen from its balconies (a favorite of photographers); the names of all of Australia's war dead are inscribed on its granite walls.

# The Arts

More contemporary attractions include the **Victorian Arts Centre and National Gallery** complex on the south bank of the Yarra, across from Flinders Street Station. The gallery, housed in the controversial building that from St. Kilda Road looks rather like a jail, houses Australia's most famous collections, including the best known works of Australian artists Tom Roberts, Arthur Streeton, William Dobell, Russell Drysdale, Sidney Nolan, and Frederick McCubbin. (Melbourne's inner eastern suburbs formed the scenic backdrop that motivated many of these artists to create the so-called Heidelberg school-style last century.) The gallery also houses works by Picasso, Renoir, Turner, Degas, Van Gogh, and Constable in its three main courts. Leonard French's spectacular stained-glass roof, the largest in the world, stretches over the Great Hall.

The main theater building is topped by a spire (which critics say makes the whole center look as if it were still under construction), and the Concert Hall is housed in the circular (and mostly underground) building closest to the river. The 2,000-seat hall is the home of the Melbourne Symphony Orchestra and is also used for major theater productions and concerts. The entire complex generates considerable comment, with architecture critics sometimes claiming it offers on the inside what the Sydney Opera House does outside (what a pity they didn't get together). The center stages a wide range of productions; tickets can be purchased from the ticket office or through the BASS (for Best Available Seating Service) booking agency. Half-price theater tickets for "same-day" performances can often be purchased at the half-tix booth in the Bourke Street Mall off Swanston. The Arts Centre complex also includes the Performing Arts Museum, with over a quarter of a million objects of performing-arts memorabilia on view, as well as an extensive video library.

Melbourne has many commercial galleries, perhaps the most fascinating of which is the **Aboriginal Artists Gallery** at 12 Liverpool Street, which displays and sells both traditional and contemporary aboriginal art.

The collection includes examples of Dreamtime art, the time before time that Australia's aboriginals believe influences all life today. Sculptures range from traditional "totem poles" to modern interpretations of subjects influential on aboriginal culture. Recent works often have a political theme. The museum also has an extensive collection of artifacts, books, musical instruments, such as the didgeridoo (a hollow log that is finely hewn to produce the haunted sound of the Outback), textiles, and posters.

The **Meat Market Craft Centre** in Northern Melbourne houses the Victorian State Craft Collection and operates as a resource and information center for artists. Its unique souvenir shop displays contemporary work by 450 local craftspeople in several mediums, including ceramics, pottery, glass, and wood, and there is a range of jewelry. The superbly restored Meat Market displays craft of almost every kind and houses frequently changing exhibitions.

Another good spot to shop for art and crafts is the **Queen Victoria Antique Arts and Crafts Centre**, a complex of laneways and old warehouses with more than 100 traders, located off Franklin Street near the Queen Victoria market.

## Melbourne's Lifestyle

It is nonetheless Melbourne's style and ambience that most visitors remember, from its elegant, lovingly restored pubs to its superb restaurants (there may be more restaurants per person in Melbourne than any other city in the world, except perhaps Paris), and its gracious manners. It has to be said, too, that the other side of Melbourne's Old-World and unhurried style is that it does not have the street life or nightlife of a Paris or New York; you have to make your own fun here.

A good way to start picking up the "vibes" is the **Colonial Tramcar Restaurant**, a 1927 tram converted into a stylish mobile restaurant. Its route passes through the city's best suburbs and the commercial district (it is a good idea to reserve at least a couple of days in advance; Tel: 596-6500). The train departs from Nolan Street, next to the National Gallery.

# Melbourne's Pubs

One of the best ways to experience Melbourne and mix in with the locals is at a pub. All Australian cities have pubs, heaven knows, but in Melbourne they are different. The city has never permitted bars that don't offer food and accommodation, and it is only in recent years that the sale of liquor has even been permitted in most restaurants. So the pubs—almost all are called "hotels"—have emerged as the focus of entertainment in the city.

They range from those that have barely changed since the days when they hosted huge crowds prior to closing the doors at 6:00 P.M. each afternoon to those that specialize in high-class food service and chic decor. In between are the suburban watering holes, sometimes described as beer factories surrounded by parking lots, and the **Melbourne pub circuit**, a series of pubs that provide various kinds of musical entertainment. The circuit, the birthplace of several bands and artists who have gone on to be worldwide stars—including AC/DC, the Bee Gees, and Olivia Newton-John—is an informal grouping, with establishments entering and dropping out on a regular basis. At any time there are about 50 pubs within 5 km (3 miles) of the commercial district. They feature a wide range of music, including jazz, folk, country and western (in Melbourne it's mostly American-style C&W), and even classical. The daily papers, particularly Friday's edition of the *Age,* offer the best guide to what is happening on the circuit.

The most interesting pubs are found in the inner city suburbs of Carlton, Fitzroy, Albert Park, South Melbourne, and Prahran. It's here that Melbourne people gather to discuss the events that really matter in this city: politics and football (cricket in summer). The best way to get to one of the pubs is by cab, as walking in most of the areas is not recommended after dark. Besides, temperatures here often fall below freezing from March through October.

The **Lemon Tree**, north of the city at 10 Grattan Street in Carlton, specializes in wine, seafood, and vocal patrons. It is a favorite of the literary set and a good spot to talk left-wing politics. **The Royal Oak Hotel** at 527 Bridge Road, Richmond, has a huge atrium, a small beer garden, and a wide selection of wines; there's often a small classical trio or a pianist playing here. **The Red Eagle Hotel**, on 111 Victoria Avenue in Albert Park, is the type of place where owning a Porsche helps conversation. The Art Deco-style **Botanical Hotel** at 169 Domain Road offers Melbourne's most comprehensive wine list. The **Fawkner Club** at 52 Toorak Road is the best spot in the city to sit outside, enjoy a cool drink, and eat a big steak. The place to really find Melbourne at play is the **Loaded Dog Pub and Brewery**, a North Fitzroy landmark known to every cab driver in the city. Its claim to fame is more than 200 brands of beer and a live-music policy that ranges from new wave to 1950s-style rock and roll. It's always crowded, loud, and fun. Similar in style and usually even louder are the **Star** in Clarendon Street in South Melbourne and the **Roxy**, just around the corner.

# Dining in Melbourne

Melbourne is very big on the good life. Its residents keep more than 2,000 restaurants in business. If you decide to eat at a non-hotel restaurant, though, check whether it is licensed to sell liquor (even wine and beer) or if it's a B.Y.O. (bring your own). B.Y.O.s account for about half of all the city's restaurants; residents often favor them because it is cheaper to buy wine or other drinks from a licensed liquor retailer than it is to purchase the same bottle in a restaurant.

Prices range from moderate to expensive, and good service is almost guaranteed because of the number of competitors. Among the top-priced eateries, **Fannys** in Lonsdale Street is a very formal French restaurant with food that would pass muster in Paris; **Mietta's** in Alfred Place also offers formal dining in an historic building that started out as the German Club and was later General MacArthur's headquarters; **Jean Jaques** on the St. Kilda beachfront has been judged to be Australia's top seafood restaurant on several occasions (it offers superb bay views and an ambience that relies heavily on discreet service and a pastel peach decor); and the Regent Hotel's 35th-floor **Le Restaurant** serves classic French cuisine with the best views of the Melbourne skyline.

More moderate are **Café Palma** in Little Bourke Street, with dining in a garden beneath a sliding-glass roof that allows diners to take advantage of the sun or a warm starlit night; and **The Bird and Bottle** at 333 Maroondah Highway about 30 km (18 miles) east of the city in the eastern suburbs, which serves a wide variety of well-cooked meals in a peaceful greenhouse environment. The atmosphere of Outback Australia is captured at **Clancy's**, at 445 Blackburn Road.

The **Gallery Restaurant** is part of the Victorian Arts Centre complex and is the ideal place for before- or after-theater dining, with its excellent service, international cuisine, and views of the city across the Yarra. **The Last Laugh** is a ten-minute cab ride from downtown and features good meals and a comedy show followed by a comedy disco. **Vlados Charcoal Grill** at 61 Bridge Road, Richmond, attracts regular visitors from Southeast Asia and Japan, who come to eat the biggest steaks served in Melbourne. (However, not everyone enjoys the large photographs of beef cattle pass as decor here.) More refined is the **Windsor Grill** at the Hotel Windsor; service and style have been the norm since the 19th century.

Melbourne boasts more than a thousand ethnic restaurants, including dozens of Chinese, Thai, Malaysian, and Indonesian places in Little Bourke Street, Italian in Lygon Street (just north of the commercial district), Greek on Sydney Road, Jewish in Acland Street, Vietnamese on Victoria Street, and Indian, Middle Eastern, and even Mexican spread throughout the city. **Fortuna Village** at 235 Little Bourke Street is typical of those in Chinatown, with a wide range of dishes from different regions of China. Most people prefer to let the chef here select their dishes.

Lygon Street's Italian restaurants offer the city's best dining value, and the quality is not matched elsewhere in Australia. It is easy to believe you are in Rome here—old men talk politics over big plates of pasta, and more often than not the decor relies on clippings of newspaper reviews. It's best just to catch a cab to Lygon Street and peruse the menu displayed outside each establishment; most places here do not accept reservations. An exception is **Florentino's**, at 80 Bourke Street, long regarded as the city's premier Italian eatery, with wood-paneled walls and homemade pasta.

## Shopping in Melbourne

Melbourne's chic boutiques and big department stores market home-grown designers such as Prue Acton, Rodney Clarke, Adele Palmer, and Sally Browne, as well as all the big-name Paris, London, Milan, and New York labels.

There are several different shopping streets in Melbourne, each with a very definite personality of its own. The bustling **Bourke Street Mall** is big. The stores are big, the selection is big, and the crowds are big. Here you'll find the major department stores David Jones and Myer Melbourne, Ltd., the latter the largest such retail establishment in the Southern Hemisphere. **Collins Street** is spoiled rotten with exclusive boutiques and stores such as Georges and Henry Buck, selling nothing but the best. The stores on Collins Street specialize in luxury clothing, imported designs, and quality goods, especially jewelry and leather.

Two interesting shopping arcades were built here in the last century: the **Block Arcade**, with a high-domed ceiling and mosaic tiled roof that make you think of Milan, and the **Royal Arcade**, which is home to some of the city's most exclusive retailers. Here you will find Australia's best shoe shops, women's high-fashion boutiques, and specialty accessory stores. Australia's most up-market shopping street is 3 km (2 miles) south of the city on **Toorak Road**; from Punt Road to Orrong Road the price tags are strictly high-altitude. **Prue Acton's Boutique** near South Yarra Station on Toorak Road offers an up-to-the-minute range of locally produced high fashion, and **The Place** in Toorak Village (last of the shops on the number 8 tram line) houses many specialist designer outlets.

The prices can also induce vertigo on **High Street** in **Armadale**, which is well known for its antiques shops, furniture stores, and exclusive boutiques. **Splashes** has a huge range of swimwear and rainwear, much of it not available anywhere else. Dozens of shops in this neighborhood offer everything from Australian-built furniture to very old books and advertising posters. Most of the shops are owned by the people who serve you, and they nearly always know their stock well.

Chapel Street in Prahran (number 78 or 79 tram from Toorak Road) is the best street for young and trendy fashion, with a style range from way-out to off-the-planet. **Cuggi**, on Chapel Street, has the city's best range of locally manufactured wool knitwear for women, men, and children. Nearby **Morrisons** has Akubra (Crocodile

Dundee) hats, moleskin trousers, and R.M. Williams boots; it's possible to walk out of here and look as if you're ready to herd mountain cattle. The **Opal Mine**, at 121 Bourke Street, stocks thousands of individually designed pieces of jewelry, especially Australian opals. Prices range from moderate to ultra expensive. **Altmann and Cherny**, at 120 Exhibition Street, displays the world's largest and most valuable opal (estimated at over $1 million), but it stocks more moderate pieces as well.

The **Queen Victoria Market**, on the northern edge of the commercial district, is one of the biggest markets in the world, with goods ranging from fresh produce, to cheap clothes, antiques, and bric-a-brac, to prints and crafts.

## Nightlife in Melbourne

Melbourne's after-dark life tends to be firmly centered on restaurants and pubs, but there are a handful of theaters on Russell and Exhibition streets that stage well-known productions such as *Cats* and *Les Misérables*. (Daily papers carry full details of theater productions and the more than 30 cinemas located within walking distance of the major hotels.) More than 20 other theaters in the inner suburbs stage everything from former Broadway or West End shows to avant-garde productions. The half-tix booth in the Bourke Street Mall sells "same night" tickets for most productions.

The **Universal Theatre** in Fitzroy is the most active of those theaters that stage original works. The **Australian Ballet** uses the Victorian Arts Centre complex as its home and performs there for about six weeks each year.

It is late at night when the dance clubs kick up their heels—patrons tend to be under 25 and definitely under 30. The most popular is the **Metro**, at the top end of Bourke Street. On a Thursday, Friday, or Saturday night upwards of 3,000 people crowd in to disco or hear top-line bands. Other favored clubs include **Inflation**, the **Underground**, and **York Butter Factory**, all on King Street in the western part of the city. The most chic club is **Monsoons**, at the Hyatt on Collins.

Nearly all the clubs feature a combination of live music and recorded disco. There are more than 20 of them listed in the newspapers' entertainment sections, and they cater to a wide range of tastes, from jazz to new-wave rock. **The Troubador** at 388 Brunswick Street in Fitzroy features live original folk music and music with a mild country feel and also serves a set menu at a good price. One of the top jazz clubs is the **Station Tavern and Brewery** in Greville Street in Prahran, about 4 km (2½ miles) south of the commercial district.

Expect to pay up to A$40 for a theater ticket, about A$15 for entry to a club and about A$4 a drink, and about A$25 for entry to a live-music venue.

# Hotels in Melbourne

Melbourne hotels offer a high standard of accommodation, which, like those in all of Australia's major cities, owes much to the standards set by Asian competitors. Business and pleasure travellers have become used to the standards offered by hoteliers in Hong Kong, Singapore, and Bangkok, a fact that has prompted Australia's big-city hoteliers to offer room quality and services rarely matched by top hotels in other Western countries. The luxury-level **Hyatt On Collins**, as an example, is considered by the Chicago-based chain to be its international flagship hotel, with a marble foyer and an arcade of shops with a busy bar sunk in its center, and rooms with views across the Yarra River and the parks on its southern bank. Its restaurant and shopping complex, called Collins Chase, is popular with Melburnians and visitors alike. The Art Deco-style decor of the Hyatt is designed to reflect the character of the eastern precinct of the city's commercial center.

The most unusual hotel in Melbourne is **The Regent**, which has its lobby at ground-floor level, function rooms on the first floor, bars and restaurants on the 35th floor, and guest rooms extending from the 36th to the 50th floor. Every room has a spectacular view, but ask for one facing the southeast toward the Dandenongs and the Alexandra Gardens. The Regent is almost as expensive as the Hyatt.

Melbourne makes good use of its wonderful Victorian architecture in some accommodations. A good example is **Gordon Place**, a complex of suites with competitive rates and their own kitchens, open fires, and antique furniture. It started as a refuge for homeless men last century, but is known now for its well-appointed rooms, its courtyard housing a tropical garden, and its superb restaurant—not to mention its New Orleans-like feel.

In East Melbourne, an old mansion from the gold-rush era has been transformed into **Magnolia Court**, a charming, moderately priced bed-and-breakfast accommodation whose rooms transport guests back a century.

It is surprising that more accommodation in Melbourne isn't built to capitalize on the city's fabulous bay views, but there is one hotel that makes up for the shortage of options; the **Parkroyal** on St. Kilda Road is the premier hotel on the city's southern side, offering unmatched views from its southern-exposure rooms across Albert Park Lake and the bay.

The **Windsor** is a century-old colonial-era hotel in the style of the Oriental in Bangkok and Raffle's in Singapore. It is operated by the Indian Oberoi chain, and its rooms are furnished in genuine antiques; its reasonable rates make it an excellent alternative to the better-known chain hotels.

The **Regency** on Exhibition Street is a favorite of visiting celebrities because of its location in the theater district, larger-than-average rooms, all with video recorders, and mid-range rates. The **Old Melbourne**, north of the city on Flemington Road (the route from the airport), is built around a cobblestone courtyard, and its rooms are designed to re-create the era of the gold rush. The **Hilton on the Park** offers superb views, particularly from its southern side, and is an easy walk across the Treasury Gardens from the major shopping and theater district.

Other good hotels include the **Menzies at Rialto,** which delights architecture enthusiasts. It occupies two 19th-century wool stores, and the laneway between serves as its lobby. The **Victoria** in Little Collins Street is more than 50 years old, but it continues to offer quality accommodation and service at rates that will let you leave with your credit rating intact. Similarly, Flag Inns operates an Australia- wide chain of motor inns, with about 20 in Melbourne that offer good-quality rooms with private facilities, free car parking, and restaurants at the lowest rates available.

**Station Pier Condominiums**, about halfway from the commercial district to St. Kilda and adjacent to the major passenger-ship terminal, offer the only rooms close to the city with beach views. Its rooms are one- and two-bedroom suites, each with a Jacuzzi, fully equipped kitchen, and a dining room.

## Melbourne Touring and Golf

Touring around Melbourne is easy, with hundreds of options including helicopter tours, chauffeured limousine tours (Budget operates chauffeured cars and has an extensive tour program), vintage-car tours, and even tours by horse-drawn coach.

The Victour office on Collins Street near the Melbourne Town Hall has information and brochures on touring, and can provide detailed maps.

One of the most popular tours with international visitors offers the opportunity to play some of the city's golf courses. Melbourne claims more golf courses than any other city in the world; they range from public courses that charge a nominal fee to exclusive, expensive clubs. An early-morning round of golf at **Albert Park Lake**, followed by breakfast at Denny's (adjacent to the course, overlooking the lake), shopping at Myer's and in the city's labyrinth of arcades, lunch in the Dandenongs (see Day Trips, below), and dinner in Lygon Street (known as Little Italy) comes close to making up the perfect day in Melbourne.

## Day Trips from Melbourne

There are some superb day trips easily made from Melbourne with several tour operators, or by rental car. Melbourne is built on the shores of Port Phillip Bay, a huge expanse of shallow water, and is about 112 km (70 miles) from the open ocean. One of the most interesting tours runs along the east side of the bay via the **Nepean Highway**. Hundreds of the city's finest houses are built facing the bay (a cool million or so will buy a two-story Edwardian home with a view). From the main street in Mornington (south of the city along the east shore of the bay), farther along to Mt. Martha and Rosebud, the coastal road winds around the bay shore, with spectacular holiday homes and safe swimming beaches contributing to an atmosphere of peaceful seclusion. It's best to drive along the Beach Road and stop at the beach that strikes your fancy.

The beaches are open to everyone, and most have changing and toilet facilities. Nude bathing is restricted to the designated areas (which are much farther from the city), but topless bathing and very small swimsuits are common everywhere. The bay provides safe swimming, but take notice if a light aircraft sounds a siren; it's telling you there is a shark in the vicinity. Don't let that put you off—it only happens a couple of times a season.

**Arthur's Seat**, along the bay just before Rosebud, offers superb views of the Mornington Peninsula on the road to Red Hill, an old farming community that is rapidly evolving into a hobby-farm area for people who want to live within commuting distance of Melbourne. It's inhabited by television personalities and former hippies turned yuppies—chopping down a tree is a crime ranked with multiple murder and drug running in these parts.

Every visit to Melbourne should include at least one day in the **Dandenong Ranges**, about an hour's drive east of the city. **Sherbrooke Forest**, a rain forest deep in the mountains, is home to the rare lyrebird (so-named because the courting male's tail feathers are shaped like the ancient Greek instrument), and hundreds of varieties of Northern Hemisphere trees provide a spectacular show when their leaves fall throughout the ranges. (Australian trees do not lose their leaves in winter, although eucalyptus trees shed their bark—but that's in summer.) It's sometimes possible to catch a glimpse of the shy and beautiful lyrebird (featured on the Australian 10-cent coin) from the secluded bush tracks that wander through the forest—but be very quiet and wear soft-soled shoes. The lyrebird is an excellent mimic, so if you hear something that sounds out of place among the trees, such as a chain saw or doorbell, there may be one nearby.

Bavarian- and Swiss-style restaurants are a feature of every village in this area; English-style Devonshire tea establishments serve scones with jam and tea. **Clover Cottage Restaurant and Strawberry Terrace**, in Manuka Road in Berwick, about 35 km (21 miles) east of the city on Highway 1, serves a wide range of French-style dishes in the dining room of a Georgian-era country mansion. It is classically tasteful, with excellent service. The **Cotswold House Country Restaurant**, in the heart of the mountains on Blackhill Road in Menzies Creek, offers

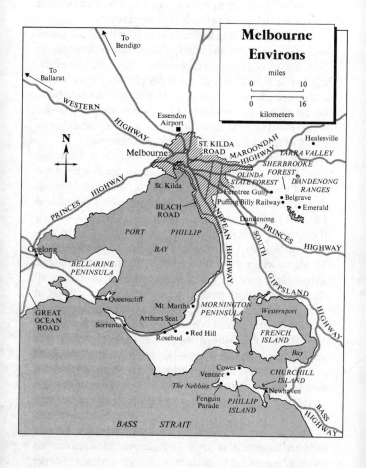

**Melbourne Environs**

miles
0 ___ 10

0 ___ 16
kilometers

To Bendigo

To Ballarat

WESTERN HIGHWAY

Essendon Airport

Melbourne

ST. KILDA ROAD

MAROONDAH HIGHWAY

Healesville

YARRA VALLEY

SHERBROOKE FOREST

OLINDA STATE FOREST

DANDENONG RANGES

N

PRINCES HIGHWAY

St. Kilda

BEACH ROAD

Ferntree Gully

Puffing Billy Railway

Belgrave

Emerald

PORT PHILLIP BAY

NEPEAN HIGHWAY

Dandenong

PRINCES HIGHWAY

Geelong

BELLARINE PENINSULA

SOUTH GIPPSLAND HIGHWAY

GREAT OCEAN ROAD

Queenscliff

Mt. Martha

Arthurs Seat

Sorrento

Rosebud

Red Hill

MORNINGTON PENINSULA

Westernport

FRENCH ISLAND

Bay

Cowes

Ventnor

CHURCHILL ISLAND

Newhaven

BASS HIGHWAY

The Nobbies

Penguin Parade

PHILLIP ISLAND

BASS STRAIT

good value *nouvelle cuisine* in an Australian homestead. It specializes in local wine, and you enjoy views across the valley as you dine. The **Fernbrook Restaurant**, on the corner of Monbulk and Gully Crescent roads in Belgrave, is set among three acres of magnificent fern glades and towering gum trees adjacent to Sherbrooke Forest. It's also a good spot to stop for Devonshire tea (scones, jam, and cream) in the afternoon. The **Baron of Beef** on Sherbrooke Road overlooks the forest and is set in four acres of rhododendron trees. It serves a good-value smorgasbord, with the emphasis on beef, and a show features bagpipes and highland dancers. It is important to reserve at any restaurant in the Dandenongs on weekends and public holidays, both for lunch and dinner.

The gardens in this region have won for Victoria the moniker "The Garden State." On a short trip, visit the **National Rhododendron Garden** at Olinda to see why.

Train buffs will be impressed with **Puffing Billy** near Belgrave in the Dandenongs, a 19th-century narrow-gauge steam train that has been restored to make a walking-pace journey from Belgrave to Emerald. It's one of the best ways to see the forest, and there are great views all the way to the so-called Australian Alps.

The **Healesville Sanctuary** to the northeast is a good place to see Australian wildlife, with koalas, lyrebirds, cockatoos (including the showy pink galah), and kangaroos living in an environment close to their natural habitat. A few miles past the sanctuary, the Maroondah Highway crosses the **Black Spur**, a rain forest with tall trees and deep fern glades.

The Dandenongs can be combined with a trip through the **Yarra Valley wine region** northeast of Melbourne near Healesville, with seven vineyards open to the public for tastings and sales. The Yarra Valley is renowned for its full-bodied reds, fruity whites such as chardonnay and Rhine Riesling, and fortified wines, including some of Australia's best ports. The region has many accommodation options, but the pick of the bunch is **Burnham Beeches**, a country house built for the Nicholas family in the 1930s. Close to Olinda, it is regarded as Australia's finest example of Art Deco architecture. The house now offers 36 very expensive suites and hosts many of the famous personalities who pass through Melbourne each year. Its expensive restaurant ranks as one of the country's finest dining rooms, and it offers excellent health and fitness facilities, including a swimming pool, tennis courts, and jogging tracks through the bush.

# PHILLIP ISLAND
## The Fairy Penguins

It is hard to imagine a visitor to Melbourne not making the journey to Phillip Island to experience one of nature's great wonders, the nightly parade of the fairy penguins as they return to their cliff-top homes at Summerland Beach after a day's fishing at sea.

Phillip Island is one of only a handful of places in the world where it's possible to see these remarkable birds at all, and certainly the easiest among those to get to. The fairy penguin is the smallest penguin, about a foot tall, and lives in several remote spots along the southern Victorian coast and on islands of the Bass Strait. These birds spend days at sea catching fish, which they then regurgitate to feed their young, who remain on Phillip Island.

The parade of birds as they flop out of the surf and waddle up the steep surrounding hills provides visitors with one of the most entertaining experiences in Victoria.

The first stop on a trip to Phillip Island should be the tourist information center at Newhaven (Tel: 059-567-447). The center has a comprehensive range of information, including maps and suggested walks along the cliff tops.

There are several tour options, with more than a dozen coach operators operating half-day and full-day itineraries, which include the island's scenic attractions and of course the penguin parade at dusk. Departure from Melbourne is usually at mid-morning (some tours leave earlier), and arrival back in Melbourne will be some two or three hours after twilight. The penguins return from their fishing expedition in the cold sub-Antarctic waters at dusk; powerful lights—which don't seem to bother the creatures—make viewing easy. The little birds do not like flashbulbs, however, and photographers are asked to use long exposures or purchase pre-printed shots rather than use a flash.

Don't forget to take warm clothing, even on the hottest summer day. On a spring or autumn night, the temperature can drop below freezing if a gale-force wind is blowing off the Antarctic icecap.

It's a good idea to arrive early during peak holiday periods because the number of people permitted to view the birds on any one night is 3,500. The Newhaven information center can advise you what time dusk is so you won't miss the parade.

A good way to experience the wonder of the fairy penguins without spending a full day in the area is to fly with Penguin Express. The flight from Melbourne's Essendon Airport begins with a glass of Champagne in the terminal and a 30-minute flight over the city's southern suburbs and beaches and along the rugged southern coast. The tour includes a chance to see koalas in the wild as well as the penguins, and the return journey provides spectacular views of Melbourne at night.

## Phillip Island Itself

Phillip Island is about a two-hour drive from Melbourne and is connected to the mainland by a bridge that permits easy access to its 58-mile-long coastline. The terrain varies from rocky outcrops and steep cliffs to superb surfing beaches and safe swimming areas. The surf is biggest at **Woolami**, but for swimming, the north coast offers dozens of equally good choices. Just drive along the shore and stop where you want. The inland houses some of Victoria's prettiest farms and several old chicory kilns (the plant was an alternative crop to coffee once widely grown on the island).

The real reason to visit Phillip Island—aside from viewing the penguin parade—is to experience the island's wildlife and scenery. Its fauna is amazing: over 200 species of birds in addition to penguins, seals, and koalas. It is one of the places in Australia where koalas can easily be seen in the wild. (Visitors and Melburnians alike are enthralled by the koalas, but the park rangers charged with their protection do ask that the animals be left alone. Simply enjoy these symbols of Australia as they lazily munch on eucalyptus leaves and look down at you, almost mocking the busy life of a traveller.) If you drive to Phillip Island, it is also important to watch for road signs that warn where koalas cross the road; you must drive very slowly at those points.

Seagulls by the millions, waterfowl, black swans, pelicans, and ibis call this beautiful island home. Coastal scenery that's a photographer's dream, secluded pockets of bushland inhabited by koalas and wallabies (small kangaroos), and huge sand dunes all combine to create a remarkable place. Beachwalking from Cowes to the Forest Caves or the Colonnades provides fantastic views of the ocean.

The island was among the first spots to be permanently settled on Australia's rugged southern coast, and has been a popular resort area for over a century. Only 13 miles long, it is a permanent home to only about 4,000 inhabitants (most of whom live in the town of Cowes), but the population in peak holiday seasons and on sunny weekends expands into the hundreds of thousands. While the fairy penguins are the highlight of any visit, there are several other attractions that make an excursion to the island memorable, including the **Island Nature Park**, home for wombats and cockatoos.

A ferry from Cowes sails out to **Seal Rock**, a remote rock formation at the entrance to Westernport Bay that is home to a colony of some 5,000 fur seals. The experience of being so close to seals in the wild is exhilarating, if a bit noisy.

**The Nobbies**, the southwesternmost part of the island, are huge cliffs that block the enormous swells of the Indian Ocean after they've built up over thousands of miles of open sea. The result is breathtaking, as the water crashes into a huge underground cavern known as the Blow Hole, creating a water spout that towers hundreds of feet into the air when the Roaring Forties are blowing their hardest. Don't be put off if the weather is cold; just bundle up and enjoy nature at its most furious.

**Churchill Island** is a small landfill connected by a footbridge to Phillip Island—simply follow the signs. It is a former farm and its historic homestead is now operated by the National Trust. The homestead is typical of country properties throughout Australia, with a rambling veranda, 15-foot-high ceilings, and more than 20 rooms furnished in colonial-era antiques. The entire island has been retained as it was a century ago, and farming here goes on much as it always has.

Phillip Island is famous for being the original home of the Australian Grand Prix, the car-racing circuit immortalized in Neville Shute's *On the Beach,* the novel that portrays Melbourne as the last surviving city on earth after a nuclear holocaust. When the book was made into a movie in 1959, there was a famous scene with Fred Astaire, Gregory Peck, and Ava Gardner at the world's last-ever motor event. Today the circuit at Ventnor in the center of the island is the site of a motoring museum that displays hundreds of vintage and classic cars and memorabilia from the racing days. The Grand Prix is long gone (to Adelaide), but the track still seems to echo with the roar of the open wheelers. The old racetrack is also the home of hundreds of exotic and colorful parrots, many of them tame enough to eat from your hand.

Accommodation on Phillip Island is mostly limited to motels and recreational-vehicle parks. **Narrabeen Cottage** is an up-market beach house (adults only) in Cowes set in expansive grounds that offer lonely walks along the beach and romantic open-log fires at night. **Trenavin Park**, one of the oldest houses on the island, is now a bed-and-breakfast with two- and three-bedroom guest wings. Accommodation can be booked on a fully inclusive basis, and Trenavin Park's restaurant is famous for its afternoon Devonshire tea.

Australian cuisine at its best can be sampled at the **Farm Shed Barbeque Restaurant**, which offers huge slabs of beef and lamb and a one-hour sheep-shearing, cow-milking, and boomerang-throwing show as part of the meal. **The Jetty** in Cowes serves seafood and beef (the island's two major products) in an indoor garden with a huge open fire and views to Westernport Bay. The century-old **Isle of White Hotel** has a good-value family restaurant. You can observe nesting mutton birds as you dine at the spectacular cliff-top **Sheerwater Restaurant Observatory**. It's moderately priced and easy to find (as is everything else on Phillip Island) on the Tourist Road. Sheerwater is closed on Mondays during the winter.

An independent traveller could easily combine Phillip Island with the Mornington Peninsula south of Melbourne, the city's major beach and resort region—and even with the Great Ocean Road—by using the 30-minute car-ferry service that operates from Sorrento near Portsea on the Mornington Peninsula and Queenscliff at the west mouth of Port Phillip Bay on the Bellarine Peninsula near Geelong.

## THE GREAT OCEAN ROAD

There can be few more pleasurable experiences for late 20th-century pleasure seekers than to be seated at the wheel of a good car anticipating a 300-km (180-mile) run along a spectacular cliff-top road with breathtaking views of the Indian Ocean.

Victoria's Great Ocean Road comes close to most drivers' idea of paradise as it snakes westward from Melbourne and Port Phillip Bay, along the southern coast from Torquay to Anglesea, through Lorne and Apollo Bay, and on to Port Campbell National Park, Warrnambool, and Portland in the direction of South Australia and Adelaide. The road provides some of the best coastal scenery to be viewed anywhere, with a backdrop of rain-forested mountains. Drivers would be well advised to keep their eyes on the road; for passengers, however, there are unmatched vistas of mountains and the Southern Ocean (known to the rest of the world as the Indian Ocean).

The coastal villages en route are Victoria's holiday playground, and the surf is recognized as among the most challenging in the world, equaling that of Hawaii and Southern California.

The Great Ocean Road is a high-quality blacktop. From it, photographers can set up some great shots, ranging from board riders hanging five at Bells Beach to coastal cliffs with sheer drops hundreds of feet into boiling sea. A two- or three-day trip from Melbourne will include: the historic port of Geelong; the wineries and pubs of the Bellarine Peninsula; the big surf at Bells Beach and Lorne; the ancient rain forest of Cape Otway; the spectacular southern cliffs and rock formations created by the ocean as it pounds the Australian continent; coves and bays where 19th-century mariners and passengers scrambled ashore from one of the more than 500 tall ships wrecked in the area; and historic fishing villages, once among the world's busiest ports and the landing points for thousands of miners bound for Victoria's goldfields.

Most Melbourne-based car-rental companies have vehicles that are certain to make the Great Ocean Road a memorable trip. Budget Rent-a-Car offers the biggest sports-car fleet, including BMW convertibles, Jaguars,

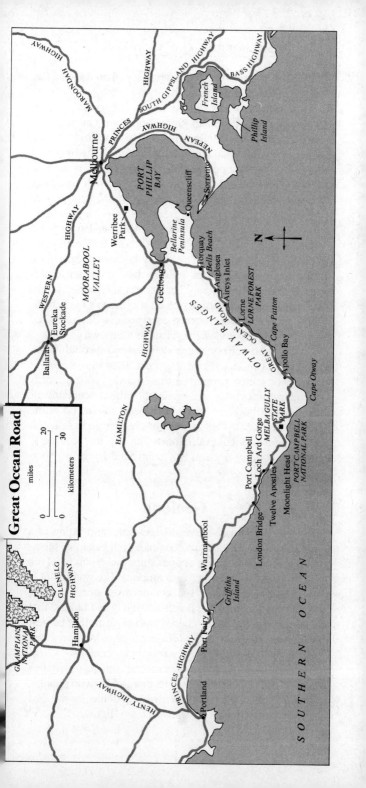

# Great Ocean Road

miles
0        20

0        30
kilometers

Nissans, and Porsches. They start at less than A$100 a day on an unlimited-mileage basis.

Coach (bus) tours of the region are conducted by Ansett Pioneer, Australian Pacific, and Trans Otway Tours, all located in the Melbourne central business district.

It is possible to undertake only part of this trip and make it a one-day outing from the city if time is limited. The first hour or so on Highway 1, through the city's western suburbs, across the giant Westgate Bridge over the docklands, and then by freeway to Geelong, is fairly dull. The only worthwhile exit is to **Werribee Park**, whose main attraction is a magnificent 60-room Italianate mansion built in the 1870s. The stately home is located in a huge formal garden that reflects the flamboyant emergence of the "squattocracy" in Victoria, the pioneer families who rode to prominence on the sheep's back. (The early pioneers were known as squatters because they simply moved in and claimed land as their own.)

Homesteads of equal grandeur extend through Western Victoria and into South Australia. They were once the centers of station properties that sprawled for hundreds of square miles. Most are retained by the descendants of the original builders; many have been able to be refurbished in recent years as wool has reemerged as Australia's biggest agricultural export. The trip to Geelong is through country once mostly controlled from Werribee Park.

## Geelong

Geelong is Victoria's second largest city, and home to a number of major industrial complexes. It began its life as a seaport, a place where clipper ships picked up wool for the mills of Europe and North America. The waterfront is still dominated by huge 19th-century wool stores bearing the names of companies (such as Dalgety and Elders) that have survived to be numbered among Australia's biggest corporations. One of the former wool stores has been turned into Geelong's biggest shopping center.

The National Trust operates several historic properties close to the city, notably The Heights and Barwon Grange, both excellent examples of privileged life in the last century. Both are well sign-posted from Highway 1.

Little evidence is left of the region's original inhabitants, the Wathaurung aboriginal tribe. They lived throughout the south coast area for more than 4,000 years until the 1840s. The probable source of one of Australia's great colloquialisms involves a white man called William Buckley, a convict who escaped to live with the Wathaurung. It was thought that he had no chance of survival, hence Australians will give a person or project that has no chance of success a "Buckley's chance." Buckley *did* survive and lived in the Geelong area as an aboriginal for 32 years, only coming out of the bush when the white settlers arrived around 1835.

Four of the area's several cool-climate wineries are open for public tastings and cellar-door sales; one of them is the **Tarcoola Vineyards** about 32 km (19 miles) northwest of the city in the Moorabool Valley. It is also the home of several hundred koalas. They range free around the property but are usually easy to find.

Wines from around Geelong are noted for their full fruity flavor, particularly the reds made from shiraz and cabernet sauvignon grapes. The tourist information office in central Geelong has comprehensive guidebooks to the city and its varied attractions, including Tarcoola Vineyards and National Trust houses.

# Queenscliff

Geelong is the gateway to the Bellarine Peninsula, a region best known for its safe swimming beaches and the historic settlement of Queenscliff.

Several pubs remain from the time when the town, at the western head of the entrance to Port Phillip Bay, was the preferred holiday resort of Melbourne's landed gentry. The **Queenscliff Hotel**, **Ozone Hotel**, and **Vue Grand** all offer high-class, colonial-style accommodation and dining rooms that have changed little since the days when tall ships stopped there en route to Melbourne. **Mietta's Restaurant** at the Queenscliff Hotel is recognized as among the best in the state serving traditional French fare.

Fort Queenscliff, Australia's largest and best-preserved military fortress, was, like many other coastal fortifications around the country, built in the last century to ward off an anticipated Russian attack.

# The Road Begins

The Great Ocean Road was built by World War I veterans as a government project designed to provide employment when they returned home from the European battlefields. It was always intended to be a tourist road; the original plans claimed it would rival the famous California coastal route. It does.

The Great Ocean Road has three parts, each with distinct characteristics: The first, from Torquay to Apollo Bay, is a Riviera-like playground with wide sandy beaches that spread out from the feet of the high, tree-clad slopes of the Otway Ranges. As you travel south the trees become bigger and the mountains taller until the landscape is dominated by rain forest and wet dark fern glades. The forest gives way to the spectacular cliffs and coastal scenery of the **Port Campbell National Park**, where the Indian Ocean swell crashes into the Australian continent. The memory of the many ships that sailed on that swell right into the cliffs is strong here. There are numerous beaches here, as well as surf that attracts many of the best board riders in the world. The region has hosted world surfing championships several times. It's easy to rent a board and try the big waves, but you're advised to stick to beaches with a lifeguard patrol unless you have already found the breakers on Honolulu's North Shore to be "no worries, mate."

**Surfing** was introduced to Australia by Hawaii's Duke Kahanamoku in 1915; since then it has become part of the national culture, with south coast beaches and the associated hedonistic lifestyle the best known images of the area. Old Holdens (the Australian version of Chevrolets) and Fords with boards on their roofs are permanent fixtures, and exotic beaches, including Winki Pop, Jan Juc, Point Impossible, and Spout Creek, are surfers' favorites.

The **Angahook Forest Park** is home to a wide range of native and European birds, including spectacularly bright parrots that will eat out of your hand. The park has several superb and well-marked trails, and is a good place to see hundreds of different wildflowers and wattle (native acacia trees whose spikes were used by early settlers to make fences), particularly in the spring, i.e., from September to November. The bushland setting of the **Anglesea Golf Course** provides the unique experience of teeing off among the local kangaroos, who live on the grounds and often refuse to move—making for another hazard on a course that wasn't easy in the first place. Anglesea is a public course and reservations are usually not necessary, unless you plan on going there on a sunny weekend or major holiday; Tel: (052) 63-1582.

Between Torquay and Anglesea is the **Southern Rose**, a lavish top-class restaurant with views over an 8-acre rose garden. It's possible to stop just for a drink, for morning or afternoon tea, or for a full meal in the late evening. Reservations are not necessary to enjoy its excellent Australian food and warm, cozy atmosphere.

The headlands that frame the surf beaches offer some of Australia's best surf fishing for whiting, snapper, gummy (a small shark), and salmon. Fishing gear and bait can be rented at most gas stations; it's best to adhere to local advice to find out where the fish are biting. Many people fish the rock pools, which act as a natural fish trap at low tide—but be careful of the incoming tide.

## The Bush Fire

As the Great Ocean Road winds into Airey's Inlet, the bush takes on a ghostly gray hue, with thousands of tall gum trees standing dead and gaunt over a lush undergrowth. This area was hit in 1983 by a bush wildfire that wiped out some 2,000 homes and destroyed thousands of square miles of forest.

Victoria and South Australia are the most bushfire-prone regions in the world, and the fire known as Ash Wednesday was the worst in 40 years. It is a natural function of the Australian eucalyptus bush to burn. Indeed, several varieties of trees need the heat of fire to germinate seed, but the 1983 fire was much hotter than normal and many of the trees never recovered. Fortunately, enough lived to provide the birth of a new generation of forest. Farther along the road, it's easy to see how the rain forest looked before the fire.

**Lorne** is the largest of the coastal towns, with an almost Mediterranean atmosphere in the summer; but in midwinter it becomes a lonely and isolated outpost bearing the brunt of the worst the Indian Ocean can provide. Its most famous attraction is the beach, but behind the town the rain forest creates a dense canopy of foliage; bush tracks here lead to high waterfalls and lookouts. **Lorne Forest Park Reserve** is lush in the extreme, with walks that make it easy to experience what much of southern Australia was like prior to white settlement. The easiest of the walks is the five-minute one from the parking lot to Erskine Falls, a walk well documented, with easy-to-follow signs. Comprehensive maps of the forest area and the various bushwalks are available at the BP gas station and supermarket as you enter the town from Melbourne.

Trail riding by horse in the area is easily arranged at **Sea Mist**, a mountain facility that also has good-quality log-cabin accommodations.

# The Shipwreck Coast

The road continues to track around the cliff tops by way of the extraordinarily rugged Cape Patton to the pretty town of **Apollo Bay**. The last of the surf beaches is not far outside town. The scenery then changes to dramatic and dark rain forest. Tall trees and ferns lap the road as it traverses the massive bulk of **Cape Otway**. **Melba Gully State Park** is particularly beautiful, its valley of ferns and glowworms covered by trees, some nearly as tall as California's giant redwoods.

An unpaved side road leads to the lighthouse, which has protected ships rounding one of the continent's southernmost points for more than a century. The 14-km- (8½-mile-) road leads to cliffs towering some 300 feet up from the ocean, cliffs that mark the start of the shipwreck coast, the graveyard of more than 500 clippers, brigantines, and barquentines from the last century. Relics of the disasters still litter some of the region's wild, isolated beaches, and tales of heroic rescues are entwined in the folk history of the fishing hamlets that dot the coast. The anchors of the *Fiji,* wrecked in 1891, and the *Marie Gabrielle* (in 1869) can be seen half-buried in sand at Moonlight Head.

The fern glens and waterfalls of the rain forest give way here to the almost unbelievably rugged west coast, and **Port Campbell National Park**. The rock formations created by the relentless ocean as it slams into Australia after an uninterrupted stretch extending from South America 15,000 miles away carry names that evoke more civilized images, such as the Twelve Apostles and London Bridge. The park extends for 21 miles and offers unmatched scenery, but it is only easily accessed in two places, at Loch Ard Gorge and another sign-posted entry about 3 km (2 miles) farther along the road.

**Loch Ard Gorge** is the best spot to experience what it must have been like on a bitterly cold night as the Roaring Forties whipped up 50-foot waves. The clipper *Loch Ard* sank in this place on just such a night; the few survivors washed up on a beach here that can now be reached by a wooden stairway. A memorial to those who were lost and a graveyard that contains the few bodies recovered lie at the top of the gorge.

The best place to learn more about the coast and its link with the days of sail is **Warrnambool's Flagstaff Hill Maritime Village**. The museum complex has its own clipper and is itself a re-creation of a 19th-century port on the city's foreshore.

The **Tower Hill State Game Reserve** near Warrnambool features an extinct volcano that, like many others in the area, has sunk into the plain and become a lake.

The Great Ocean Road continues on to the pretty fishing village of **Port Fairy**, which has excellent colonial accommodation available at the **Dublin House Inn**, an 1855 pub whose facilities rival the standards of big-city hotels. The inn has at times been a general store, a bakery, and a liquor store. **The Cottage**, reminiscent of the farm cottages of England, has three bedrooms and every possible modern convenience, including a couple of bikes you can ride around the village.

Close to the coast is **Griffiths Island**, home each summer to thousands of mutton birds. These remarkable birds leave the area every year on or about April 26 to spend the northern summer in Siberia, and return around September 22.

There are several places along the Great Ocean Road where it's possible to return to Melbourne along more direct Highway 1. All are well sign-posted and the highway will return you to Geelong and to Melbourne via the Westgate Freeway. (Take Alternate 1 from the Princes Highway.)

Your trip along the Great Ocean Road could be extended easily to include Victoria's oldest town, the coastal city of **Portland** (which includes several historic buildings), and then branch off through the Western District to the **Grampian Ranges**. These undulating hills from the coast to the mountains comprise part of the world's biggest volcanic plain, with extinct craters dotting the landscape. Take the Henty Highway north to Hamilton and turn right onto the Glenelg Highway in the direction of Ballarat and Melbourne. A well sign-posted road to the left in the town of Dunkeld will take you north through the mountains to Halls Gap and ultimately to Highway 8, the major Adelaide/Melbourne route. It would be best to allow at least two days for this trip and stop overnight in Hamilton, Stawell (on Highway 8), or Ballarat.

The Grampians were named after similar rugged ranges in Scotland, and offer a rich variety of native flora. The easiest spot in Victoria to pet a kangaroo is here at Zumsteins, a small town about a half-hour drive across the Sierra Range from the main center of Halls Gap. It is easy to find; only two roads traverse the Grampians and the area is well sign-posted. The Grampians are brilliant with wildflowers in spring, and several significant aboriginal sites are found in the ranges. Stop at the ranger station at Halls Gap for information.

If you turn left and stay on Highway 1 at the town of Heywood on the way north from Portland to Hamilton, you will continue west along the coast through the town of Mount Gambier in the state of South Australia and on up to Adelaide.

## Ballarat and Back to Melbourne

The return journey to Melbourne is via Ballarat, once the site of the richest gold mines in the world. A pitched battle was fought here at the Eureka Stockade in 1854 between British forces and miners seeking political representation (and the repeal of mining licenses)—the nearest thing Australia ever had to a revolution. Ballarat is the site of **Sovereign Hill**, a re-creation of life in a gold township in the 1850s, and the new **Gold Museum**. There are displays of the huge nuggets, which attracted miners from around the world, as well as exhibits of 19th-century mining equipment and original miners licenses. The story of Eureka and the events that led to Victoria's independence from England is told with original documents and photographs. Particularly interesting is the story of the California Militia, a group of miners who organized under the U.S. flag in 1854.

A visit to Sovereign Hill can easily take most of the day. It has a main street complete with boardwalks, the New York Bakery, the United States Hotel (now a restaurant), a working mine (a gold-train ride down the shaft is great fun), and the museum, which details the huge Ballarat and Bendigo strikes.

Superb accommodation in a colonial-style structure is available at the **Miners Retreat**, a Victorian-era home with iron-lacework verandas and suites furnished with antiques. It's a good value too. The return journey to Melbourne from Ballarat is via the Western Highway and takes about two hours.

## GETTING AROUND

Melbourne is the gateway to southern Australia, with good domestic air connections to Sydney and other cities and direct international services from North America, Asia, and Europe to Tullamarine Airport. The airport is about 20 km (12 miles) from the central business district and the major hotels; cab fares average A$18.

It is easy to find your way around Melbourne, but if you rent a car and drive beware of trams (you'll know this already if you've seen the charming 1986 Australian film *Malcolm*). Trams travel on fixed rails. They will not swerve in front of your vehicle, but they will continue exactly where they intended to go—regardless of where you are at the time. Cars must stop when trams stop, to permit disembarking passengers to use the road with safety. You may only pass a tram on the left.

The commercial district has several unusual intersections where right-hand turns are made from the left-hand lane in order for drivers to avoid the unpleasant experience of being sandwiched between two trams.

Travelling out of the city is easy; major freeways and highways are clearly marked. To get onto the freeway to Geelong via the Westgate Bridge, simply proceed to the southern end of the city and turn right into Flinders Street; signs will clearly direct you from there. To get to the road to the Dandenongs, drive east on either the Eastern or South Eastern Freeway, and to the Mornington Peninsula travel straight down St. Kilda Road. If you are heading to Phillip Island, a sign will direct you from St. Kilda Road onto the Princes Highway and then onto the South Gippsland Highway at Dandenong.

Good maps can be obtained from Victour on Collins Street, just down from the Melbourne Town Hall. Victour also has an excellent "Excursion Planner," with detailed touring information.

The two peak holiday seasons correspond with major festivals in March and November. The city enjoys sunny autumn weather in March for the **Moomba Festival** (*moomba* is aboriginal for "Let's get together and have fun"). The festival includes one of the world's outstanding water-skiing events (on the Yarra River), dozens of concerts of all types, a huge carnival in the Alexandra Gardens, and a street parade that attracts up to half a million people. In November, the Spring Racing Carnival includes the **Melbourne Cup** on the first Tuesday.

## ACCOMMODATIONS REFERENCE

▶ **Burnham Beeches Country House.** Sherbrooke Road, **Sherbrooke**, Vic. 3789. Tel: (03) 755-1903.

▶ **The Cottage.** 28 Campbell Street, **Port Fairy**, Vic. 3284. Tel: (055) 681-592; in U.S., (213) 553-6352.

▶ **Dublin House Inn.** 57 Bank Street, **Port Fairy**, Vic. 3284. Tel: (055) 681-822.

▶ **Gordon Place.** 24-32 Little Bourke Street, **Melbourne**, Vic. 3000. Tel: (03) 663-5355; in U.S., (800) 44-UTELL; in Canada, (800) 387-1338; Telex: AA 35468.

▶ **Hilton on the Park.** 192 Wellington Parade, **East Melbourne**, Vic. 3002. Tel: (03) 419-3311; in U.S., (800) 445-8667; Telex: 33057.

▶ **Hyatt on Collins.** 123 Collins Street, **Melbourne**, Vic. 3000. Tel: (03) 657-1234; in U.S., (800) 228-9000; in Alaska and Hawaii, (800) 228-9005; Telex: AA 38796.

▶ **Magnolia Court.** 101 Powlett Street, **East Melbourne**, Vic. 3002. Tel: (03) 419-4518.

▶ **Menzies at Rialto.** 495 Collins Street, **Melbourne**, Vic. 3000. Tel: (03) 620-111; in U.S., (800) 44- UTELL; in Canada, (800) 387-1338; Telex: AA 136189.

▶ **Mietta's Queenscliff Hotel.** 16 Gellibrand Street, **Queenscliff**, Vic. 3225. Tel: (052) 521-982.

▶ **Miners Retreat.** 602 Eureka Street, **Ballarat**, Vic. 3350. Tel: (053) 316-900.

▶ **Narrabeen Cottage.** 16 Steele Street, **Cowes, Phillip Island**, Vic. 3922. Tel: (059) 522-062.

▶ **Settlers Old Melbourne.** 5–17 Flemington Road, **North Melbourne**, Vic. 3051. Tel: (03) 329-9344; in U.S.,

(800) 44-UTELL; in Canada, (800) 387-1338; Telex: AA 32057.

▶ **Ozone Hotel**. 42 Gellibrand Street, **Queenscliff**, Vic. 3225. Tel: (052) 521-931.

▶ **The Melbourne Parkroyal**. 562 St. Kilda Road, **Melbourne**, Vic. 3004. Tel: (03) 529-8888; in U.S., (800) 421-0536 or (800) 252-2155; in Canada, (800) 251-2166; Telex: AA 152242.

▶ **The Regent of Melbourne**. 25 Collins Street, **Melbourne**, Vic. 3000. Tel: (03) 653-0321; in U.S., (800) 545-4000; in Canada, (800) 626-8222; Telex: AA 37724.

▶ **Rockman's Regency Hotel**. Corner Exhibition and Londsdale streets, **Melbourne**, Vic. 3000. Tel: (03) 662-3900; in U.S., (800) 223-6800; in Canada, (800) 341-8585; Telex: AA 38890.

▶ **Sea Mist**. Corner of Wenslaydale and Gum Flat roads, **Winchelsea**, Vic. 3241. Tel: (052) 887-255; in U.S., (213) 553-6352.

▶ **Station Pier Condominiums**. 15 Beach Street, **Port Melbourne**, Vic. 3141. Tel: (03) 266-3743.

▶ **Trenavin Park**. Ventnor Road, **Phillip Island**, Vic. 3922. Tel: (069) 568-230.

▶ **Victoria Hotel**. 215 Little Collins Street, **Melbourne**, Vic. 3000. Tel: (03) 630-441; Telex: 31264.

▶ **Vue Grand Private Hotel**. 46 Hesse Street, **Queenscliff**, Vic. 3225. Tel: (052) 521-544.

▶ **Windsor Hotel**. 103-115 Spring Street, **Melbourne**, Vic. 3000. Tel: (03) 630-261; in U.S. and Canada, (212) 841-1111 or (800) 223-0888; Telex: AA 30437.

# ADELAIDE AND SOUTH AUSTRALIA

*By Kerry Kenihan*

*Kerry Kenihan, a journalist, travel writer, and author of four books—two of which have been published by Penguin—is a member of the Australian Society of Travel Writers. She lives in the Adelaide Hills.*

After Edinburgh, there's Adelaide. Australia's best-known biennial arts festival (the next is in March 1990) is one reason that visitors come in ever-increasing numbers to South Australia—called the Festival State. They also come for November's Formula-One Grand Prix, and to gamble at Australia's most elegant casino.

Surrounded by acres of parkland, the capital, backed by a crescent of hills, is a city of pubs and churches. Its gracious Victorian and Edwardian buildings do *not* reflect a history of English convict labor; Adelaide was early Australia's only non-convict settlement.

But it is ironic that the concept of colonizing the state with free men was planned by Edward Gibbon Wakefield while he served three years (from 1830) in England's Newgate Gaol for marital indiscretions.

Adelaide, with only one million people, has a small-town, almost folksy atmosphere, and it can launch you to many South Australian attractions that can be seen in a day each. It is the gateway to the colorful Flinders Ranges, the Outback, the wine country, and the Riverland, where, from Renmark, the Murray River can be cruised on the Southern Hemisphere's biggest paddle wheeler. Farther afield are one of the world's finest nature sites, Kangaroo Island, and the unusual opal-mining town of Coober Pedy in the Outback.

In Adelaide you can swim from 18 miles of safe beaches, cycle the parklands, and play golf and tennis within a mile of downtown. More than 500 restaurants and pubs offer international cuisines and superior wines.

MAJOR INTEREST

**Adelaide**
North Adelaide for street life and shopping
The Hills

**South Australia outside Adelaide**
The wine country, especially the Barossa Valley
Kangaroo Island
Coober Pedy: opal mining, underground living

# ADELAIDE

Colonel William Light, son of Captain Francis Light, who was the founder of Penang in Malaysia, designed his utopian walking city (named after Queen Adelaide, consort of England's King William IV) like a chessboard, interspersed with and encompassed by parks and gardens. Light had been appointed South Australia's surveyor-general, with executive power over even the governor, to locate and plan the city. The parks include Himechi Garden, recently developed to honor Adelaide's Japanese sister city. (Other sister cities are Austin, Texas, and Penang.)

Orient yourself with an hour's pedicab tour (about A$11) or take the Explorer replica tram (it's really a bus) from the SA (South Australia) Travel Centre, 18 King William Street. Commentary accompanies the journey, which takes in the Adelaide Casino, Old Parliament House on North Terrace (now the Constitutional Museum), and the nearby contemporary-style **Festival Centre**, which is the Adelaide Arts Festival's home. You can alight from the tram at any stop along the way and reboard 90 minutes later at no extra cost.

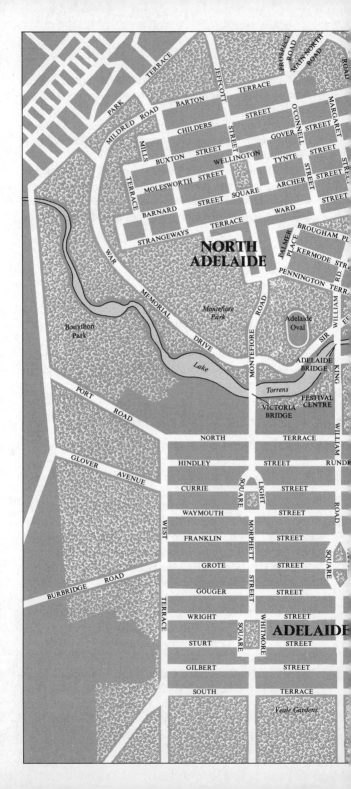

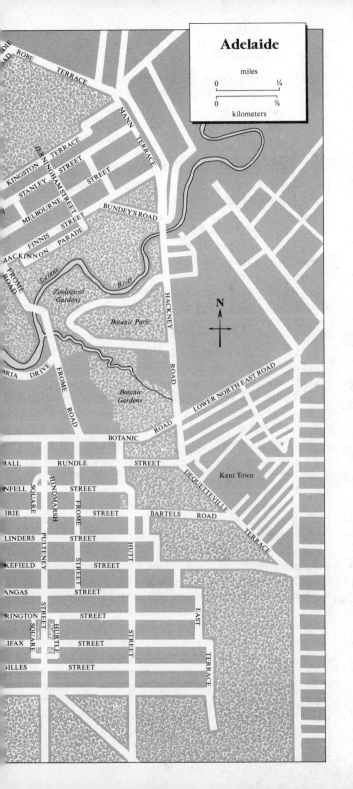

The Festival Centre includes the concert hall, the Lyric and experimental theaters, an open-air amphitheater and plaza, and the Playhouse Gallery, which has changing exhibitions. **Lyrics Restaurant** and the less formal **Playhouse Bistro** overlook the small, slow river Torrens and are open for lunch, dinner, and supper.

The tram passes the **Botanic Gardens** and the hundred-year-old **zoo**. The trip includes suburban, seaside **Glenelg** where, just off Anzac Highway, you can see the replica of HMS *Buffalo,* which brought the first governor to South Australia. The **HMS Buffalo** is an intimate seafood restaurant—and a museum. Glenelg, with a marina and a safe beach, has other economical to medium-priced seafood restaurants, and several others that reflect the ethnic backgrounds of European and Asian settlers.

# Exploring the City

Adelaide is a small city, bordered by North, South, East, and West Terraces, and it's easy to walk. A good beginning is at **Victoria Square**, where the 380-room **Hilton International** is located. The spacious marbled lobby is a favorite meeting place for locals, who often breakfast at the busy Marketplace Café.

Just around the corner is **Grote Street**'s colorful market. Walking north along King William Street, you will pass the Post Office (1867), Town Hall (1863), and Treasury buildings.

Three streets north from Victoria Square is **Rundle Mall**, which has Adelaide's best shops—from department stores to boutiques—and buskers. Opposite, boisterous Hindley Street (or Little Europe) boasts clubs and outdoor cafés that are good for people-watching and reflect the mix of nationalities.

North just one street is tree-lined **North Terrace**, which includes the train station, the Convention Centre, and the Monte Carlo–style **Adelaide Casino**, which has a 1930s atmosphere, internal Corinthian columns, and magnificent crystal chandeliers above the gaming tables. Next to the casino, which is in a 61-year-old former railway station, is the **Hyatt Regency**, which is only two minutes from the Festival Centre. The Hyatt is in the high price range, with its presidential suite equipped with telescope for 360-degree views. The Hyatt is almost an art gallery within a hotel, with the works of painters, ceramicists, potters, and glassblowers who were commissioned to reflect South Australia past and present and also Japan. The Hyatt's Scoops is Adelaide's first liquor-licensed ice-cream parlor, fun and friendly.

To the right of King William Street, North Terrace includes the **South Australian Museum**, with Australian bird, mammal, fish, and reptile exhibits. The Art Gallery of South Australia at North Terrace hosts visiting exhibitions, and the University of Adelaide nearby features many fine old buildings, including castlelike Bonython Hall, where concerts are held.

**Ayers House**, on the opposite side of North Terrace, is the restored Regency manor of former state premier Henry Ayers and is now headquarters of the National Trust of South Australia. Open for public inspection (except Mondays), it includes the **Henry Ayers Room**, Adelaide's most prestigious restaurant, where you dine on local seafood and fresh produce served elegantly. Tables are set well apart and, surrounded by antiques and paintings, you will almost be transported into the past as a personal guest of Henry Ayers. (Yes, the famed Ayers Rock was named after him.)

Off North Terrace and close to the bisecting King William Street is Kintore Avenue, where Australia's only Migration and Settlement Museum stands on the site of the former Destitute Asylum of the 1870s (in which children were imprisoned).

Just down from the angular Festival Centre on King William Road you can get a motor-launch cruise of the river Torrens, or hire a paddleboat, at Captain Jolley's next to the bridge. Above is the externally uninviting **Jolley's Boathouse Bistro**, but inside and on the balcony overlooking the river you'll lunch with local executives on artistically presented and moderately priced *nouvelle cuisine*. The decor is simple: potted plants and director's chairs in a casual atmosphere that nonetheless requires you to dress nicely.

Walk or take the bus to North Adelaide past parks with floral displays and tennis and golf facilities along King William Road, which becomes O'Connell Street after you reach Brougham Place. The **Hotel Adelaide** is situated there on the corner. With parkland at your feet, you'll enjoy one of the best views of the city, particularly at night, if you request a high-level, south-facing room (at upper-medium cost) or dine in the hotel's **Brougham Restaurant**.

**North Adelaide** is the city's oldest urban area, with restored bluestone cottages, mansions, terraced houses featuring intricate iron lacework, and many restaurants, pubs, and small, contemporary art galleries. You'll find them along O'Connell Street and the streets branching off it for a short distance: the **Tynte Gallery**, for example, at 83 Tynte Street, and **Gallery Bonython-Meadmore** at 88 Jennings Street.

A short walk right from Brougham Place off O'Connell is Melbourne Street, which has exclusive boutiques, a few restored pubs, and Adelaide's best Mexican food at **Zapata's** at number 42. Open for lunch and dinner, except Mondays, it has a white stucco interior complemented by dark wood furniture, lamps, and Mexican rugs. The food is not heavy or expensive; a special feature is the unusual liqueur coffees.

One street back from Hindley Street in the city center is Currie Street, where you can take a bus to **West Beach**, not far from the airport, and see dolphins and sea lions perform at seaside **Marineland**. While the cuisine at Marineland does not rival Adelaide's most elegant, it may be a novelty to dine with dolphins swimming to your table.

Buses depart from Grenfell Street, an eastern continuation of Currie Street across King William Street, for **Port Adelaide**, where South Australia's maritime heart is exposed in impressive restored 19th-century buildings. This is a compact area, so walk and discover the **Maritime Museum**'s seven separate locations around the port, beginning at 119 Lipson Street. There's an 1869 lighthouse, and a *son et lumière* show at the 1854 Bond Store.

End a leisurely stroll around the port at the restored boutique-brewery-brasserie, the **Port Dock Hotel** on Todd Street. This public bar has changed little since its days as a meeting place for former seafarers and clients of its the brothel. A lofty covered extension is the place to taste Old Preacher Ale, mischievously named after a temperance preacher who forced pub closure for 77 years. Sunday lunch here in summer with seafood, pasta, and jazz is relaxed and inexpensive.

# The Adelaide Hills

The Mount Lofty Ranges, more commonly known as the Adelaide Hills, embrace the city. Green for most of the year, they brown off in summer. Take a route 100 circle-line bus from Currie Street for one and a half hours of city, southeast suburbs, and sea views from the lower hills.

Most bus companies have Hills tours, but it's best to rent a car, especially in spring, for panoramic views of Spencer Gulf, Adelaide, and the suburbs. Pause, particularly at night, at **Windy Point**, a scenic vantage point in the foothills. (To get there, drive 12 km/7 miles from the city along shop- and restaurant-lined Unley Road, which becomes Belair Road.)

Windy Point has an excellent, formal, and expensive à la carte restaurant and a more casual Italian bistro, **Beppi's**. In both, city and suburbs are at your feet, with magnificent sunsets over the ocean in winter.

**Mount Lofty** is the highest point in the ranges, and there are spectacular city views from the summit. Close by is Cleland Conservation Park, where you can cuddle a koala. Just below it, on Summit Road, Crafers, is **Mount Lofty House**, the first South Australian country-house hotel, and Australia's third to be admitted to the prestigious French Relais et Châteaux country-estate association. It's 25 minutes from Adelaide and has an atmosphere of grand country living, with formal dining at **Hardy's**, an intimate, elegant restaurant. Its **Piccadilly Restaurant** is stone walled and less formal for breakfast, light luncheon, or dinner.

The Hills' hub is **Hahndorf**, about 40 minutes from Adelaide on the South-Eastern Freeway, resembling a German village with an interesting clock museum, galleries, and craft shops selling calico, lace, copper, and woolen goods in one main street. Each January it hosts Schuetzenfest, which means shooting festival, but the festival is really an excuse to get into German costume, sing, dance, parade, and eat and drink German-style.

Hahndorf was home to the great landscapist Sir Hans Heysen. The Academy and Art Gallery has some of his renowned works, and the active can follow the Heysen Trail, hiking through the hills that he so loved and depicted (ask locally).

Hills towns are not far apart, being separated only by valleys, orchards, and groves that are most beautiful in spring and fall. Several towns spin off the freeway, though it's nicest to drive through the back roads to, for example, **Aldgate**, with its award-winning craft shop featuring local woolen goods, pottery, art, and leatherware, or **Bridgewater**, an old flour-mill town. **The Mill** is now a casual but up-market restaurant nestled into a hill, and the water wheel still works. Get a map in Hahndorf from the Tourist Information Centre and wend your way on back roads to the city.

Although not far from Adelaide, the Hills should be explored for more than a day, which means overnighting. You will find old world, English-style, low-priced, high-quality country cottage accommodation by a lake and apple orchards at **Apple Tree Cottage**. With bed-and-breakfast and self-catering by an open fire, and two period-furnished bedrooms, it's a tranquil experience not to be missed. Apple Tree Cottage and its sister, Gum Tree Cottage, are at Oakbank, not far from the freeway.

More homey but by no means substandard accommodations that will enable you to mix with locals and gain their touring knowledge in the city, Hills, Barossa Valley, and farther afield are listed in the *South Australian Home Style Accommodation Guide,* available from the SA Travel Centre at 18 King William Street in Adelaide.

## Shopping in Adelaide

You'll find Crocodile Dundee hats at **Adelaide Hatters**, 39 Adelaide Arcade, or aboriginal arts and crafts at 28 Currie Street.

There's fine leather at Shop 14 in the Renaissance Centre in Rundle Mall. For antiques, browse the **Adelaide Antique Market**, 45 Flinders Street. If you are not going to Coober Pedy, visit **Olympic Opal Jewellers**, 5 Rundle Mall, which has a simulated opal mine offers and discounts to overseas visitors. Up from Rundle Mall is Gawler Place, where the **Opal Mine**, at number 30, also offers discounts.

# Dining and Entertainment
# in Adelaide

Competition among the large number of restaurants in Adelaide has resulted in high standards and lower prices.

King George whiting is a fish specialty of South Australia that many restaurants feature on their menus. Prawns (or shrimps, as North Americans know them), lobster, and fresh fish are superior and caught locally. In all of Australia, only South Australia offers kangaroo meat, which is gamey and tender after hanging, marinating, and roasting or broiling. It is featured at **Chloe's** in an elegant mansion at 36 College Road, Kent Town, five minutes by cab northeast of the city center. The reasonably priced menu at Chloe's includes a wonderful abalone mousseline. There are more than 20,000 bottles of Australian and imported wines in the cellar.

At 73 Angas Street, an unprepossessing, central, business location just a short walk east of the Hilton, you will find authentic, spicy, northern Chinese cuisine at **The Beijing**. It's quietly informal, inexpensive, the food is excellent and nicely presented, and the Peking duck doesn't require 24 hours' notice.

*Kaiseki-ryori,* a refined, delicate form of Japanese cuisine, isn't on the menu at the **Matsuri Sushi Bar and Restaurant** at 167 Gouger Street, a stroll west from the Hilton, but devotees of this hard-to-find artistic style can order it in advance. Decor is authentic, floor-level tables are available, traditional dishes are on the menu, and good wines include Japanese imports.

Try the pubs. You'd never know South Australia was once a temperance state, as pubs proliferate. Some pubs provide very cheap fare. In Adelaide there has been recent restoration of many splendid old colonial hotels (pubs) that had fallen into disrepair.

The counter lunch or counter tea is inexpensive, hearty, but fairly unimaginative in pubs that *haven't* been restored, but in those places you'll meet the earthier of the locals.

Other pubs, like the **Earl of Aberdeen**, on the corner of Carrington and Pulteney streets, not far east of Victoria Square, provide nightlife. You can mix with business people and, often, tourists—and also enjoy excellent food. The pub's **Gazebo Restaurant**—exposed brick, glass roof, and lush greenery—specializes in aged steaks, and there are boutique and imported beers and a variety of characters in the bar, especially Saturday nights.

The **Colonel Light** in Light Square (west off King William Street at Currie Street) is also newly restored to recapture the old colonial atmosphere.

The **Old Botanic Hotel** (corner of North and East Terraces) is a good watering hole for a convivial pint or two, plus either a light or substantial meal after wandering the city's museum and art gallery on North Terrace, where students and the fashionable people mingle at sidewalk cafés in summer.

After shopping in Melbourne Street, North Adelaide, sample the boutique beers and ales at **The Old Lion**, which has a 100-year-old grapevine as a feature of its brasserie.

The **Directors Hotel** (247 Gouger Street, a short walk west from the Hilton) is favored by Adelaide's yuppies. The pub's menu is international and reasonably priced. Decor is a Hollywood theme of days gone by.

There are several discos and night spots in central Hindley Street (west off King William Street, opposite Rundle Mall). Action starts around 9:30 P.M., mostly with deejay music. At **Limbo's** the younger crowd enjoys new wave music; to escape the kids try **The Cargo Club**. Crowded and jumping, **Braestead's Club New York** is up-market. At 171 Greenhill Road, Parkside, it is a five-minute cab ride south from downtown. **Juliana's** at the Hilton provides an intimate setting (brass decor) Wednesday to Sunday for late-night dancing and drinking. You'll meet out-of-towners here.

**Regine's**, at 69 Light Square, is elegant yet high-spirited, and open late. The Hyatt's **Waves** (opened June 1988, on North Terrace, just west of King William Street) claims to feature the world's most advanced computerized video and light technology. The crowd is mixed, from international visitors to local yuppies.

The **Adelaide Casino**, next door to the Hyatt, stays open until 4:00 A.M. The handsomely decorated, 30s-style **Pullman Restaurant** presents buffet-style lunches, dinners, and late suppers, often carrying a specific European or Asian theme. Bars include the cozy **Wine Bar**, with more than 300 choices of top South Australian wines.

Do not leave town before experiencing Adelaide's pie floater (meaty pie in thick pea soup) from curbside carts, evenings until late, on North Terrace by the casino and outside the General Post Office in Victoria Square. It's a wake-up or a settler after a night on the town.

# SOUTH AUSTRALIA'S WINE COUNTRY

South Australia's five major wine regions encourage wonderful self-indulgence.

The red-soiled **Riverland** starts one hour's drive northeast of Adelaide on the **Murray River**, where you can rent a **houseboat**. (Book at Tourism South Australia Travel Centre, 18 King William Street, Adelaide 5000; Tel: 08-212-1644.) Drive-yourself, self-contained vessels are based at many locations on the Murray, including the towns of Renmark, Paringa, Berri, Loxton, and Waikerie.

To reach these river towns, drive the South-Eastern Freeway out of Adelaide to Tailem Bend, leave the freeway, then follow the clearly sign-posted road along the river. A houseboat stay will reveal the prolific bird life of the Murray, spectacular red cliffs, ancient gum trees, and historic towns. There is good fishing and also water sports on most reaches of the river. The citrus fruit here is Australia's best.

The Riverland is one of Australia's biggest wine producers, and most of the 44 grape varieties cultivated in South Australia's wine-growing areas are represented. Main varieties of white grapes produced are chardonnay, chenin blanc, frontignac, Rhine Riesling, sauvignon blanc, semillon, and traminer. The Riverland's red grapes are cabernet sauvignon, malbec, pinot noir, and shiraz. Fine sherries are also produced.

The wineries of the **Southern Vales**, edged along the Fleurieu Peninsula facing Gulf St. Vincent, are Australia's tightest concentration of wineries (more than 40), just 40 km (25 miles) south of Adelaide. You can sun on one of several wide, sandy beaches before tasting elegant whites and full-flavored reds and perhaps lunching at a winery. Several have excellent tables in a vineyard atmosphere.

The wineries' directions are well sign-posted as you drive above and along the coast on South Road out of Adelaide.

**Coonawarra**, about 400 km (250 miles) southeast of Adelaide, is a small region—a cigar-shaped plain of red volcanic soil about eight miles long, which, since the beginning of the century, has produced some of Australia's finest reds. This is particularly true of its cabernet sauvignons. The region also produces Rhine Rieslings, which are emerging as whites of great quality. Labels to look for include Penfolds/Wynns, Mildara, Hungerford Hill, and Petaluma.

You can discover the Coonawarra region while driving from the state of Victoria along the Great Ocean Road, one of the nation's most spectacular drives (for coastal views from high cliffs) till you deviate to **Mount Gambier** just over the border in South Australia. Mount Gambier's mysterious Blue Lake changes from gray to brilliant blue from November to March. The puzzle of the blue was solved in 1979, when Australian scientists discovered that the lake's deep bottom was composed of pure calcium carbonate and that tiny suspended crystals of this material refracted mainly the blue line of the light spectrum.

After visiting the Coonawara area north of Mount Gambier, you can explore several spectacular caves with marine fossils north of the town of **Naracoorte** before continuing via the town of Keith to Adelaide. If you return to the coast, you'll cross the **Coorong**, an unspoiled, virtually uninhabited region of dunes, ocean, and inland waters abounding with bird life.

The narrow **Clare Valley**, 135 km (84 miles) north of Adelaide, has traditions in 21 wineries that stem from 1851 plantings by Jesuit priests needing sacramental wine. A unique style is the Clare Riesling introduced by the priests. The vines are a variety of *croushon,* widely grown in Europe. Other white grapes grown are Rhine Riesling, white hermitage, and white pinot with some verdelho, mainly used in blending. Red varieties, mirroring most of the other South Australian wine districts, are principally shiraz, cabernet sauvignon, and pinot noir.

## The Barossa Valley Wine Area

The most popular wine district, however, is the Barossa Valley, an hour northeast of Adelaide. Australia's best-

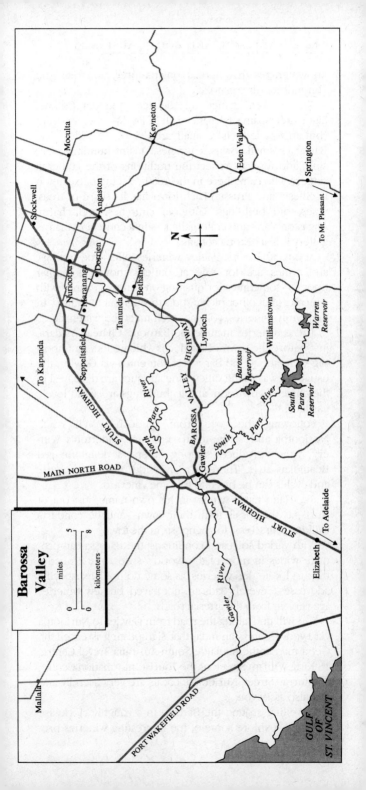

known grapes grow here among pastures, gum trees, and almond and olive groves.

The Barossa, named by Adelaide's founder Colonel Light after Spain's Barrosa—Hill of Roses—sherry region (but misspelled), is a small area, 5 by 19 miles. The Barossa's small towns, churches, quaint buildings, cuisine, and festivals reflect the traditions of the Lutheran settlers who came here in the 1800s, fleeing persecution in Silesia and Prussia. Each town has its share of trees, vines, old buildings, Lutheran churches, and charm. Angaston's arts and crafts gallery is in a church; Bethany's gallery is in a historic cottage.

About 50 Barossa Valley wineries offer free tastings, and wines are for sale at outlets known as "cellar doors"—sometimes for quaffing on winery grounds with a picnic, or at other picnic spots throughout the valley. In the family wineries, you may well meet the winemakers.

These wineries include the Baroque **Château Yaldara**, just before the town of Lyndoch, which offers an imposing welcome to the Barossa if you enter via Gawler, the usual gateway to the valley. Fine antiques are displayed in the château's ballroom and its buildings are set in lovely gardens.

Following the road from Lyndoch, you'll reach **Nuriootpa** and, at the town's entrance, **Elderton's Winery**, which produces, among others, a delightful red Beaujolais style. There is a riverside picnic area here, and cycles can be hired to tour the vineyard.

Ray Hahn has a winery in his own name, just out of Nuri—as the locals term their town—and he conducts walking tours. Look for signposts in the town.

With varied soils and conditions, the Barossa can produce wines in most of the world's styles. You'll need a map to locate the wineries, as some do not have specific addresses. Several roads are not paved, but few wineries are very far from the arterial roads.

You will find, along the road from Gawler to Nuriootpa via Lyndoch and Tanunda, that sign-posting is excellent. Get a map at the Adelaide South Australia Travel Centre, 18 King William Street, or the Tourist Information Centre, 66 Murray Street, Nuriootpa. Locals are very friendly and will also assist you.

Travelling around the Barossa in a roughly clockwise direction, explore some of the interesting wineries producing various, quality styles, beginning with **Peter Lehmann Wines** at Tanunda.

Peter is a winemaker's winemaker, highly representative of the valley's diverse quality styles, but his brilliant semillon sauternes stand out along with his cabernet sauvignon. His riverside winery has picnic facilities.

**Wolf Blass**, Sturt Highway, Nuriootpa, is Australia's most successful red wine exhibitor. His black-label reds, cabernet sauvignon or shiraz, are great wines, particularly for putting down for at least ten years. His large vine-draped tasting area is German in style.

**Saltram's**, on the road just before the town of Angaston, is famed for its Mr. Pickwick port, and its selection of reds and whites is commendable. There is a picnic area. **Yalumba**, just out of Angaston as you head north, is a big old bluestone winery set in lovely gardens. Its Heggies's Rhine Riesling is most appealing.

**Moculta Wine Company**, Truro Road, Moculta, is a bit out of the way but worth the deviation for its Portuguese oak-matured cabernet. Drive through Angaston toward Keyneton and go left at the Moculta turnoff for tastings in a historic bluestone building. Circling back to Tanunda, you'll find **Rockford Winery** on Krondorf Road. Here, try the big bold reds in the old Australian tradition.

**Barossa Settlers**, Trial Hill Road, Lyndoch, is a small premium winery set in an 1860s stone stable, where you can sample its distinctive late-harvest Rhine Riesling.

Come to the Barossa Valley in spring blossom time, summer, or fall; dress casually.

On the Sunday of Australia Day weekend (a three-day weekend falling on or just after the official date of January 26), the Oom Pah Fest brass-band festival, with frolic and food, takes place in Tanunda. Also at Tanunda on the first Sunday of every March is Essenfest, the German food festival. Biennial Easter Monday (the next in 1991 after 1989's) is the best time to visit for the week-long Barossa Valley Vintage Festival.

Adelaide Cup weekend (including the third Monday in May) brings a hot-air balloon regatta to **Seppeltsfield**, a large winery with manicured picnic and barbecue grounds. To get there turn left at the tiny hamlet of Dorrien, opposite the **Barossa Junction**, a motel-restaurant incorporating vintage railway carriages.

At Marananga, a village on the way to Seppeltsfield

(there are lovely views and cozy accommodations at **The Hermitage**), begins the date-palm avenue planted by the Seppelt family's employees during the Depression.

The winemakers welcome connoisseurs to the August Barossa Valley Classic Gourmet Weekend. Participating wineries team up with South Australia's best chefs to serve the finest food and wine in friendly settings, with live music appropriate to each winery's atmosphere. The host wineries vary from year to year, as does the date, which always falls on a mid-August weekend. Inquire at the SA Travel Centre, 18 King William Street, Adelaide, for the specific dates and wineries. You'll have to drive from winery to winery in the Barossa, but distances are short, and the food, wine, and entertainment—from jazz bands to string quartets—will be forever memorable.

While in the Barossa area see the old coopering craft's revival at the Keg Factory, St. Halletts Road, Tanunda. It's from goat to garment at **Merindah Mohair Farm**, Springton Road, Mount Pleasant, which sells garments hand-crafted from goat hair.

## Exploring the Barossa Valley

It is probably too challenging, but you can attempt the Barossa in one day by rented car or chauffeured limousine, helicopter, or cab from Adelaide with the option of getting around locally by limo, car, cab, or moped (at Tanunda). The region may seem confusing but you'll find that it's not, once you arrive in Gawler or Nuriootpa with map in hand. All accommodations, attractions, and wineries are proudly sign-posted.

Sturt Highway skirts the valley, with Barossa Valley Highway as its spine. Try to allocate three days if you are doing it on your own. Tight schedules will likely come unstuck despite the short hops between towns.

You can arrange a hot-air balloon ride over a rolling landscape, with Champagne on descent, at the Orlando Winery, the valley's first (1847), located in Rowland Flat. Booking is essential; Telephone (085) 24-4383. Or have a leisurely lunch at the gourmet **Vintners Restaurant** in Angaston (perhaps trying tender kangaroo) to extend your day.

If you're driving up, head for Nuriootpa—via old Gawler to see its historic pubs and heritage buildings around Church Hill if there's time; otherwise, take the bypass road. For information, maps, and advice, especially on wineries offering your preferences, consult with the Tourist Information Centre at 66 Murray Street in Nuriootpa. It's a logical beginning for your visit.

Travel the area roughly clockwise, gradually zigzagging south. For its crafts gallery, country pub, and hollow tree, include Springton on your itinerary.

Celtic music is featured at April's folk festival in Kapunda (at the area's north), Australia's oldest mining town (copper).

Return to Adelaide via the spectacular **Torrens Gorge** in the southern Mount Lofty Range above the river Torrens, which flows to the city. It's winding, lush with forests, and includes the National Motor Museum at the Mill, Birdwood, south of Springton in the Barossa Valley. There are a trout farm, wildlife park, and conservation and recreation areas.

## Staying in the Barossa Valley

Motels and pubs in the area have adequate, moderately priced bed-and-breakfast accommodations, but the most interesting places to stay are restored homesteads or cottages.

The homestead of the pioneer winemaking Seppelt family, **The Lodge** (the licensed country guesthouse with four rooms opposite Seppeltsfield), is not cheap but offers a most gracious environment. Romantic for two, The **Landhaus**, a restored shepherd's cottage, is a bed-and-breakfast accommodation with a spa, at Bethany. Up to 12 can dine by appointment at one of the valley's most elegant tables here. The peaceful four-room **Lawley Farm Cottage and Barn** (1850), on Krondorf Road in Tanunda, has been restored as a bed-and-breakfast accommodation.

**Stonewell Cottages**, between Tanunda and Seppeltsfield, is a new German-style hotel with lake views for a maximum of only eight guests. **Collingrove Homestead**, Angaston, has been classified by the National Trust. Accommodation is in nicely refurbished maids' quarters. Formal dining is available here by arrangement.

## Dining in the Barossa Valley

Informal cafés and coffee shops here reflect German/ Northern European traditions, while old pubs, many restored, provide reasonably priced, no-nonsense to good fare—and opportunities to meet the locals. For a palate-cleansing ale, pause at the beer garden at the 1846 **Tanunda Hotel** on the main street. The **Lyndoch Hotel** has good steaks. **Barossa Bakery** on Murray Street, Nuriootpa, offers traditional German lunches. Enjoy coffee at the **Linke's Family Bakery**, also in Nuriootpa. **Die Gallerie**, Murray Street, Tanunda, retains its old, country-store atmosphere; snack here or dine at leisure in the *wiengarten*.

Several restaurants and some wineries (lunch only) have interesting menus but two, plus the Landhaus, stand out. Well-presented, stylish dining—with an emphasis on fresh local produce—in an informal, vine-shaded atmosphere can be had at **The Vintners**, mentioned above, on Nuriootpa Road in Angaston. Game is the specialty of the award-winning **Pheasant Farm**, an operating pheasant farm with a lake, off Samuels Road near Marananga (closed February).

Delicious picnic fare from old German recipes can be bought from the valley's butchers, bakeries, and delicatessens, and it goes well with local wine and local fruits dried by Angaston's Angas Park Fruit Company.

Picnic hampers, from a ploughman's lunch to a gourmet's picnic (24 hours notice for the latter), are available from **Gnadenfrei Estate Winery**, Marananga, which also has restaurant facilities; Tel: (085) 62-2522.

Several wineries have pleasant picnic spots. There's also Bethany Reserve, a tranquil spot in the village with a trickling creek and gum trees, and Warren Park, near Mengler Hill, where a panoramic view of the valley can be enjoyed. Both lie on a scenic route east from Tanunda to Angaston.

# *KANGAROO ISLAND*

Australia's third-largest island, Kangaroo Island, is a place of spectacular natural contrasts.

South Australia's first official English settlement was near **Kingscote** in 1836. Earlier, in 1803, unofficial settlers arrived—brutal sealers and renegades. Tales of their exploits can be heard at the coastal town of American River, where they lived a primitive existence.

Kangaroo Island includes farmland as well as natural wildlife areas. Five days is an adequate stay, although day-trippers come just to mingle with the seals 60 km (36 miles) south of Kingscote, at Seal Bay. But they miss so much in so little time.

Some areas require permission from park rangers to enter, but rangers are helpful and conduct independent travellers on special-interest activities, sometimes even to usually inaccessible places.

It's quite an experience to stroll among rare sea lions at **Seal Bay**, one of the world's largest colonies; visitors can also camel-trek in southwest **Flinders Chase** (the largest of 15 national and conservation parks on the island); whale-watch in August; and swim with the seals or scuba dive around shipwrecks circling the rugged 281-mile-long coastline.

Visitors can also game-fish, or join National Parks and Wildlife Service rangers to descend escarpments for swimming in secluded bays, and to explore the Kelly Hill Caves. They can stay—with minimal amenities, but comfortably—at lighthouses.

The less intrepid sun on the superb beaches on the island's northern side. At the sea or lagoons, the hundreds of migrating and native birds include albatross and fairy penguins. Visitors can also see protected kangaroos (first observed by Captain Matthew Flinders, who named the island while passing it in 1802), wallabies, koalas, possums, bandicoots, New Zealand fur seals, goannas (a kind of monitor lizard), and platypuses in natural habitat. Or photograph some 50 orchid and hundreds of wild-flower species August to November.

## Touring Kangaroo Island

Kangaroo Island, 91 miles long, has 1,000 miles of roads, paved ones running among only three main towns at the east—Kingscote, American River, and Penneshaw—with a bit more beyond central Parndana. There is no public transportation. Rental-car charges include expensive insurance, because the many unpaved roads mean accident risks. Many signposts reflect the 1802 island circumnav-

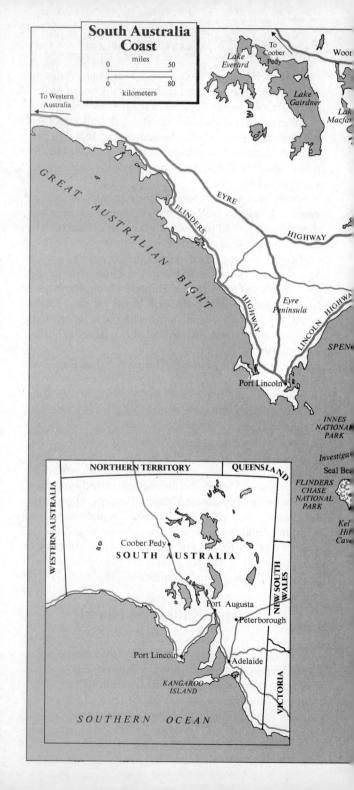

## South Australia Coast

| 0 | miles | 50 |
| 0 | kilometers | 80 |

To Western Australia

To Coober Pedy

Woor

*Lake Everard*

*Lake Gairdner*

*Lake Macfar*

GREAT AUSTRALIAN BIGHT

FLINDERS

EYRE

HIGHWAY

HIGHWAY

*Eyre Peninsula*

LINCOLN HIGHWAY

SPEN

Port Lincoln

INNES NATIONAL PARK

*Investiga*

Seal Bea

FLINDERS CHASE NATIONAL PARK

Kel
Hil
Cave

### Inset map

| NORTHERN TERRITORY | QUEENSLAND |

WESTERN AUSTRALIA

Coober Pedy

**SOUTH AUSTRALIA**

NEW SOUTH WALES

Port Augusta

Peterborough

Port Lincoln

Adelaide

VICTORIA

*KANGAROO ISLAND*

SOUTHERN OCEAN

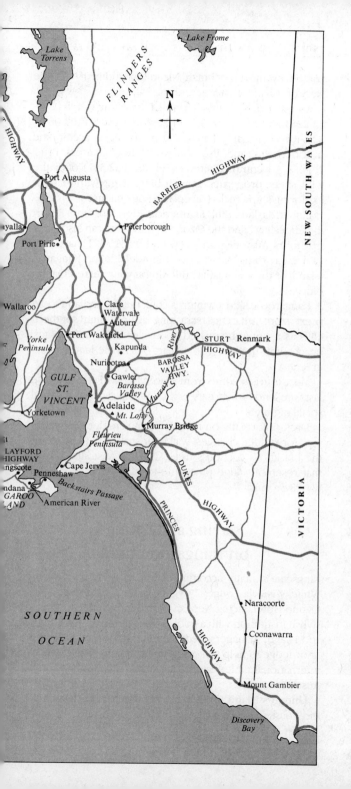

igation by the Frenchman Nicholas Baudin. If you are
wary of driving, consider tours.

Kingscote's Kangaroo Island Holiday Tours (Tel: 0848-
22-225) and Kangaroo Island Explorer Tours (Tel: 0848-
22-640) have daily-changing trips to major scenic and
historic areas, and also four-wheel-drive charters. Peter
Telfer's Adventure Charters (Tel: 0848-22-357) offer the
wild, sheep properties, game-fishing, diving with seals, or
exploring shipwrecks (divers must be qualified).

Linnett's Island Club in American River, Sorrento Resort
in Penneshaw, and the Ozone in Kingscote can also organize tours. Australian Odysseys (Tel: 08-315-321) have one-
to five-day camel safaris. Book in Adelaide, on Kangaroo
Island, or through Qantas/Bill King at your nearest Qantas
office.

Kangaroo Island's winter is cold, but the Indian Ocean
(next stop, Antarctica) crashing against high southern
cliffs is a not-to-be-missed spectacle. Swim in summer;
beachcomb the rest of the year—when the landscape is
greenest.

Most tourists come from December to February. The
last weekend in February is K.I.'s racing carnival, a casual
social highlight.

Dress informally on the island. In summer take warm
tops for sudden changes. Watch for snakes, particularly in
the blackboys (or grass trees, a native Australian plant)
that resemble huge pineapple tops. Walking shoes and
hats are a must.

## Staying and Eating
## on Kangaroo Island

Kingscote's main accommodations are right in town.
While **Wisteria Lodge**, 7 Cygnet Road, is the newest, the
**Ozone Hotel**, facing Nepean Bay's sunset reflections, is a
stylish institution with a pool. Known as Mr. & Mrs. Kangaroo Island, managers George and Ann Murphy have vast
knowledge to help visitors plan excursions. Their quality
international table features local seafood with top South
Australian wines.

**Linnett's Island Club**, overlooking American River and
the coast, has comfortable fully serviced and self-con-

tained units and excellent facilities, including pool, spa, sauna, and tennis. The food emphasis here is also on seafood.

The local lobster is good eating; do ask for it.

In Penneshaw there is the **Sorrento Resort**; see Getting Around, below.

The surprise in Penneshaw is **Muggleton's General Store**, with its B.Y.O. restaurant. The atmosphere is old-world; good Mediterranean-influenced lunches are prepared here by Rowan Muggleton, a former Melbourne Cup caterer who now presents gourmet fare at the K.I. Cup. Penneshaw's 1911 **Old Post Office Restaurant** is brasserie-style and inexpensive.

Nightlife (animal, not human): Fairy penguins parade at Penneshaw and on the Kingscote foreshores. On Kangaroo Island, buy the local honey (mainland bees are prohibited) and jams (perhaps from the first mulberry, planted at Queenscliffe near Kingscote in 1836). Try the eucalyptus oil that is manufactured locally; it's marvelous for rubbing into aching muscles or congested chests, and will clear nasal passages instantly.

# COOBER PEDY

A moonscape of craters and hills from the air, at ground level much of Coober Pedy resembles a wrecker's junkyard.

Coober Pedy (pronounced "Coober Pee-dee"), 863 km (536 miles) north of Adelaide—and the Outback's last frontier—hides its wealth beneath its pockmarked surface: It produces 80 percent of the world's opals and is rather an offbeat destination for visitors to South Australia.

And about 70 percent of its residents live underground, following the example of the miners who arrived after the discovery of opals here in 1915. The miners escaped the searing desert heat and night cold by remodeling disused mines into homes, or digging them from bare hillsides.

You can sample a bit of this unique lifestyle by staying in one of the five underground motels. Just don't expect views! The **Desert Cave** is claimed to be the only international-standard underground motel in the world, and it offers a novel experience in complete comfort. The **Underground Motel**, a little away from the main action of Hutchinson Street, is on Catacomb Road, while the **Opal Inn Hotel-Motel**, built on the surface, is at the throbbing epicenter of Coober Pedy's nightlife. **Radekas Dugout** has self-contained underground units alongside youth accommodations beneath the surface.

Like early Christians in Roman catacombs, visitors worship underground in the Catholic St. Peter and Paul's Church and the Anglican Catacomb Church.

Coober Pedy, from the aboriginal *kupa piti*—white fellow's burrow—is a place of polarized fortunes where dynamite is discounted at the supermarket! This polarization is instantly experienced at play in the Opal Inn Hotel-Motel, the town's social hub. Order a schooner of beer and chat with the colorful characters in the hotel's public bar.

The 4,000 people—give or take a thousand who avoid the census or drifters seeking the big strike—comprise about 45 nationalities.

Visitors come for the underground museum, pottery, and art galleries, to buy fiery opals more cheaply than in the cities, and to noodle or fossick (rummage) for them on the lunarlike surface.

But heed local boasts that the town is so progressive that everyone moves forward. Walking backward you would risk falling down one of the thousands of deep mineshafts no one has bothered to fill in.

If you are serious about mining, get a permit from the South Australia Department of Mines and Energy on Hutchinson Street.

It's best to visit Coober Pedy between pleasantly warm April and October. Summer temperatures can reach 54 degrees C (129 degrees F), although buses and many aboveground buildings are air-conditioned. Underground temperatures remain at 25 degrees C (77 degrees F).

In Coober Pedy, wear light, casual clothes, with a warm jacket or wrap for cool nights. Hats, sunglasses, and walking shoes are essential.

Coober Pedy is colorfully rambunctious on October's second weekend, during the annual race meeting and Outback Festival of arts and crafts. July's Greek Glendi Festival is fun.

# Around the Town of Coober Pedy

Walk Main (Hutchinson) Street at least. Hotel staff can arrange scenic flights or hire cars, but if you're driving beyond town, be careful. While sign-posted, many of the narrow, unpaved roads through rubbled hills have few landmarks. You can easily lose your sense of direction. As an alternative, there are taxis and comprehensive, locally operated tours.

Main Street yields the **Umoona Opal Mine Museum and Motel**, which has seven motel-style units, communal facilities, and above- and below-ground camping. The facility also features local aboriginal heritage, art, an underground mine, and a display home. There are also the **Underground Gallery and Bookshop** and various shops (some underground) selling opals, local art, and souvenirs.

With spectacular views, **The Big Winch** off Umoona Road is a retail complex atop a hill, the highest point in town. Paintings and opals (set or unset) are offered for sale, and cutting demonstrations are given. There are tables outside for picnicking in the cooler months. The giant winch and bucket symbolize the determination of the miners. Down the road, noodling (fossicking, or searching with your bare hands) is permitted.

It is worth the drive of 6 km (3¾ miles) along 17 Mile Road to the underground home of Crocodile Harry, a former Latvian baron, who made his converted-mine home into a gallery of eccentric art.

The **Breakaways**, an exposed sandstone range, is 28 km (17½ miles) north of town. The plain beneath it, the so-called **Painted Desert**, was the movie setting for *Mad Max Beyond Thunderdome*. The reserve is so-named because the sun's position constantly alters the vibrant colors of the landscape. A round trip north of 40 miles by four-wheel drive from Coober Pedy returns visitors along part of the 5,937-mile-long Dog Fence, erected to protect grazing sheep from dingoes, that stretches from Surfers Paradise on the coast of Queensland to the Great Australian Bight, the wild, open stretch of water that pounds the state's south coast. The fence is regularly checked by boundary riders in three states. Fossilized shells 100 million years old can be found along the fence and on the desolate Moon Plain to the east, about 20 km (12 miles) from Coober Pedy.

# Eating and Nightlife in Coober Pedy

Main Street's casual cafés, two licensed Greek barbecue restaurants, motel, and pub dining rooms also provide nightlife. Ethnic clubs welcome visitors and the food, particularly at the Greek club, is inexpensive and authentic. You can eat almost any hour of day or night in Coober Pedy.

## GETTING AROUND

Night entry into Adelaide by air is a spectacle of lights emphasizing the square-mile city's geometric layout. Transit airport bus and cabs meet international and domestic flights at opposite terminals. It's 15 minutes by bus or cab to central Adelaide. Interstate trains disembark passengers for Adelaide at inner-suburban Keswick Station, an easy, ten-minute cab ride to the city.

Adelaide's climate is Mediterranean. Summers can include heatwaves; winter is cool, June the wettest month. September to May is best for a visit. Bring casual dress, of course, but also semiformal wear (coat and tie for men) for the casino and the top restaurants.

### Kangaroo Island

Lloyd Aviation has a separate terminal sign-posted on the right just before Adelaide's small domestic airport building where through-passengers are met for the flight to Kangaroo Island. Flying southeast in an 18-seater airplane to the island takes 25 minutes. It's ten minutes from there by airport coach to Kingscote, "the big smoke" (slang for metropolis) of 1,700 people. Albatross Airlines and Air Transit operate smaller planes into the island.

From Port Adelaide along Gulf St. Vincent to Kingscote in the car-ferry *Island Seaway* is six hours. Alternatively, drive or take the bus for two hours through scenic, mainland Fleurieu Peninsula to Cape Jervis for the hour crossing of Backstairs Passage on the *Philanderer* ferry from Cape Jervis to tiny Penneshaw on the island. There's one modern motel, **The Sorrento**, in Penneshaw.

Buses leave the Adelaide bus terminal, at 101 Franklin Street (Tel: 08-272-6680) to connect with the ferry at Cape Jervis. Book the ferry passage at: Philanderer Ferries, P.O. Box 570, Penneshaw, South Australia 5222; Tel: (0848) 311-22.

Kingscote Yacht Club welcomes charter yachtsmen from American River or the mainland.

### Coober Pedy

From Adelaide, Kendall Airlines has four weekly flights. Make independent ground arrangements or take a three-day air package or a four-day package combining Coober Pedy with Ayers Rock, the spectacular sand and rock formations known as the Olgas, and Alice Springs. (See the Northern Territory chapter.) In Adelaide, call Kendall at (08) 231-1282, or phone the main office in Melbourne, (03) 670-2677.

Bus Australia's six-night Outback tour includes Coober Pedy, as does Deluxe's five-day package. With Greyhound and Ansett Pioneer, through-coach services extend to Ayers Rock and Alice Springs. Inclusive stopovers can be arranged. Treckabout Safaris has executive charters and four-wheel-drive Outback packages that include Coober Pedy. Organize in Adelaide or with Qantas abroad. Self-drivers can rent cars or mobile homes in Adelaide.

The ten-plus hours' self-drive from Adelaide to Coober Pedy becomes tedious after the Stuart Highway leaves coastal Port Augusta. Brief or overnight stops can be scheduled at Eldo Mess in Woomera, a former British rocket range, and/or the Glendambo hotel-motel.

Carry drinking water. Glendambo's roadhouse sign says: "No fresh rain water. Don't ask." When driving at night, beware of emus and kangaroos, who may damage vehicles more than the vehicles will damage them.

## ACCOMMODATIONS REFERENCE

▶ **Apple Tree Cottages**. P. O. Box 100, **Oakbank**, S.A. 5243. Tel: (08) 388-4193.

▶ **Barossa Junction Motel**. Barossa Valley Highway, **Tanunda**, S.A. 5353. Tel: (085) 63-3400.

▶ **Collingrove Homestead**. Eden Valley Road, **Anga-ston**, S.A. 5353. Tel: (085) 64-2061.

▶ **Desert Cave Motel**. Main Street, **Coober Pedy**, S.A. 4500. Tel: (086) 72-5004.

▶ **ELDO Mess**. Town Center, **Woomera**, S.A. 5720. Tel: (086) 743-271.

▶ **Gateway**. 147 North Terrace, **Adelaide**, S.A. 5000. (08) 217-7552; in U.S., (800) 44-UTELL; in Canada, (800) 387-1338; Telex: AA 88325.

▶ **Glendambo Hotel Motel**. Stuart Highway, **Glen-dambo**, S.A. 5170. Tel: (086) 72-1030.

▶ **The Hermitage of Marananga**. Seppeltsfield Road, **Marananga**, S.A. 5235. Tel: (085) 62-2722.

▶ **Hilton International**. 233 Victoria Square, **Adelaide**, S.A. 5000. Tel: (08) 217-0711; in U.S., (800) 445-8667; Telex: AA 87173.

▶ **Hotel Adelaide**. 62 Brougham Place, **North Adelaide**, S.A. 5006. Tel: (08) 267-3444; in U.S., (800) 624-FLAG; Telex: AA 82174.

▶ **Hyatt Regency Adelaide**. North Terrace, **Adelaide**, S.A. 5000. Tel: (08) 231-1234; in U.S. and Canada, (800) 228-9000; in Alaska and Hawaii, (800) 228-9005.

▶ **Landhaus**. Bethany Road, **Bethany**, S.A. 5352. Tel: (085) 63-2191.

▶ **Lawley Farm Cottage and Barn**. Krondorf Road, **Tanunda**, S.A. 5353. Tel: (085) 63-2141.

▶ **Linnett's Island Club**. Government Road, **American River**, S.A. 5221. Tel: (0848) 33-053.

▶ **The Lodge**. Seppeltsfield Road, **Seppeltsfield**, S.A. 5360. Tel: (085) 62-8277.

▶ **Mount Lofty House Country Estate**. 74 Summit Road, **Crafers**, S.A. 5152. Tel: (08) 339-6777.

▶ **Opal Inn Motel**. Main Street, **Coober Pedy**, S.A. 5723. Tel: (086) 72-5054.

▶ **Ozone Hotel**. Commercial Street, **Kingscote**, S.A. 5223. Tel: (0848) 22-011.

▶ **Radekas Dugout**. **Coober Pedy**, S.A. 5723. Tel: (086) 725-223.

▶ **Sorrento Resort Motel**. North Terrace, **Penneshaw**, S.A. 5222. Tel: (0848) 31028.

▶ **Stonewell Cottages**. Stonewell Road, between **Ta-nunda** and **Seppeltsfield**, S.A. 5352. Tel: (085) 63-2019.

▶ **Umoona Opal Mine Museum and Motel.** Hutchinson Street, **Coober Pedy**, S.A. 5723. Tel: (086) 725-288.

▶ **Underground Motel.** Catacomb Road, **Coober Pedy**, S.A. 5273. Tel: (086) 72-5324.

▶ **Wisteria Lodge.** 7 Cygnet Road, **Kingscote**, S.A. 5223. Tel: (0848) 22-707.

# PERTH AND WESTERN AUSTRALIA

*By Janis Hadley*

*Janis Hadley was the first woman editor in the Hong Kong business press, for* Asian Business *magazine. Born in the United Kingdom, she has lived in Western Australia for the past eight years, working as a free-lance travel writer for publications in Australia and overseas.*

Western Australia, like most other parts of the country, is immense. Most travellers—even those who have lived in the state all their lives—find it hard to come to grips with the distances here.

As Australia's largest state, Western Australia covers a staggering 1.5 million square miles—1,550 miles north to south and 1,055 miles west to east. Driving from the capital, Perth, to the beautiful northern tropical tourist town of Broome would take the average motorist 20 hours; it is roughly the equivalent of driving from London to Athens.

Along with these immense distances comes isolation. Perth is credited with being the most isolated provincial capital in the world. It takes half an hour longer to fly from Melbourne to Perth than from Perth to the Indonesian island of Bali. Singapore and Jakarta are as close to Perth as Sydney.

But it is this relative isolation that gives Western Australia its most endearing qualities. The fierce determination of West Australians to succeed against the odds has turned out world-famous entrepreneurs like Alan Bond (whose yachting syndicate snatched the America's Cup away from the United States in 1984) and financier Robert Holmes à Court. Perth allegedly has proportionately more million-aires than any other city in Australia.

As well as being isolated, Western Australia is the most sparsely populated state of Australia. More than two-thirds of the population of 1.4 million live in Perth, with the remainder living in small mining and agricultural towns hundreds or thousands of miles from one another.

For the tourist, this means that planning a trip here takes a little bit more thought than usual. If your stay is only a short one, then concentrating on the lifestyle and sights of Perth will make a lot more sense than spending hours—and lots of money—making epic journeys to the far corners of the state.

If you do have the time and the extra cash to cover the distances, you will be treated to some of the most rugged and seldom-visited scenic grandeur on earth, and a friendly country way of life that is a world away even from that of Perth, let alone the usual travel destinations.

MAJOR INTEREST

**Perth**
Historic buildings
Shopping arcades
Western Australian Art Gallery and Museum
King's Park
Foreshore parkland
River cruises
Water sports (catamaraning, sailing, water-skiing)
Indian Ocean beaches

**Around Perth**
Hillarys Boat Harbour and Underwater World
Yanchep National Park
Cohunu Wildlife Sanctuary
Armadale Pioneer World
York historic town

**Fremantle**
Fishermen's Harbour

South Terrace's open-air cafés and restaurants
The Round House
The Maritime Museum
Fremantle markets
Arts and crafts galleries
Antique shops

**Elsewhere in Western Australia**
Rottnest Island paradise near Fremantle
Margaret River wine country
Southwest beaches and rugged coastline
Gold Country's boom town of Kalgoorlie
Abrolhos coral islands
Kalbarri coastal retreat
The Pilbara
The Kimberley wilderness area

Separating Western Australia into regions is difficult; even within regions there are immense contrasts. Nonetheless, touristically speaking, it can be divided up into six regions:

- *The Southwest* (which includes Perth), the state's most populated area, containing a host of varied attractions.
- *The Gold Country,* centered east of Perth around Kalgoorlie, a fascinating mining town blending the old and new.
- *The Nullarbor Plain,* a huge expanse of nothing near the South Australia border.
- *The Central Coast,* an area of beaches, coral reefs, and wild dolphins about five hours' drive north of Perth.
- *The Pilbara,* the mining heart of Perth inland between Perth and The Kimberley, with some of the state's most impressive gorges.
- *The Kimberley* at the north end of the state, with an unspoiled tropical coastline, vast rivers and gorges, and some of the biggest cattle ranches in the world.

# *PERTH*

Perth's big attraction is its affluent lifestyle—made possible by the spin-off effects of the state's great minerals and other natural resources industries—that tends to focus largely on the outdoors.

This is hardly surprising considering that most of the city's population is spread around the picturesque banks of the Swan River and along 30 miles of Indian Ocean white-sand surf beaches.

On most summer Sundays the Swan is awash with colorful yachts and private pleasure cruisers (Perth people really are boat-mad). Getting together for sports, on the beach, or around the family barbecue is a way of life here.

Many visitors' general impression of Perth is one of wealthy people, yachting, and beautiful parks—and they're not far wrong. No matter where you come from you're likely to be impressed by Perth's neat and clean environment. There are parks everywhere; the only concentration of high-rise buildings is in the very center of town; and the entire urban area only has one industrial smokestack.

The best place to start a visit to Perth is in **King's Park**, the huge elevated tract of natural Australian bushland at the western end of the main street, **St. George's Terrace**. For a few dollars you can rent a bicycle here and explore the park as well as take in some great views of the city, its suburbs, and the Swan River. You'll see the sparkle of the river, softened by the gray-green bush trees on the Daring Range, which fringes Perth's flat river plain. The suburbs sprawl out to the shallow Darling foothills, and the Swan meanders along the main street in the heart of the business district. From this vantage point see Perth by day, the sunset at dusk, and the colorful cityscape lights at night.

The city center consists of four main streets running east-west: St. George's Terrace, closest to the river; Hay Street, the main shopping drag to the north; Murray Street; and Wellington Street, nearest to the railway on the northern side. Barracks Arch, just down St. George's Terrace from King's Park, was part of the original Perth barracks. The Old Court House, built in 1836, stands in

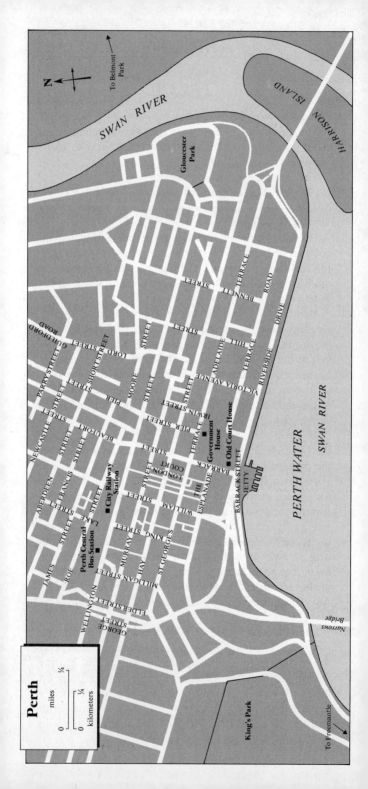

the middle of the Supreme Court Gardens near the river. The Government House, on Adelaide Terrace, was built by convict labor in 1863.

Shoppers will no doubt appreciate the traffic-free atmosphere of the **Hay Street Mall**, right in the center of the city, which is joined to Murray Street by shopping arcades selling everything from the famous Argyle diamonds to local wildflowers. In fact, best buys in Perth are dried Western Australian wildflowers, attractively boxed and mailed home for you. Other good buys are crafts turned from local woods and attractive silk-screened tee-shirts with sailing and aboriginal motifs. **London Court**, off Perth's **Hay Street** pedestrian mall, is an easy one-stop shopping place for these gift items.

If you have a little more money to spend you shouldn't pass up Broome pearls and Argyle diamonds. The Argyle diamond mine in Western Australia's Kimberleys has the world's largest output, based on the total number of karats produced. Most prized are the rare pink diamonds—with a price tag to match—but you'll find white sparklers to suit every pocketbook.

Broome's pearls are cultured on underwater farms and are of the type known as South Sea pearls. They are large by comparison to Japanese pearls and start in size at 10 millimeters in diameter. The pick of the crop can be more than double this size. Avoid the huge markups these goods attract when sold overseas by buying them here in the state where they are produced. **Linneys** in Rokeby Road, Subiaco, specializes in stunningly designed jewelry featuring both pearls and diamonds. (**Subiaco** is a district just on the other side of King's Park from the city center.)

The **Aboriginal Art Gallery** in St. George's Terrace is the place to buy quality aboriginal art and crafts. Here you'll find large emu eggs meticulously decorated with stylized animals; carved wooden birds with colorfully painted plumage; and paintings on bark depicting kangaroo hunts and other bush scenes. The most dramatic items are huge canvases stippled with thousands of multicolored paint dots, which are rudimentary maps designed to pass on the stories of the age-old aboriginal culture.

For maps of a more modern kind—dating back to the first European discovery and settlement of Australia—

**Trowbridge Prints** in Claremont has a fine selection. (**Claremont** district is southwest of King's Park on a bay off the Swan.)

Just north of the railway line, and an easy walk after a day's shopping, is the **Northbridge** area, the cultural, nightclub, and café center of Perth. Here, all within the space of three blocks, you will find the excellent **Perth Art Gallery** and **Perth Museum**, and a host of small restaurants and exotic food stores.

# The Swan River

A visit to Perth is incomplete without a river trip. Walk to the Barrack Street Jetty to choose your cruise. You can spend an hour or two gazing at the millionaires' mansions along the river, have dinner aboard a paddle steamer, or take the excellently priced trip upriver to the historic Swan Valley vineyards. The price of that last includes lunch and wine tasting.

For the more adventurous there are numerous places along the river where you can rent a catamaran or windsurfer to experience what the locals enjoy doing best.

West Australians of all ages are almost fanatical about sports—both playing and watching them. The city is sprinkled with sports arenas, including the centrally located WACA (pronounced "Whacker") or West Australian Cricket Association, which becomes an Australian Rules Football venue in winter. Horse racing is held on Saturday afternoons at Belmont Park in winter and Ascot in summer, both excellent racetracks within ten minutes of the city; Gloucester Park, next to the WACA, is the place to see pacers.

With 30 miles of white sand coastline within 20 minutes from the main street, there's always room on Perth beaches. One of the best is **Cottesloe Beach** just above North Fremantle on the north side of the Swan's mouth. Nude bathing is not legal in Western Australia, but that hasn't worried the generations of sun lovers swimming au naturel at popular **Swanbourne Beach** just above Cottesloe.

# Dining and Entertainment
## in Perth

Perth has a lot of restaurants, and there is a wide ethnic diversity among them. Many are B.Y.O. or B.Y.O.G. (bring your own grog), which makes a meal economical because you don't pay the restaurant wine markup. The better restaurants are closed on Monday nights.

Restaurants on South Terrace in Fremantle and James Street in Perth's Northbridge area provide a good selection of the world's cuisines, and it is possible to dine handsomely there for as little as A$25 a couple. A bit more upscale, the **Matilda Bay Restaurant** in Crawley, right next to the Royal Perth Yacht Club south of King's Park, is moderately priced and specializes in seafood. It combines elegant dining with one of the best Swan River views.

Lunching in the garden of the pricey **Mediterranean**, on Rokeby Road in the suburb of Subiaco, is the way to see Perth's leading businessmen and socialites, and dine on top international-style food served with excellent local and other Australian wines.

Enter most Perth nightclubs feeling sprightly and you'll come out feeling like Methuselah—they are the province of the affluent under-25s. **Chicago's**, in the Orchard Hotel on Wellington Street, or **Juliana's**, in the Parmelia Hilton, close to King's Park on Mill Street, just off St. George's Terrace, however, cater to the over-25s.

Popular Australian and international entertainers regularly play the theater restaurants of the **Civic** on Beaufort Street and **Romano's** on Stirling Street, both just north of the central city block. **Dirty Dicks**, on Cambridge Street just 3 km (2 miles) northwest of the city center, provides an Aussie dinner with bawdy music-hall skits. Most hotels provide live entertainment by local musicians from rock to jazz and bush bands. There will be colonial and Irish folk songs and a raucous atmosphere at **Clancy's Tavern** in Fremantle, and jazz at the **Railway Hotel** in East Fremantle each weekend.

Popular cultural events include the **Festival of Perth** in February, and, year-round, ballet, music, and drama at several venues. Check the daily *West Australian* or Friday's *Daily News* for details of what's on while you're in town.

# Staying in Perth

Nowhere is far from anywhere in Perth or Fremantle, so you don't need to opt for a centrally located hotel. You can choose from international-standard resort complexes, beach-side venues, or older-style accommodation refurbished to turn-of-the-century glory.

**Burswood Island Resort and Casino,** located on the main highway running from the airport to the city center, is Perth's newest hotel, expensive by West Australian standards but well worth it. It's a five-star, ten-story hotel where every room affords splendid views over the Swan River. The resort complex includes Australia's largest one-level casino, the vast Superdome entertainment venue, a golf course, and a very wide range of entertainment facilities. The only trouble staying here is dragging yourself away to see the sights.

Great Eastern Highway, Victoria Park, W.A. 6100. Tel: (09) 362-7777; within Australia, (008) 999-667, Telex: AA 92450.

Located just across the Swan River at Adelaide Terrace, the eastern extension of the main St. George's Terrace, is the **Merlin Hotel**. Popular with businessmen, this upscale hotel is famous for one of Perth's finest and most expensive restaurants, **The Langley**. The hotel has a soaring lobby, great views, and a quality shopping arcade and restaurant complex.

99 Adelaide Terrace, Perth, W.A. 6000. Tel: (09) 323-0121; within Australia, (008) 999-090; in U.S., (800) 44-UTELL; in Canada, (800) 387-1338.

For a more moderately priced accommodation in the heart of Perth's shopping center in Murray Street, try the **Wentworth Plaza**. This pleasant older-style hotel has recently been refurbished. It's a short stroll from here to the best shops, theaters, and restaurants.

300 Murray Street, Perth, W.A. 6000. Tel: (09) 321-6005; within Australia, (008) 999-270.

The place to stay if you want a top beach-side venue is the **Observation City Resort Hotel**. Prices are on the high side but you are paying for a great Indian Ocean location. Built to capture views of the 1987 America's Cup racing, it's situated on Scarborough Beach, just 20 minutes northwest of Perth. Unlike many of the other top hotels, the shops in Observation City stay open seven days a week.

The Esplanade, West Coast Highway, Scarborough, W.A. 6019. Tel: (09) 245-1000; within Australia, (008) 999-494; in U.S., (800) 4-UTELL; in Canada, (800) 387-1338.

## FREMANTLE

Although only 20 minutes by taxi from Perth's central business district, historic Freo (as it's affectionately known) is completely different from skyscrapered Perth. Originally a separate port city servicing Perth, Fremantle has now been engulfed by Perth's suburbia. Fortunately this has not destroyed its special resort-like character. To get a good feeling for Fremantle, stroll around the port's nooks and crannies—the busy dock areas at the mouth of the Swan River, and the narrow Mouat and Cliff streets, which date back to early settlement days—then walk the broad promenade of Marine Terrace with its shoreside park and elegant 19th-century buildings.

Thanks to impetus from Fremantle's role as host city for the 1987 America's Cup race, its old features have been renovated rather than destroyed. Cafés, restaurants, and historic pubs abound in a fun-filled atmosphere where eating, drinking, and socializing never seem to stop. (And indeed, during the America's Cup they didn't.)

Cup-inspired meeting places include **Lombardo's Restaurant and Bar** complex built over Fishermen's Harbour; the central courtyard restaurant and coffee lounge of the **Esplanade Plaza Hotel** on Marine Terrace; and **Papa Luigi's**, the best-known of the open-air cafés on South Terrace.

In South Terrace you'll also find the bustling **Fremantle Markets** (open from Thursday to Sunday), where it's easier to spend time rather than money. For interesting gifts and souvenirs, try the nearby **Bannister Street Craftworks** on Bannister Street.

The Cup transformed many of the old run-down sailors' hotels. Today, a pub crawl in Fremantle is a delight. Typical is **The Sail and Anchor** on South Terrace, which makes its own "real ale." Two minutes' walk from here brings you either to the **Norfolk** or to the **Newport**, both great pubs with real Fremantle atmosphere. Western Australia's lobster, known as crayfish, is a specialty at **Oyster Beds Restaurant** set on the Swan River at the top end of

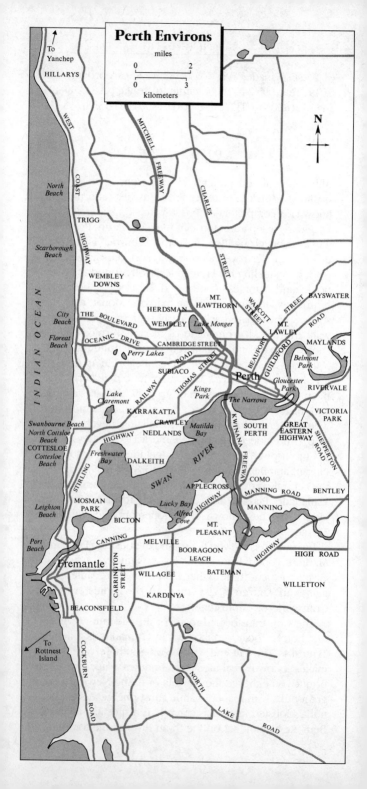

town. Spend a leisurely afternoon here watching the yachts while dining alfresco on superb seafood at very reasonable prices.

Fremantle's most interesting building is **The Round House** at the waterfront end of the main street, High Street. It was a small and rudimentary jail for convicts in the 1850s, when the area was a penal colony. Whales were dragged from shore and through a tunnel underneath the Round House to be stripped of blubber. The **Fremantle Museum** on Finnerty Street, originally a lunatic asylum, is considered one of the finest examples of convict-built colonial Gothic architecture in Australia. It is worth spending time here discovering the hardships of the early days, Fremantle's interesting convict history, and its role in providing Britain and other Commonwealth countries with wheat, meat, and wool.

Old sea stories abound in Fremantle. The **Maritime Museum** on Cliff Street graphically shows how Dutch mariners bound for the Spice Islands (Indonesia) were blown east by the Roaring Forties to hit the treacherous Western Australian coast. (Closed mornings and Monday, Tuesday, and Thursday.)

The **Esplanade Plaza Hotel** in Marine Terrace is the place to stay if you want to make Fremantle your base. Popular with those who love Fremantle's relaxed atmosphere, this 19th-century hotel had a splendid refitting for the America's Cup racing and offers the best of the old and the new at a moderate cost. The **Atrium Restaurant**, under the conservatory roof, is the place to be seen for the buffet lunch; bookings are essential.

# ROTTNEST ISLAND

Perth's island playground, just 11 miles from Fremantle, gets its name from the first Dutch mariners, who called it "Rat's Nest," believing that the small animals they found on the island were vermin.

Actually they are quokkas: small, friendly marsupials that delight in being fed from your hand. By day they stay under shady trees and at night, when they get more adventurous, they are everywhere.

Rottnest is a special getaway spot. Only the locals have

cars and there are few phones. It's what vacations must have been like before resorts were invented.

You can't take a motor vehicle to Rottnest, so island transport is by bicycle or on foot. But that's no hardship since the island is only about seven miles long and a round-island trip on the coast-hugging road is under 17 miles—a two-hour cycle at the most. Rent a bicycle at Thomson Bay from the shop behind the pub at a very economical rate.

If pedal power isn't your style, you'll find most of the interesting spots are within easy walking distance. There's also a bus at the ferry berth to take you around the island to get your bearings and see the sights.

Rottnest's many protected bays, with white-sand beaches and fringing coral reefs, are ideal boat havens. The beaches at Thomson Bay, and Longreach and Geordie bays to the north, just a 20-minute stroll away, are best for safe swimming. Fishermen may prefer the wilder waters at Rocky Bay or West Point at the western end of the island. Divers can call into the museum at Thomson Bay for the Rottnest Wreck Trail brochure, which shows locations of 11 wrecks accessible to scuba divers or snorkelers. You can rent gear at Thomson Bay. Rottnest is a reserve, so no spear guns are allowed. If you're not quite so adventurous, take in the best of the coral and shipwrecks on the mini-submarine at Thomson Bay.

The settlement in **Thomson Bay** is the center of activity. In January the bay is covered with yachts and power boats, and the settlement hums day and night. There are two hotels. Young people gather at the **Rottnest Hotel**, originally the summer home for West Australian governors. This moderately priced hotel is nicknamed the Quokka Arms by young locals, and its beer garden is the scene of much raucous activity during summer weekends. It has a great location right on Thomson Bay beach, but can be noisy during school vacations and public holidays. The more upscale **Rottnest Lodge Resort** is a popular getaway spot with the smart set. The resort is peaceful, yet only a couple of minutes' walk from the main action at Thomson Bay, and moderately priced.

**Rottnest Island Self Catering Cottages** are budget-priced family accommodations in well-equipped cottages dotted around Thomson, Longreach, and Geordie bays, which, except for school holidays, can be booked at relatively short notice (see the Accommodations Reference section at the end of the chapter).

Rottnest has an interesting history. The old church, warders' cottages, jail, and military establishments are relics of days gone by. Read the visitors' book at the jail (now an economy lodging house).

Getting to Rottnest is easy. If you want to combine a sea trip with a river trip, take a ferry from the Barrack Street Jetty in Perth, or, alternatively, catch ferries directly from Fremantle or from the boat harbor at Hillarys on Perth's northern beach area. The trip down river from Perth takes about 40 minutes, and it is half an hour over the sea from both coastal exit points.

Alternatively, you can fly to Rottnest in just 12 minutes at a very economical rate from both Perth and Jandakot (a 30-minute drive south of the city, off the Roe Highway) airports.

## *ATTRACTIONS NEAR PERTH*

Drive north on West Coast Highway to Perth's new beachside suburbs and you probably won't be able to resist a cooling dip in the Indian Ocean. Two special beach spots are **Mettam's** and **Hamersley Pools**—between Trigg and North Beach—where natural rock formations have formed shallow, safe swimming areas that are pleasantly warm year round.

Farther along the highway—some 30 minutes from the city—is Hillarys Boat Harbour and Underwater World. The fishy story continues at Atlantis Marine Park, 30 minutes farther north in Yanchep. The nearby **Yanchep National Park** has a colony of koalas, typical bush birdlife, and limestone caves.

Just over an hour's drive east of Perth through the Avon Valley is the old town of **York**, with its fine historic buildings. The Residency Museum should not be missed. Accommodation options include the four-poster beds of the gracious **Settlers' House** on the main street. It's not inexpensive, but well worth the experience.

A 25-minute drive south from Perth on the Albany Highway leads to **Cohunu Wildlife Sanctuary** at Gosnells. This is your chance to be photographed with kangaroos, wallabies, and emus, and to cuddle a koala.

At **Armadale**, 10 km (6 miles) south of Cohunu, artists and craftspeople at Pioneer World colonial village create and sell unusual and interesting artifacts.

## THE SOUTHWEST

A couple of hours' drive from Perth to the country's Southwest corner, leads to a cooler, mixed-farming area, important for wheat, wool, and beef. Its lush green landscape has a perfect climate for vines. At the town of **Margaret River**, more than 20 boutique-style wineries welcome visitors to taste and buy from their cellars. Perhaps the most impressive of these wineries, **Leeuwin Estate**, is a showpiece for its wines, with an elegant restaurant featuring local produce—including the freshwater crustacean the marron—and a magnificent natural amphitheater fringed by tall karri trees. Leeuwin's chardonnay is internationally acclaimed, and the winery also produces Rhine Riesling, pinot noir, and cabernet sauvignon styles, which are all Australian medal winners.

Other important attractions in the Southwest include the beautiful rugged coastline, the wide beaches—great for fishing, surfing, camping, and just relaxing—limestone caves, forest drives, and the many craft outlets. Some interesting towns to visit are the old whaling towns of Albany (on the southern coast of the Southwest corner) and Esperance (much farther to the east), the quaint timber town of Pemberton, between the Margaret River and Albany, and the lovely estuary town of Denmark, west of Albany.

**Captain Freycinet Motel**, on Tunbridge Street on the outskirts of Margaret River, is a new, moderately priced hotel built to cater to wine lovers visiting the vineyards. **Margaret River Hotel Motel** is a favorite with young people for its moderate prices and lively atmosphere. A recent refitting has turned a seedy hotel into a comfortable venue with elegant Victorian architecture.

## THE GOLD COUNTRY

It was the discovery of gold in the 1880s that made the powers in the east of Australia sit up and take notice of

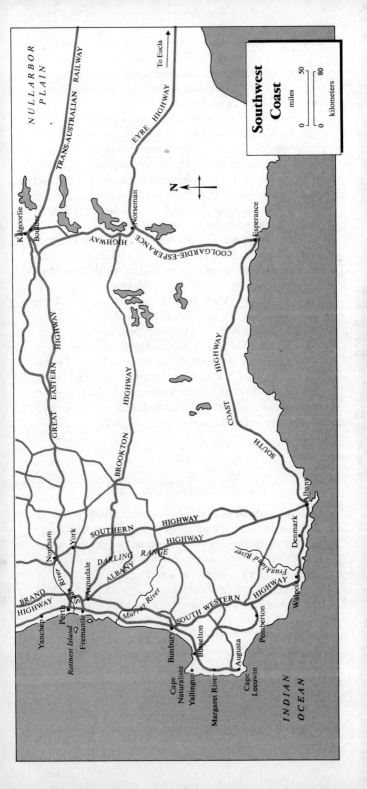

Western Australia. With another gold boom now well under way, the goldfields—centered around **Kalgoorlie**—have hit the jackpot again.

Located about six hours' drive east of Perth (or overnight by train), Kalgoorlie is an unusual combination: Old shops, which look much the same as they did 150 years ago, stand side by side with modern supermarket complexes, and the old underground mines are located within easy view of huge new open-cut gold mines. Be sure to go down the Hainault Tourist Mine in nearby Boulder to observe traditional mining methods.

There are legalized brothels in town, many hard-drinking bars, and the Two-Up game, a traditional Australian gambling game played by tossing two coins. Most hotels and bars here are basic but full of atmosphere. For comfort stay at the **Plaza Hotel** in Egan Street, just off the main Hannan Street. It is modern, comfortable, and reasonably priced, with none of the hard-drinking, hard-talking action for which Kalgoorlie is renowned. For atmosphere try the **Palace Hotel**. This gracious old hotel on the corner of Maritana and Hannan has seen better days, but is brimming with ambience. Its bars are the haunts of many a local character with a tall tale to tell. And do visit the other hotels—there are plenty to choose from.

## THE NULLARBOR PLAIN

This huge expanse of nothing (Nullarbor comes from the aboriginal word meaning "treeless") on the central southern coast of Australia between Perth and Adelaide is more memorable for the sense of achievement you feel in crossing it than for what you see along the way. The trip by car leads west from Adelaide on the world's straightest road. Towns to stay in include Eucla and Norseman. Whatever you do, don't run out of gas; there is virtually *nothing* in between towns.

## THE CENTRAL COAST

Centered around the major port town of **Geraldton**, five hours north of Perth, this area offers many sightseeing opportunities, perhaps the most outstanding of which are the protected, unspoiled coral islands of the **Abrolhos group**, which can be visited by charter boat, and the now-famous wild dolphins that come into the shallows farther up the coast at **Monkey Mia** to be fed and patted.

You can take a weekend cruise to the **Abrolhos Islands** from Geraldton aboard a 75-foot schooner equipped with diving and fishing gear; check Geraldton's tourism office in Chapman Road for details. The islands are a six-hour motor-sail from the port, so this is a trip in itself. A visit to Monkey Mia is best combined with a general Central Coast trip taking in Geraldton, the seaside retreat of Kalbarri and nearby gorges to its north, and the eerie Pinnacles limestone formations near Cervantes, halfway between Perth and Geraldton.

**Kalbarri** is an ideal base from which to see the region. You can choose from river or sea for your recreation activities. The tiny town is at the mouth of the Murchison, the river that has scoured the landscape to form 50 miles of spectacular gorges, and there is top fishing on white-sand Indian Ocean beaches. The river estuary is the place for safe swimming and water-skiing. The **Kalbarri Beach Resort** on the estuary is more upscale than the other family-style accommodations in the town, but moderately priced, with a wide range of sporting facilities.

There are three flights a week from Perth to Kalbarri, where you can rent a car for side trips. However, if you have the time, a drive from Perth to the Central Coast is worth it. You'll see craggy, windswept coastlines, rolling farming country, and historic stone flour mills and farm cottages at Dongara and Greenough, halfway between Perth and Geraldton.

## THE PILBARA

This rugged area is the center of much of the state's iron-ore mining operations and is very interesting for its mountains that literally move. There is some spectacular gorge country here north of Geraldton and about halfway between Perth and the Kimberleys in **Hamersley Range National Park**, near **Wittenoom**, which, not surprisingly, has become a prime tourist attraction.

You can't take a scheduled flight directly to Wittenoom,

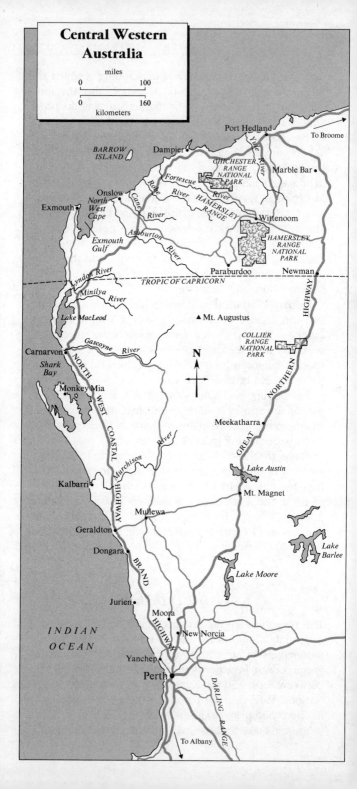

but there are daily flights with a coach connection to **Tom Price**, the heart of the state's iron-ore mining district. Visit the mine to get an idea of the huge scale of the operation. Wittenoom is 110 km (67 miles) north by car from here. The dramatic, craggy gorges are close to Wittenoom town and most are accessible by road. Stay at the moderately priced **Dumar Motel** in Carey Street.

Drive north-northwest from Wittenoom to Karratha (a four-hour drive on unpaved roads) and you'll pass through a region of large jagged ranges tinged red from the iron-ore deposits in the rocks, sparse bush, and arid landscapes. This is cattle country and home of some of the state's biggest stations.

At **Millstream**, halfway between Wittenoom and Karratha, is a lush tropical oasis, complete with cool, deep pools, date palms, and fruit bats. It's a beautiful spot and well worth the 10-km (6-mile) detour off the main road.

**Karratha** is a modern town built to service the huge northwest shelf natural-gas project. Dampier, 20 km (about 12 miles) northwest of Karratha, is where natural gas from ocean fields is piped ashore and processed for shipment overseas or piped south to Perth. The complex is worth a look. Flights leave Karratha daily for Perth and once a week for Broome to the north. You can also take a bus tour of the gorges from Karratha—Nor West Explorer Tours in Karratha City Shopping Centre (091-85-2474) offers a range of tours.

## THE KIMBERLEY

The Kimberley region in the northwest is Western Australia's last frontier, poised to become one of the country's major tourism drawing cards.

It's an awesome area. In the remote hinterland you can gaze over craggy, million-year-old landscapes, dramatic gorges, and thousands of miles of rugged bushland on which no one has ever stood. To the west is the historic pearling port of Broome, magnificent beaches, and a magnificently rugged coast deserted except for isolated aboriginal missions. And in the northeast, close to the Northern Territory border, is tropical Kununurra and the largest man-made lake in Australia.

The best time to visit The Kimberley is in the dry

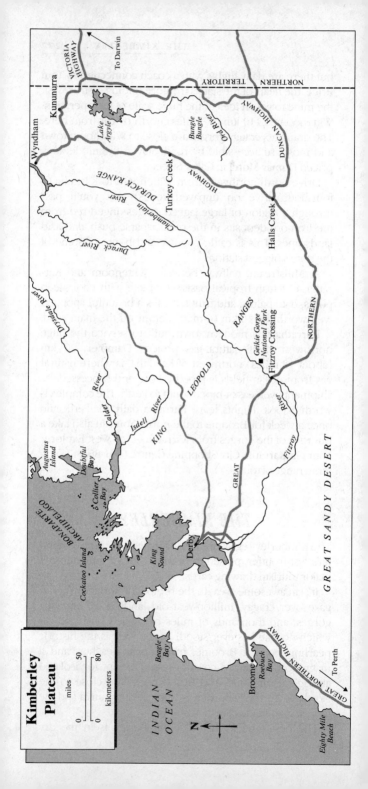

## Kimberley Plateau

miles
0        50
0        80
kilometers

INDIAN OCEAN

Eighty Mile Beach

To Perth

GREAT NORTHERN HIGHWAY

Roebuck Bay

Broome

Beagle Bay

King Sound

Derby

BONAPARTE ARCHIPELAGO

Cockatoo Island

Augustus Island

Collier Bay

Doubtful Bay

GREAT SANDY DESERT

Fitzroy River

Fitzroy Crossing

Geikie Gorge National Park

GREAT        RANGES

LEOPOLD        RANGES

KING

Calder River

Isdell River

Drysdale River

Durack River

Chamberlain River

DURACK RANGE

Halls Creek

NORTHERN        HIGHWAY

Turkey Creek

Bungle Bungle

Ord River

DUNCAN HIGHWAY

NORTHERN TERRITORY

Lake Argyle

Kununurra

Wyndham

VICTORIA HIGHWAY

To Darwin

N

season from April to September, when there's a warm to hot tropical climate. At other times the weather is unbearably hot and humid, and there is the likelihood of being cut off by flash flooding.

It is impossible to see everything in the vast Kimberley region, so first-time visitors might make their base in the Kununurra region, a four-hour flight from Perth, then take a four-wheel-drive tour with experienced bush guides to the remote wilderness of the Bungle Bungle, and finish with some R & R in Broome, just a two-hour flight from Kununurra. Seven days is the minimum for this Kimberley experience.

# The Kununurra Region

Flights leave Perth daily for Kununurra. Make sure you ask for a window seat on the plane so you can marvel at the thousands of miles of rugged coast and the remote, red interior you'll see en route.

**Kununurra** is a modern town, built in the 1960s to service the huge **Ord River** dam and irrigation scheme. The innovative plan was to turn desert into a major fruit- and sugar-producing area—and the area is certainly green—but falling sugar prices and the area's remoteness from main markets have impeded the scheme's success.

However, the region has a big plus for visitors: When the Ord was dammed, **Lake Argyle** was formed, and it is now the biggest man-made lake in the Southern Hemisphere. Here you can take your pick from a wide range of water sports or hire a boat to fish or picnic on the lake's lush banks.

Some travellers stay in Kununurra—the **Swagmans Inn** is moderate, modern, and comfortable—but it is much more fun to take the regular coach service 75 km (46 miles) to Lake Argyle via the fruit fields of the irrigation project. Here the **Lake Argyle Tourist Village**, a scenic complex on the banks of the lake, provides camping gear for you to stay on an island in the middle of the tranquil lake, or offers the softer option of a night at the inexpensive **Lake Argyle Inn** on its banks. With shops, restaurants, and tours, in addition to the accommodations, it really is a village. Prior booking is advisable (see the Accommodations Reference section at the end of the chapter).

Close by is the pioneering Durack family's early home,

**Argyle Downs Homestead**. It is now a museum and has exhibits and photographs that show the hardships of station life at the turn of the century.

Reserve at the tourist village for an adventurous day trip to raft on the Ord River through magnificent gorges and thick tropical undergrowth—and to see, from a safe distance, those famous crocodiles.

You'll see plenty of other Australian wildlife in the area. Animals and birds that come to drink at the lake include all types of marsupials, from large red kangaroos to tiny rock wallabies, colorful bush parrots, storks, cormorants, and pelicans.

# The Bungle Bungles

Be prepared for breathtaking primeval landscapes and unique experiences when you venture into the remote Bungle Bungle region, the most dramatic of the interior sights, which lies due south of Kununurra about 200 km (122 miles).

The only way to reach the Bungle Bungle mountain range is by four-wheel-drive vehicle, but it is unwise to attempt the trip on your own into this largely uncharted, uninhabited area. It's much safer to take a four-wheel safari run by skilled bushmen. Safari tours originate in Kununurra, and there are many operators to choose from who offer adventure trips of up to ten days duration. But if you're on a limited timetable, you can see the best of the sights on a three- or four-day trek. (SafariTrek Australia includes many extras to make the adventure more comfortable. They operate a variety of tours from May to August and can be contacted at their Perth office; Tel: 09-474-1707. Prices are moderate and are all-inclusive.)

If time is really short you can take an air charter from Kununurra for a bird's-eye view of the Bungle Bungle and surrounding district.

When you join a four-wheel-drive adventure trek there's a 150-km (90-mile) drive south from Kununurra on paved roads through cattle country, then it's unpaved roads through the bush some 50 km (30 miles) to the Bungle Bungle.

You'll need to hang on to your hat—and your stomach—as the vehicles grind up huge rock inclines and down precipitous slopes, but any discomfort is offset by the overwhelming beauty of the terrain. This is a magnificent world of cavernous gorges, sheer massifs, fragile sandstone pinnacles, and eerie landscapes that more resemble the moon's surface than anything on earth. The Bungle Bungle range itself covers 270 square miles and is at least 350 million years old. It is characterized by beehive-shaped formations banded by lichens whose life support are water droplets trapped in the rock.

Peer down the deep gorges and you'll see thick, lush plant life. These palms and creepers are remnants of prehistoric tropical vegetation. Yet far above on the craggy slopes the searing heat makes even the desert lizards shudder.

There are plenty of stops on the way: to clamber up a rock slope where no one has ever set foot, to picnic overlooking awesome, age-old ridges, to listen to the silence. Each night of the safari is spent under canvas at scenic watering holes on the banks of one of the many tributaries of the Ord River. The sunsets are breathtaking in this dramatic setting. After a bush barbecue watch the Southern Cross constellation rise in the night sky and listen to the yarns of your bush guides around the campfire.

# Broome

Broome (a two-hour flight from Kununurra) on the coast on the southwest tip of The Kimberleys, is a perfect spot for some relaxation after a rigorous Kimberley safari. There are daily flights from Perth or from Kununurra. The main drawing cards are the 18-mile Cable Beach on the town's western edge and the opportunity to buy pearls directly from pearl farmers.

It has a leisurely, tropical atmosphere—warm in winter, the best time to visit, and hot and humid in summer. The town is green and lush year round, with colorful tropical vegetation, palms, and the unusual baobab trees that look as though they are growing upside down.

Broome is built on a small inlet, so there's an interesting mix of landscapes. On the coast, the broad white sands of **Cable Beach** stretch for miles and miles. It's never crowded and nobody minds if you bare it all. To the east of the town are the low-lying mangrove flats, which experience two tides a day, and at the southwest tip are the rugged cliffs of Gantheaume Point, where at low tide you can see dinosaur tracks embedded in the sandstone rocks.

Broome was founded in the 1880s when pearls were discovered in the Indian Ocean. The find sparked a huge export trade to Europe, where the pearl shell was made into buttons and the pearls adorned the necks of European wives and mistresses. When plastics came along Broome's pearl shell trade died, but pearling has more recently been rekindled on cultured-pearl farms.

The **Broome Historical Society Museum** on Saville Street tells the story of pearling and the many Asian people, particularly from Japan, who came to Broome at the turn of the century to dive for pearls. At first they free-dived, then they wore rudimentary suits with oxygen pipes in order to pluck the oysters off the sea bottom. Many didn't live long to spend their riches—as you'll see by the many rough-hewn rock gravestones at the large Japanese cemetery on Port Drive.

The Asian influence is evident in Broome's **Chinatown** area between Dampier Terrace and Carnarvon Street. Here, even the telephone boxes have curled roofs. Chinatown is the place to buy pearls, cheaper mother-of-pearl jewelry, and aboriginal carvings of native animals. **Linneys** of Broome in Dampier Terrace supplies pearls to the finest jewelers in Bond Street and Fifth Avenue, but here you can buy direct, and the prices reflect the elimination of the middlemen. Nearby, **Buccaneer Pearls** offers regular factory tours to see the craftsmen at their work.

The **Shinju Matsuri Pearl Festival**, in early August, is a week-long salute to the pearl that attracts thousands of people to the town. Flight and accommodation bookings well in advance for this time are a must.

The **Roebuck Bay Resort Hotel**, at the southern end of Broome overlooking the small town beach, offers cottage-style accommodation and stunning modern architecture in the main bar. The recently completed **Cable Beach Resort** overlooks the beach and is a popular spot to sip a drink and watch the sun set over the Indian Ocean. You'll pay a little more at both these resorts than at other accommodations in Broome, but if you've come all this way they are worth it.

It's a good idea to rent a car—all hotels can arrange this for you—to get around the town and to and from the beach. MiniMokes and Volkswagen convertibles are the popular vehicles. You can't drive far out of town before the paved roads turn into un-signposted bush tracks only suitable for four-wheel-drive vehicles. It's safer to take a day tour with a local guide, or get a group together and see the dramatic bush landscape by air. Check with your hotel for details on the various excursions.

Divers will doubtless appreciate the pristine coral of the **Rowley Shoals**, 120-odd miles off Broome's coast. This remote spot in the Indian Ocean is considered to have the finest unspoiled atolls left in the world. Boats leave Broome for the Rowley Shoals in the winter months for a 12-day charter. For details check with the Holiday Western Australia Centre in Perth (09-322-2999).

## GETTING AROUND

Perth is the main entry point to Western Australia by air, train, bus, and car. The international airport is modern and efficient. The only delay is customs processing, which usually takes about an hour. The domestic terminal is straight across the runways from international arrivals, but it's 10 km (6 miles) around by taxi or bus. Allow 15 minutes for the trip if you have to make a connection.

From any arrival point, there are no tricks to getting to the city, never more than 20 minutes away, or to your hotel. Many hotels have courtesy mini-buses. All entry points have bus services, and Perth taxis in particular set very high standards. Taxi drivers are friendly, and many are well-educated and multilingual.

Getting around in Perth and Fremantle is exceptionally easy by bus, train, or rental car. Perth even has free Clipper buses that circle the city center. Fremantle has a distinctive tram circling the main attractions. There's also a good train service between Perth and Fremantle— worth a ride. The Perth rail and bus stations are located on Wellington Street. Coach tours are available from the major hotels to sights both in the city and nearby. Or you may prefer the independence of a rental car. Apart from short peak-hour bursts of traffic, you can go anywhere quite quickly in Perth.

There are daily flights from Perth Airport to all major towns in Western Australia, and this is the way to go if you don't want to spend hours on long, straight roads. However, direct flights between some major towns are not as frequent, and sometimes involve returning to Perth before flying on. A trip from Kalgoorlie to Geraldton, for example, requires a plane change in Perth.

If you rent a car, note that gas stations generally open from 7:00 A.M. to 6:00 P.M. After 6:00 P.M., there is a gas station on duty in each Perth suburb or in major towns. Renting a car in the larger provincial towns can be considerably more expensive than in Perth. That's mainly because provincial operators have awakened to some of the inhospitable places people take rental cars in the countryside.

Travelling to the southwest of the state is easy by car (and fairly expensive by air). Distances are quite manageable in a day—Albany is about 400 km (251 miles) from Perth via Albany Highway and through the wheat belt of the state, or a little longer through Bunbury on the coast and via forested Manjimup in the tall timber country. Many communities in this area use the money from speeding fines to repair their roads and for other worthy causes, so watch out for the speed signs. There is a train service from Perth to Bunbury. There are daily flights and a train service from Perth to Kalgoorlie, and a taxi service in the town, but you'll need a car to venture farther afield. The roads are good but there are few facilities.

### Driving Precautions

If you're venturing across the Nullarbor or driving in the Pilbara, Kimberley, or goldfields areas, you're in remote country with few facilities, low rainfall for most of the year, and flash floods in the summer months, so a few driving precautions are advisable.

The vehicle should be fully serviced; see that tires are in good condition—including the spare—and tire pressures are correct. Make sure the vehicle has a full tool kit and, for the Nullarbor and more remote areas of The Kimberley, take a range of spare parts. It is advisable to carry ample water—for drinking *and* for the car's radiator.

It is not a good idea to drive at dusk because kangaroos, emus, and stray cattle choose this time to go foraging for food and can wander across the road and cause major accidents.

Most inland roads in the Pilbara are unpaved, but you can tackle the main highways easily in a sedan car. Move off the major tracks and you'll need a four-wheel-drive vehicle. Check with the tourism departments or gas stations in each town about the state of the roads, especially if you are travelling during the wet season.

Distances are so vast in The Kimberley that most visitors fly between the main towns of Broome and Kununurra. However, if you have the time and the stamina the drive is 1,200 km (almost 750 miles) on the Great Northern Highway, which loops around the lower edge of The Kimberley, adjacent to the Great Sandy Desert. The interior is four-wheel-drive country and it is unwise to tackle it without proper preparation. This is remote, uninhabited wilderness with no facilities, so everything must be taken with you. Even in the Bungle Bungle area, now a national park, there are few signposts and it is easy to get stranded with vehicle problems or no water.

### When to Go

Perth's hot summers and mild winters attract visitors year-round, but September to December is ideal sightseeing weather. For those who don't mind the heat, January to March is consistently 90 degrees F or warmer, but the humidity is low. The occasional bursts of 100-degree heat in late January and February do not suit everybody.

When the mercury rises in Perth you can always head south, where it is cooler; high summer is a very pleasant time in the southwestern corner. Not so the northwest and Kimberley regions, which get very hot and rainy from November to March, much like the climate during the Wet in Asia. In the northwest, 100-degree days are the norm rather than the exception. Traditionally, the best time to visit up north is April to September, when days are clear and warm.

### What to Wear

In Perth people dress up to go to work, but apart from that, Western Australia is delightfully informal, opting for color and comfort in fashion, day and night. Exceptions are a few places (such as the International Room at the Burswood Casino) that require a jacket at all times. Some visitors might be surprised to find notices outside bars and restaurants along the coast insisting on minimum dress standards—usually no bare feet or bare chests.

# ACCOMMODATIONS REFFERENCE

▶ **Cable Beach Resort.** Cable Beach Road, **Broome,** W.A. 6725. Tel: (091) 921-824.

▶ **Captain Freycinet Motel.** Tunbridge Street, **Margaret River,** W.A. 6285. Tel: (097) 57-2033; in Australia, (008) 015-540.

▶ **Dumar Motel.** Carey Street, **Wittenoom,** W.A. 6752. Tel: (091) 897-088.

▶ **Esplanade Plaza Hotel.** Corner Marine Terrace and Collie Street, **Fremantle,** W.A. 6160. Tel: (09) 430-4000 or (008) 999-120; Telex: 96977.

▶ **Kalbarri Beach Resort.** Grey and Clotworthy streets, **Kalbarri,** W.A. 6532. Tel: (099) 37-1061 or (008) 07-4444.

▶ **Lake Argyle Tourist Village. Lake Argyle,** W.A. 6743. Tel: (091) 68-1064.

▶ **Margaret River Hotel Motel.** Bussell Highway, **Margaret River** W.A. 6285. Tel: (097) 57-2136.

▶ **Palace Hotel.** Maritana Street, **Kalgoorlie,** W.A. 6430. Tel: (090) 21-2788.

▶ **Plaza Hotel.** Egan Street, **Kalgoorlie,** W.A. 6430. Tel: (090) 21-4544.

▶ **Roebuck Bay Resort Hotel.** Hopton Street, **Broome,** W.A. 6725. Tel: (091) 921-898 or (008) 094-848.

▶ **Rottnest Hotel** (Quokka Arms). **Rottnest Island,** W.A. 6161. Tel: (09) 292-5011.

▶ **Rottnest Island Self Catering Cottages.** For information and bookings, Rottnest Island Board, **Rottnest Island,** W.A. 6161. Tel (09) 292-5044.

▶ **Rottnest Lodge Resort. Rottnest Island,** W.A. 6161. Tel: (09) 292-5161.

▶ **Settlers' House.** Avon Terrace, **York,** W.A. 6302. Tel: (096) 411-096.

▶ **Swagmans Inn.** Duncan Highway, **Kununurra,** W.A. 6743. Tel: (011) 81-204.

# CHRONOLOGY
# OF THE HISTORY
# OF AUSTRALIA

- **circa 50,000 B.C.:** The first Australians arrive, crossing the land bridge from New Guinea.
- **c. 15,000–7,000 B.C.:** Rising seas cover the land between the mainland and Tasmania and the other islands, finally cutting the New Guinea land bridge.
- **A.D.1567:** Alvaro Mendana sails from Peru hunting the fabled *Terra Australis Incognita.*
- **1606:** Dutchman Willem Jansz discovers Cape York Peninsula, but doesn't realize it's part of a continent.
- **1606–1700:** *Terra Australias Incognita* becomes *Hollandia Nova* on Dutch East India Company maps.
- **1642:** Dutch explorer Abel Tasman discovers Tasmania, but the discovery is ignored.
- **1688:** The English buccaneer William Dampier lands on a bleak stretch of the northwest coast.
- **1770:** The *Endeavour* reaches the southeastern corner of Australia, and Captain James Cook then sails north, charting 2,500 miles of coast. He names the land New South Wales and claims it for England.
- **1773:** The first picture of a kangaroo circulates in England.
- **1788 ( January 26):** The First Fleet with its cargo of convicts anchors in Sydney Cove, Port Jackson.
- **1790:** Ships of the Second Fleet arrive.
- **1792:** The young Aboriginal Bennelong goes to England.

- **1793**: The first free immigrants arrive.
- **1797**: Merino sheep are imported from Cape of Good Hope.
- **1803**: Publication of the first newspaper, *Sydney Gazette and New South Wales Advertiser*.
- **1804**: Hobart is settled.
- **1811**: Reverend Samuel Marsden ships the first commercial cargo of wool to England.
- **1824**: Wine grape cuttings arrive with James Busby; he plants some at his Hunter River estate.
- **1829**: Settlers land at Fremantle on August 10; Perth is founded two days later.
- **1836**: South Australia settlers land on Kangaroo Island.
- **1837**: A year-old settlement on the banks of the Yarra River is named Melbourne.
- **1851**: Nuggets found at Bathurst, Ballarat, and Bendigo start a California-style gold rush. Work begins on the University of Sydney.
- **1853**: The paddle wheeler *Lady Augusta* carries the first cargo of wool from Swan Hill down the Murray River in South Australia.
- **1854**: First steam train runs from Melbourne to its port.
- **1855**: Striking stonemasons win an eight-hour workday. Shakespearean actor G. V. Brooke and Lola Montez Kelly arrive to entertain Melbourne citizens and miners.
- **1859**: European rabbits are introduced near Geelong; by 1868 they've eaten most of Western Victoria.
- **1860**: The Burke-Wills expedition leaves Melbourne for the crossing of the continent to the Gulf of Carpentaria. Burke and Wills die at Cooper's Creek on return.
- **1861 (November 7)**: A crowd of 4,000 watches first Melbourne Cup horse race.
- **1862**: John McDouall Stuart succeeds in his third try to cross the continent south to north.
- **1868**: Arrival of the last transported convicts.
- **1872**: The Overland Telegraph is finished between Port Augusta and Port Darwin.
- **1878**: The Melbourne telephone exchange opens.
- **1880**: Bushranger Ned Kelly is captured after

shoot-out at Mrs. Jones's Hotel, Glenrowan. He hangs at Melbourne Gaol in November.

- **1883**: Claims are pegged for silver lode, leading to the founding of Broken Hill.
- **1886**: Wolseley's powered shearers are introduced to wool sheds.
- **1891**: Delegates from the six colonies gather at Sydney to draft a national constitution.
- **1893**: Patrick Hannan's gold strike sparks the Golden Mile rush in Kalgoorlie, Western Australia.
- **1895**: Andrew Barton (Banjo) Patterson composes "Waltzing Matilda," now the unofficial national anthem.
- **1896**: Runner Edwin Flack represents Australia at the first modern Olympic games.
- **1901 ( January 1 )**: Birth of the Commonwealth of Australia.
- **1901 (May 9)**: The Commonwealth Parliament convenes in Melbourne.
- **1902**: The "Australian Nightingale," Nellie Melba, comes home for a concert tour after 16 years abroad.
- **1909**: The first Australian flight of a Wright biplane, in Sydney. The craft stays aloft for 90 meters.
- **1912**: Swimmers Fanny Durack and Mina Wylie, the first Australian women in the Olympics, place first and second in the 100-meter race.
- **1913**: The New Australian Capital Territory is named Canberra.
- **1914**: Australia joins England in the war against Germany.
- **1915**: Australians land at Gallipoli.
- **1923**: Vegemite is concocted by chemist Cyril Percy Callister. The brown paste is now the national elixir.
- **1927**: Parliament House is opened at Canberra.
- **1928**: Charles Kingsford Smith makes first transpacific crossing from the United States to Brisbane.
- **1932**: Sydney Harbour Bridge opens. The same month, Phar Lap wins the Agua Caliente Handicap.
- **1933**: The Flying Doctor Service is established.
- **1939 (September 3)**: Australia joins England in the war against Germany.
- **1942 (February 19)**: The Japanese bomb Darwin.

- **1942 (May):** The Battle of the Coral Sea ends the fear of a Japanese invasion.
- **1946:** The start of postwar immigration: a flood of 2,500,000 British, Greeks, Italians, Dutch, Germans, Poles, and other New Australians.
- **1951:** The first School of the Air is broadcast in Alice Springs.
- **1951 (January 1):** 8,250,000 citizens celebrate the Commonwealth of Australia's 50th birthday.
- **1954:** Queen Elizabeth II makes a 58-day state visit.
- **1956:** The XVI Olympic Games take place in Melbourne; the Aussies win 13 gold, 8 silver, and 14 bronze medals.
- **1959:** Construction starts on the Sydney Opera House.
- **1962:** 30 Australian military advisers go to Vietnam.
- **1963:** Mount Tom Price, Western Australia, is recognized as one of the world's greatest iron-ore deposits.
- **1965:** Robert Helpmann, the Australian Ballet leader, is named the nation's "Man of the Year," and Demetrios Stathopoulos becomes the nation's greatest "gun shearer," with a record clip of 370 sheep in a seven-hour, 48-minute day.
- **1973:** Sydney Opera House opens after 13 years and a cost of $100 million—all lottery money.
- **1975:** Peter Weir's film *Picnic at Hanging Rock* wins international acclaim as the first export in new wave of Australian arts.
- **1983 (November):** The yacht *Australia II,* owned by Perth millionaire Alan Bond, wins the America's Cup.
- **1987:** The tally of Australia's millionaires exceeds 30.
- **1988:** The new Parliament House in Canberra is formally opened by Queen Elizabeth II.

*—Shirley Maas Fockler*

# INDEX

## WHEN TRAVELLING, PACK

All the Penguin Travel Guides offer you the selective and up-to-date information you need to plan and enjoy your vacations. Written by travel writers who really know the areas they cover, The Penguin Travel Guides are lively, reliable, and easy to use. So remember, when travelling, pack a Penguin.

☐ *The Penguin Guide to Australia 1989*
  0-14-019905-5 $11.95

☐ *The Penguin Guide to Canada 1989*
  0-14-019906-3 $12.95

☐ *The Penguin Guide to the Caribbean 1989*
  0-14-019900-4 $9.95

☐ *The Penguin Guide to England and Wales 1989*
  0-14-019901-2 $12.95

☐ *The Penguin Guide to France 1989*
  0-14-019902-0 $14.95

☐ *The Penguin Guide to Ireland 1989*
  0-14-019904-7 $10.95

☐ *The Penguin Guide to Italy 1989*
  0-14-019903-9 $14.95

☐ *The Penguin Guide to New York City 1989*
  0-14-019907-1 $11.95
  (available March 1989)

# FOR THE BEST IN PAPERBACKS, LOOK FOR THE

In every corner of the world, on every subject under the sun, Penguin represents quality and variety—the very best in publishing today.

For complete information about books available from Penguin—including Pelicans, Puffins, Peregrines, and Penguin Classics—and how to order them, write to us at the appropriate address below. Please note that for copyright reasons the selection of books varies from country to country.

---

**In the United Kingdom:** For a complete list of books available from Penguin in the U.K., please write to *Dept E.P., Penguin Books Ltd, Harmondsworth, Middlesex, UB7 0DA.*

**In the United States:** For a complete list of books available from Penguin in the U.S., please write to *Dept BA, Penguin, 299 Murray Hill Parkway, East Rutherford, New Jersey 07073.*

**In Canada:** For a complete list of books available from Penguin in Canada, please write to *Penguin Books Canada Ltd, 2801 John Street, Markham, Ontario L3R 1B4.*

**In Australia:** For a complete list of books available from Penguin in Australia, please write to the *Marketing Department, Penguin Books Australia Ltd, P.O. Box 257, Ringwood, Victoria 3134.*

**In New Zealand:** For a complete list of books available from Penguin in New Zealand, please write to the *Marketing Department, Penguin Books (NZ) Ltd, Private Bag, Takapuna, Auckland 9.*

**In India:** For a complete list of books available from Penguin, please write to *Penguin Overseas Ltd, 706 Eros Apartments, 56 Nehru Place, New Delhi, 110019.*

**In Holland:** For a complete list of books available from Penguin in Holland, please write to *Penguin Books Nederland B.V., Postbus 195, NL–1380AD Weesp, Netherlands.*

**In Germany:** For a complete list of books available from Penguin, please write to *Penguin Books Ltd, Friedrichstrasse 10–12, D–6000 Frankfurt Main 1, Federal Republic of Germany.*

**In Spain:** For a complete list of books available from Penguin in Spain, please write to *Longman Penguin España, Calle San Nicolas 15, E–28013 Madrid, Spain.*